ALL
HALLOWS

Also by Christopher Golden and
available from Titan Books:

Road of Bones

Titan anthologies featuring
Christopher Golden:

Dark Cities
Cursed
Hex Life
Christmas and Other Horrors

ALL HALLOWS

Christopher Golden

TITAN BOOKS

All Hallows
Print edition ISBN: 9781803364520
E-book edition ISBN: 9781803364537

Published by Titan Books
A division of Titan Publishing Group Ltd
144 Southwark Street, London SE1 0UP
www.titanbooks.com

First edition: Sep 2023
10 9 8 7 6 5 4 3 2 1

A CIP catalogue record for this title is available
from the British Library.

Printed and bound by CPI Group Ltd (UK),
Croydon CR0 4YY.

For Bracken MacLeod

TONY BARBOSA

In the woods behind Tony Barbosa's house, the autumn leaves screened out so much daylight it seemed like dusk had already arrived. The paths through these woods had been his happy place for all the years he and his wife, Alice, had owned their house, and never more so than in October and November, when neighbors set fire to raked leaves during the day and the scent of their wood-burning stoves lingered on the chilly air at night. Alice had never been fond of autumn, had no real love of Halloween, and felt uneasy anytime he cajoled her into walking the trails that meandered through their woods. Too creepy, she said. He should have realized the first time she'd said it that their marriage would run into trouble.

He wiped a sheen of sweat off his brow and let out a breath.

Tony and Alice had enjoyed about two years of smooth sailing before they hit their first rough seas. The births of their two children had kept them afloat for a long time, but circumstances had become so difficult that he worried they were sinking now.

"Sinking," he said quietly to himself. "Or sunk?"

"Dad?"

He turned to see Chloe headed toward him down the path,

a big cardboard box that looked even bigger in the arms of a girl so short. Chloe had inherited big brown eyes and thick hair from her dad, but the diminutive stature she got from her mom.

"You talking to yourself back here?" she asked.

"First sign of madness," he admitted. "But you're not really crazy until you start answering yourself back."

"You're only half-crazy, then. Good to know."

Tony felt the twinge of melancholy he always got when he looked at his now-seventeen-year-old daughter. She was a good kid—smart and confident and ambitious. Her mother's daughter, really. Tony wished he could take credit. He and Chloe had been close until she turned twelve and decided her parents were idiots. The teenage animosity had lasted for years but had finally dissipated over the summer. Now she was just trying to navigate the sometimes whiplash-inducing back-and-forth of her parents' relationship.

She set the box down. "What've we got here?"

"Open it. Let's find out."

Chloe tore into the box like it was Christmas morning instead of Halloween, but in the Barbosa house, October 31 was just as important as December 25. Sometimes even more so. During what Alice lovingly referred to as their daughter's "hormonal years," prepping the Haunted Woods every October was the one thing that had brought Tony and Chloe together. Barbosa's Haunted Woods had taken on legendary status in town, enough so that the neighbors tended to get a little miffed about the traffic it brought to Parmenter Road.

When it had drawn mostly people from their own neighborhood, they'd all loved it. But now that the Haunted Woods brought people from all over town, dozens of cars clogging the street just as trick-or-treat was wrapping up for the night, some of the Barbosas' neighbors weren't as thrilled as they once had been.

Now it didn't matter anymore. Tonight would be their swan song.

Chloe pulled a bunch of Bubble Wrap out of the box, digging deeper. "Hey! This is cool."

She revealed a thin, almost skeletal hand and what appeared to be some kind of face mask, and at first, Tony didn't recall having ordered them. With all the haunted attraction props they had accumulated over the eleven years they'd been doing this, he had plenty of skeletons and scary masks. Then Chloe stood and walked to the nearest oak tree, and it clicked for him. The rough pattern on the arm and the mask were imitation bark, the gray-brown hue meant to match the trees. When Chloe held the demonic tree face in place and the skeletal evil-tree arm up to the side of the oak's trunk, Tony grinned like a little kid.

"That is going to freak people out," he said. His most glowing review. After all, that was their great ambition.

They'd been putting the whole display together as a team since Chloe was six. She had loved it even then, never scared of the terrifying props. Her little brother, Rick, was thirteen years old and in the eighth grade, and he still refused to even walk through the Haunted Woods. Once it had been fear that drove the kid, but Tony thought now it was simple disinterest. Either that, or Rick thought of the Haunted Woods as "Dad and Chloe's thing," with himself and his mom on the outside.

And maybe that was okay. Tony and his daughter had Halloween and scary movies and the Haunted Woods, but Chloe had zero interest in going fishing with her father and brother. As a first-generation Portuguese American kid growing up in Quincy, on Boston's south shore, Tony had gone fishing with his father, Silverio, almost every Saturday morning from the time he could hold a fishing pole until the day he got married. When Ricky had been born, Tony's dad had been first to the hospital, beaming with pride. A machinist, he'd worked his body to ruin to support his family and always seemed exhausted to Tony, but that afternoon, holding his grandson in his arms and crowing about the day he would be able to take both his son and grandson fishing, Silverio Barbosa had never seemed more vividly alive.

Less than a year later, cancer had taken him. He had never taken his grandson fishing.

But even now, with Ricky a teenager, old enough to demand they call him Rick, Tony took the boy fishing on Saturday mornings. Sometimes they settled into silence, enjoying the solitude, and sometimes Tony reminisced about his dad and his childhood and tried to share what little wisdom he felt he'd acquired in his life till now.

So if Rick didn't want anything to do with the Haunted Woods, wanted to leave that to his sister, that was more than okay. It was nice for Tony and Chloe to have something just for themselves, especially since Chloe was older, and while her grandfather had shown up at the hospital after her birth and pronounced her the most beautiful child he had ever seen, Silverio Barbosa had never declared any intention to one day take her fishing. Born in another time and another culture, he viewed that as entirely something the men did. Tony sometimes wondered if he had done the wrong thing, excluding Chloe from his fishing excursions with her little brother, but when it started, he had viewed it as time to bond with Rick and time for Alice to bond with Chloe.

He didn't know what was right. He just tried to do his best by the people he loved.

This year had been a little different. It would be the last time, the end of the Haunted Woods, so he and Chloe had tried everything short of physical violence to get Rick involved and excited. He had made excuses, his disinterest clear. In the end,

Tony didn't mind—this thing had always been his and Chloe's, and it seemed right that it would end that way. He hadn't explicitly told her this would be the last one, but she lived in the same house, had eyes and ears and a little intuition. She knew how long he had been out of work before he'd finally found a new job in August, knew not to answer the phone to avoid the bill collectors. Tony and Alice casually mentioned to neighbors that they were "considering downsizing," so maybe people wouldn't realize they hadn't had a choice. Chloe could see the writing on the wall.

"How many of those did we order?" Tony asked, admiring the tree demon again.

"There are three sets," Chloe replied, studying the contents of the box. "The eyes glow—there's a switch. If we get some soft blue lights angled just right and put them on those trees at the third bend in the path—"

"With one of the fog machines—"

"It'll be perfect."

Chloe had a smile full of mischief. Her eyes gleamed with delight that matched his own. People came to Barbosa's Haunted Woods, donated money to whatever charity Tony and Chloe had chosen that year, and took a walk along the path that would scare the crap out of them.

"Happy Halloween, kid," Tony said.

"Happy Halloween, Pops."

He hoped she wouldn't look up at him right then. She knew him too well. His little girl might not be his little girl anymore, but she'd see his pain. The pain of the kind of failure it took to raise your kids in a home like this one and then lose it.

"I'm still trying to get this banshee moving properly," he said, turning to go back to his current task. As visitors rounded the second turn in the path, the banshee should have come shrieking along a thin wire, pale green funeral rags fluttering around its wraithlike body, but something had gummed up the wire and the banshee kept hitting a snag. There were two of them—the second one, near the exit from the Haunted Woods, was working perfectly, which made this even more frustrating.

"The scream is scary all by itself," Chloe replied.

"Yeah. But I didn't buy them for the scream. I bought them for the shock."

The same could have been said for most of the props and animated mechanisms he'd accumulated over the years. Growing up, his love for Halloween had always been more about the experience than the candy. Running across neighbors' front yards with a little bucket or pillowcase, he'd felt a delicious thrill no movie could provide. In those days, just like now, some neighbors would do nothing at all and some would way overdo it, but there had been a few who got it just right—a fog machine and creepy music, a little fake cemetery, an animatronic figure that would move or unleash an evil laugh at just the right moment.

On the street where he'd grown up, there'd been a family called the Shipkas, and Mr. Shipka had a scarecrow he would tie to the lamppost at the end of their driveway that he had hooked up to a speaker system. He hid inside with a microphone and peeked out the window, waiting for kids of just the right age and the perfect combination of innocence and fear. As they passed the scarecrow . . . it would *talk* to them. And the voice he would use . . .

A kid named Ed Korski had literally pissed himself. Tony had been there—both of them ten years old at the time—and once his own initial fear had passed, he had first laughed and then felt awful for Ed, who'd run home with his head down and skipped the following Halloween. Tony's guilt for laughing had eventually subsided, but his fascination with the power of that moment—the rush of feeling so afraid and the relief when he had realized it was all just meant for fun—had stayed with him.

At sixteen, he'd begun working at the Haunted Farm over in Amesbury every autumn. It had been a glorious mix of scary attractions, a spooky hayride, a walk through "demon woods," and an old barn converted to a "horror circus," complete with clowns so scary that every night, people screamed. After the screaming would come laughter, and both the terrified patrons and the workers responsible would go home buzzing from the experience. When Tony was twenty-one, the farmer who leased the land to them every year passed away, and his kids wanted to sell the farm. The Haunted Farm lost its home, and the organizers discovered it was simply too much trouble to find a new one. They allowed it to die, but not before auctioning off every last plastic spider, bloody chain saw, demon mask, and fake gravestone. Tony had bought as much of that stuff as he could afford and stored it in his parents' basement until he and Alice moved to Coventry. The house on Parmenter Road had the perfect backyard; the woods already had trails worn through them by decades of local kids.

Barbosa's Haunted Woods was born.

Now it would die.

But Tony would make its last Halloween glorious.

"Coming through!" Chloe said.

Tony stepped off the path and let her by. She hurried past with the big shipping box in her arms.

"You want help with those?"

Chloe glanced over her shoulder, purple hair a veil across the left side of her face. "You think it's my first day on the job? I got it. You get that banshee flying."

Then she was gone, around the next bend. The trail snaked through the half acre of woods behind the house, up and down the incline amid the trees. Fall had arrived, but there were still enough leaves on the branches to screen out the view from one part of the trail to the next. Where the trees weren't thick enough to keep people from seeing through to another part of the path, he'd curtained off the areas with black cloth. Where even that wasn't enough, fog machines pumped dry ice mist into the air. In the dark, you could hear the screams, of course, but with the leaves and curtains and mist, and the way they staggered admissions, you could rarely see anyone else in the woods. Much creepier that way.

Tony loved his props and took great care of them. The most unsettling one was the glowing-eyed creepy doll with the cracked porcelain face who rocked back and forth on an antique carousel horse. There were zombies in cages, hooded witches, and hideous scarecrows with jack-o'-lantern heads. But what made Barbosa's Haunted Woods so great were the volunteers. Many of them were local actors, but even the amateurs took the night very seriously. Props were one thing, but people made up like zombies and demons and whiteface clowns were what really got the screams going. The best were the spots where hissing zombies lunged up out of graves to claw at the feet of passersby.

His grandfather had drummed it into his skull that nothing could ever be perfect, but Tony had disagreed. Nothing could *stay* perfect, but if you were lucky and diligent, you could steal a few perfect moments in your life. This afternoon was one of them. Whatever else might be wrong, he had made the Haunted Woods as perfect as it could be, and he and Chloe would always have this memory.

With a huff that cleared his head, he turned his focus back to the guide wire for the banshee. He ran his fingers carefully over the wire. The spot where the prop kept snagging didn't seem to be tree sap, so he guessed it must be bird shit. Disgusted, he wiped his fingers on the rag hanging from his belt. Bird shit might be zero fun, but it was a hell of a lot easier to clean off than sap would have been.

Tony turned and scanned the path for his toolbox. He kept a little bottle of industrial cleaner in the box. It wasn't environmentally friendly, so he used it sparingly, but one little squirt and a scrub with the rag ought to do the trick.

Somewhere over his left shoulder, a branch snapped, Chloe coming back.

"That was quick," Tony said, crouching to dig around the toolbox. He snagged the squirt bottle and when he straightened up, his knee cracked louder than the broken branch. "Jesus. I'm getting old."

Chloe didn't argue with him, and that sort of stung. He was only forty-five, after all.

Tony turned, ready to feign insult, but his daughter was nowhere in sight. He glanced into the woods, toward the spot where the snapping sound had originated. Black cloth curtains rippled, blocking his view, but behind that cloth, dry leaves rustled and crunched as someone scuttled away.

"Funny girl." Tony grinned. Occasionally, he and Chloe would try to spook each other back here in the woods while they were setting up their scares.

A whisper came from behind the black cloth.

It wouldn't be dark for hours yet, but the shadows were deep back here, and the curtains made them deeper. Tony chose his steps carefully, creeping toward the edge of the path. He would have loved to scare the crap out of Chloe, but the leaves were crunchy. If he tried to grab her, he'd end up pulling down the curtain, and there was no time to rehang it.

That whispering came again, almost like the hiss of a snake.

"Okay, let's save the fooling around for when the job is done," he said. It was one of his reliable bits of wisdom. His kids called them *dad-isms*.

Still Chloe didn't respond. He wanted to keep things light so as not to spoil the fun, but they had work to do if they were going to be ready in time. Tony stepped off the path, not bothering to try to soften the crunch of leaves underfoot. He reached for the curtain.

"Are you talking to me?" Chloe asked.

Blinking in surprise, he turned to find her twenty feet away, coming around a bend in the trail. She had the cardboard box in her arms, but he could tell it was empty by the way she carried it.

Tony looked back to the black curtain, which danced lightly in the breeze. He reached out again to pull it aside, even as Chloe kept speaking to him, wondering why he'd gone suddenly silent.

From behind the curtain there came a grunt and another crunch of leaves, followed by light footfalls and the snapping of little branches. Tony whipped the cloth aside and saw the back of a retreating child, a little girl darting deeper into the woods. Or he assumed it was a girl, no more than ten, dressed in a costume he recognized immediately. With her faded, old-fashioned dress and a wig made of red yarn, she had to be planning to trick-or-treat as Raggedy Ann. In the dark woods, she almost looked gray, the red wig nearly black except the moment she passed through a shaft of sunlight. But then she lost herself in the trees and the shadows, and in seconds, even the rustle of leaves from her running footsteps had gone silent.

"Friend of yours?" Chloe asked.

Tony laughed softly. "I'm gonna guess one of the neighbor kids trying to get an early peek at what's in store for tonight."

"A little young to be out in the woods on her own."

"Maybe on a dare," Tony said. He knew it probably wasn't good parenting to have let that girl run around the neighborhood unsupervised, but secretly he approved. He loved the idea that she must have been excited enough about tonight to sneak around for a look. It made him think maybe she was a little bit like he'd been as a boy.

"Check this out," Chloe said as she knelt and reached for something just beyond the drawn-back curtain.

When she stood, Tony saw that she'd retrieved a fallen Raggedy Ann doll. He reached out and took it from Chloe's hands to examine it. The doll must have been an antique, he thought. It was so worn and yellowed with age, and one of its eyes hung loosely, ready to tear free at the slightest provocation.

"Part of her costume, I bet," he said. "Gotta belong to her grandmother or something. This thing's ancient. Maybe this was her inspiration."

"What do you mean?"

Tony smiled again as he looked down at the old doll. "I haven't seen a kid in a Raggedy Ann costume in years."

"You know everything old comes back around eventually," Chloe said.

Raggedy Ann in hand, Tony nodded. "True. Let's make sure Mom and Auntie Helen keep an eye out for her tonight. When she comes here, I want to give this back to her. It's in rough shape, but it's probably worth something. I'm sure her parents won't be happy that she's lost it."

"I'll remember," Chloe said. She took the doll back from him and laid it on top of his toolbox. "Now get back to work, old man. Daylight's wasting."

Tony gave her a wistful grin, bent over, and kissed the top of her head. "I love you, kid. Thanks for doing this with me."

Chloe brightened. "You kidding? This is our day, Pops. We're gonna scare the shit out of them."

Tony laughed as she picked up the box again and headed toward the house. He plucked the rag from his belt, took his squirt bottle, and went to clean off the banshee's guide wire. He heard the breeze rustling through the branches, but other than that, the path was quiet. Tonight, though, it would be very different.

Tonight, the woods would be full of screams, and he intended to cherish every last one.

VANESSA MONTEZ

When she spotted the little girl putting her hand in Winnie the Pooh's mouth, Vanessa wondered if Pooh would bite it off. For better or worse, that was how her brain worked. She'd take something ordinary and boring and think, *And then . . .* , and something awful would happen. It was a little fantasy game she'd played in her head ever since she could remember, mostly to combat the mundaneness of growing up in Coventry, not to mention having John and Lucy Montez as her parents.

Her parents were so boring. She loved them to death. They were literally her best friends and she hugged them every chance she got, but they were forty going on ninety, content to be together, sort of a world unto themselves. It would've been charming if it wasn't such a snooze. Not that Vanessa wanted any drama between her parents. God knew she'd seen enough of her friends going through it with their families. By the time she hit sixth grade, some of her friends' parents were already separated or getting divorced, and Jennie Collins's dad even died that year, which was deeply messed up. Then divorce started going around like it was contagious. Kids gossiped about one another's parents, but Vanessa kept her mouth shut, afraid of jinxing her mom and dad.

But there they were, a few years later, and more quietly in love than ever.

Sometimes boring could be wonderful, that was an inescapable truth. But at the end of the day, it was still boring, and Vanessa Montez hadn't been built for that.

Especially not now that she had her driver's license.

"Steve, how bad do you really need this?" she asked, rolling her eyes. "You know it's, like, poison. You're waiting in line for poison."

"I do, I do," he replied, grinning that stupid grin he'd been winning arguments with since he was four years old. "But it's delicious, cheesy poison."

Steve Koenig was a junior, at sixteen too young to have his driver's license, but when Vanessa had gotten hers last week, Steve had been even more excited than she was. He'd assumed that she would be his chauffeur from that moment forth, and though Vanessa bitched about it, truth was that she had assumed the same thing. She might be a year older, but she could never stay mad at him. Steve knew her like nobody else. Knew everything about her. Some people thought their friendship was weird, that boys and girls didn't get that close, but Vanessa had never cared much what people thought.

Hence the way she clapped her hands and cheered for the girl working the register at Orange Julius when she finished taking payment from the chubby grandpa in front of them. The old guy should absolutely not have been eating that chili cheese dog. If the cheese and the disgusting animal parts inside the hot dog didn't kill him, the farts the chili gave him later might make his wife stab him in the throat.

Vanessa hoped.

"Well done, Sheila!" she cried, with the slow clap of sarcasm. "You got this."

Sheila shot her the middle finger—which her manager would

surely frown upon—and smiled at the next customers in line, a pair of twelve-year-old boys who had been stealing glances back at her. One of them looked over his shoulder while his friend ordered, and Vanessa growled at him, then smiled. The kid blushed and stammered a little when it was his turn to order.

Vanessa liked twelve-year-old boys. They were fun to mess with. In a couple of years, they'd be assholes, she was sure, but for now they entertained her.

"Would you take a chill pill, please?" Steve whispered in her ear. "Go and play with Winnie the Pooh."

She scowled. "Eat me. I'm just trying to encourage Sheila to hurry. I'm bored."

"You're always bored. And you're gonna get her to spit in my food if you keep it up."

Vanessa smiled. "The closest you'll come to kissing her."

"You're gross. Go play with Pooh."

"Like you don't want to kiss her."

Steve flushed pink. Their little sparring match had ended as such matches always did, with him embarrassed. She knew he didn't have any particular lust for the Orange Julius girl, but he was a sixteen-year-old boy, which from what she'd always heard meant he spent half his waking hours and all the sleeping ones with a boner hard enough to hammer nails. Steve was different from most of his species, though. Still horny, yes, but sweet. Uncertain and shy, no idea how to talk to girls other than his lifelong best friend, and awkward as hell anytime Vanessa drew attention to that fact.

"Vee," he said, a raspy whisper.

She nodded and whispered as well. "Okay, okay. I'll play with Pooh. Get me a soft pretzel."

His eyes widened. He started to berate her for wanting something to eat after giving him no end of shit for having to wait in line, but she laughed and walked toward the center of the food court, where the costumed Winnie the Pooh was waving and nodding and just generally being adorably fluffy for the amusement of parents and little kids. It wasn't a Halloween thing—Pooh Bear was a promo for the toy store deeper into the mall and sometimes wandered around in an attempt to lure unsuspecting consumers to his toy-selling lair.

Vanessa found an empty table. She dragged out a metal chair, its feet screeching against the floor, and plopped down to people-watch. Mostly she was aggressively hunting for people at whom she could glare. There were occasional racists, but mostly it was just dudes of all ages who were checking her out. She wasn't dressed for Halloween any more than Winnie the Pooh, but there weren't many girls in Coventry, Massachusetts, into the things she loved. As far as the typical mall rats were concerned, a Dominican girl whose makeup and hair made her look like Siouxsie Sioux was something to stare at. Okay, she did steal some of her eyeliner and shadow designs from pictures of Siouxsie and the Banshees, but she usually wore a T-shirt, a hooded sweatshirt, jeans, and boots—all black. Nothing sexy, nothing that hugged her body extra tight. It was just men, and boys. Dudes in general. They saw this girl whom they might normally find mildly attractive, but who dressed and behaved like she couldn't give a shit what they thought of her, and her indifference to their dicks made them want to either fuck her or hurt her, or both, in whichever order they could swing it.

Her dad was a man. Steve would be a man someday. She loved them both, would take a bullet for either one of them, so she knew there must be a lot of wonderful guys out there. She just wished the rest of them weren't always doing their best to make her feel nasty.

Vanessa glared reproachfully at a fiftyish guy walking with

his daughter, carrying her shopping bags from Tape World and Jordan Marsh. He was with his daughter, but examining Vanessa pretty thoroughly.

"What?" she snapped. Loudly.

The guy pivoted, guiding his daughter away from the food court. Vanessa smiled, but she didn't feel like smiling at all. She hated the mall so much, couldn't wait to be done with high school so she could get out of the Merrimack Valley. New York City called to her, maybe even Los Angeles, but of course she'd never go to LA. Too far from her parents. And that was the great irony of her life. Punks always seemed to hate their parents, but she couldn't bear to think of leaving hers behind.

"Here comes your poison!" Steve said as he wove through the maze of food court tables. She wondered what people thought, seeing the two of them together—her, this death-punk rocker girl, and him with a stylishly stonewashed denim jacket over a Huey Lewis and the News T-shirt, looking like a John Hughes movie had fucked MTV and borne a child.

Vanessa smiled again, this time for real, as he slid into the chair opposite her. Steve handed over her pretzel, but she also grabbed his Orange Julius and took a big drink from his straw.

"Oh, you bitch."

"Poison is delicious." She smiled, knowing he could never really be mad at her. It just wasn't in the DNA of their friendship.

The conversation ceased while he chowed on his cheese dog. Vanessa ripped off one loop of her hot pretzel and bit off a hunk. Steve had dragged her out of the house to drive him to Methuen, mostly because he wanted to drift through Chess King and the other shops that sold clothes he didn't think he was cool enough to wear just yet. Coventry wasn't a bad place to grow up, but Steve longed for college just as much as she did. An opportunity for a fresh start. When you're young and in school with the same kids year after year, you start defining yourself before you can even tie your shoes, and by the time you realize that's what you've been doing, it's too late. They've all made up their minds about you already. College would be a new beginning, a time when they could both choose to be anything or anyone they wished.

"Do you want to hit the arcade?" he asked in between bites.

But she knew the answer he was hoping for. Despite his feathered hair and stonewashed jacket, he hadn't come to the mall hoping to run into girls. He just wanted to do some window-shopping and let Vanessa cajole him into cruising the aisles of the bookstore. They were here because it was away from Coventry, and because she had her license, and it made them both feel a little grown-up, as crazy as that seemed with a mall full of kids.

"Nah. No arcade today," she said, though she did have a small video game addiction that cost her many quarters. Many, many quarters. "Your parents would be pissed if I kept you too long today. I'm sure there's stuff they want you to help with for the party."

Steve took a sip of Orange Julius. "You're coming, right?"

Vanessa squirmed in her seat.

"Vee. You are coming, right? I mean, we both know you're not hanging around with Owen and those assholes. They'll probably be smoking crack or something."

"They don't smoke crack," Vanessa said. "None of those pussies would dare."

"Oh, like you would."

"I wouldn't," she agreed. "But that's because I'm too smart for that shit, not because I'm scared. Now, if Owen's got shrooms, I will go and smoke with him, and you will not say a word about it."

Steve rolled his eyes and took another bite of his hot dog. They both knew that he would have plenty to say if she went off and did drugs with Owen O'Leary and his gang of imbeciles later, and she would agree with most of what he said. But she would be high at the time.

"Yes," she promised. "I will be at the big Koenig Halloween Bash of '84. Then, later tonight, I will watch scary movies with you until the crack of dawn and then make scrambled eggs for your parents and crow like a rooster and bring them breakfast in bed, just like last year."

Steve sat back in his chair. "But between the party and the movies, you might get super fucking high on shrooms so the movies will freak you out even more."

Vanessa pointed a finger at him. "Bingo. And if you want to get high instead of me, and this year, I'll take care of you while you freak out, I will do that for you because you are my best friend on this earth or any other. You're too young, of course."

"Says the girl who's eleven months older than I am."

"I'm an adult now. I have my driver's license."

"True. And I love you for it."

"You only love me for my chauffeuring skills."

Steve nodded to confirm the accusation. They both laughed as they cleaned up the trash from their table, dumped it in a can, and left the mall to go home, celebrate Halloween, and get high. They were eagerly looking forward to being terrified that night.

Just like every Halloween.

BARB SWEENEY

Barb didn't mind driving around town doing errands—usually she appreciated the time to herself, away from the constant push and pull of being a wife and mother—but this afternoon, she'd planned to carve pumpkins and decorate the front door with fake spiderwebs and little rubber spiders that would hang from the light fixtures on either side of the door. Somewhere in there, she had also planned to make dinner. Barb had never been much of a cook, but it didn't take a lot of skill to prepare the pepperoni mac and cheese that her kids loved so much.

Of course, to do all that, she'd have needed to stay home and not be running around doing things that her husband, Donnie, had promised to get done this afternoon. Instead, Donnie had decided to clean out the garage, something he'd been vowing to do since July. It would have been a relief to know that he'd finally gotten around to it, except, as usual, he had chosen precisely the wrong moment. An hour into the job, he had gotten a phone call about one of his court cases, and that had dragged him back inside to sift through the files and argue over the phone, and by the time he'd emerged, two o'clock had come and gone with half the contents of the garage scattered about the driveway.

Barb didn't want an argument. Not today. Donnie meant well. He was a good attorney, a halfway decent father, and a passable husband when he felt like it. For the rest, he skated by on charm and dimples and too much to drink.

A burst of static came over the radio. Then another. The song had been "The One That You Love" by Air Supply, and she'd been musing on strangling the one that she loved, but now the static seemed to claw at the music, tear it up. Another voice broke in, like the ghost of one radio station overlapping with Kiss 108. But this wasn't the voice of Sunny Joe White. The voice sounded like someone amused, caught in the middle of telling a joke, but then it changed, as if the man had something caught in his throat. The sound was awful, almost hateful, like an animal . . . and then it was just static again. Barb twisted the dial, trying to tune back in to Kiss, but all that came out was static and squealing, so she jabbed the power knob and the inside of the car went silent.

Barb Sweeney didn't like silence. Too much time to think.

And now the goddamn radio was broken. One more thing Donnie would promise to handle and then leave to her to fix. Sort of like their marriage. And that was the problem, wasn't it? Donnie was always handling things he ought not to touch and breaking the promises he ought to keep.

"Stop it," she told herself, interrupting the quiet inside her Cutlass, which looked new but which her mother had forced her brother to sell her secondhand on the cheap, just to keep up appearances. The neighborhood knew Donnie was an attorney, knew he'd served two terms in the statehouse, but those days were over. He was still a lawyer, but she didn't know where his money went and was afraid to find out.

Heart racing, Barb pulled over at the entrance to Parmenter Road, just beside the Dead End sign. She cranked the window down all the way and took a few deep breaths. She loved the son of a bitch. Loved him for the same charm that got him into trouble all the time, and she'd known exactly who he was when she married him—pregnant at the time, and him engaged to someone else.

A smile touched her lips. "Jesus, Donnie," she whispered. "What am I going to do with you?"

With a few more deep breaths, shivering at the chill of the late October air sweeping through the open windows, she hit the gas and drove up Parmenter Road. The trees in front of number 15 Parmenter were festooned with sheets and pillowcases made into ghosts that flapped in the breeze. Tonight, they would be spooky as heck, and she hoped the breeze would still blow. Some of the houses gave no hint of their owners being aware it was Halloween, but most of the neighbors had made at least some effort, a few cardboard decorations taped to the storm door or some pumpkins. But of course, nothing would compare to the Barbosas' Haunted Woods later tonight. Alice Barbosa and her husband—Barb could never remember his first name—kept mostly to themselves, but on Halloween, they pulled out all the stops.

They'd have competition tonight, though, with the block party the Koenigs were throwing. Barb drove past the Barbosas and saw their daughter, Chloe, carrying a box around from the backyard. They'd gone the extra mile this year, with a fake stone entryway and fake wrought iron gate to lead into the backyard. Barb admired the heck out of their charitable efforts. She'd done a lot of charity work herself, mostly with the Coventry Hospital Aid and the planning committee for the town's upcoming tricentennial celebration. But what the Barbosas did was just pure fun. She envied them the fun they had together and the way they seemed so content just to be in each other's company.

Chloe glanced up as she drove by, and Barb gave her a quick

wave to avoid seeming rude. The girl managed to clutch the box with one arm long enough to flap her hand in something like a wave, smiling as she nearly dropped her burden. Barb glanced in her rearview mirror, hoping she hadn't caused Chloe to damage anything in that box, but it looked as if the girl had it under control.

Distant strains of music greeted her as she rounded the bend and 48 Parmenter Road came into view. Barb and Donnie had moved into the split-level in the summer of 1972. In that time, they'd painted it twice, but the clapboard siding soaked up paint like Donnie soaked up scotch, and it desperately needed a new coat. They'd made a deal with their kids—if they were willing to commit to a schedule and get the job done, Barb and Donnie would pay them instead of hiring a contractor. What they hadn't told the kids was that they'd pay less than half as much, but what they didn't know wouldn't hurt them.

Barb smiled when she saw Julia up on the ladder. At eighteen, she'd been in more than her share of trouble—Barb didn't like to think about it—but she had straightened herself out and would be off to community college next fall. Barb's fiery red hair came from a bottle at her hairdresser's, but Julia came by her ginger status naturally, a gift from her dad's side of the family, though Donnie himself had the dark hair his mother had told him came down from the "Black Irish," the descendants of Spanish sailors who'd survived the sinking of the armada and washed up on Ireland's shores.

At the foot of the ladder, thirteen-year-old Brian was stirring a freshly opened can of paint, the spitting image of his dad. Her youngest, Charlie, had the pale blond hair and blue eyes he'd inherited from his mother, and Barb had a special place in her heart for Charlie because of it. Of course, she would never admit that to anyone.

Eleven-year-old Charlie was half-hidden behind the bushes in the mulch beds in front of their split-level, slathering on the eggshell-blue paint while bobbing his head to the music blaring from the battered radio the kids had put on the grass. Some kind of twangy Southern rock blasted from the speaker. At his age, Charlie didn't have much of his own musical taste to go on, but he loved anything his older siblings listened to.

He also loved Chinese food, which was why Barb had two paper bags of takeout on the seat beside her instead of pizza, which would've been quicker and cheaper.

Brian looked up from stirring the paint and spotted her. "Hey, Mom!"

"Foooooood!" Charlie called, emerging from the bushes with a grin on his face and paint spatters all over his clothes. There was a reason she asked him to paint where the mulch would soak it up instead of having him do the garage doors and drip all over the driveway.

Barb exhaled, the sight of her happy kids relieving much of her stress as she pulled the car into the driveway.

Then she hit the brake, staring through the windshield. "What. The. Fuck?"

The stress came roaring back. She slammed the shift into Park and killed the engine, popped the door, and stepped out, forgetting all about the Chinese food and the trick-or-treat candy she'd bought and her husband's dry cleaning that hung on the hook in the back seat. If she'd thought of it, she might have tossed that dry cleaning onto the driveway and backed up over it, maybe spun the tires right on top of the tailored suit Donnie was so damned proud of.

Barb didn't use a lot of profanity. The kids noticed. They halted any further work and just watched her. She saw them out of the corner of her eye, but she didn't care, couldn't shake herself from the paralysis of fury.

The kids' bicycles had been put back, and so had the trash cans, but at least half of the boxes and other crap Donnie had pulled out when he'd started "cleaning" the garage had been left out, stacked and arranged just outside the still-open garage doors. From the looks of it, he'd kept at the job for maybe fifteen minutes after she'd left, and now there was no sign of him.

She swiveled her head around to stare at Julia. It wasn't fair, but she was the oldest and often served as Barb's sounding board. Sometimes those sounds were just a flurry of angry words, things she shouldn't dump on a teenage girl, especially her own child. But with Donnie gone, and the neighborhood gossips to think of, who else was she supposed to unload on?

"Where is your father?"

Julia shrugged. "No clue."

A lump of ice formed in Barb's chest.

"He said he had to call a client or something," Brian said. "Then he came outside and said he had to go to the office but not to worry, 'cause he'd be back before dinner."

Barb clenched and unclenched her hands and bit her lower lip, not wanting to say something to her children that she'd regret. When did Donnie think dinner was going to be? The kids were all going out to enjoy Halloween with their friends, and they—Barb and Donnie—were due at the Koenigs' party when most of the trick-or-treaters had come and gone. The kids were going to eat their Chinese food right now, and Barb had figured she and Donnie would eat their own dinner shortly thereafter. Instead, he'd taken off and left her with the kids, the candy, and a bunch of crap to stow back into the garage.

No. Just, no.

"Kids, come and get all this stuff out of the car. Eat your dinner and then put all that stuff back into the garage for me before you get cleaned up for tonight."

They stared at her. Young Charlie took a step toward the car. "Mom, where are you going?"

Barb bent to reach into the car and grabbed the Chinese food, the smell wafting from the two bags making her stomach growl. Or maybe that was just her temper finally eradicating the last of her patience.

"I'm going out to find your father." She handed the take-out bags to Julia. "If he comes home before I do, tell him he's in the doghouse."

Charlie smiled at that—he loved references to any of them being in the doghouse, the imagery of it. Julia and Brian knew better. There was nothing here to smile about. Barb climbed back into the car and slammed the door. She took one more glance at her kids but said nothing as she started it up and reversed out of the driveway.

When she found Donnie, he really would be in the doghouse, because no way would she allow him to sleep in her bed tonight. Not when she was pretty sure he'd spent the afternoon in someone else's.

The tires skidded in road sand as she gave the car some gas. Then it leaped forward, and she didn't spare a thought to the possibility of early trick-or-treaters. Reason and caution had been left behind.

Donnie had hurt her too much, at last.

The time had come to see if she could hurt him back.

VANESSA MONTEZ

Vanessa liked to take her time making up her face. People seemed to think that her aesthetic was just slathering on makeup, but it took time and meticulous effort to achieve just the effect she was going for. The fact that she would be attending a Halloween party only added to what she deemed her obligation to perfect her look. Her lipstick tonight would be a dark, frosted blue, her cheeks albino white, and her eye makeup blacker than black. Boys and men fetishized her looks—some thought her beautiful and others ugly, but most of them wanted to slot her into some category they called "exotic" without realizing how racist their whole thought process was. She was something other than white, so automatically, she was mysterious.

Idiots.

Her mother was Vietnamese and her dad Dominican, and these boys didn't know what to make of her, which was just fine. Vanessa had never been interested in boys.

"Aren't you a little old for trick-or-treat?"

Vanessa flinched, heart racing as she turned to see her mother standing on the threshold of her bedroom. The door had been halfway open, so she wasn't exactly intruding, but a knock would have been nice.

"Mom! You scared the crap out of me!"

Lucy Montez's expression softened with hurt. She had a mischievous side, but she always hated to think she'd upset anyone she loved. "Sorry, honey. I didn't think." Then her eyebrows lifted. "Although, isn't this the day for scaring?"

Vanessa had to give her that. "It's fine. But try not to give me a heart attack, okay?"

"Not to worry. That's your job as a teenager. Giving your parents heart attacks."

"Fair," Vanessa replied. "Anyway, I'm not trick-or-treating, but I'm gonna go over to Steve's early and give out candy with him tonight, if that's okay. His parents are still going to be getting ready for the party, and he asked me."

Her mom pondered that for a moment. "I guess it's okay. I'm sure your dad won't mind."

"Thanks!" Vanessa saw the way her mother scrutinized her outfit and glanced at herself in the mirror on her bureau. "You don't like my costume?"

"It's a costume?"

That got a laugh. "Yes, Mom. I know it's hard to tell sometimes with me. I'm going as Siouxsie Sioux."

"Siouxsie Sioux. Always with you, it's Siouxsie Sioux."

Vanessa smiled. "You like the music. You know you do."

"It's okay. The hair and the makeup, though—you look like a ghost!"

"I look like a girl who doesn't give a damn what the world thinks."

Her mother's eyes narrowed, examining her more closely. Then she nodded. "Yes. I think you do." She kissed Vanessa on the temple. "But it's not a costume, my girl. It's only you."

Vanessa felt her chest swell. That was just about the nicest thing her mom had ever said to her. And then she had to go and ruin it.

"It must be nice on Halloween to walk around and not have people think you're strange."

She wanted to groan, but she kept quiet. Her mother meant well. In Lucy Montez's mind, that was probably a kind thing to say. But Vanessa could read between the lines—her mom had just sort of approved of her not giving a shit what people thought and then two seconds later snatched back that approval.

Vanessa forced a smile and wondered if her mother could tell it was a mask. Her parents were sweet and indulgent with her, and she loved to hang around with them, to watch TV or play board games or walk around Boston and just see the sights, but she knew they had never understood her and that they were uncomfortable when people shot puzzled or disapproving looks at their only child. They loved her unconditionally, but they didn't realize that Vanessa wanted to be seen as strange. She disapproved of the world and its people, and she wanted to set herself apart from it. If people saw her and thought she was a freak or an alien—something that didn't belong—that was precisely the response she desired. But how could she explain that to John and Lucy Montez, who struggled so hard to *belong*?

"I do love Halloween," she said. A safe reply. The truth.

She turned back to her mirror, adding more sharpness to the edges of the black diamonds she'd painted around her eyes. The wildly teased hair looked perfect right now, and she wondered how long it would stay like that—without it, the odds of anyone guessing she was masquerading as Siouxsie plummeted.

"So, you and Steve are spending a lot of time together," her mother observed with added gravity.

Vanessa snickered. "We've been spending a lot of time together since the first grade."

"I know. But it seems . . . more."

Fixing her spiky hair, Vanessa turned to face her mom. She'd never come out and *told* her parents she was gay, but she was sure both of her parents knew. It felt obvious to her in the little things they said and didn't say, the glances they gave each other when other parents talked about who their sons or daughters were dating, and asked if Vanessa had a boyfriend yet. There had never been a conversation, but she could see that they knew, and they didn't seem to love her any less. But she never brought it up, left it unsaid, because what if she was wrong?

No, she had never come out and told anyone aside from Steve. Even then, it was only because on her thirteenth birthday, Steve had told her that he loved her. He'd still been twelve and had been worried that when she started high school a year ahead of him, she would start hanging out with older boys and get swept off her feet by some guy with chin scruff and a guitar. She'd told him that she loved him, too, but that it would have to stay just the kind of love it had always been. Somehow that worked. Steve was the only one she trusted, the only one who knew. Owen and the other guys might tease her and call her *lezzie* and *dyke*, but they were mostly kidding. They didn't know any lesbians, and imagining she might actually be gay was, for them, like imagining she was a Martian. She didn't like it, but she tried not to hate them for being ignorant little pricks.

Steve, at least, was smart enough to love her for who she was.

Now Vanessa smiled at her mom and wondered if she would love her daughter any less if Vanessa opened up to her and confirmed what she had probably already guessed.

She will. She'll love you no matter what.

Her mom had always promised that, and Vanessa believed

it—most days. But she only had half a year left until college, and unless she met a girl and fell madly in love before then— which, let's face it, was pretty unlikely at Coventry High School—she planned to wait until after graduation to officially come out. That way if they were disappointed or disgusted with her, she'd only have to live with that reaction for a couple of months.

Until then, leaving it all unspoken felt safer.

"I've gotta go," she said, and she kissed her mom on the cheek.

"Have fun," her mom replied. "We'll see you at the party. Don't eat too much candy before dinner."

"It'll be fine," Vanessa promised. "One piece of candy for the kids and one for me, right? Even split?"

Her mother wagged a finger. "I haven't forgotten the year you threw up all over my bedroom."

Vanessa rolled her eyes as she hustled down the stairs. "I was nine years old! Move on, woman!"

With a wave, she went out the door and pulled it shut behind her, resisting the temptation to sample the candy that already waited in the Halloween-themed bowl on the little table her mom had put there this afternoon. Outside, she felt a twinge of yearning for the years when her dad brought her around the neighborhood on Halloween night, holding her hand as she engaged in the most important ritual of childhood commerce—the plea for free sweets.

The afternoon shadows had grown long, the street quiet in that strange almost postapocalyptic hush that enveloped them in the hour or so before trick-or-treat began. Parents would be struggling to dress their kids in costumes. Some of those kids would be throwing tantrums. Moms would be trying to cajole children to eat something now, early as it was, because if they had no dinner before they went out, they would be full to bursting with candy before they made it home, and dinner would be ruined.

Autumn leaves skittered along the pavement as Vanessa walked toward the Koenigs' house. Parmenter Road was a dead end, with three houses on the cul-de-sac, all of them surrounded by towering pines and oaks. The Koenig house was on the left, the Montez home on the right, and the Sullivans in between. Most afternoons, the Sullivans would have left their dog out on his own in the yard, leashed to a wire run that let him roam back and forth barking at passersby. Today, the dog was as scarce as the rest of the neighbors. It was like October had decided to hold its breath until November arrived.

Vanessa enjoyed the quiet. In her dark makeup and black combat boots, with her spiky hair, she felt like the ringmaster at some kind of nightmare circus, and the thought made her sublimely happy. If a life meeting that description were offered to her, she'd have jumped at the chance. Instead, she had this one night a year to pretend the world understood her. For now, that would have to do.

BARB SWEENEY

B arb went to Giovanni's first. The place styled itself a "trattoria," but that was just a fancy word for an Italian restaurant. Like most of the eateries in Coventry, it had a dining room space but also an attractive bar on one end, all brass and wood and gleaming bottles, with a big fat TV bolted to a shelf in the corner behind the bartender. The volume never went up—this wasn't that kind of bar—but there was always some type of sports match on, and they didn't require much narration.

When Barb pushed her way into Giovanni's on her own, she felt her face flush. Maybe nobody would notice her pink cheeks, but she thought they would. It infuriated her to know that she blushed, that she felt embarrassed to be searching the town for a husband who couldn't stay away from the bars for forty-eight hours in a row. Donnie's drinking she could handle, most days, but he didn't just come to bars for the drinks. He came for the scenery.

How many times had she done this—searching bars for her wandering spouse? Six or seven by now. Several times, she had failed to locate him, but others, she had spotted his car in a parking lot and gone inside, pasting a smile on her face. Instead of reminding him that he had children at home or that she had made dinner that was now in the trash, or that he had to be in court in the morning and he had lost several clients in the past year because he had been unprepared . . . Instead of any of those things, she would slide up next to him, put an arm around him, and ask him to order her a drink. If he had been flirting, his flirtation partner would look the other way, Donnie would order Barb a drink and greet her with a little kiss, as if he'd been waiting for her all along.

They would wait until they reached home for the fighting to start.

She had made an art form out of keeping her shit together when a lot of women would have made a scene. Barb Sweeney had not been raised to be one of those women.

Tonight, though, she felt brittle and on edge. How many more times would she go out searching for a man who did not want to be found, who cared nothing for his obligations to his wife, his children, or his clients? Donnie's charm had once been like magic, but tonight, it felt like a poison that had been eating away at her insides for years.

The owner of the place—a little Sicilian woman who'd stepped into the role when her father, the real Giovanni, had died—spotted Barb from across the restaurant the moment she came through the door. She didn't know the weathered little woman's name, but they shared a moment of recognition, and then, almost as one, they both glanced toward the bar. Yeah, the woman certainly recognized Barb, enough to know precisely what had brought her through the door. *Not embarrassing*, Barb thought. *Humiliating*.

If Donnie had been there, she'd have bitten her tongue, smiled through her teeth, and gotten him outside before she could break into shouts or tears, before she could say the things on her mind, maybe play out the scene with him for the last time. But Donnie wasn't there. The bar was sparsely populated by a pair of older divorcées drinking martinis and a wizened, old, dark-skinned man who might have been Giovanni's brother, given the look of him.

"Are you here for dinner?" the owner said, sidling over to the hostess stand, where Barb had paused to survey the bar.

"Not tonight, I'm sorry to say. Just looking for someone."

The woman smiled wistfully. "I understand. But he's not here tonight."

Tonight. The word carried extra meaning, and Barb did not need it spelled out for her. How often did he come into this place? More than Barb had known, that much seemed certain.

"If he comes in, you want me to tell him to go home?" the old woman asked.

Most of the time, Barb could forget it, push the sick feeling in her stomach aside—the disgust and the humiliation and the anger. But the way he had taken off this afternoon, leaving his kids to paint the house while he couldn't even finish organizing the garage—the way he'd left all that stuff on the driveway, lied to the kids that he had to go to the office, and about what time he'd be back—she'd had enough.

"If he comes in, tell him *not* to come home," Barb said. "Tell him to fuck himself." She turned her back, blushing even more deeply as she pushed through the door.

The owner let out a soft little exclamation, something in Italian, but Barb didn't bother trying to translate. She went to the car and started the engine, pulled out of the parking lot, and hesitated at the next intersection. Crosstown or downtown? Unless he'd added more to his repertoire, those were likely to be the stops on his bar crawl. River City Billiards was a pool hall that also happened to serve a hell of a surf-and-turf special for a reasonable price. The restaurant sported a very busy bar with low lighting and a music selection that included everything from the Rat Pack to current soft rock, as if to draw in the married men nostalgic for the days when they were young and single, and the divorced women who came out in twos and threes and didn't mind being the "other woman."

Barb didn't understand that part. These divorcées had been hurt, even broken, but every night, they were out here in their makeup and latest outfits, happy to be the reason some wife would end up hurt and having to rebuild her own life. She couldn't deny there was something inherently more attractive about a man who could take care of his family, who was good to his wife and loved his children. A man who had strength but also stability . . . that increased any guy's attractiveness dramatically. But you were never really going to meet those men in a bar, were you? If they were so trustworthy, they'd be sitting in the restaurant with their wives, not in the bar with someone else's ex.

She didn't bother looking in the restaurant. If Donnie had met some woman here, he wouldn't be treating her to a lobster dinner. A song by the Carpenters was playing through the speakers in the bar, and Barb couldn't help inwardly mocking these middle-aged lonely hearts still grasping at the past. There was nothing cool about this place.

A too-tan-for-October bleach-blonde with the posture and hip sway of an airline stewardess bumped into her, spilling her own fruity drink. She turned to cuss at Barb for the pink stain on her shirt, but something about Barb's glare shut her down. At work, at her kids' schools, almost anywhere else, Barb tried to be friendly and accommodating. Not here. The stewardess didn't dare say a word.

Halfway along the bar, in the press of bodies, Barb spotted Ted Oliphant and Alex Frankel flirting with women who were not their wives. She knew both men and she knew their wives, so when Ted spotted her, he raised a glass and gave the redhead beside him a few extra inches of distance.

"Barb! Great to see you," he said, tapping Alex Frankel with his free hand. "Hey, Franky, look who it is."

Alex paled, then caught himself and mustered a smile as Barb ignored him, striding up so she was face-to-face with Ted, closer to him now than the redhead whose charms he hoped to enjoy later.

"Where is he, Teddy?"

Ted frowned thoughtfully, put on his best, most understanding lawyer face. *Fucking lawyers*, she thought.

"You're looking for Donnie." As if she hadn't done this schtick with them before. "I'm not gonna lie to you, Barb. He was in here earlier, had a few drinks, but he left at least half an hour ago. Said he was supposed to be home for Halloween tonight."

Barb glared at him. Her lips were pressed together, and she had to force her mouth to hold back the words she wanted to say—and her eyes to hold back the tears of anger and frustration and years of turning the other cheek. She shot a glance at Alex, but he turned away, tried to pretend he wasn't a part of the conversation.

How much humiliation, how much insult, how much heartache did a person have to endure before she was allowed to stop behaving? How did the world expect her to maintain composure on a night like this?

She turned back to Ted. "What about you, counselor? Don't you have two little girls at home that you're supposed to take trick-or-treating? Seems to me both of you gentlemen have pumpkins to carve."

Ted blushed a dark red, visible even in the gloom of the bar. A moment or two passed, filled with the sounds of the restaurant, the clink of glasses in the bar, the chatter of diners and drinkers. Alex had stiffened, but now it was the buxom brunette who'd been keeping him company who finally answered Barb's question.

"You Donnie's wife?" the brunette asked, giving her a disdainful look of appraisal.

That disdain did it. The look in this woman's face. She couldn't take one more humiliation.

"Yes. I'm Donnie's wife. You Donnie's slut?" Barb replied.

"Hey," Alex said. "You've got no right to talk to her like—"

Barb held up one hand. "Shut your mouth, Alex. Or my next stop is your house, with a full report."

Alex shut his mouth.

The brunette, though, seemed to take it all in stride. She lifted her chin so she could look down on Barb. "Donnie's had plenty of sluts, honey. I'm not one of them. I'm a little too obvious for him. From what I hear, he likes more of a challenge. But be that as it may, these boys are telling the truth. Your husband was here and he left, said something about Chinese food. Could be he just wants to climb on top of that waitress at the Sampan, but I got the feeling he was actually going home for once."

The *for once* was what pushed Barb's last button.

She snatched the drink from Ted's hand, drained the scotch from the glass, coughed a little, and then slung the half-melted ice into the brunette's face.

Alex grabbed her wrist while Ted took the empty glass from her hand.

"What the hell was that for?" Ted demanded.

Barb held her hands up in surrender and backed away from them all. "I like your wives, that's why. Maybe they're too nice, too normal to come looking for you in every dive in Coventry, but I'm not. And I'll bet it's only a matter of time before they get tired of pretending they married good men. Someday maybe they'll be right where you're standing, picking up other women's husbands and spending your alimony money while your kids learn to hate you. They deserve better than you."

She turned her back on them, pushing through patrons to escape the bar.

"Jesus," Alex said to her retreating back, "what's her problem?"

Ted, though, at least had the decency to tell him to shut up. Maybe Barb had made him feel just the slightest hint of shame. If so, she was glad—she just wished someone else's wife would have done the same to her own husband.

Out in the parking lot, she sat in the car in the last hour of daylight, and she cried out of anguish, and then out of rage.

Then Barb drove home, wondering what she would find when she got there. Wondering how they could just keep going on like this.

VANESSA MONTEZ

The sun had become just a flare of orange above the tree line. Stars had begun to emerge along with a quarter moon, enough illumination to turn the oncoming evening a ghostly blue. In the Koenigs' backyard, golden lights had been strung around the deck and over the sliding glass door to the kitchen. Some of the biggest pumpkins Vanessa had ever seen sat atop small tables, candles flickering eerily behind their carved, evil faces. The enormous deck had a tiki bar set up on one end that didn't really go with the Halloween season, but Mr. Koenig had hung rubber bats from the thatched roof, and the speakers behind the bar were playing a spooky music mix that included haunted house sounds, evil laughter, and various scary songs. Vanessa and Steve liked "Thriller" and "Monster Mash" well enough, but they'd been helping to decorate the deck and backyard for an hour and already heard each of those songs more than once. Musically, it was going to be a long and repetitive night.

The party wouldn't start for quite a while still. Not until trick-or-treat had begun to wind down. For now, Vanessa and Steve had the deck to themselves while Steve's mom and dad handed out candy. Through the screen of the open slider, Vanessa heard the doorbell and a cheer from Mr. Koenig—it

46

seemed the first of the Halloween frighteners had arrived to claim their candy.

"This feels weird," she said. "Almost, like, adult."

Steve glanced over at her. They were sitting on the wicker sectional that filled one corner of the deck, relaxing on cushions. Vanessa had her legs folded beneath her, comfortable in full Siouxsie Sioux makeup. Even her spiky hair seemed to be holding up fairly well. Steve sprawled on his back, his head just a few inches from her hip, the cowboy hat he'd acquired for tonight's costume resting over his heart.

"Boring, you mean?" he asked.

"You're bored?" She looked at him curiously. It was his house, after all. His parents' party.

"Nah. I'm here with you, and it's quiet, and I like looking at the stars. When the party starts and all the neighborhood hypocrites start showing up, that's when I'll be bored."

Vanessa smiled. "You have any hypocrites in mind, specifically?"

Steve didn't take his eyes off the stars overhead. "All of them. I like some of the neighbors, don't get me wrong. But aside from yours, can you think of one family that lives on Parmenter who isn't full of shit in one way or another?"

"The Colemans?"

"He pretends he's the world's greatest dad because he drills his sons until they're the best athletes in town, but have you ever seen him talk to either of those kids about anything else? He snaps at them, makes them miserable, they look like they'd rather jump off a bridge than swing another bat, but everyone pats the dad on the back, like he's some kind of hero instead of a turd."

"The Kenneys?"

"Mrs. Kenney and my mom despise each other. They go to the same hairdresser," Steve said. "It's like there's a weird tug-of-war, where people have to decide to be friends with the Kenneys or friends with my parents, but it's an unwritten rule. Nobody talks about it. But are the Kenneys invited to the party tonight? Yes, they are. And will they show up?"

Vanessa tipped the brim of an invisible hat. "You bet your ass they will."

"Hypocrites."

"Point taken. What about the Barbosas, though? The dad does his whole Haunted Woods thing for charity. That's pretty cool of him."

"I guess," Steve allowed. "But he never waves."

"What do you mean?"

"When I'm out for a walk or something, or when we used to wait for the bus back before the miracle of your driver's license, if you saw him going out somewhere in his car, he'd never wave. Not very friendly."

Vanessa sighed. "Or just unhappy. Maybe some people are just not overly friendly because they've got their own troubles, something else on their mind. When I'm Mr. Barbosa's age, I doubt I'll wave at random kids waiting at their bus stops. I'll be too grumpy in the morning for that crap."

"I guess."

"You just want *him* to notice you because you want *Chloe* to notice you."

Steve didn't try to deny it. "Nothing wrong with that. She's lived maybe ten houses away from me for years and barely knows I exist." He shifted on the cushions, craned his head back so that he could look at her face without sitting up. "You're right, okay? I know you are. But none of that means I'm in any rush to join the grown-up world of hypocrisy and, like, muddling through my days, needing coffee to keep from murdering people."

They fell into a comfortable silence. Their long friendship

allowed for such things. The ruckus of trick-or-treaters around the front of the house grew louder and more frequent. Kids squealed, and parents called after them to slow down, or to say, "Thank you," or to only take one piece of candy per house. Vanessa missed being that young, when nothing else mattered but how many Reese's cups she could score over the course of the night.

She'd told Steve it felt weird to be back there, just waiting for the night to begin. They were too old to trick-or-treat but too young to have kids. Too young to go to bars, too young for college parties. They could give out candy with Steve's parents, but that seemed weak, and they could have gone to the party the CYO was throwing at the church hall at St. Francis tonight, but that was even worse. It felt like they were just floating in this weird space, not willing to commit to juvenile delinquency but with college still waiting in the distance.

Yet, out here on the deck, just the two of them, Vanessa felt content. She wasn't eager to go off to college and leave him behind—something that would happen in less than a year. Sitting out here and relaxing with her best friend felt the way she imagined adulthood to be. It might be boring— she suspected it would be—but it also felt sweet and safe, like something she ought to cherish.

She grabbed him gently by the ear, gave it a little tug. It was something she'd done to him out of affection since they were in elementary school.

"I don't know what I'd do without you," she confessed.

"Ditto." He smiled.

"Really. So many kids call one another best friends and that lasts for a year or two, and then they switch around like it's musical chairs. I just have you."

"I just have you, too," Steve said, reaching up to hold her hand. "But that's enough."

Vanessa laid her head back against the cushions and looked at the moon and stars. The doorbell rang again, and a little girl made spooky ghost noises, an *Ooooooooooooo* that carried from the front door all the way out to the back deck. The party would start in a couple of hours, and Vanessa would hang around, mostly for her parents' sake. They were a bit shy themselves and appreciated that she could whisper a reminder to them when they forgot the names of this or that neighbor. But for now, it was just her and Steve.

"Just so you know, I'm over Chloe," Steve said, his voice quiet. "It's been Julia Sweeney for a while now."

"I know," Vanessa replied, squeezing his hand. "Me, too."

Steve sat up, grinning like a conspiratorial fool as he leaned toward her. "Wait. You, too?"

Vanessa laughed and sat up. "I know. I'm an idiot. She's clearly not looking my direction."

"Don't worry, Vee." He sighed. "She's not looking my direction, either."

She'd been worried that Steve would be annoyed when he found out they were both crushing on the same girl. Now she knew how dumb she'd been. He was her best friend. Of course he wouldn't mind. If anything, he seemed happy.

"Oh my God, she's so damn cool," he said.

"Right?" Vanessa said. She glanced around, still protective of her secret. "And those eyes kill me."

"Is that blue even a color human eyes can be?"

They both laughed quietly, grinning with their shared secret.

And then they heard a third voice laughing along with them. It came from the woods behind the house, from the darkness there, and Vanessa felt as if her heart had seized in her chest.

"Who's there?" Steve called, slowly sitting up, eyes narrowed as he tried to peer into the woods.

The voice began to call to Vanessa, speaking her name in a loud rasp meant to sound like a whisper, like something that hadn't spoken in a long, long time. Steve shrank back against the cushions, but Vanessa felt something give way inside her. Whatever had made her freeze a moment earlier now shattered, and she shot to her feet.

"The party's not for a couple of hours yet, asshole," she snapped, jumping down the three steps to the grass and striding across the Koenigs' backyard. "If you want some fun and games before then, go and hang out with the little kids. Maybe they'll fall for your spooky bullshit."

For a few seconds, nothing moved in the trees. Vanessa held her breath. If there were some kind of ghost or flesh-eating ghoul in the woods, she felt pretty sure it wouldn't know her name. Plus, she thought she'd recognized that voice, even raspy as it was. She told herself she was 100 percent certain that nothing waited in the woods for them, no evil lurked back there, full of malice and hunger. One hundred percent.

Okay, maybe 99 percent.

Footsteps crunched leaves, and she exhaled in relief as Owen O'Leary emerged from the woods behind the Koenigs' house. He'd made himself up as a hobo clown, with patched-up rags for clothes and some fairly impressive makeup that his sister must've done for him. As he stepped out of the trees, Owen reached into his jacket and pulled out a hard pack of Marlboros and a Bic. He lit up with the smooth reflexes of a gunslinger, a move she suspected he'd practiced in a mirror, and then held the pack of cigarettes out to her.

"Smoke?"

Vanessa gave him the same look of disgust she always had, the same expression she had whenever she spotted roadkill in the street.

Steve came down off the deck, spine straight, in the same

way billions of young men had confronted billions of other young men since time began, hiding his fear of personal harm beneath a mask of disdain and false bravado.

"What's your problem, O'Leary?" Steve asked.

Owen took a drag of his cigarette, eerie behind his clown makeup. The orange tip of the Marlboro glowed more brightly and cast a strange shadow on his face. "I don't have a problem, man. Your folks say the whole neighborhood's welcome at this bash they're throwing, but honestly, I'm not feeling real welcome."

"We told you," Steve said. "It doesn't start till later. You know that."

"I do." He nodded, head ducking low, out in front of his shoulders. It was a strange little affectation, but even though Vanessa didn't like him sometimes, she had always found this endearing. It made him seem more ordinary, less like the tough asshole he so often seemed to want to be.

"What are you doing back here, then?" she asked, no longer angry.

Owen used his cigarette to point into the woods. "I put a big cooler full of beer back there, plus a bottle of Southern Comfort and a two-liter of 7 Up for mixing." He tilted his head toward Steve. "I know your parents wouldn't be cool with kids drinking at the party and wanted to respect that."

Steve laughed, but there was no humor in it. "Sorry, what? How is that respecting their wishes?"

"Me and the guys won't drink at the party, not on the deck or in the house," Owen replied as if the whole thing were eminently reasonable. "Maybe in the yard, if it's in a cup, but we'll be cool about it. This way we have our party and they have theirs, and nobody has to get upset."

He patted Steve on the arm. "You're welcome to imbibe along with us, Stevie. I know you're not a big drinker or anything, but it's Halloween. Some of us are going off to college next fall. Might be the last big neighborhood party we're all at. Kind of got me feeling a little . . . what's the word?"

"Nostalgic?" Vanessa suggested.

"That, yeah. But I was going for something else. Wistful. It's got me feeling wistful. I don't want any trouble. It's all about love, tonight."

Vanessa and Steve were both speechless, unsure how seriously they ought to take this thoughtful turn from Owen O'Leary, who'd never been an especially bad human but who had frequently been an arrogant prick, too immature to waste time being courteous or kind.

"You're serious," Vanessa said.

Owen pushed his long, bushy hair away from his face and took another drag on his Marlboro. "I mean, later on, I'm sure I'll behave like an ass. That's what whiskey and beer are for, basically. But yeah. You know I'm cool with you, Vanessa. You got a wicked sharp edge to you. Stevie, you're a dweeb, but you're our dweeb. Who knows, probably end up working for you someday—"

"You think I'd hire you?" Steve said, but he was joking now, which surprised Vanessa more than anything. She got along all right with Owen and his crew, but Steve had never had a kind word to say about them.

Voices were raised inside the house, and they all turned to look at the deck and the lights beyond the screen door and the slider. From the moonlit yard, they watched Steve's dad hustle into the kitchen to retrieve more bags of candy from the counter. Apparently, the excellent Halloween weather had the trick-or-treat trade booming.

"Okay, I gotta bolt," Owen said, raising his cigarette in farewell. "But I'll see you guys later."

For a second, Vanessa thought he meant to return to the

woods, which would be stupid, because none of the paths back there would lead him home. Instead he started cutting across the backyard and onto the property of the house next door.

Owen hesitated, then turned back to them. "Hey, Vanessa."

"Yeah?"

"Watch what you're drinking tonight. The freaks are coming, and you don't want to end up in the Love Shack or the back of that asshole's van."

Her stomach twisted with a wave of nausea. "I'll be careful. Thanks, Owen."

He waved again, and then he was gone.

Vanessa turned to look at Steve. "Your parents invited Zack and Ruth?"

"The whole neighborhood, remember?" Steve said. "It'll be fine. Even if you believe all those stories, they're not gonna do anything here. Who's that stupid?"

Vanessa felt that queasy twist in her gut again. Zack and Ruth Burgess had moved to Parmenter Road two years ago, thirtysomething, no kids. They'd moved in with Ruth's parents, basically overnight, a surprise to even the next-door neighbors. A few days later, the local newspapers were full of details about a New Hampshire couple who'd been kicked out of their rented house after police had arrested them on charges stemming from accusations that they'd been running a brothel out of their house. The details and rumors that emerged hinted that rather than a brothel, they'd been hosting regular swingers' sex parties and the people who lived in nearby houses wanted them gone. Supposedly, there'd been drugs involved, and because the guests had to kick in some money—like a cover charge—to cover the costs of the food and drinks and drugs, the cops had been able to charge them with prostitution, distribution of drugs, and other crimes.

Zack and Ruth Burgess were never named as the couple

in the "Love Shack" story, which was soon replaced by some other bit of scandal in the newspaper, but somehow, many of the residents of Parmenter Road had come to that conclusion. Zack and Ruth—who insisted that the teens in the neighborhood call them by their first names—were rumored to have done all kinds of other things, including abducting and drugging kids in the back of Zack's van. Stories swirled about them getting people drunk and having sex with them at the house, only to have them wake up at the house and slink out in shame.

Vanessa had believed a lot of those stories at first. Everyone talked about Zack and Ruth—and Ruth's parents had since retired to Florida, leaving the younger couple alone in the house—so it seemed like some of it had to be true. And maybe some of it was. But she had serious doubts about anyone being abducted and raped in Zack's van. As far as she knew, the police had never been to visit them. Vanessa figured they were just the boogeymen of Parmenter Road now, a nasty little suburban myth. She felt sort of bad for them, really.

But that didn't mean she wasn't going to be very careful with what she drank tonight, just in case something ended up in her cup that she didn't want there.

"You worried?" Steve asked.

"Nope. Just hungry," she said. "I'll murder someone for a fucking cheeseburger."

He laughed. "I don't think murder will be necessary."

RICK BARBOSA

When the doorbell rang for the first time, Rick did a fist pump and leaped from the sofa. He'd been sitting with his mom, watching the ridiculous old movie *The Blob* on Channel 38 because Alice Barbosa didn't think her "little man" was old enough for scary movies. Even though they had a VCR and Chloe had rented *The Exorcist* for later on tonight—and even though Rick was in eighth grade and a teenager now—Mom was totally stonewalling him. As if he hadn't watched R-rated movies before, after she'd gone to sleep. Dad objected to those, too, but at least he didn't try to stop Rick from watching the old ones that were always on local stations on the weekends. Monster movies. A lot of them were cheap, old black-and-white things, but he didn't mind. Rick liked them all, from boring, foot-dragging Mummy movies to his very favorite film, John Carpenter's *The Thing*. If he thought any of the goons he would be trick-or-treating with would understand the costume, he'd have dressed as Kurt Russell from that movie, fake beard and all.

Good thing you didn't, he thought now. *Chilly night or not, it would've been sweaty trudging around the neighborhood in that jacket.*

The doorbell rang a second time.

"Jeez, we're coming!" Rick called.

His mom had ducked into the kitchen to check on the lasagna baking in the oven, but now she poked her head out. "One piece of candy per kid. It's going to be a busy night."

"Yeah, yeah." Rick wished she would realize that he wasn't six years old anymore. Thirteen might not make him a high school kid, but he had a working brain. She didn't need to repeat everything ten times.

He opened the door and was surprised to find his friends had arrived on time for once. The little kids would show up for their treats any minute, but now he wouldn't have to deal with them. He could start his own trick-or-treating. At thirteen, he figured it might be his last year.

"Mom!" he called. "The guys are here."

Rick barely listened to her reply. He grabbed his old rubber Frankenstein mask and tugged it on. Chalky, rubbery, a little moldy, the smell inside the mask should have been gross, but it made him happy.

"Ready!" he said, picking up his pillowcase as he rushed out the storm door.

Then they were off, laughing and cussing and shoving one another across the lawn. In the back of his mind, Rick knew they were still little shits, that as tough as he imagined himself to be, the trouble they were likely to get into was small-time. Kid stuff. But that was okay with him. If they played ding-dong ditch at some houses or broke a couple of streetlights to make the street darker, they could definitely get grounded for that kind of thing, but probably not arrested. Probably not beaten up or put in jail. Some of Chloe's friends did drugs, and one girl had gotten pregnant and been beaten up by her dad and thrown out of the house. That was a whole different level, and Rick felt no rush to get older. For him, thirteen was like Baby Bear's bed felt to Goldilocks—just right.

Quinn and Tommy were friends from school who happened to live in the neighborhood. They weren't his best friends at school, not even his best friends in the neighborhood, but they were "the guys." His actual best friend on earth—Billie Suarez—didn't go to school with them, but she lived two doors down and Rick had grown up racing through the next-door neighbor's backyard to get to her house. The couple who lived in the middle, the Panzas, were cranky old racist assholes who didn't like Black kids in the yard and yelled anytime they saw Billie back there, but Rick and Billie had worn a path along the back edge of their property anyway. Anytime Mr. Panza yelled, they ducked into the woods, and then he had no right to complain, as he didn't own anything past the first trees. The woods back there actually belonged to Rick's parents, so Mr. and Mrs. Panza could eat shit and die for all Rick and Billie cared.

Of course, the racist bullshit bothered Billie. She told her parents a few times when she was little, but as she got older, she decided it wasn't worth it. The Panzas weren't getting any less racist, and the Suarezes were sure as hell not moving. Billie's parents were stubborn. They'd come from Cuba as little more than kids themselves, and they weren't going to let anyone push them out.

Billie's Halloween costume was Storm, from the *X-Men* comic book. Rick had read a couple of dozen *X-Men* comics at Billie's insistence, and he thought the stories were pretty cool, but reading comics wasn't for him. He found it hard to figure out the natural flow of the pictures on the page—like, up or down or to the side? Where were his eyes supposed to go next?—but Billie loved them so much that he had absorbed plenty of information about the characters, and her passion for Storm was infectious, maybe even a little aggravating at times. Quinn was the only other one of their friends who seemed to read a lot of comics, but he seemed mostly obsessed with *Justice League of America*. If Rick had to pick between Batman and Storm, it was definitely going to be Batman, but he wouldn't ever have admitted that where Billie could hear him.

Her mom had done the costume for her. In recent comics, Storm had gone from her white-haired African goddess superhero look to a kind of white-mohawked punk ass-kicker look, but Mrs. Suarez would never have let Billie get a mohawk. Instead, she had a long white wig and a black cape that had been tailored with gold edging and swooped up to attach to Billie's wrists, and with the white wig and the little headband Mrs. Suarez had made, it was enough that anyone familiar with the character would recognize her. But unlike the usual costumes, the pirates and hoboes and Darth Vaders, most people would have no idea. They'd assume Billie was dressed as a witch or a vampire, and Rick thought that was a real shame. Most kids their age just threw together anything so they could trick-or-treat, like Rick relying on his old Frankenstein mask, but Billie had passion none of them would recognize or appreciate.

Side by side, they set off up the street with purpose.

"The usual arrangement?" he asked Billie, by which he meant the long-standing compact that Billie would get all the Baby Ruths, and Rick every single Reese's Peanut Butter Cup. After trick-or-treat, the two of them always ended up at the house of one family or the other, dumped out their candy, and began their usual trading and bartering.

This year, there were going to be some extra items on the agenda, however, since they intended to go to the Koenigs' party for a little while, and Billie had made Rick promise to take her through his dad's Haunted Woods. She'd been too terrified every year up till now—and Billie still wasn't completely sure she wanted to subject herself to screams and terror in the dark woods on Halloween night. But Rick had told her this was the last year for the Haunted Woods, her last chance. He'd offered to hold her hand and protect her, but Billie had reminded him that she was a month older and didn't need to hold his stupid hand. She'd punched him in the shoulder, and Rick had gritted his teeth and pretended it hadn't hurt.

Billie's real name was Guillerma, but nobody called her that except her dad, and the only time most people remembered she wasn't just Billie was the first day of every school year when the teacher took attendance. Teachers invariably mangled the hell out of Guillerma until Billie explained it was the feminine of Guillermo, which translated to "William" in English, and to please call her Billie.

"Hey, hey!" Quinn said, racing to catch up with them on the street. "Can I get in on this candy trading thing?"

Billie looked over her shoulder, and down her nose. "Depends what candy you like."

"Charleston Chew are my favorite."

Rick burst out laughing.

Quinn frowned, looking a bit hurt. "What's so funny?"

Billie patted his shoulder. "He thinks you're joking. Rick says Charleston Chews taste like dog turds, so yep. All yours, Quinn. You don't even have to trade anything back. If anyone's handing out dog turds tonight, you get 'em all."

Even Tommy, who usually had Quinn's back, laughed at this.

Quinn just shrugged. "Fine by me. If they're dog turds, they're the tastiest friggin' dog turds on earth."

Rick held out a hand to shake. "Fair enough."

They shook, and then Billie bolted for the front steps of the next house and Rick pursued her. It was too early to worry about which houses might run out of their best candy, but racing one another was fun. Other kids were all over the place now. Witches and vampires, hoboes and clowns. Little kids were made up like princesses, cowboys, superheroes, and the occasional Indiana Jones or Luke Skywalker.

When it was their turn, Billie and Rick were the first two kids in their group to hold out their open pillowcases. The woman at the open door, Mrs. Standish, wrinkled her nose when she saw Billie. "Aren't you a little old to be trick-or-treating?"

"She's tall for her age," Rick said, voice muffled inside his Frankenstein mask.

Mrs. Standish sniffed and dropped a couple of mini candy bars into each of their pillowcases. Rick spotted the telltale blue of a Nestlé Crunch wrapper and grumbled to himself, then thanked the old woman and trotted down the steps with Billie. They both hated Nestlé.

"Hey," Billie said quietly, coming to a halt on the grass.

Rick turned to her, wondering if she had a hole in her pillowcase or something, but her attention was entirely on him. She stared at the eyeholes in his mask, and for a moment, he felt badly and wondered if he should take it off, show his face.

"I can stand up for myself," she said.

"I know, Bill. But that old lady—"

"Gives me the same look every time she sees me on the street, Halloween or no Halloween."

"She was being—"

"It doesn't matter," Billie interrupted. "I mean, it does. But let's just have fun, okay? I know it's not why she said it to me, but the old bat's not wrong. We're almost too big for this, and I just wanna enjoy it."

Rick thought about his father and his sister, Chloe, running their Haunted Woods tonight for the last time. About how he'd overheard his parents fighting about selling the house, how they couldn't afford to keep it and needed a smaller, cheaper place to live. He hadn't told his friends, not even Billie, that he'd be moving away, but he had a feeling she must know. The adults would have gossiped about it. She didn't ask him and he didn't tell her, as if that would stop it from happening.

Now Billie was accepting that they were getting too old to trick-or-treat. They'd talked about it before, but in her expression, he saw for the first time what a change it really was. Not just Halloween, but everything about the way they'd grown up together, the two of them. Maybe not tonight but soon, all that would truly be over, in the rearview mirror, and they'd have to leave it behind.

Not tonight, though. Rick was determined. He wasn't moving out of the neighborhood yet.

"Rick—"

"Okay," he said. "Sorry, I was just thinking. But I've got it, Billie. Only fun tonight."

She smiled. "Good. Then I won't have to punch you again."

A voice called out from behind them. Rick turned to see another group of kids rushing to catch up, but then he realized they were more interested in Tommy and Quinn. The one in the Jason Voorhees hockey mask had to be Vince Spinale, based on size alone. Vince wasn't much older—fifteen—but twice the size. Even so, nobody was going to turn him away if he went to the door in search of candy . . . unless they just screamed and called the cops when they saw him in his Jason mask. The image made Rick smile inside his stinky rubber Frankenstein face.

"You know those kids?" Billie asked as they hustled up the walk toward the next house.

Rick glanced back again. It was hard to tell in the dark and with costumes on, but he thought he could identify a couple of the others with Vince. One girl in a Red Riding Hood outfit might have been Heather-something, who had a crush on Vince.

A kid in a baseball uniform with whiteface makeup might have been Vince's cousin, who hung around the neighborhood a lot, but Rick couldn't remember his name. One kid looked like he was dressed as the Scarecrow from *The Wizard of Oz*, but only at first glance. At second glance, his costume seemed freakier than that. His jacket looked dirty, with rips that had been badly sewn, and the hat looked more like a clown's than a scarecrow's. His makeup looked creepy and sad, with rose-pale smears on his cheeks and drawn-on stitches. Something about the way the kid hung back behind the others suggested he was shy, quiet, and Rick figured he wasn't going to make any new friends with that costume. It gave Rick a chill just to look at the kid, and he smiled, thinking, *Mission accomplished.*

Billie rang the next doorbell, and a dad came to the door dressed as the devil himself. He offered them their choice of full-size candy bars, and Rick gave him a thumbs-up.

"If hell offers full-size Snickers, sign me up," Rick said.

The devil laughed and ushered them back so he could serve the rest of the kids who had come up behind Rick and Billie. When they'd all had their turn and were moving on to the next house, cutting across the lawn, the haunted scarecrow kid fell in behind Rick, following him in silence. The others were talking, laughing, gossiping savagely about kids who weren't there to defend themselves. But that scarecrow stayed behind Rick, almost too close.

Rick wouldn't have said the kid gave him the creeps, but he did pick up his pace, rushing with a laughing Billie to the next house. Rushing to keep ahead of the silent scarecrow, who kept following with small, inexorable steps, his head down as if afraid someone would notice him out there in the dark, among the other kids.

What's your story? Rick thought.

But then Billie grabbed his hand, excited to see the next

house was giving out cans of cold soda. They kept racing ahead, house to house, and soon the ratty old scarecrow had been mostly forgotten. But he hadn't gone anywhere. He kept up with the group, speaking to no one, almost as if the others barely noticed him.

"Do you know that kid in the scarecrow outfit?" he asked Billie.

"Isn't it Alan Tylden?" she replied.

"Definitely not. Alan's taller, and wider."

"No idea, then. But it's a creepy costume."

It really was.

BARB SWEENEY

When Barb pulled her car into the driveway, her headlights washed over a group of trick-or-treaters that included five little kids, a baby in a stroller, and a trio of moms who looked like they were having more fun than their kids. One of them had a longneck Budweiser in hand and a witch's hat on her head. The kids were an assortment of Disney characters who didn't exactly go together—Tigger, Snow White, Peter Pan, and Minnie Mouse. The baby was clad in something pink that Barb assumed was a Piglet costume, even though she didn't get more than a glimpse.

She hit the brakes. The moms all whipped around to make sure the car hadn't killed any of their children. Barb ignored them, staring instead at the buckets and other painting equipment just inside the still-open garage. Her kids had finished for the day sometime before sunset, put the stuff into the garage, and just left it there. The ladder remained up against the house. She killed the engine, and the headlights went dark. Inside the garage, the door that led into the kitchen opened, illumination spilling into the concrete gloom of the garage, and her thirteen-year-old, Brian, stuck his head out. He must have heard the car arrive, she knew, and now he was checking on her.

Guilt flooded her heart. Brian hadn't gone trick-or-treating or gone to a party. He'd stayed home, waiting for her, which likely meant that Charlie had also not gone out collecting candy with his friends.

Donnie, she thought. *You son of a bitch.*

She'd gone searching for her asshole husband and left her kids to wrap up their work on the house and deal with Halloween plans on their own. And she'd apologize to them, take the blame, allow them to be angry with her because she did share some of the responsibility. But when they weren't home, it would be Donnie she blamed, Donnie she fucking crucified. Barb had endured so much as Mrs. Donald Sweeney, but the party bus her husband had been driving all these years had just run out of goddamn road.

The mom in the witch's hat rang the bell while the others glanced warily over their shoulder at Barb's car. Barb opened the door, climbed out, and shut it quietly, not wanting to make a scene. Then the front door opened, and her breath caught in her throat. She had been expecting Julia. As the eldest, she would have taken charge of Halloween, handing out candy, waiting for mom to come home from her dad-hunt. But it wasn't Julia who came to the door. After Barb had searched all over town for him, learned more than she wanted to know about Donnie's nocturnal activities around Coventry and beyond, there he was, answering the doorbell on Halloween night as if everything were perfectly ordinary. As if that were the kind of man—the kind of father and husband—he was.

Barb lost her shit.

"What the hell do you think you're doing?" she demanded, striding toward the front door.

The little kids must have felt the wave of fury radiating from her, or just seen it in her face, because they scampered down the three granite steps and scurried back toward their moms—all except Minnie Mouse, who held a plastic pumpkin bucket out toward Donnie even as she turned to stare defiantly at Barb. Tiny Minnie hadn't gotten her candy, and she wasn't going away without it. Donnie had turned at the sound of her voice, but the presence of the formidable little Minnie Mouse forced his attention back to the bowl of candy in his arms. He dropped a couple of pieces in her pumpkin bucket and smiled at her. The smile gave him away, as it always did. Alcoholics were often excellent actors, and Donnie had bullshitted his way through many an encounter, claiming he'd only had a drink or two. But his smile changed when he was drunk, became lopsided and relaxed, and he squinted when he'd gone way overboard.

Like right now.

"Look at you!" she said, reaching the steps just as Minnie Mouse finally retreated with her prize. The little girl squeaked in delayed fear and raced back to her mother, the woman brandishing her Budweiser longneck.

All three of the moms were staring. Barb ignored them.

"I've been all over town looking for you, *again*." She jabbed a finger at Donnie's chest. He clutched the candy bowl to him and leaned against the doorjamb. "I've had enough, Donnie! You took off in the middle of cleaning the goddamn garage, left your kids to cover your ass while you went out to drink with the sluts who'll laugh at your jokes and feed your ego, stick their tits in your face—"

"Lady, hey! Jesus Christ!" Budweiser mom snapped. "Maybe now's not the time?"

Barb turned to jab that same finger in the air, pointing at all three moms and their kids. "Oh, mind your business, for God's sake! Do you think I wanted this? You think I said, 'Sure, let's have a meltdown in front of the neighborhood—'"

"Barbara, hey—" one of the other moms began. The way she tilted her head, and the way her curly brown hair fell across her face, summoned her name from Barb's memory—Janis-something. Her daughter had been in Scouts with Julia, a thousand years ago.

"Take it inside," Janis-something said. "You don't need to share this with anyone else."

Barb stared at her, at the little kids shrinking away from her front door, holding their candy as if they were afraid she might try to snatch it, and she began to tremble. When she blinked, she understood that at some point she had begun to cry. Tears slid down her face. Angrily, she wiped them away and nodded to Janis-something, wordlessly waving at them to move on. As she did so, a quartet of slightly older kids started across the grass from the house next door, no parents accompanying them.

A hand landed on her shoulder. Barb flinched, turned, and found herself eye to eye with her drunken, cheating motherfucker of a husband. She could've taken kindness from him in that moment, and she could have taken anger. If he'd been ready for a fight, that would have been okay. Instead, he looked at her with disdain, as if her display of emotion there in their front yard had embarrassed him—embarrassed *him*!

"Barb," he began.

She put both hands on his chest and shoved him backward through the open door. He stumbled, nearly lost his footing, but managed to stay upright as he grabbed hold of the banister at the bottom of the stairs. Barb did not bother to look back at the people out in her yard, the audience who'd had a front row seat to her breaking at last. Now she brought the curtain down, slamming the door behind her.

Donnie repeated her name. Barb wiped again at her tears, sickened by her inability to stop crying. He reached out a comforting hand, and she slapped it away.

"I really did have to go to the office," he said.

"I wasn't aware you'd moved your office to River City Billiards."

His left eyelid twitched, like a crack appearing in thin ice. "You really were out hunting for me. Christ, you need your head examined."

She almost forgot how to breathe. Her face felt so hot, and she knew she must have flushed deep red. "I need my . . ."

Barb had never slapped her husband's face before. Not ever. Her hand flashed out before her brain even registered the action. The sound of that slap, her palm and fingers against his cheek, echoed through the foyer. Her engagement ring had been turned inward—she hadn't wanted to flash it around while she was by herself, searching bars for Donnie—and the prongs around the diamond scratched his face. A red line rose up on his skin, along with a few beads of blood.

Donnie stared at her as if she had removed her mask to reveal a wolf underneath. "What the hell was that?"

The floorboards at the top of the stairs creaked. "Mom, stop! Please stop!"

She looked up to see her sons staring down at her, as if she was the one responsible. Her youngest, a tearful Charlie, had been the one to speak. Behind him, Brian wore a lost expression, his face red but without tears. Beyond them, in the shadowy interior of the darkened kitchen, Barb could just make out her daughter. The boys just wanted this to stop, but it was Julia's eyes she felt burning her from the darkness. Julia only watched, and Barb knew that whatever happened next would hang in the air between herself and her daughter forever. She wondered how many other moments like this had passed by without her recognizing how they would color her daughter's view of her, and of men, and of herself.

"Barb," Donnie said, gentle again, taking advantage of the boys' interruption.

"This isn't the first time I've gone looking for you, or have you forgotten?" she asked. Somehow her spine felt straighter. When she wiped again at her eyes, the tears were drying up.

"If you're asking do I remember the other times you've humiliated me in public, then yes. I haven't forgotten."

She smiled thinly, nodding. "Of course. I humiliated you. Not the other way around? You don't think it's humiliating for a grown woman with three children to fetch her husband home so he can fulfill his responsibilities to her and to those children?"

The kids were there, listening to every word. She'd fought with their father in front of them, but not like this. Not with them looking on, watching as if their parents were performing some grotesque marriage theater.

The doorbell rang. Laughter came from outside.

Trick-or-treaters.

Donnie reached for the doorknob. Barb beat him to it, turned the dead bolt, and flicked off the outside lights.

"Sorry!" she called through the door. "Candy's all gone."

Someone slapped a hand against the door. "Jerks!"

The kids rang the doorbell a couple of times and then ran, shouting to one another. Whoever had been out there, they were too old to be begging for candy tonight. Halloween, she'd always believed, should be a night for the ones still young enough to be sweet. And scared. Halloween was for both.

Barb and Donnie studied each other like bull and toreador, but she couldn't be sure which she was. She sure as hell was seeing red.

"I've had enough," she said, voice a quiet rasp.

"Mom, stop," Charlie said at the top of the stairs. Eleven years old was too young to understand.

"You're a husband and a father. All your life, you've been dodging responsibilities because you charm everyone. It's a blessing and a curse. Your mother knows it, your brothers and sisters know it. Your children know it, Donnie, and you'd better believe I know it. My guess is that the trashy divorcées who fall all over you at these bars . . . they know it, too. I can't take it anymore, and we don't deserve it, your kids and I. So as of right this moment, it's over."

Donnie had seemed almost sober while they fought. Now his eyes narrowed, and he wetted his lips with his tongue. He swayed a little, betraying his drunkenness anew. "What's over? What the hell are you saying, Barbara?"

"Your party. It's over. You're going to come home after work and have dinner with your family. No stopping at bars on the way home. You're not going to take a drink of alcohol for at least six months. You're going to be the man you promised to become on the day we were married."

"Or else what?" He ran a hand across his chin, where his five o'clock shadow had darkened to at least 9:00 p.m.

"Or you get out. Right now."

She pointed at the door.

Donnie hesitated. The boys were silent at the top of the stairs. Julia slowly emerged from the shadows of the kitchen to stand just a few feet behind her brothers.

"Dad?" Julia asked, her voice plaintive. Unsure.

"You want me gone, Barb?" Donnie said.

Barb sighed. "That's not what I'm saying, and you know—"

"No. You want me gone." He threw up his hands. "Fine. I'll go."

Barb felt sick. Bile burned up the back of her throat. Her tears returned and her cheeks flushed, and she stepped between her husband and the door. This wasn't what she had expected, wasn't what she had wanted. Faced with his sins at last, when she had finally had enough, he was supposed to apologize and promise to be better. Other husbands ran around on their wives, other husbands drank. She'd heard stories from other women, from cousins and friends and even from her grandmother. Those husbands might go back to their old tricks eventually, but for a while at least they would behave, and it was in those periods when the marriage could be saved. When things could be rebuilt, and fresh beginnings were possible.

"I don't want you to go," she replied. "I want you to be a good husband."

"You want me to be your house pet. Jump when you say. I've got clients, Barbara. You think it helps my reputation with clients to have you chasing me around town? I take those clients out for dinner sometimes, and yes, I buy them drinks, and I drink right along with them. That's a big part of the relationship with my clients. You want to make it out that I'm some kind of womanizer—"

"Jesus, Donnie, you are! Everyone knows you are. You already have a reputation, and it's not the one you think you have. Or how do you think it feels knowing you've slept with women whose kids go to school with our children?"

"Goddamn it, Barb, you shut your mouth!" he roared, spittle flying from his mouth. His cheeks had turned red, and a blood vessel in his right eye had spread pinkness across the orb. "Don't you put that filth in our kids' heads!"

He spun and barked at the boys, "Go to your rooms! Don't listen to this shit!"

Barb pointed at the boys, but her gaze went past them, to Julia. "No. You stay right there, boys. If your father wants to leave us, you should see just the kind of man he is!"

Donnie threw up his hands, shaking his head. "You're nuts. Listen to yourself. You're the one who told me to go!"

"I don't want you to go! I want you to stay and be a better husband. To stay sober for a while and keep your prick in your pants, for God's sake! Is that so impossible for you?"

"I can't listen to this. You're insane. Enough of this bullshit."

Donnie reached past her and unlocked the door. He pulled it open, and Barb felt herself sliding into some kind of trance state. This couldn't really be happening. She grabbed hold of his wrist, and he shook her off. Her left foot knocked over the bowl of Halloween candy, and the bright little packages went sliding across the foyer. The boys were calling to their father as he went out the door. Barb went after him, ran onto the lawn to put herself between Donnie and the garage door. His car sat in the garage and it would take him away, and she had to figure out some way to get through to him, some way to clear his head so he would understand what he was destroying here tonight.

They were shouting at each other then. She heard herself, heard Donnie, too, but it was as if she'd separated from her own body. Barb had no idea what either one of them was saying. His face had turned redder—even in the light from the lamppost at the edge of the driveway, she could see that, could see the dark red of broken capillaries in his nose.

"Get out of my way, Barbara!" he screamed.

Out on the street, a family crossed the road and picked up their pace so their trick-or-treating children would not witness much more of this. Some teenagers stopped to watch as if a car accident had just occurred and they were curious if the driver had survived.

"Donnie, please!" Barb said. She grabbed the front of his shirt with both fists. "Stay and fix this. Don't just run away!"

He shoved her backward. Barb had slapped him for the first time just a minute or two ago, and now she balled her hand into a fist and punched him in the face, shocked even as her fist found its mark. Donnie stared at her, then cocked his arm back and slapped her so hard that it spun her around and dropped her to the grass. Barb tasted her own blood in her mouth.

A voice growled one word: "Assssshole!" A dark figure leaped onto Donnie's back, and it took a few blinks before Barb saw it was Julia. Her beautiful daughter clung to her father's back, one arm around his throat.

"Don't you fucking touch her again!" Julia screamed through anguished tears.

Donnie bent forward, flipped Julia onto the ground next to her mother. Barb heard Julia grunt all the breath from her lungs, and neither of them could do anything but watch as Donnie stormed over to the garage, hauled up the door, and climbed hurriedly into his dented Cutlass.

The engine growled to life, brake lights coming on.

Barb looked up as her sons burst from the house. Charlie came first, his face flushed, lips pressed tightly together. He wiped at his tears as he bolted across the lawn away from the house, away from his family, away from the pain. Brian called after his little brother, told him to come back, that it was going to be okay. He might have gone after Charlie, but then the Cutlass reversed out of the garage and the driveway, and Brian stood frozen beside his mother and sister as they all watched Donnie Sweeney leave them behind.

She thought she might have caught a glimpse of Charlie running off in the red glow of the Cutlass's taillights, but then they were both gone, father and son.

Barb broke. She crumbled to the grass, body racked with sobs. Julia knelt there, arms around her. Brian stood nearby as if paralyzed by the realization that he ought to do something, without knowing what that something might be. At thirteen years old, he'd watched his family shatter, and there was nothing he could do about it.

After a moment, Brian took off running in pursuit of Charlie, calling out for his little brother, and Barb's heart broke a little further. Her boys needed her, but right then, it was all she could do to keep breathing.

CHARLIE SWEENEY

Charlie's feet knew where he wanted to go, even before he realized it himself. Eleven-year-olds knew their neighborhoods better than anybody—every path that led to a friend's back door, the length of every barking dog's leash, which moms were generous with cookies, whose big sister might tousle a younger boy's hair with a hundred-watt smile. There were no conscious thoughts in his skull right then, only a kind of rushing noise, the sound it made when he plunged into the water doing a cannonball off a diving board. The rushing noise pushed out all thoughts and nearly all the breath in his lungs.

There were kids in the street. He heard someone call his name, but he kept his head down to hide his tears. Down the street a few young voices called out, "Trick or treat!" at someone's front door, the kids so cheerful that he cried all the harder. Snot ran from his nose, and he blubbered out loud and then felt so mortified that it happened again.

Charlie'd felt pain before. Embarrassment and humiliation. Grief when his nana died. How many times had he seen his parents fight, seen the sneers on their faces as they slashed at each other with sharp words, and felt sick in his gut? How many times had he wanted to scream at them to stop? How many times had he wanted to make them feel what he felt, make them hurt the way he hurt?

To hell with them! They didn't deserve him!

Charlie ran, shaking his head, his navy-blue Pumas slapping the dirt when he left the road and darted between the Spinales' house and the crumbling wreck that belonged to old Mr. Robideaux, who lived alone in the big, old house and still taught history at the high school even though he had to be about a billion years old.

Only when he saw the bushes did Charlie realize where his feet had been taking him all along. Between those two houses, just before the road hit its dead-end cul-de-sac, there was a tightly clustered circle of tall evergreen shrubs. Mr. Robideaux trimmed the outside of that circle but never paid any attention to the inside, where a hidden sanctuary awaited.

He ducked low and pushed through the prickly branches into the dark interior of the shrub circle, where he collapsed to the ground atop dirt and roots and generations of dried brown pine needles. Or fir, or spruce, or whatever other evergreen these shrubs might be. For Charlie and his siblings and other kids in the neighborhood, this place had been a secret fort, a place of quiet safety, where beers and cigarettes and joints were shared, where kids had their first kisses and more. Just a week ago, Charlie had been here in the midst of this sacred space with Brian and Vince Spinale and a few other kids. Anyone passing by on the street could have caught the scent of weed smoke drifting from within, but none of them seemed as worried about that as Charlie had been—though he hadn't said a word, unwilling to draw attention to himself and have Vince call him a pussy.

Vince had offered him a puff of the fat joint he'd rolled in Zig-Zag paper, and Charlie had refused. When Vince rolled his eyes and started trying to pressure him into it, Brian had stepped in. The Sweeney brothers didn't always get along—in fact, they fought more often than not—but when it came to stuff like that, Brian did what big brothers were supposed to do. No matter how much shit he gave Charlie himself, he sure as hell wasn't going to let other kids do the same. There was something safe about fighting with your brother, Charlie thought. When the fight was over, you still went home and ate dinner at the same table, slept in the same house—sometimes the same room.

He used to think the same was true about parents, but now he knew better.

"Dad," he whispered to himself, breath hitching. "I hate you. . . ."

On his side, curled up on the ground, needles pricking his cheek, he squeezed his eyes closed and tried to stop crying, but that only made it worse. The sound coming from inside him made him flush with embarrassment, but at the same time, there was something so necessary and satisfying about letting it out. Charlie had been holding this sound—this pain—inside him for a long time.

"Ass . . . ass . . . asshole," he said, struggling to get it out, then halfway laughing, halfway sobbing at how ridiculous it sounded to stammer that word.

His father enraged him. Charlie loved him so much, found it impossible not to love his dad even on the days when he hated him. Donnie Sweeney had a magic touch. Charlie might be having the worst day ever, but his dad could always cheer him up with that big voice, that joyful smile, like Santa before he got old and fat. He'd never have spoken that comparison aloud, especially not in front of his mom or one of his siblings, but that's what it always felt like when his dad smiled at him, cajoled him, or just gave him any attention at all. Like the man who would one day become Santa had just shared a little bit of magic with him.

How could someone so full of laughter also be so cold, so selfish? How could his father love him one moment and not spare him a single thought the next? Everyone loved Donnie Sweeney, but nobody more than Donnie himself, and for the first time, Charlie wondered if that wasn't his dad's defining characteristic. He loved his wife and his kids right up to the moment it threatened his ability to have a good time, to be adored. Toddlers were like that. Charlie had seen little kids throwing tantrums at the swimming pool, and how different was that, really, from what his father was doing every time he went out drinking and then acted shocked when Mom got angry with him? The second you said no to a toddler, they lost their minds. That was his dad.

"Asshole," he whispered, and this time, he didn't stammer.

His mother wasn't innocent, either. She always tried to pretend everything was fine until suddenly it wasn't, and the dam broke, throwing her into fury and panic and sorrow. Why wasn't there anything in between? Charlie couldn't blame his mom for the things his father did or for finally snapping and drawing a line in the sand, but hadn't there been some kind of middle ground, ever? Some way they could have stayed a family?

A ripple of laughter carried to him, there in his hiding place. He heard kids talking, and then some adults. A little jangle of metal, like a dog's chain or tags, and then the scratching of its nails on the pavement and the snuffling of its snout in the grass just outside the shrub circle. Charlie stiffened—he was a bit afraid of dogs, but also afraid of being discovered here, like this, helpless as a baby. Tears and snot on his face.

"Come on, Lucky!" someone called, and the dog growled a bit and then went quiet, the clinking of its tags moving away.

Charlie tried to catch his breath. He managed to sit up and

wipe his face and nose on the sleeve of his faded sweatshirt. Then he wrinkled his nose in disgust. *That'll have to go right into the wash*. As if his mom was going to give a damn about the laundry tonight or anytime soon.

What would happen now? That was the real question.

Exhaling, Charlie began to cry again, but the tears were different this time. They came not with sobs and snot but with a bone-weary sadness, a kind of surrender. It felt like an ending, and he realized that was exactly what it was. From now on, everything would be different.

"Dad," he whispered, only this time the word wasn't spoken in anger or even sadness but in confusion and disappointment. If he knew anything now, at eleven, that he hadn't known at ten years old, it was that he wasn't going to grow up to be his father. Charlie never wanted to make anyone feel the way he felt right now.

Something shifted in the darkness behind him. He spun and stared at the deepest bit of shadow, a black lump beneath the lowest branches inside the shrub circle. The shrubs grew together overhead, but some moonlight still filtered through. Enough to show the carpet of brown needles beneath him and the mostly bare branches around him, dried up and skeletal, not thriving and green like those on the outside, exposed to the weather and the sun. During the day, it felt quiet and secret in here, but at night, it seemed somehow sacred. Haunted.

The thing tucked under the dead branches shifted again, its weight making brown twigs and needles crunch beneath it.

"I don't think your dad is coming," a voice whispered.

Charlie couldn't move. How did it know, this thing? How could it know?

A hand came from the shadows. He flinched, and a little squeak came from his lips, and then he felt foolish. The hand belonged to a child. A kid, maybe even younger than he was.

"Hello?" Charlie said.

The lump of shadow crept out from beneath the branches, and in the moonlight, Charlie could make out a second hand and a face covered in clown's greasepaint. He might have screamed then, but he'd already embarrassed himself, and besides, the little girl's eyes were so wide and copper-penny bright that his concern for her overrode his fear of clowns. Which was a good thing, because she couldn't have been more than nine years old.

"I'm Sarah Jane," she said. "What's your name?"

"Charlie. Charlie Sweeney."

She laughed softly. "Charlie-Charlie." But then the sadness returned to her eyes, along with a little bit of fear.

"Why did you say my dad isn't coming?" Charlie asked.

"He isn't, is he?" Sarah Jane replied firmly, as if daring him to produce his father on the spot.

Charlie glanced away, toward the low opening in the shrub circle that he'd used to enter. "No. I don't think so."

Sarah Jane exhaled. "They never do. Dads. When you really need them, there's always something more important."

Spine stiffening, Charlie locked eyes with the little girl in the clown costume. "I don't think that's true. Lots of people have dads who show up for them. My dad's got a pretty good batting average, really. It's just that he and my mom . . . he's not there for her enough."

The little girl glanced away, as if she'd revealed something she wished she had kept to herself. Or Charlie had. Either way, she seemed uncomfortable. The quiet gave him a moment to study her. Black hair in tight curls, a bit wild and with leaves and twigs sticking out. A scratch on her left cheek, a red line right through the white paste of her makeup. The costume had seen better days, its bright colors washed out by time and laundering, which made Charlie wonder how many kids had owned it and handed it down before it got to Sarah Jane.

She had a little accent, maybe Spanish, but he didn't know enough people who spoke other languages to try to sort out where that accent came from.

More voices came from out on the street, followed by a squeal of delighted terror. He overheard one of the kids tell the others to hurry, that Mr. Barbosa was going to open the gates to his Haunted Woods soon. That meant trick-or-treat had already been going on for at least an hour and a half, and he was missing the whole thing, thanks to his father. He'd overheard his siblings talking while Mom had been out searching Coventry for their dad, and his sister saying Dad couldn't keep his dick in his pants.

The little girl started to cry, softly, her shoulders shaking.

"Sarah Jane?" he asked. "Where's . . . where's *your* dad?"

She let out a shuddery breath and spoke without looking up. "Charlie, will you . . . will you help me? Is there somewhere you could hide me?"

He didn't understand. "You're hiding right here."

Her head snapped up, and those tearful eyes were even wider, and desperate. "He'll find me. He always finds me."

"Your dad?"

Sarah Jane laughed then, and it was an awful sound. An old sound, heavy with a pain not meant for little girls. "My father is dead. He's been dead for ages."

"Then who are you hiding from?"

She looked at him as if he were an idiot. "The Cunning Man. He'll come for me, and I'll never get away a second time." Her eyes were red, and she wiped at her tears. "Please, Charlie. You've got to—"

Footsteps scuffed pavement, then grass and dirt. Someone approached the shrub circle, and for just a moment, when he saw the flare of alarm in her eyes and the way Sarah Jane stiffened, Charlie was sure the Cunning Man had come after all.

Branches cracked. Charlie heard a grunt and turned to see a dark shape crawling through the opening in the shrubs, and then his brother Brian's face appeared in the cross-hatched moonlight.

"Hey, bro," Brian said as if this had been just another day. "I thought I might find you here."

The shrubs quivered and more branches cracked, and Charlie glanced back to see that they were alone. Sarah Jane had forced her way through the lowest part of the shrubbery on the other side. He thought she must have scratched the hell out of her face and arms. He pictured her running around the neighborhood, bleeding, frightened of some guy she thought was coming for her. And who was to say? Awful things happened to kids all the time. They were the sorts of things his mother didn't want him to hear about, but she also always said he had "big ears." Charlie heard everything.

"Come on," he said, pushing past Brian and crawling out onto the grass facing the Colemans' house.

His brother came out after him, swearing as he stood up and brushed off his jeans. Charlie looked around for the little clown, thinking her white makeup would glow in the moonlight, that he would see her for sure.

"Sarah Jane?" he called.

Brian grabbed him by the shoulder and turned him around. "Hey, hey, bro. What are you doing? Who's Sarah Jane?"

There was no sign of her. Charlie exhaled, thinking about the Cunning Man and about Sarah Jane's dead father.

"Dad's gone, isn't he?" Charlie asked.

"Come home, Charlie. Mom's freaking out. She'll be thinking something happened to you."

Charlie turned to look at his brother. He tasted salt on his lips and realized he'd started crying again. "But Dad . . . ?"

Brian nodded. "Yeah. He's gone. And fuck him for leaving."

Charlie wished he could be angry, too. Instead, he felt like trash. Discarded and forgotten, no more important to his father than yesterday's newspaper.

"Why doesn't he . . ." Charlie began. But the rest of the words wouldn't come, and instead, he only sobbed.

Brian pulled him into a hug—they hadn't hugged since they were little—and Charlie let his big brother hold him as loss racked his body. They stood like that for long minutes, brothers in pain, brothers in abandonment. No matter how often they fought, they would always have this to bind them.

Again, Charlie thought of Sarah Jane. He ought to look for her or send someone else to look for her. He would tell his mother when he got home, he thought. Deep down, though, he wondered if Sarah Jane might be the lucky one of the two of them. Her dead father might be gone, but he probably hadn't chosen to leave her.

Donnie Sweeney, though? He'd just had enough.

He didn't care what happened to them next.

RICK BARBOSA

Rick knew the scarecrow was gonna be trouble. The kid gave him the creeps, following behind him so close it seemed like the other boy might be breathing down his neck any second. Their cluster of trick-or-treaters had hit more than a dozen houses. At every door, they spread out into a disorderly gang, each impatiently waiting their turn. Rick used those opportunities to put space between himself and the scarecrow, but somehow the kid always ended up right behind him once they started walking toward the next house. At first, he didn't like it because that closeness felt like an intrusion. He was out here trying to enjoy Halloween with his best friend, and he didn't even know this kid's name.

You're being a jerk, he thought.

But was he? Yeah, his mom always told him to be nice to everyone, and he understood that this kid must be new to the area. But if the scarecrow was already friends with Vince Spinale and that crew, then why the hell did he seem so eager to get closer to the younger kids?

To me, Rick thought, but then he shook that idea from his head.

Quinn and Tommy were cool. He didn't mind hanging out with them. But tonight, that meant having the older kids along for the ride, and having Vince Spinale and his cousin and Heather What's-her-name apparently meant having the scarecrow, too. They were walking toward the Burgesses' Love Shack house, and that made him uncomfortable enough, but having the scarecrow breathing down his neck made it worse. He wanted to turn on his heel and confront the kid, to tell him to back the hell off. Maybe back the *fuck* off, because even though he was thirteen and his mom hated him to swear, the scarecrow was freaking him out.

"Hey," Billie said, reaching out to brush her hand against his. A little electric shiver went through him when she touched him.

He glanced at Billie through the holes in his sweaty mask, saw the concern in her eyes, and felt disappointment when she let her hand fall away. He laughed nervously. This was Billie. He might crush on some of the girls in his class, but not Billie. She never made him feel awkward or gave him that hot flush in his cheeks that some girls did.

Not till now, in the tight black jumpsuit and the long white wig of Storm, she looked like someone else completely. Beautiful. Storm was a goddess, after all.

"What's going on with you?" she asked.

"Just a weird night."

Billie brushed at his hand again. "You feeling okay? We could just go back to your house and check out your dad's haunted maze a little early."

Rick muttered something about being fine and kept his eyes forward, not wanting to look at her just then, and maybe not for the rest of the night. He'd never thought about kissing Billie before, but suddenly his mind went there and he wondered what it would be like. *Weird*, he knew. *Too weird*.

But now he pictured it in his head, imagined her lips would be soft, and he thought in addition to being weird, it would also be really nice.

"I need more candy," he said. "I'm on a mission. A contest is in order."

"What contest?" Quinn asked, glancing over his shoulder at them. He and Tommy had taken the lead in the group, with Rick and Billie in the middle, and the older kids bringing up the rear.

Rick pulled off his Frankenstein mask, relishing the fresh air. "Whoever gets the most Reese's Peanut Butter Cups wins," he said.

"What do we win?" Quinn asked.

"Ooh, how about whoever gets the most, everyone else has to give up their own Reese's to the winner?" Billie said.

A debate ensued.

In the middle of that, the scarecrow stepped on the back of Rick's sneaker, gave him a flat tire, so Rick stepped out of his shoe and stumbled a bit. A flash of anger went through him and he spun around.

"What's wrong with you?"

The scarecrow backed up a couple of steps, but said nothing. Just raised his hands in surrender and apology.

"Rick?" Billie said.

"He's been up my butt the whole time, like he's trying to whisper in my ear or something!"

The scarecrow gave a tiny shrug, curling in on himself in embarrassment. "It was an accident."

Rick picked up his shoe, gripped it tightly as he fought the urge to throw it at the scarecrow. He glanced around at the others. Some of the faces were behind masks, but even then he could see from their eyes what they all thought of his flaring temper. They shifted, embarrassed for him, or stared in disapproval as if he were having a tantrum. And maybe that wasn't too far from the truth. He felt himself flush, regretting the outburst. The guy had gotten on his last nerve, but now even Billie was watching him, waiting to see if his anger would subside.

He gestured with his shoe. "You guys keep going. I'll catch up."

Quinn broke the tension with a laugh. "Eat some candy, Ricky. Feed the beast."

Rick shot him the middle finger and grinned, but it was all performance, acting as if he didn't still feel anger and embarrassment. He went to the curb and sat down, started unlacing his lost shoe to put it back on.

Vince and his cousin were the first to get bored now that the momentary drama had ended. They started toward the next house, and the rest streamed after them. Tommy and Quinn muttered to each other, and Rick knew they were mocking him. They were his friends, but he didn't hold it against them. He'd have done the same.

Only Billie stayed behind. She sat on the curb beside him, setting her trick-or-treat pillowcase between her feet on the road.

"You okay?"

Rick glanced up the street at the rest of the group, staring at their backs. The scarecrow seemed to be keeping a healthier distance from the other kids after Rick's blowup, but still just looking at the skinny kid's retreating back gave him a sour twist in his gut.

"Not really," Rick admitted. "He was creeping me out. I felt like I had a stalker or something. Whoever it is, I'd rather not be around him or Vince and those guys, to be honest. If you want to catch up with them, I don't mind—"

Billie sucked her teeth. "Don't be a drama queen. I'd rather it's just the two of us anyway."

Rick smiled. He felt the same way. He stuffed his Frankenstein mask into his pillowcase with the candy. If anyone wanted him to show his costume, he'd dig it out, but right now he felt like it might suffocate him.

Billie stood, offered Rick her hand, and helped pull him up. "Let's go. I want to hit as many houses as we can before we go back to your house for the Haunted Woods."

The minute they started walking again, his agitation seemed to evaporate. For a while, the hair on the back of his neck had been bristling and he had felt outside of himself, somehow, observing his body from far away. Now he took a deep, long breath and let it out with a sigh.

Billie nudged him. "You okay?"

Of course he wasn't. His sister had been working with their dad on prepping the Haunted Woods, having that time to bond over this thing they shared and to experience the sadness that came with it being the last time they would ever do it. But there had been lots of "last times" in the house in the months since his mom and dad had told Rick and Chloe that they were basically bankrupt and had to sell. The last first-day-of-school photo in the driveway. The last birthday they'd celebrate at the dining room table. The last time his height would be measured against the wall in his bedroom, where the wooden ruler was bolted to the wall, zoo animals painted along its length. Rick knew he was already too old for that last one, but still, it had been weird to know without question that it would never happen again.

Soon there would be more last times. The last time he and Billie would hang out in the house, or explore the woods in the back. The last time they would get late-night pizza delivery. The last time Rick would sit at the old, round Formica table in the kitchen and eat the cinnamon pancakes his mom made every Sunday. The last time they would sit as a family around that table.

So many last times still to come.

Like this, his last time trick-or-treating in the neighborhood. Maybe his last time trick-or-treating at all.

As they crossed the lawn of the next house, Rick laughed softly.

"What's funny?" Billie asked, blowing a lock of white hair out of her face.

"Just kinda laughing at myself, I guess." He glanced at her but quickly looked away. "I guess your parents probably told you what's going on with my folks. With the house."

For a few seconds, he thought she must not have heard him. But when they reached the front steps of the next house, she paused to look at him.

"Yeah." Billie's forehead creased. "I was mad at first that you didn't tell me. But my mom said it must be hard for you, and then I figured me being mad was selfish. I mean, it's not me moving." She lowered her gaze. "It just sucks."

"Totally, totally sucks." Rick glanced away. In that moment, he didn't even want to risk her looking at him. "I've been thinking I'm doing okay with it all. But now I think maybe that's not true."

Billie swung her candy bag at Rick. "You'd better not be okay with having to move. It's kind of insulting when you act like it's no big deal."

The awkwardness and sadness popped like a bubble. "So this is about you now?"

"Of course!" Billie said. "Your dad should never have gotten laid off in the first place, for my sake! It's really inconvenient for you to move. What if some assholes move in there? What if they have kids I hate?"

"Yeah. It was shitty of my dad's old company not to take your feelings into consideration."

Billie stepped up and rang the doorbell. "It really was. Life won't be the same without you."

The words seemed to linger like the sound of the doorbell. Suddenly, he wished he were older, that he could make decisions for himself. He had seen Billie almost every day since he was old enough to play in his backyard, and now if he wanted to hang out with her, he would have to get a ride to her house. Sure, he could call on the phone, but that wasn't the same.

The door opened. He had barely noticed the care that had gone into decorating for Halloween, but now he saw the extra lines elderly Mrs. Mathiesen had added to her face. She wore a witch's pointed hat and a flowing black dress, and she cackled as she answered the door, but only for a few seconds before her smile broke through.

"Trick or treat!" Billie said as if she were small again.

Rick said the words as well, that traditional invocation that summoned candy from strangers. He was late responding to his cue, but at least he got it in there. You didn't really deserve the candy if you couldn't muster up a hearty "trick or treat." He finally noticed the evil faces carved in the two jack-o'-lanterns by the door and the fake spiderwebs and plastic spiders that covered the door itself. Rick hoped that if he got to be her age and had to move into a house all by himself, he would still be able to find the fun in Halloween the way Mrs. Mathiesen could.

"Thank you," he said, smiling at her.

"You're very welcome. Happy Halloween," she said as she closed her door. "Don't be a stranger!"

Yeah, he was going to miss this place.

They angled across the lawn to pass between the shrubs that separated the widow's home from the house next door. His thoughts had strayed, so it took him a second to realize this was the Love Shack house, and he faltered.

"Do we want to skip this one?"

Billie didn't have to ask for an explanation. The whole

neighborhood knew the rumors about Ruth and Zack. Anytime Rick heard the roar of Zack's motorcycle going down the street, he thought of it. Sex might as well have been an alien planet for him, but he knew the basics. Weird as it was for him to think anyone might have sex parties—like, orgies or whatever—that didn't really bother him. He figured it was like anything else. If they were having a good time, then good for them. He envied adults the freedom to make those kinds of decisions. Drinking, sex, driving a car, staying out all night if they wanted to.

But some of the rumors about Zack and Ruth involved violence. And there were whispers about them doing stuff to kids. The police had never shown up as far as he knew, so Rick figured rumors were just rumors, but it made him queasy even to think about it, so skipping their house was a definite possibility.

Vince Spinale and the scarecrow and the others had already rung that doorbell and collected their candy from Ruth, and now they were nearly to the house beyond. Rick was glad—the last thing he wanted was to catch up with those kids right now. He just wanted to be with Billie, safe with his closest friend on this last Halloween together. It occurred to him that if they skipped Zack and Ruth's house, they'd be close to catching up, which might prompt Tommy and Quinn to beckon them to join the larger group again.

"Do *you* want to skip it?" Billie asked him.

Rick hesitated, glancing again at the larger group of kids from whom they'd detached themselves.

"Nah," he said. "Pretty sure they still give out full-size bars."

And we're together, he thought. His mom said Ruth and Zack probably weren't the pervs that neighborhood gossip suggested or the police would have arrested them by now. But he also knew if they actually were some kind of freaky sex maniacs, they weren't likely to try anything on two kids walking together, especially not with so many other kids and parents walking the street.

They started toward Ruth and Zack's house. There were lanterns on either side of the door, but one of them had burned out, leaving just the glassed-in bulb on the left, surrounded by moths and flies drawn to the light.

They had emerged from the shrubs and were half a dozen steps across the lawn when two shadows came around the house from the other side. One of them was Zack, instantly recognizable with his long hair and thick, drooping mustache and the oversize leather wallet he kept in his back pocket, clipped to his belt with a chain. A boy was with him, thin and pale and shaking. A little blond kid maybe nine years old. Zack had a hand on the kid's shoulder, guiding him past the garage.

Rick froze, breath catching in his throat. Billie halted, too, seeming paralyzed as they watched Zack usher the little blond boy toward the steps. The kid tripped on the bottom step, fell, and then curled on his side on the concrete stairs. When Zack bent to help him up, they could hear the man talking to the boy.

"You'll be okay. We're gonna take care of you," Zack promised.

Weakly, the boy nodded and let Zack help him up. Although the doorbell hadn't rung, Ruth came to the door. She opened the storm door and whispered urgently, drawing her husband and the little boy inside, then shut the door behind them.

The light beside the front door went out, signaling that they were no longer giving out candy.

"Wow," Billie said, "you don't think . . ."

She left the question unfinished, but Rick didn't need her to elaborate. "What else am I gonna think?"

"We should go home," Billie said. "Get our parents. Call the police or something."

"There's no time for that."

"You have a better idea?" Billie asked.

"Yeah," Rick said. "We keep trick-or-treating."

He started for Ruth and Zack's house again. Billie hurried to catch up, tugged on his sleeve, tried to change his mind. But Rick knew that if they ran home for help, they might be too late to stop whatever was about to happen to the little kid inside the old split-level house. His stomach churned, but he didn't hesitate when he got to the front steps. He climbed the concrete stairs, ignoring the fact that the front lights had been turned out.

Rick rang the doorbell.

Only when he heard the sound echoing in the foyer on the other side of the door did it occur to him to wonder what he ought to say if they actually answered. He clutched his pillowcase full of candy and smiled thinly as he realized there was only one thing he could say.

The door yawned open with a creak. Ruth stood in the shadows just inside.

"Trick or treat!"

The words came from behind Rick. Billie had stuck by him, two steps lower.

"Sorry, kid," Ruth said. "The lights are off. We're all out of candy."

Behind her in the darkened foyer, the half-full bowl of full-size Reese's and Snickers and Milky Ways sat on a table, in full view despite the shadows.

Ruth started to close the door again. Rick couldn't let that happen, not with the little kid inside.

"That's a lie!" he snapped.

Ruth's eyes widened in surprise, then narrowed in anger.

"What the hell did you just say?" she demanded.

Rick froze. The door remained open, but he had no idea what to do next. All he knew was that he couldn't walk away.

TONY BARBOSA

There were hidden speakers all through the Haunted Woods. He'd created mixtapes of creepy music that thumped and floated through the trees, and various screams and eerie moaning. He wanted people to hear one another screaming, too, but not to hear footsteps and muttering and talking from the folks who didn't take it seriously, so finding the right volume was important.

The night had turned darker and a bit colder—perfect for Halloween—and it was time to let the first people come through. Still, he wanted it to be perfect. Usually, Tony did his final walk-through with Chloe, but she had gone around front to coordinate with her mom and her aunt, and it seemed to be taking longer than anticipated, so Tony decided he had to do the walk-through on his own.

Despite the bittersweet elements factoring into this year's Haunted Woods, he smiled as he walked the trail. Voices called to him. Ghouls in dirt pits along the path raised their hands to wave to him and give a thumbs-up to assure him they were in place. Around a turn, he spotted Alexandria, who did a lot of the horror makeup, putting the finishing touches on a walking corpse whose face had been split in two by an axe . . . which the corpse now held in his hand. A black-lace-veiled widow with impossibly long, skinny white fingers held up a little flashlight to guide Alexandria's work.

"How we coming?" Tony asked.

"Last touch-ups," the makeup artist said. "I'm not responsible for anyone who wets their pants when this face comes running at them with an axe."

Tony laughed. "Five minutes."

"You got it."

"Five minutes!" he called out.

A chorus of voices replied in kind, confirming they'd gotten the message.

"Places!" said one of the actors in the group.

"Thank you, places!" the ghosts and killers, witches and zombies replied. Tony had never been onstage, but he loved the way actors and theater people had their own subculture. It added to the sense of family among those involved with the Haunted Woods. He was going to miss so many things about it, and losing this camaraderie was chief among them.

He kept on along the path. A dry ice machine chugged mist through the trees. The blue gels over the angled lights cast eerie shadows. A bloodstained whiteface clown with a knife loomed from the mist and uttered a high-pitched laugh that sent an actual shiver along his spine.

"Oh, that's really good," Tony said.

"Thanks, Mr. Barbosa," the clown replied.

He spotted a flash of bright red through the trees. Black fabric had been stapled to posts to create more of a claustrophobic feeling in the woods, but there were breaks. A small figure darted behind the black fabric, offering another glimpse of red. The music had quieted for just an instant, and he heard the rustle of dry, old lace. Tony frowned as he left the trail.

"Mr. Barbosa?" the clown ventured. "Something wrong?"

Tony ignored him. Whatever his real name was, the clown hadn't been there earlier and seen the little girl dressed in her old, yellowed Raggedy Ann costume. He wasn't sure that was whom he had just seen and didn't feel like trying to explain it now. Instead, he went to the break between those fabric banners and slipped through, moved past several thick trees, and glanced around. No sign of anyone back there, not Raggedy Ann, not an evil clown or a creepy doll, not even an actor practicing her menacing witch cackle or a madman slavering as he tried to escape his straitjacket. They were all in place, ready to open. He patted his back pockets, trying to remember where he'd left the antique doll the little girl had left behind earlier.

"Places," Tony said to the clown as he returned to the path. "Three minutes."

"Thank you, places," said the clown.

He covered the rest of the trail in under a minute. Nobody jumped out at him, but the mechanized attractions with motion sensors went off, and though he had been through the Haunted Woods a dozen times already and had been the one to set them all up, he still jumped a couple of times. That brought the smile back to his face.

Exiting the trail, he spotted Chloe crossing the back lawn toward the entrance, and he flagged her down.

"Hey," she said. "Sorry I got held up. Mom had me advising some woman from her work about where to park—"

"Parking's always a nightmare," Tony said. "People kind of have to just do their best."

Chloe shrugged. "Which is basically what I said. But that Mrs. Kincaid or whatever her name is—"

"Kenton, I think."

"Whatever. Mom was dealing with her bullshit, so I wanted to help."

Tony exhaled in frustration. Mrs. Kenton didn't even live on Parmenter. She lived on Jewell Street, which was a short dead-end road half a dozen houses away. The old witch knew this was their last time, that the house would be sold after the first of the year, that it was all for charity, and yet she still had to come out and make a nuisance of herself in person. Tony understood how irritating it must have been for the neighbors to have people parking up and down the street on Halloween night every year, sometimes blocking their driveways, or at least pulling in them to turn around. But it was maybe three hours, once a year, and this was the last one. Mrs. Kenton could jump off a bridge as far as Tony was concerned.

"You did the right thing," he told his daughter. "I hope you don't mind, but I did the walk-through."

Chloe smiled sadly and stepped up to hug him. "I don't mind. It's great, Dad."

"We did it again."

"Definitely."

This time, they didn't bother to acknowledge that this would be their final Haunted Woods. They had talked about it enough.

Tony kissed the top of her head and stepped back. "Everyone's ready to go. You want to head up and tell your mother?"

"You go," Chloe told him. "I might go out later on, but I saw the Spinales in line, and I'd like to be part of scaring the shit out of them."

He laughed. "That's my girl."

They squeezed each other's hands, and Chloe headed into the Haunted Woods while Tony walked around to the front of the house. In his quiet moments when he'd been setting the whole thing up, he'd daydreamed about massive lines snaking all the way down the street, and yet he had also entertained fears that the Koenigs' planned block party would prevent most of the neighbors from showing up. As he approached the plastic cemetery-style gates they'd put at the end of the driveway for the event, he craned his neck to scan the people lined up on the sidewalk, and his fears were put to rest.

At the gate, Alice waited patiently. This was entirely his thing—his and Chloe's—but as many small disputes as they'd had about the Haunted Woods over the years, this year, she had just gone along with their plans. It was their swan song.

Alice stood with her sister, Helen, and two women he didn't recognize but who wore the bright orange T-shirts of the volunteers. They would be taking donations and guiding people, and Tony appreciated them.

He opened the gate. A girl of about seven raised both fists and cried, "Yes!" to the delight of the people around her.

Alice met him at the plastic gate. Her smile seemed real enough, if tentative. "You ready for this?"

"We're set. Yeah."

With a grin, she began to turn back to the dozens of people already in line.

Tony put a gentle hand on her arm. "Hey, Alice? Thanks for this. For all your help. Chloe and I couldn't do it without you."

He half expected a wiseass reply, but Alice patted his chest with one hand and showed him a sad smile. "Have fun, Tony. You and all these freaks who love having the crap scared out of them."

He laughed. Alice had never understood the appeal of horror, but she knew all of this made him happy, and that was enough. She caught his gaze, and they locked eyes for several long, bittersweet moments. Tony felt his laughter give way to a deep sadness he'd been suppressing for months.

This was the moment. Not losing his job, not fighting with

the bank, not being forced to put the house up for sale, not telling the kids. This was the moment he felt the failure of the past year really hit home. His dad had worked hard to give Tony a bright future, and Tony had done the same for his family. He had a new job, but the time he had been out of work had unraveled so much of what he had struggled to build. Now it felt like starting from nothing.

"Hey," she said, maybe sensing the turn of his thoughts. "The folks are getting restless. We letting them in?"

Tony looked at the excited little girl again, saw Alice's sister explaining to the girl's parents that if they took one of the available glow sticks, they could go through and get the less-scary version of the Haunted Woods, but the little girl loudly protested this suggestion.

"Absolutely. Let 'em in. Let's scare the shit out of them."

Alice caught his hand, gave it a squeeze, and then let it go.

An ending. There would be a new beginning soon.

The people began to enter, and soon the screaming would start. Tony knew it would make him feel better, at least for a little while.

ALICE BARBOSA

Alice watched her unhappy husband trot along the side of the house and felt a weight lift from her shoulders. It was all simple now. She'd often said that all the hard parts of a wedding happened before the organist started to play. A thousand things might still go wrong, but they were out of your control at that point. Wedding planning came with a million headaches, but a wedding itself was pure pleasure.

It turned out bankruptcy was a lot like a wedding. Once you hit the bottom, the rest was like toppling dominoes. The things that came next were immediate and unavoidable. She hoped their marriage could survive everything that had gone wrong and the bitterness of losing the house, but they had both made some terrible mistakes. Maybe they could rebuild, save their family, find a new path—and maybe not.

"Three, please?" said a dad leading his twin boys, who were maybe ten years old. One of the boys already had a glow stick in hand, supplied by Alice's sister, Helen. The other twin shot a little sneer at his brother, clearly disapproving of the glowing green glow stick. He'd wanted the full scare tonight, it seemed, while his twin was more anxious.

"The donation is whatever you want to give," Alice said. "We suggest five bucks a person or ten for a household."

The dad dropped a five-dollar bill into the donation box. Alice smiled and kept her thoughts about the man to herself. They were raising money for the Jimmy Fund Clinic at Dana-Farber Cancer Institute. The guy couldn't manage a ten-dollar donation when his kids had certainly eaten at least that much in candy tonight?

Then again, who was she to judge? Lots of people couldn't spare ten dollars. On the other hand, not many of those people lived in this neighborhood.

"Hey!" Helen said. "You awake?"

Alice smiled and gave her a little wave. Her big sister, always looking out for her. Alice spoke to the next group and the next after that, and the line streamed toward the backyard. There were a couple of volunteers who were timing out the entrances, so that the groups weren't right on one another's heels. If you could see the people ahead of you, then you'd see when the actors would jump out or the mechanisms would give a fright, and the experience would be ruined.

Helen handed a glow stick to a girl about fifteen, said something friendly, and then backed toward where Alice stood by the gate.

"Anytime you want to switch places, let me know," Helen said.

"I'm good!"

Helen studied her. "You sure? You're a little bit of the old Wonderland tonight, I think."

Alice wanted to tell her to fuck off. She loved her sister, but she didn't need to be reminded of the childhood nickname Helen had given her and kids in the neighborhood had adopted. "Alice in Wonderland" always had a tendency to let her mind wander. She insisted it was because she had more imagination than the others, but secretly thought she probably had undiagnosed ADHD or something.

That wandering tendency hadn't helped her marriage. How many times had she been tempted to stray? She loved Tony and cherished their children, but she always yearned for a different kind of attention, the kind of hunger that men sometimes got in their eyes. Alice could not have honestly sworn that she regretted having cheated with the one man she had allowed to seduce her—only that he lived on the same street. His children knew their children. Of all the self-destructive things she had ever done, this was the dumbest.

The line had grown longer. Alice knew Tony would be relieved. He'd been so worried that the Koenigs' party would draw too many people away from the Haunted Woods, but it had only made them show up earlier.

From over her left shoulder, she heard one of the traffic controllers ask her to hold off. The next group in line was a happy couple in their twenties. They didn't look familiar to Alice, but then she had lived in the neighborhood long enough for most of the houses to turn over at least once, so they might have been recent arrivals to Parmenter or one of the other nearby streets. Once upon a time, people in neighborhoods like theirs knew everyone, but the country was changing. People had no time, usually both parents had to work. Neighbors were often strangers, which Alice felt was a very sad evolution. That was one of the reasons she'd always supported Tony's love for Halloween, and the Haunted Woods.

On the other hand, she knew it might be better for her that the neighbors didn't know one another a bit better. This way, her sins could stay private.

"What's the holdup?" Helen asked, striding over.

Alice glanced at the traffic controllers who were still holding the next group from going into the Haunted Woods. Ahead of them, there seemed to be a family squabble.

"Looks like a kid who's losing his nerve," she told her sister. "Happens every year."

Helen sighed. When she spoke next, it was under her breath, so the people next in line wouldn't hear. "What a circus. Thank God you won't have to deal with this nonsense anymore."

Alice winced. She didn't know how to put her thoughts into words without getting into a fight. Instead, she hoped her sister would read it in her eyes. She had always thought of the Haunted Woods as a nuisance, and yes, she would be happy never to have to deal with it again, but Tony had already taken enough punches. She had no desire to keep hitting him.

"The line's moving again, Helen. If you're going to help with our 'nonsense,' maybe get back to handing out glow sticks."

Helen looked stung. "Wow. Bite my head off. I just meant I'm not going to miss this geek stuff, and I figured you weren't going to miss it either. Looks like I was wrong."

She turned and went down the line of waiting people, explaining the glow sticks to potential scaredy-cats. Alice saw that the backup on the lawn had cleared, so she began taking donations again and ushering people into the darkness.

RICK BARBOSA

Rick flinched when the door slammed in his face. His ears could hear Billie muttering behind him, but his brain wasn't processing anything she said. They had seen Zack Burgess bring a little kid into his house—no parents in sight and definitely not a child who lived there. They'd rung the doorbell for trick-or-treat, and Ruth Burgess had come to the door and lied to his face, said they had run out of candy, but Rick had spotted the bowl of candy right on a little table against the wall just inside.

He had tried to come up with some argument, some way to force her to let them in. But while he'd been thinking, Ruth had shut the door.

A little buzz filled his head, like a tiny nest full of wasps had started growing there. What the hell were they supposed to do now?

Billie tugged his sleeve, and he jerked back as if she'd punched him.

"Whoa. Relax!" she said. "Just getting your attention. You totally spaced out for a minute."

Rick glanced at the Burgesses' door again. If Zack Burgess had caught that little kid on his fishing line, he'd have had to throw him back. The kid was a minnow. Too innocent even to know enough to be scared.

"We can't just leave him in there," Rick said.

He turned, raised his fist to pound on the door, but Billie grabbed his other arm and tugged.

"Get over here," Billie whispered, moving past the bushes in front of the house, over to the side where they'd seen Zack emerge with the kid.

"We should call the cops," Billie whispered. "Our folks are home. Let's run back, get them to call."

"No. Think about it," Rick said. "The time it'll take us to get back there, convince our parents, have them call the cops, and for the cops to show up? Anything could happen to that little guy by then."

Billie glanced at the house. "So we just barge in?"

"We have to get a look at what's going on inside. We do a little window-creeping. If we see the kid is really in danger, we'll scream, we'll get every neighbor and every other kid to come running. And if the kid seems okay, then one of us will run home and get help that way."

Billie nodded. Rick hurried into the backyard, keeping his head down and his footsteps as light as possible. The cape on Billie's costume made a quiet shushing noise as they crept around the side of the house, and it felt ridiculous, the two of them thinking they were actual heroes instead of kids dressed as a monster and a mutant. But that kid in the Burgesses' house—that kid wasn't pretending. This wasn't a story.

The property sloped down from the street to the woods behind the house. Rick and Billie crept alongside the house and around the back, where old wooden steps led up to the deck.

"Those stairs are gonna creak," Billie whispered. "Are we really gonna climb up there and stare at them through the kitchen windows?"

Rick ignored her and ducked underneath the deck. His

treads scuffed the concrete pad and he froze, whipping around to stare at the house, holding his breath. He glanced down at his pillowcase. All those little pieces of Halloween candy were wrapped individually, and the wrappers made a kind of rasp or crackle. It might give him away, and if they had to run, he didn't want to be carrying it. Instead, he stashed it in the low shrubs at the foot of the deck and gestured for Billie to do the same. She didn't seem happy about it, but candy would have been a stupid reason for them to get caught, and she knew that. Billie stashed her pillowcase beside his.

The basement was a walk-out, which explained the concrete pad. There were some chairs under the deck, too, plastic things stacked in one corner, already put away for the coming winter. The basement door had three small glass panes in its upper panel, too high for them to look through without standing on one of those plastic chairs. But there were windows back here as well. Two of them were covered from the inside, like someone had hung black curtains over them. The other two were under the deck, right by the door. When Rick crept toward the windows, he glimpsed fake wooden paneling on the walls, a TV stand, an ugly sofa upholstered with something that looked like a hobo's coat, and a little corridor leading out of the room toward a door at the bottom of stairs that would lead up to the first floor.

Someone moved inside. Zack Burgess.

"Shit," he whispered, dropping into a crouch. He gestured for Billie to do the same.

Now he could only see the crappy-looking drop ceiling.

Zack wasn't alone. He had the little boy with him, one hand on his back, bringing him downstairs and guiding him through the corridor toward the cellar TV room.

Rick lowered himself to his hands and knees and made his way to the back of the house. The lights were on in the TV room, and he knew that would make the darkness under the deck seem darker still, and make it harder for those inside to see out. He braced himself against the concrete foundation and lifted his head. The nearest window was open a few inches, and he could hear voices from inside.

"You're gonna be okay, buddy," Zack said, not unkindly. "We'll get you cleaned up, get you something to drink, and then we can call your folks. Have someone come get you. How does that sound?"

The kid's reply floated out the window like the slightest breeze. "Okay. My knee hurts."

"I know," Zack said. "I don't think you broke anything. Maybe just gave it a twist. My wife, Ruth, is gonna bring down some bandages and something to clean those scrapes. You'll be okay. Why don't you tell me your name?"

"It's Leonard," the boy said, still so quietly. "Not Lenny or Len. My mom never wanted anyone to call me those names. Always Leonard."

Eavesdropping at the window, Rick couldn't help smiling. He glanced at Billie and saw from her expression that she could not hear the conversation. The two of them had nicknames, diminutives of the names their parents had given them. But not this little guy. Not *Always Leonard.*

He became that in Rick's mind. Always Leonard.

A commotion came from the TV room, and for a moment, Rick felt sick in his gut, but then Zack started talking again, and Rick realized he was just dragging the coffee table over for Always Leonard to put up his leg. Zack wanted a closer look at the kid's knee.

"Try to move it like this," Zack said.

Always Leonard let out a dreadful howl and then whimpered the way only a little boy could. Rick knew that whimper well— third grade hadn't been *that* long ago, and he'd whimpered like that when he'd fallen at recess and smashed his elbow on the pavement.

"Aw, man. Sorry, Leonard," Zack said. "It doesn't look nearly as bad as all that. I'd never have tried moving it otherwise."

The boy muttered something Rick couldn't hear. There came a creaking noise, and then Ruth Burgess's voice, which meant the creak had been the hinges of the door that led upstairs.

"Okay, here we go!" Ruth announced. "Band-Aids, a little alcohol to clean the scrapes, and you'll be good as new."

There was more conversation. This Ruth sounded so much brighter, so much friendlier, than the one who had answered the door a few minutes earlier. So different, in fact, that Rick actually craned his neck a bit to peer through the window for a look. He heard Billie hitch her breath behind him, probably worried he would be spotted, but he couldn't help himself. The woman had lied to him, told him they were out of candy, and where had Always Leonard come from, anyway? This random kid, definitely not familiar to Rick or his friends, not from the neighborhood, with no parents around and no group of kids to keep him company while out trick-or-treating? Why had Zack Burgess discovered the kid in his backyard? It didn't make any sense.

And yet . . . as he looked through the window, the scene unfolding in that basement TV room appeared to be precisely what it was supposed to be. Ruth had just set a tray on the coffee table with a tin of Band-Aids and a bottle of what must have been rubbing alcohol. Rick saw that she'd also brought a couple of cans of Coca-Cola and a little plastic bag full of cotton balls to help clean Always Leonard's cuts.

"Okay. Let's fix you up," Zack said.

They seemed genuinely concerned about Always Leonard,

which didn't jibe with the awful things Rick and Billie had been thinking, or with the rumors about the Burgesses. Maybe they were sex freaks, sure. Those other windows at the back of the house were blacked out, and there was a door off the TV room that had a lock on it, which really made Rick wonder what might be on the other side. Some kind of kinky sex dungeon where they had orgies with strangers, probably.

But his fears for Always Leonard seemed groundless. Maybe they didn't need to sound the alarm and get the rest of the neighborhood to come running.

"Where are the kids?" Always Leonard asked. He reached for a can of Coke while Ruth dampened some cotton with alcohol.

"Kids?" Zack asked.

"The kids. Where are the kids you have in here?"

Outside the window, Rick stiffened. What the hell was Always Leonard talking about? The boy's eyes were bright and searching, as if he thought the Burgesses had sons or daughters hidden under the sofa or behind the TV.

"There aren't any kids here," Ruth said as she cleaned his scrapes.

Always Leonard didn't even wince at the dabbing of alcohol. He took a long sip of his Coke and then frowned as if Ruth had started speaking a different language.

"There are children here," Always Leonard said. "I know there are. I can *smell* them."

What the hell, Rick thought, and he was sure Zack and Ruth must have been thinking the same.

But then the Burgesses looked at each other, and there was something more in that look than just confusion. Zack and Ruth didn't just seem bewildered by what Always Leonard had said. They looked worried, maybe even a little bit scared. And suddenly, all of Rick's fears flooded back.

He turned toward Billie, and the sole of his Nike scraped concrete.

Rick pulled back from the window.

Inside, Ruth's voice broke the quiet. "Zack," she said. "I think there's someone outside."

VANESSA MONTEZ

Vanessa watched as Mrs. Koenig handled the finishing touches for the party, moving in and out of the house like a cartoon mouse zipping into its hole. Mr. Koenig sat on his deck with a few of the neighborhood husbands who had shown up early to drink beers and talk about sports and their jobs, and to complain about their wives, who had stayed home to give out candy so these guys could pregame their evening's drinking and complain about everything. Their sports teams sucked; the coaches were amateurs who should be fired. Their bosses were arrogant pricks who were all promoted because they'd kissed enough ass, not because they had any discernible skills. And their wives—oh, their wives were incessant nags who were capable of finding fault in anything their husbands did, no matter how thoughtful they might have been.

A quartet of perfect men—the apex of masculine evolution, Vanessa thought while wanting to drown them all in a shallow pool.

"We should've gone trick-or-treating," Steve said.

Vanessa smiled. "We decided we were too old, remember?"

"Yeah, but your costume is killer. I feel like it's wasted."

She glanced down at her black punk garb and nodded.

"Possibly. But the party doesn't officially start for, what, another half hour? I'll dazzle the world later."

Steve exhaled, maybe a bit louder than he'd intended. Vanessa tracked his gaze and saw that he kept glancing at his dad and the other husbands on the deck. His parents might not pay much attention to him, but they weren't abusive, and he had everything he needed in his life. Millions of kids would envy him. But that didn't make Steve blind to what an asshole his father seemed to be.

"Hey," she said. "I've got some of those bug-repellant tiki torch things in my garage. Do you want to walk over and get them with me? It might help with so many people in the backyard tonight."

He nodded. "Good idea."

They pushed off the picnic table where they'd been seated and strolled over to the deck. Vanessa hoped Mrs. Koenig would pop out of her mouse hole again, but she must have been preoccupied finishing up her taco salad or something. Instead, Steve got his father's attention.

"What's up, Stevie?" his dad asked, gaze flickering toward Vanessa.

She didn't like the way his eyes landed on her breasts. She was seventeen, and she had a figure. Normally, she wouldn't have worn anything that would draw such looks from men, but it was Halloween, the time of year when "come as you aren't" was the rule. The other dads glanced at her, too. One of them—a tall, athletic guy with a sheen of sweat on his forehead despite the chilly evening—looked her up and down as if he had x-ray vision.

"Vanessa has some bug torches at her house. We thought we'd go get 'em and put them around the backyard."

Mr. Koenig's eyes narrowed. "We've got plenty of torches."

"More couldn't hurt, right?"

Steve's father glanced at Vanessa again. For a moment, she saw him not as the money man he was now but the spoiled teenager he must once have been.

"I have a better idea," Mr. Koenig said. "Why don't the two of you go down to the Haunted Woods and tell the crowd down there that the party's starting?"

Steve glanced at Vanessa as if to ask what she wanted to do.

She shrugged. "I did want to go. Probably the last time, right? We can get there and back before the party really gets started."

"Don't worry, kids," the sweaty husband said. "There'll be plenty left to eat when you get back."

Mr. Koenig looked right at Vanessa. "Yeah, no worries. We'll fix you up a nice box lunch."

All the breath went out of her. She went numb, staring at him.

"Vee. What do you think?" Steve asked. "Haunted Woods?"

She barely heard him. Mr. Koenig had gone back to talking sports with his buddies as if the exchange had been completely innocent, but had it been? Was that just something he said, some kind of clichéd phrase she didn't know, or had he just made a reference to "box lunch" as a euphemism for going down on a girl?

Vanessa blinked. Had that just happened?

Mrs. Koenig came outside. She smiled at them. "Another batch of brownies in the oven, guys. I hope people eat them all, because my waistband can't have those leftovers."

Normal.

Ordinary.

Steve nudged her. "Vanessa. You wanna go?"

She looked at him. Realized her expression remained slack and forced a smile.

"Let's head down there. But no glow stick for you this year."

The joke came out of her almost on autopilot, the same kind of teasing she and Steve always engaged in. Somehow it woke her up, made her feel a little better.

"No glow stick," he promised.

Then they were walking around toward the front of the house and onto Parmenter Road, among all the parents and kids out trick-or-treating. The grotesque men on the deck had been left behind, but the cloud of swaggering douchebaggery that emanated from them seemed to follow.

Vanessa did her best to forget, to tamp it down. It would be better later, she told herself. There would be dozens of people there, and she wouldn't have to deal with Mr. Koenig and his friends again. And Owen would have alcohol. She had not intended to drink tonight, but she had a feeling she was going to change her mind. A drink or two would do wonders for her anxiety.

She hoped.

RICK BARBOSA

Rick pressed his back to the house and closed his eyes, praying Ruth Burgess wouldn't spot him when she looked out the window. He knew how stupid it was—closing his own eyes didn't make him invisible or Ruth blind. He shifted a foot to the side, as quietly as possible.

Billie slipped out from beneath the deck and hid as best she could behind one of the support posts. Even in the dark, her bright white Storm wig sort of glowed, but if they were lucky, the post would be enough to obscure the view from the basement window.

Rick could hear the Burgesses talking to each other inside the TV room.

"I'm telling you, I heard something," Ruth said.

Zack swore. "A skunk. Maybe a bear."

"Or kids trick-or-treating."

"In our backyard?" Zack asked.

He approached the window as he spoke. Ruth had glanced out quickly, but then arguing with Zack had distracted her. Now it was Zack's turn. Rick closed his eyes again and said a little silent prayer in his head.

He held his breath.

"I don't know," Zack muttered at the window. "I can't see a fucking thing out there."

"Go out and—" Ruth began.

"Don't be stupid," her husband snapped. When his tone softened, Rick realized Zack had focused on Always Leonard again. "Hey, kid. Don't look at us like that. Everything's okay. Grown-ups get cross with one another sometimes. I bet even your parents argue."

The answer came so softly, it took a moment for Rick to realize he'd heard it.

"They used to," Always Leonard said.

From the darkness, up against the house, Rick listened to Ruth and Zack offering comfort to the child they had taken in. Zack actually used the words *Oh, hey, champ*, like a TV sitcom dad. But something about the way they spoke made Rick's skin crawl. It reminded him of the animated snake Kaa in Disney's *Jungle Book* movie, like their voices were meant to lull Leonard into feeling calm.

"I know how you feel," Ruth said, there in the cellar. "I lost my parents young, too. Nobody really understood what it felt like. I got lucky, though. I had a neighbor, Mr. Kasovich, who knew how to make me feel better. He knew what I needed."

Rick didn't want to risk looking back through the window, but he didn't have to. He heard the springs of the sofa creak, the sound of someone moving, sitting next to Always Leonard, and the way Ruth and Zack were talking—it wasn't just comfort. It was Kaa, that mesmerizing tone, the false comfort of the snake.

He slipped out from the darkness under the deck and into the moonlight, gesturing for Billie to follow. They stepped quietly, carefully.

"Hey," Billie whispered. "Let's get out of—"

Rick gave a quick shake of his head. "Something's wrong. For a second, I thought they might be okay, but they're not. They're nasty. Like, pedos or something."

"So what do we do? What if they have knives?" Billie's eyes were wide. "What if they have *a gun*?"

Rick bowed his head. He didn't pray much—usually, he figured if God was even there, the state of the world made it pretty clear he wasn't listening to the typical thirteen-year-old's prayer—but he cast a thought heavenward, a two-second plea for help. Even then, he knew what had to be done.

Billie glanced toward the basement windows and the light gleaming from within. "You know I've always got your back. But as much as you and me talk tough and try to act like we're older than we are . . . we're kids, too."

"Not little," he whispered. "Not like him. I can't do this without you, Billie."

She looked frightened, but she nodded.

"Go bang on the front door," he whispered. "As hard as you can. Make a ton of noise—we've gotta make sure Zack goes upstairs. They're not going to want anyone coming inside, but if it sounds like an emergency, or like the cops or something, he's going to have to go and see what's going on."

Billie stared at him. "And then what?"

"Then we get the kid out of there."

Billie turned to run alongside the house, past the bushes, and around to the Burgesses' front yard.

Rick moved back toward the windows, a knot in his belly. He knew he ought to look inside again, but the idea of peering through that glass and seeing Ruth and Zack doing something to that kid brought tears to his eyes. From the window, he heard Leonard say something, and Ruth hushed him as if he were a toddler she was hoping would go back to sleep. It occurred to Rick that they might have drugged the kid, and he hoped that wasn't the case. Getting him out of there would be a hell of a lot harder if they had to, like, carry him or something.

What happened to calling his parents?

The thought stilled the nausea in his gut. Anger flooded into him. Hatred. Everyone whispered rumors about the Burgesses, even joked about them, the same way they did about rumors that this girl had sex with that guy, or somebody's dad got fired from his job. But this was different. This was . . .

Rick couldn't find the words.

And then he did.

This was the kind of thing only monsters did.

The thunderous banging at the front door made Rick stand up straight.

"What the fuck is that?" Zack barked.

Rick took another step, deeper into the darkness under the deck, where he could get a glimpse inside the TV room. Zack had stood up from the sofa. He had a camera in his hand. Ruth remained on the couch with Always Leonard, whose shirt had been cast aside.

Rick clenched his fists, stifling the fury that made him want to cry out. If he acted now, they would never get that little boy out of there. The pounding upstairs became even louder. Zack Burgess cussed a blue streak and stormed down the corridor and up the stairs, leaving his wife on the sofa with Leonard.

Quietly, Rick approached the basement door. Ruth might be alone down there for a minute, but she was still an adult and he was a kid—and Zack might be back downstairs anytime. He tried the knob, but found it locked. He thought he might be able to smash the door in with his shoulder, but he was in the eighth grade, not yet physically formidable.

Raised voices floated out through the slightly open TV room window. Rick hesitated in confusion.

"Show them to me!" Always Leonard demanded, almost whining.

Ruth Burgess had been gentle with him until now, cajoling, sweetening him up like a forest witch in her candy house. Now she lost her cool. "I told you, goddamn it! There aren't any kids here except you."

The little boy in the Burgesses' TV room let out a kid-size roar of frustration. "I know they're in the house. You've got kids in here!"

Ruth started to argue, but Leonard hissed at her. "I can smell them. I know they're here . . . or their souls are."

Rick froze. *What the hell?*

"That's enough of that weird shit," Ruth sneered. "Get your ass over here."

Rick took a few steps back to get up momentum before launching a kick at the door. His boot struck the wood under the knob—right by the lock—and with a splintering crack, the door smashed open. He rushed in so fast the door hadn't even swung all the way inward before he had barreled into Ruth Burgess.

Ruth let out a cry of alarm as Rick bodychecked her. The woman stumbled into the coffee table and crashed on top of it, then rolled off the other side. But Ruth was tougher than she looked. She hit the floor and sprang back up, shoulders dropped like a linebacker, ready for a fight. In that moment, Rick wished they'd never seen Zack leading Leonard into his house.

"I know you," Ruth snarled. "You're the Barbosa boy. Your father's gonna love this."

Rick couldn't stop a laugh of disbelief. "Are you kidding me? We know what you're doing here, you sick freak!"

Somehow she hadn't counted on this. Ruth had been so angry at his intrusion that she hadn't realized what his presence meant. Rick saw the change on her face, the calculus going on behind her eyes as she tried to figure out how to bullshit her way out of this, and then he saw her realize she and her husband were fucked, and there was only one way out.

She turned toward the corridor that led to the stairs and shouted for Zack.

Always Leonard stood paralyzed in front of the television set, watching the quick back-and-forth. Rick reached for him to drag him out of there, but Leonard leaped out of his grasp. The kid lunged at Ruth, and though he might only be nine years old and probably didn't weigh more than seventy pounds, he bent into it and pumped his legs, and the impact was enough to knock her onto the sofa. Leonard started to slap and punch at Ruth, fists striking her eyes and nose and throat. Ruth gasped and clawed at the kid's hair, then managed to get a knee up between herself and him, and she tossed Leonard off her.

Eyes bulging, nose bleeding, she rasped for breath and clutched at her own throat, and Rick knew something had happened. Ruth couldn't catch her breath. Leonard had damaged her windpipe. For a second or two, Rick couldn't breathe either, just thinking about what to do.

But then he heard footsteps pounding across the floor upstairs and the sound of the cellar door smashing open—Zack was coming—and he knew he had no choice.

Rick grabbed Leonard by both shoulders and propelled him out the back door. They darted from under the deck and saw Billie running around from the front of the house.

"Book it!" she snapped. "Run faster, Rick!"

They raced for the trees. Rick had been slowed down by Leonard, but now the little guy picked up his pace and turned out to be almost as fast as Billie. They were halfway across the grass when Rick realized they should have headed for the front yard. On the street, they would have found a neighbor or other kids—witnesses, in case Zack tried to stop them, maybe hurt them—but back here, the only place to run was into the woods. Billie had come back here to get Rick, and her momentum had turned them toward the trees. They knew the woods better than the Burgesses, Rick was sure. They spent a lot of time on the paths among those trees. But that didn't mean they were going to get out of this.

Zack Burgess came roaring out through his basement door. "Fuckers!" he shouted. "You little shits, I'll fucking kill you!"

The trees were just ahead. Rick saw the opening of a path, a sliver of moonlight showing the way. Always Leonard passed him and darted in just ahead of him, and then all three of them were in the woods, running their asses off, sneakers pounding dirt and pine needles. Rick's heart thumped hard and his breath rasped loudly in his ears, but suddenly he felt good. Leonard was going to be okay. The Burgesses might be monstrous perverts, but he and Billie . . . they had saved this little kid.

They were goddamn heroes.

As he ran, he thought of their pillowcases full of Halloween candy, and even as frightened as he was, he mourned for the loss.

"Come on, this way!" Billie called from up ahead, darting to the right, cape flying behind her, cutting through trees toward another path they all knew very well. A path that would lead them home.

Rick heard branches snapping behind him as Zack Burgess smashed through the trees in pursuit. He ranted at them for a few seconds, but then the only sound Rick could hear coming from back there was the thump of Zack's boots on the trail. No more talk. No more threats. Panic fluttered in Rick's heart, and he ran faster, catching up to Billie and Leonard, urging them onward. No more threats meant that Zack meant to do more than threaten. He intended to stop them, to keep them from telling the police what they'd seen. And there would only be one way to keep them quiet.

A branch tagged his forehead, scratching a furrow in the skin. It burned, but Rick barely noticed as reality set in. None of this was supposed to happen. There were sad things happening in his life—his parents had given up on their marriage and were selling the family house, he'd be leaving his best friends behind—but tonight had been about having fun, reveling in Halloween. Now . . .

Were they really running for their lives?

Rick stared at Leonard's back, saw the nerdy way the skinny little kid pumped his arms as he ran. *You'd better be worth it, kid.*

The thought made his stomach churn. Rick wouldn't have left any kid in those circumstances, down in the Burgesses' TV room, not even the worst brat in the world. They would get back to his house, or Billie's house, and they'd call the police. Leonard would tell the cops what happened. Ruth and Zack were going to jail.

Ruth.

Oh, shit. Ruth.

What would the police find when they went to the Burgesses' house? How badly had Leonard hurt her? What story would Zack tell when the police caught up to him?

Rick forced himself to stop thinking and just run. Whatever happened next, there was nothing to be done about it now. Events had been set in motion. The only thing they could control tonight was how hard they fought to keep themselves and Leonard safe. How hard they ran to escape Zack Burgess, and the awful things that happened in his basement.

A voice came swimming up from his memory. Leonard's voice, from just a minute ago.

He'd said he knew there had been kids in that basement

because he could smell them—or their *souls*—and what the hell was that about? Leonard had gone nuts on Ruth, and that was okay, that was self-defense. Good for him. But the things he had said . . .

Something wasn't right. Something more than just how evil the Burgesses were.

Suddenly, all Rick cared about was getting out of the woods. Getting back into the neighborhood, where there would be other people. Suddenly, all he really wanted was to be home, with his family.

Home, where he'd be safe.

BARB SWEENEY

Barb felt as if the world had slowed nearly to a halt. She sat at her kitchen table in a chair with a plastic cushion and a wrought iron back, part of a set that had belonged to her grandmother. Donnie had once said the chairs were uncomfortable, but beyond that, he seemed not to care about household furnishings, as if over the course of all these years he had really only ever been a visitor. Never attached to anything, able to walk out the door whenever he liked without leaving behind anything that really mattered to him.

She had a Diet Coke in front of her, half-empty, long since having lost its fizz and any coolness from the fridge. A package of Benson & Hedges menthols lay beside the soda can, the top torn open. It had been in the back of her bedside drawer for over a year, ever since she'd mostly succeeded in quitting smoking. Year-old cigarettes weren't ideal, and the menthol flavor on the stale cigs tasted more like ammonia, but the nicotine hits were like a massage with every puff. If she kept smoking, she knew that in the end it would be her lungs that killed her.

But not tonight, you bastards. Not tonight.

"Mom?"

She blinked. Reacted in slow motion. Turned to see Brian

126

standing in the kitchen doorway. Middle child. Eldest son. Handsome, well liked, generally well behaved. She had good kids, in spite of them having Donnie for a father. But as good as Brian might be, she almost sneered at him. Maybe offered him a cigarette.

Instead, Barb put on her most understanding Mom face. "Brian James Sweeney," she said. "You're the cure for what ails me."

Brian always smiled at that, but not this time. "You okay, Mom?"

Of course not. You must be old enough by now to understand what a troublesome and pointless question that is.

"I'd be lying if I said yes, babe. But this was coming for a long time, so I can't say I'm surprised."

Brian exhaled. He came into the kitchen and stood with both hands on the back of one of the wrought iron chairs, but he didn't sit down. Barb picked at the Formica at the table's edge, chipping it away.

"I guess I'm not real surprised, either," Brian said quietly, glancing over his shoulder as if he didn't want his brother or sister to hear.

The phone on the wall started to jangle. It rang so loud that they both jumped, but neither of them moved to pick it up. Chances were nine out of ten that it would be one of Julia's friends—they'd been calling off and on for an hour. One of them had come to the door. Julia had spoken quietly with the other girl and sent her away, but now she was in her parents' bedroom fielding one call after another.

"Do you . . ." Brian began, but then he glanced down as if in shame.

Barb smiled. "Do I think your dad will come home?"

Brian nodded, and in that moment, he looked as if he must be the youngest in the family instead of Charlie.

"I don't know, to be honest," Barb admitted. "But listen good, kid. We're going to be okay with or without him. Might be that we'll be better off without, if you really want to know. Better to know you're relying only on the real and tangible, on the people you can count on, than to put your hopes on the shoulders of a man who's cast them aside a thousand times. He's just not reliable, your dad."

"But you loved him."

"I still do. But my first duty is to you kids and making sure you're taken care of. I can't count on your dad for that, and I guess this is my wake-up call to make me stop pretending that I can."

Brian fell silent then, thinking it over. After a few seconds, he exhaled, then went to the refrigerator and got himself a can of Sprite.

"Is Charlie okay?" Barb asked and instantly chided herself. Moments ago, she'd been frustrated with Brian for asking the same about her. "I mean, do you think he'll try to run off again?"

Brian sat down at the chair across from her and cracked open his soda. The can gave a hiss that echoed through the kitchen.

"I was gonna talk to you about it in the morning," he said. "He seems okay, but I'm not sure. I think he's kinda off in fantasyland or something."

"What do you mean?"

"The place he hid—it's this open space in some bushes, like a little secret spot," he said, and Barb could see that he regretted mentioning it, but Brian continued, "Anyway, I had checked a couple of backyards and the corner where we get the bus, and then I realized that was where he'd run. It wasn't like he could drive off somewhere, and he definitely wasn't gonna go into the woods at night by himself."

"That makes sense," Barb replied. "But it doesn't sound like 'fantasyland.'"

"I'm getting to that. When I caught up to him, Charlie didn't give me a hard time about coming home at all. He said there'd been a girl in the bushes with him—"

Barb took a long drag on her Benson & Hedges menthol. "A girl?"

She exhaled after the question. Donnie had always thought it some kind of magic trick that she could talk with smoke in her lungs.

"A girl. Younger than him, he said," Brian went on. "Sarah Jane. She was running away, too."

"That seems like a pretty big coincidence."

"That's what I thought," Brian said. "But I didn't argue with him. He was already upset enough."

Barb studied her middle child. "Did you see this girl?"

"Supposedly, she ran off just before I got there."

The numbness in her retreated a little. Barb had been sitting in the kitchen and letting the seconds tick by, waiting for the moment she had to be a mom again. She hadn't been eager for the moment to arrive—after tonight, she needed a break. Was that too much to ask? Her husband had walked out on her. Her ribs hurt from the way she had fallen, and the left side of her face, around her eye, had swelled a little from the smack she had received when she blocked Donnie's departure. She didn't think he had struck her on purpose. They had both been flailing their hands like idiot kids in a slap fight. But if she were being honest with herself, it wouldn't have been the first time he had bruised her.

She had wanted the seconds to slow down, give her time to catch her breath. To think about the way her budget had to change, and if she had to switch careers, and how each of her children would handle the night's violence and tomorrow's separation, and the eventual divorce. Brian going out to find Charlie and bringing him home in one piece had been the work of angels. The moment they had walked into the house, she had hugged and kissed them both and told Julia they wouldn't need to call the police to search for Charlie after all. Charlie had turned red and his eyes had welled up, but after she'd hugged him and kissed his forehead, he'd mumbled something about watching television and gone into the room he shared with Brian.

"Mom?" Brian said.

Barb nodded. "Just thinking it over." She stubbed out her cigarette and rose, the chair legs scraping the floor. Her mane of dyed red hair had become unruly, but there was no point in trying to tame it now.

Brian stood. They both abandoned their sodas on the kitchen table, and Barb led him down the corridor toward the boys' bedroom. She could hear Julia laughing about something on the phone in the master bedroom, almost as if her father hadn't thrown her on the ground outside. As if her parents' marriage hadn't ended.

Barb knocked softly on the doorframe, even though the door was open.

"Hi, Mom," Charlie said, barely looking up from the TV. A rerun of *The A-Team* was on.

"Hey, kiddo." Barb moved into the room and leaned against the bureau. "Mind if I interrupt Mr. T for a second?"

"Okay." Charlie glanced at his brother, who still stood in the doorway of their room, and wrinkled his nose as if he'd smelled something unpleasant.

"This girl you saw tonight, when you went up the street."

Charlie lowered his gaze. "Yeah?"

"You really saw her? Talked to her?"

He frowned, raising his eyes again. Pinning her with a questioning look. "Yeah?"

Barb nodded, pondering. Whatever Brian thought, Charlie had never been a kid who made up little fantasies. He had never had an imaginary friend, and he wasn't a liar. If he said there had been a little girl in the bushes, Barb had to believe him.

"Do you know who she is? Where she lives?"

"Her name is Sarah-Jane-something. But I don't know where she lives."

"Do you know who she was hiding from? Bullies, maybe? Her sister?"

Charlie's expression turned dark. Troubled. "She called him 'the Cunning Man.'"

Barb felt her mouth go dry. Her back stiffened. She didn't think she'd ever heard the phrase before, but it seemed as if she had, and it unnerved her.

"No name?" she asked.

"Was it her dad?" Brian asked from the doorway. "Her mom's boyfriend, maybe?"

Charlie rolled his eyes. "I don't know! And why are you acting like a grown-up all of a sudden? You're not Dad!"

Barb felt all the air go out of the room. Those three words, and Charlie's anger, struck them all a hard blow. Of course Brian knew he wasn't his father, knew he wasn't in charge of his little brother, but he had been the one to go out and bring Charlie home safe tonight. Sexist or not, if Donnie really was not coming home, Brian was the man of the house now.

"Your brother's not trying to be your dad, Charlie—"

"I'm not," Brian said. His face flushed, either in anger or in sadness, and Barb thought he might yell at Charlie. Instead, he went over and sat on the floor beside his little brother's bed. "We're in this together, Charlie."

"So, you're gonna stop being a butthead to me?" Charlie said, clearly dubious.

131

Brian smiled. "Well . . . tonight, yeah. But tomorrow, I intend to be a brand-new butthead."

Charlie couldn't help smiling in return. "Fair enough . . . butthead."

"Y'know," Barb said, "it might not be too late for you guys to hit a few houses for trick-or-treat."

"We still have most of the candy we were going to give out tonight, right?" Brian asked. "And there are plenty of scary movies on TV."

Barb laughed, surprised she was able to do so. They were going to be all right without Donnie. They were going to be just fine.

"I'll get the candy," she said. "We can set you guys up out on the porch. I think one of my favorite Dracula movies is on later."

Charlie's eyes opened a bit wider. He wasn't usually able to watch bloody movies, and he gave his mom a double thumbs-up.

Barb went down the hall and descended the stairs to the front door. The outside lights had been shut off all night. Only a handful of kids had bothered to ring the bell, and Barb had only opened it twice. The bowl of Halloween candy sat on the tiled landing in the shadows, and as she picked it up, her stomach growled. Propping the bowl against her hipbone, she dug around and extricated several mini Snickers bars and stuffed them in the pockets of her blue velour sweatpants. Chocolate might make her fat, but she figured it was better than lighting another cigarette.

Though, who was she kidding? She'd be lighting another cigarette soon enough.

She turned to go back up the stairs, and something moved in her peripheral vision. Barb glanced at the tall, narrow, frosted-glass window beside the front door. She stared at it, sure that a figure had passed by. Probably some straggler, a kid getting toward the last half hour or so of trick-or-treating who didn't understand the no-lights rule. Or maybe a little punk who wanted to egg their house for not participating in trick-or-treat. Barb had heard stories in previous years about kids who did that.

Or it's Donnie, she thought.

Her chest tightened, heart aching. What was this feeling, really? It tasted a little like hatred, but then why did she want to wrap herself in a blanket and cry? She had loved him once, so damn much, and she still did. But that was the source of her pain, the thorn in her side. The man had poisoned her with her own feelings, and she'd had enough.

If Donnie stood out there on his own stoop, no way would Barb let him in. Not tonight. And not tomorrow, unless he had come to collect his stuff.

On the other hand, if it was a couple of little bastards trying to egg her house—

Balancing the candy bowl, Barb put her free hand on the doorknob. Something moved again, just beyond that frosted glass. A shape that darted aside, abandoning the stoop.

"What the heck?" she whispered.

Floorboards creaked at the top of the stairs behind her. "Mom?"

Barb whipped around. When she spotted Julia on the top step, backlit by the light from the kitchen, she exhaled loudly. "Jules, you scared me."

"Sorry," Julia said. Her face looked pale, her eyes rimmed with red. She'd cried her share of tears tonight, mostly alone in her parents' room, if those eyes were any evidence.

"It's okay. What do you need, sweetheart?" Barb asked. "If you want some of this candy, take it now before your brothers get through with it."

Julia glanced away, guiltily. "I'm good. I just . . ."

"Go on, Jules. Whatever it is, you can talk to me about it. Are you worried about what's going to happen now?"

She didn't have to explain what she meant. Julia nodded slowly. Of course she would be worried. At seventeen, college was around the corner. And even without worrying about that expense, Julia was old enough to realize that her mother wasn't prepared to pay the mortgage on her own, never mind the food bill for three kids.

"All I can say right now is that we will work it out," Barb said. "You keep all your dreams, kid. Give me a couple of days, and then if you want to sit down and talk about the nuts-and-bolts stuff, finances, and everything, I will have that conversation with you. But you don't need to worry. I will make it work."

Just speaking the words made Barb begin to feel better. She hadn't put those thoughts into sentences before that very moment, but as they left her lips, she believed them. No way would she let her kids down. She had problems. She wasn't perfect. But she could be solid for her kids. Stable. They needed her to be steady and strong, and so she would be that.

And she'd never go out driving in search of Donnie Sweeney again. Let him put his dick wherever he pleased.

Barb didn't quite feel that last part 100 percent. But she told herself she would, in time.

"Are Charlie and Brian okay?" Julia asked, pulling her ginger hair into a ponytail.

Barb started up the steps, and her daughter stepped aside to let her pass. "They're watching TV, and I'm going to let them stay up as late as they want, and eat candy and drink soda till they puke. No rules for anyone tonight. Tomorrow we start fresh."

Julia followed her into the kitchen, where Barb picked up Brian's Sprite. He hadn't asked for it, but she knew he would remember that he wanted it the second she handed him the candy bowl.

"I'm glad to hear you say that," Julia said. "I got a few calls tonight—"

"You don't say."

"A bunch of my friends are going to the Haunted Woods. It's the last year for it," Julia reminded her. "They're all bugging me to go, but after tonight, I figured you'd want me home. And I guess I'm not really feeling like it anyway. I'll probably start crying halfway through—"

"Through the Haunted Woods?" Barb said. "Nobody would notice. And anyone who did would think you were scared out of your wits."

Julia frowned. "So, you think I should go?"

Barb walked to her daughter, arms laden with candy bowl and soda can, and bent forward to kiss her daughter's forehead. "You should absolutely go. It's the last time. The end of an era."

"Yeah. I guess it is."

The end of an era. The words echoed in Barb's mind.

"Just no drinking, okay?"

"Yeah. Of course," Julia said, shifting her eyes to the left as she lied.

Barb saw it, knew the lie right away, and she smiled sadly. "You know what, my girl? I take that back. Drink if you want to. Have one for me, 'cause I could really use one. But just stay safe, you and your friends look out for one another, and you come home to me in one piece."

Julia blinked in surprise and then gave a small chuckle at how easily her mother had seen through her. She kissed her mom on the cheek, and Barb felt the shards of her heart start to knit back together, just a little. It would be a lifetime's work, fixing that, but suddenly, she felt it must be possible.

"Thanks, Mom. We'll be okay," Julia said. She fixed her mother with a meaningful look. "We'll *all* be okay."

Barb bumped her with the candy bowl. "Damn right we will. Now go get ready."

Julia scurried back down the corridor and Barb followed. The boys were arguing about who was the second coolest guy on the A-Team, because of course Mr. T was number one. She stepped into the room with their candy and Brian's Sprite, and she told herself that Julia was right. The Sweeneys were going to be okay.

They just had to get through tonight.

JULIA SWEENEY

Julia wore no costume, but she felt as if her face had become a mask. At seventeen, she was too old for trick-or-treat but felt too young for some of the sexy costume parties she'd heard about from friends who'd gone off to college. She'd been to her share of campfire bashes in the woods, where lots of her friends from school and the neighborhood would drink till they puked, as if vomit were the gold medal victory in the evening's competition. But that sort of thing had lost its charm before she had even finished junior year.

Tonight, she'd turned to Cynthia Walukevich for comfort. They'd been on-and-off best friends since the fourth grade, and though Cynthia might not be the sharpest knife in the drawer, she usually knew when to speak and when to listen, when to offer a shoulder to cry on and when to rage and be angry at the people who'd hurt Julia. That's what friends were for—to have your back—and Julia and Cynthia had been that for each other. Tonight, Julia had cried, and Cynthia had been smart enough to temper her rage at Julia's dad with sympathy. No matter how much Julia hated her father tonight, she loved him, too, and Cynthia knew that.

It'll be better at home, Cynthia had promised her. *Quieter, no more fighting. You and your mom and your brothers will be happier with your dad out of the house. You know it's true, Jules. And your dad loves you so much. Anybody can see that. You're like his friggin' princess, right? You'll see him plenty. And when you do see him, your mom probably won't be there, which means none of that stress, right? You'll have a better time. Trust me, Juju, this is for the best.*

Julia had asked Cynthia when she'd gotten so wise, but she knew the answer. Cynthia's parents had gotten divorced three years earlier. She'd been through it already. As frantic as Julia had felt, freaking out about her parents fighting, about her dad being such an irresponsible drunk, about Charlie taking off in the dark and Brian having to go after him, somehow Cynthia had managed to calm her down—and then talk her into leaving the house and coming to the Barbosas' Haunted Woods. To clear her head, Cynthia had said, and that had seemed like the most reasonable suggestion in the world.

Now she strode up the sidewalk toward the Barbosas' house, and the moment she spotted Cynthia, Julia wanted to strangle her.

There were about forty people in line for the Haunted Woods. Julia saw Mrs. Barbosa near the big fake cemetery gates. A woman she thought she recognized as Mrs. Barbosa's sister was handing glow sticks to the fraidy-cats. Up at the front of the line, four people away from being let in, Cynthia waved her hand for Julia to hurry and catch up, but Julia didn't quicken her pace in the slightest.

Cynthia had said she and "the girls" were meeting up for the Haunted Woods before they went over to the Koenigs' block party. That should have meant at least a few of the neighborhood girls they had been friends with over the years. Most of them were shallow and untrustworthy, but they were her friends and they made her laugh. Instead, it was just Cynthia and her latest shitty boyfriend, a tall, oily, second-string quarterback named

Hunter Kenney. Julia had never told Cynthia exactly why she despised Hunter—didn't tell her about the time Hunter had taken her hand and pressed it over the bulge in his jeans as if he were surprising her with a priceless gift. Julia had yanked her hand away, given him a disgusted sneer, and told him to fuck off, but still he persuaded himself that she'd been impressed and enthusiastic. She'd made it as clear as possible that if he ever tried anything like that again, she would rat him out to Cynthia. He'd wondered aloud which of them Cynthia would believe when he explained that Julia had been the one to grab his junk and proposition him.

Julia had assured him that she knew whom Cynthia would believe, but in truth, she wasn't sure, and that made her feel sick.

Now here he was, the oily bastard himself.

Julia went up to Cynthia and took her by the hand, leading her across the street. Cars were parked up and down Parmenter, but several groups were leaving. They weaved between two vehicles, silhouetted in headlight beams.

"I need to talk to you," Julia said.

Cynthia called back to Hunter to save their place in line.

On the sidewalk, Julia rounded on her friend. Her guts churned and her head spun with a dozen different emotions. "What the fuck, Cyn?"

Cynthia flinched. "Hey. Why are you mad at me?"

Julia took a deep breath. She had never been one of those girls who cried about everything, but tonight, she had a reason. Tonight, her father had broken her heart, not to mention throwing her on the front lawn. For the first time in her life, he'd physically hurt her in addition to the emotional hurt. So when her eyes welled up, staring at Cynthia, she grew even angrier because she didn't want Cynthia to think these tears were about her.

"Don't pretend you don't know what I'm talking about."

Cynthia sighed. "Look, I knew you wouldn't come if I told you Hunter was with me, okay? But you needed to get out of the house. I love you, Jules. You know that. I just wanted you to be able to breathe."

Julia gave a brittle laugh. "Great job."

"I just don't get why you hate him so much. Okay, you think he's not good for me, but you never say why."

"He's a scumbag, Cynthia. You know how many girls he's hooked up with before you, and he's cheated on, like, every last one of them. You think you're gonna be different? Never mind that you lied to me. Where are the rest of the girls?"

Cynthia's expression darkened. "I wasn't lying. They were here. We had to get out of line, like, three times, and they got tired of waiting for you. But I waited, Julia. I made my boyfriend wait because I was trying to do something nice for you."

Julia's chest rose and fell as she stared at Cynthia, trying to get her anger under control. She believed Cynthia had other motives, that this had been more about getting her and Hunter together to try to force her to accept him.

She hung her head. "I've had enough fighting for tonight."

Cynthia took her by the hand. "I don't want to fight either. I didn't mean to make it worse."

Hunter called to them from across the street. It was their turn. He didn't say it, but Julia heard the impatience in his voice—he didn't want to step out of line a fourth time. She didn't care if she inconvenienced him, but she couldn't handle any more conflict.

"We're coming!" she barked at him as she grabbed Cynthia's hand. They rushed across the street just as Hunter was handing a ten-dollar bill to Mrs. Barbosa for their entry-fee donation. Even so, she leaned over to whisper in Cynthia's ear, "I can't promise to be nice to him."

"That's okay," Cynthia said with a grin. "I'm *never* nice to him."

Julia smiled. She felt brittle inside. The scene at her house earlier had left her in no mood to forgive, and even less willing to trust anyone who said they loved her, but she also felt as if she couldn't afford to lash out at anyone tonight. She was in no state to be judging behavior. Tomorrow she would decide how to react to Cynthia's well-meant deceit. Tonight, she needed her friend.

Mrs. Barbosa waved them through the big fake gate. Cynthia tried to reach for one of the glow sticks that meant "don't be too scary," but Julia grabbed her in a bear hug and trapped her arms, propelling them past the point of no return. If she had to put up with Hunter, the least Cynthia could do was suffer a few extra moments of cozy terror in the Haunted Woods.

"If I pee myself, it's on you," Cynthia said.

Hunter laughed. "Remind me to stay a few feet ahead of you, babe. Away from the splash zone."

Julia laughed. She wanted to knee him in the balls, but that didn't mean he wasn't funny on occasion.

True to his word, Hunter started out ahead of them as they passed alongside the Barbosa house, but as they walked into the backyard accompanied by the soundtrack of excited screams and monster moans from the woods, Julia grabbed the back of his T-shirt.

"What are you doing?" Hunter asked sharply.

"If you're in front, you'll spoil some of the surprises," Julia said. "Cynthia should go first."

Hunter flashed a mischievous grin. He bowed and gestured for them to precede him.

Cynthia shot Julia a petulant look. "You're evil."

Julia replied with her deepest, evilest laugh, linked arms

with her best friend, and the two of them marched into the darkness. Somewhere in the trees up ahead, they heard the rev of a chain saw. Cynthia whimpered, straining to go back the way they'd come, but in the glow of an electric pumpkin, Julia saw the smile on her face. Terror could be fun.

They passed a massive oak tree, and a pair of zombies lunged from a ditch beside the path, reaching for their legs. The girls shrieked in harmony and stumbled ahead with Hunter snickering behind them. A second later, he let out a cry and a stream of profanity, and Julia whipped around to see him clutching his chest as a bodiless head zipped past him on a metal wire. A bit of gristle and dripping spinal column dangled beneath the head. It was grotesque but not exactly high-quality makeup effects—perfect to startle the hell out of whoever had decided to hang back in each group that went through.

Cynthia clung tightly to Julia again.

"No, no, no," she said. "Jules, tell them no."

Julia looked ahead and saw a whiteface clown looming from between two trees, holding what looked like a bloody human face—peeled right off—in his hand. Cynthia was deathly afraid of clowns, and for a moment, Julia regretted forcing her friend to come through without a glow stick.

"Close your eyes, Cyn. I've got you." She escorted Cynthia past the spot where the clown loomed. Calliope music, the kind of creepy, tinkling melody you'd hear at a carnival merry-go-round, played softly in the woods, and beneath that, Julia could hear someone crying softly.

"Is he gone?" Cynthia asked.

"Yeah."

Behind them, Hunter muttered something about the clown. Apparently, they scared the shit out of him, too. Julia pushed Cynthia forward, reminding her that the only way out was through. They laughed nervously as they passed a few displays that had become familiar over the years. Zombie hands thrust up over the edge of a fresh grave, a long gravedigger's shovel leaning casually against a cracked faux-marble headstone splashed with blood. A demonic figure hissed at them from up within the branches of a tree, and they shrieked again. An awful wail began off to the left, and they looked over to see a soft light begin to glow behind an antique baby carriage, and a tiny, clawed hand reach out from within.

Something dashed from between two black drapes, right across the path in front of them. A little girl in a stained Raggedy Ann costume with smeared kohl around her eyes and blood splashed on one side of her face. She crashed into Julia, who stared down into those wide, young eyes. Cynthia screamed, and Raggedy Ann shoved Julia away and ran off into the darkness just as a hockey-masked killer burst from the other side of the path, reaching for them, only to be dragged back by the chains that bound him to a stake in the ground.

"Dude!" Hunter cried. "That scared me shitless."

The girls kept clear of the murderer's reach, and Hunter tried to get him to high-five. It took Julia a few seconds to realize the chained killer was a friend of Hunter's, and she appreciated the fact that the actor wouldn't break character. Mr. Barbosa had always been super serious about the Haunted Woods, and she loved that even now, on the last night ever, people were dedicated to making the experience everything it ought to be.

Julia wore a huge grin. She was having a fantastic time.

Then another figure stepped out onto the path, lifted her arms, and shouted, "Boo!" at the top of her lungs. It was ridiculous instead of scary, because there was no gory makeup, nothing spooky here. Cynthia jumped and screamed anyway.

Chloe Barbosa broke down laughing. "Oh my God," she said between breaths. "You're such a loser."

But she said it with love.

"Don't be too hard on her," Julia said as Chloe fell into step with the group. "I wouldn't let her take a glow stick."

"Good," Chloe said, linking arms with Cynthia. "My dad went all out. Come on, I'll protect you guys."

Hunter grunted in disapproval as he quickened his pace to keep up with them. "I'm protecting them just fine."

"You screamed like a little bitch back there," Cynthia reminded him.

The three girls laughed together. Julia was glad to be with Chloe. The Barbosas were all so kind, and Chloe had never been anything but sweet to her. People didn't have to be shitty all the time. It was good to remember that.

More screams came from up ahead. Cynthia whimpered.

Julia didn't want it to end.

VANESSA MONTEZ

Trick-or-treat wasn't over yet, but the early rush of trick-or-treaters had filtered back to their homes to dig through their buckets and bags and argue with their parents about how much candy they were going to eat tonight. The lights remained on outside of homes, the beacon to older kids and families that had gotten a late start. One little Cape-style house had its windows open and spooky music blaring from within. At another house, the owner had put their television set up against the window, with *It's the Great Pumpkin, Charlie Brown* running in a loop on their VCR.

Vanessa Montez soaked it all in. If she could have made every day Halloween, she would have done it with the snap of her fingers. In her witchy punk outfit, she felt more herself than any other night of the year.

"People are going to be showing up back at the house by now," Steve said.

Vanessa shot him a sidelong glance. She smirked and gave him a little shove. "Your dad wanted us to come down and let people know the party's starting soon. He'll survive without you there to bully for an hour."

"Oh, that's nice," Steve replied. "My dad's not a bully."

She gave a short laugh. "Okay."

Did Steve actually believe that? Of course he must love his parents, but like most kids, he wanted to escape them most of the time. Could it be possible that he didn't see how much of a bully his father was? From the tone of his voice—hurt, even stung—Vanessa supposed he really did not see it, but Steve's father had always fit a certain stereotype. In movies, Mr. Koenig would never be the main character. He would have been the arrogant boss, thinking his salary made him better than anyone with less in the bank. There were way worse than Steve's dad, but his country club attitude was pretty obvious.

Yet Steve didn't see it.

An awful, ugly question rose in Vanessa's mind. If Steve didn't find fault with his father's behavior . . . what did that suggest about Steve?

"You have something to say?" he asked.

Vanessa smiled. "Duh, no. I like to give you shit. Learn to love it."

Steve couldn't help but laugh and roll his eyes. That should have been the end of it, but Vanessa found the moment lingered in her thoughts. Before they had left Steve's house, his father had made a comment that might have been meant to offend her. She had brushed it off, assuming she was misinterpreting, but she had to wonder. For the first time, she wondered what Steve would say if she mentioned it to him, and she discovered she did not want to know the answer. Not if they were to remain best friends.

"Monnn-tezzzzzzz!" a voice called from the darkness ahead.

Vanessa and Steve had been passing through the glow of a streetlight. As they returned to the darkness, the figures approaching them resolved into Vince Spinale and his usual gang of idiots.

"Spinale!" she called in return.

"Oh, this guy," Steve muttered.

She mostly agreed with the sentiment implied by his tone, but as much of a loudmouth as Spinale could be, Vanessa enjoyed sparring with him. He was loud and crass, but he wasn't a bully. Sometimes, at the bus stop when they were younger or hanging around the smoking area outside school, he could be excellent company.

They traded barbs for a few seconds, until Vanessa realized they were on their way to the Koenigs' block party and told Spinale that the party hadn't really gotten started yet—just a few adults cracking their first beers of the evening. Moments later, she had turned the tide, and the whole group was headed for the Haunted Woods together, though Steve seemed unhappy about it.

As they walked, Vanessa glanced around at the kids with Spinale. Most of them she recognized, but they had a kid with them she could tell wasn't anyone she knew. Tall and lanky like Steve, he wore a scarecrow costume that looked stiff and tweedy, like he'd meant to go as Ichabod Crane or something and added the hat and straw stuffing at the last second to pull off the scarecrow look. As they walked, the scarecrow kept looking over his shoulder, not at Vanessa and Steve but anxiously, as if he expected to see someone following them—someone who made him nervous.

With him lagging behind, Vanessa and Steve caught up quickly.

"I'm Vanessa, by the way," she said to dispel the awkwardness of being strangers. "This is Steve."

The scarecrow kid glanced at her. He exhaled, almost as if he hadn't wanted to be friendly but had given in.

"I'm Arthur," he replied. "Arthur Griggs."

"You somebody's cousin or something?" Steve asked.

Vanessa whapped him on the arm. "Jerk." She turned to Arthur. "Don't mind him. The manners of a Morlock."

Through slits in his hood, Arthur's eyes lit up. "Morlocks! You've read H. G. Wells?"

"I mean, yeah, but . . . confession. We read *The Time Machine* in school. I do love reading all the weird stuff, though."

The stranger nodded. "I'm new in the neighborhood. My family moved in last week, a couple of streets away, but my parents felt your street might be safer for All Hallows."

"You mean Halloween," Steve said.

"Of course." Arthur glanced at his shoes as they walked toward the Barbosas' house and the line of people waiting to be let into the Haunted Woods. "My parents are sort of old-fashioned. They embrace a more antiquated approach."

"They sound interesting," Vanessa said.

Arthur had stopped listening to her. Once again, he peered over his shoulder.

"What are you afraid of back there?" Steve asked.

Arthur winced, then stared straight ahead as they got into the line for the Haunted Woods. "Being somewhere new is always a little scary, I suppose."

But Vanessa had seen the look in his eyes, and this wasn't just anxiety from being in a new place, among new people. Whatever had Arthur Griggs so nervous, he obviously thought it might be following them.

And that scared the shit out of him.

TONY BARBOSA

In previous years, Tony had donned makeup and costume, relishing every shriek he could pull out of his neighbors, but it always flew by much too fast. This last time, he wanted to soak it all in, so he had forgone participation to simply observe. He had chosen a spot about sixty feet before the end of the trail, hidden from view, and it had been just as wonderful as he'd imagined.

He shivered, leaning against the trunk of an oak, thinking about going inside to grab a coat. A ripple of nervous laughter reached him from the path, and he looked up to see a familiar tumble of ginger hair shining in the eerie light. Catherine Sullivan laughed again and turned to reach back for her companion's hand. With that girlish laugh and the delight in her eyes, it surprised Tony a bit to see that the man who took Catherine's hand was her husband, Kev. Tony usually tried to ignore local rumors, but he'd been unable to avoid hearing the Sullivans' marriage had been on the rocks. Tonight, they looked delighted to be together.

A motion sensor made the orange light snap off, and a prop ghost made of torn gray fabric burst from the trees accompanied by a banshee wail that sounded like a mother's rage and grief. Catherine jumped back at least three feet, stumbling so that

Kev had to catch her before she careened into the pine trees on the opposite side of the path. Her cry matched the banshee's, and Tony had to resist the urge to cheer. Her fear was his success.

Alice came up behind the Sullivans, nearly colliding with them, and the three of them laughed together.

"Whooo," Kev said to his wife. "You'll need to change your trousers after that one."

The orange light reset in time for Tony to see Catherine's upper lip curl in amused disgust. "You're so gross."

Alice grinned. "But is he wrong, Cath? That's the question."

The resulting laughter seemed warm and genuine. Whatever troubles the Sullivans might have been having were clearly in the past, but a clock had begun ticking in Tony's head. Guests of the Haunted Woods were prompted from the beginning to keep moving along the trail. That wasn't just as a courtesy to the people coming behind them but to preserve the quality of the scares. The whole thing was calibrated for maximum effect, and if the next group caught up with Alice and the Sullivans, it would diminish the experience for all of them. They were nearly to the exit, but all Tony wanted was for everyone to have the best experience possible.

He slipped from among the trees, but was still in darkness when the orange light winked out again and the banshee came screaming from the other side of the path. Catherine jumped again and cried out, though not with the same level of panic as before. Alice and Kev brayed with laughter, until a man came the wrong way along the trail and spoke to them in the dark.

"What the hell are you laughing at?" he asked, his voice slurred, but full of low warning, the growl of a wounded bear.

The orange light clicked on again, and in that sickly illumination, Tony could see Donnie Sweeney. His hair was a mess, his shirt untucked, and there were deep scratches on his cheek and neck as if he'd just come from a fight. He listed to the left, toward the trees where the banshee prop had retreated.

All the laughter drained from the faces of the two couples.

Kev Sullivan stiffened. "You're going the wrong way, Donnie. How drunk do you have to be? This is the exit."

Tension seethed in the air between them. The motion sensor had reset, and now they set it off again. The orange light clicked off and the banshee came screaming out for the third time, but now Catherine Sullivan didn't so much as flinch. She kept her gaze locked on Donnie, and even just in the glow of half moonlight through the trees, Tony could see she looked sick. Horrified in a way not even terror had prompted before.

Alice, though, stepped back into the trees as if hoping she could vanish like one of the ghosts.

Donnie took a step toward Kev Sullivan. He smiled a leering, whiskey smile. "*Wrong way, Donnie*," he mimicked. "*This is the exit*. Y'know, your wife said almost the same thing to me that first night."

Catherine sucked air so sharply it sounded as if she'd cut herself.

Kev shot out a hand and grabbed Donnie by the throat. He shoved Donnie backward, his whole body tensed, poised in warning. "Get the fuck out of here, Sweeney. Go right now."

Donnie laughed, touching his throat. The orange light clicked back on, and he glanced up at Kev as if Catherine and Alice weren't even there. The words were meant for Kev, and only Kev.

"Funny thing is, that second night, she let me do whatever the hell I liked. And turned out, *she* liked it, too."

Tony strode from the shadows, fists clenched, ready to drag Donnie Sweeney out of the woods and all the way back to his house if necessary. He wanted to beat the shit out of the guy himself. The Haunted Woods was probably the happiest memory he would be taking away with him when this house was sold, and he wouldn't let Donnie ruin that.

"Get off my property," he said.

Donnie scoffed. He wasn't even acting like a tough guy in that moment, just like a man to whom threats from Tony Barbosa meant nothing at all.

"Relax, Tony. I didn't come here to mess with you, but since you're here, you should probably know I fucked Alice, too."

Tony felt hatred or disgust or humiliation, or some cocktail of all three. He might have doubted the man's words, but for the gasp that came from Alice the moment he spoke them. She followed it with a tiny sob, and when he darted a glance her way, she couldn't meet his eyes. There were tears in hers.

Something collapsed inside Tony, then, like his spirit had surrendered. He had suspected Alice had been unfaithful, but he had imagined someone better than an alcoholic attorney— taller, more charming, smarter. But *this guy*?

Tony wanted to kill him. He took a step. . . .

But Kev Sullivan got there first. Catherine didn't bother trying to call her husband off. She didn't cry out. If all of this was true, if Donnie Sweeney had been the reason for the rumored tensions between the Sullivans, then maybe she didn't dare try to stop Kev from what came next, for fear that he might misinterpret her concern.

Kev stepped into the punch like a baseball pitcher, put his whole torso into it. The punch smashed Donnie's head to one side, crunched his nose with such force that blood spattered the path. As Donnie fell, he set off the motion sensor again, and the orange light clicked off. The banshee screamed out of the trees as Kev leaped on top of Donnie and began to beat the hell out of him. His right elbow pistoned back and forth, fist smashing Donnie's face over and over. Tony didn't even consider trying to break it up.

Another scream tore the night, and this one hadn't come from the banshee, and it sure as hell hadn't come from Alice or Catherine Sullivan, who had both turned to look away.

Tony looked toward that other scream. The real one.

The next group of guests in the Haunted Woods had come around the corner and through a curtain of black drapery. Tony couldn't have said how long they had been there, how much they had seen or heard, but he recognized the girl who had screamed.

Julia Sweeney. Donnie's daughter.

Seeing Julia, Kev jerked away from beating on Donnie and rose to his feet. Julia stared at her bleeding father in a way that implied the rest of them were invisible. She took several shaking steps toward him. The Sullivans and their friends moved out of her way, which was when Tony got a good look at the other kids who had come through the curtain behind Julia. One of them was his own daughter, Chloe. Tony had no idea if she'd heard what Sweeney had said about her mother, but it was Chloe who spoke first.

"Dad," she said. "Jesus Christ, do something."

Julia Sweeney walked over to her father, her face a wretched mask of loathing, tears filling her eyes. She tried to speak, but no words came out. Her father started to rise. He spat a gobbet of blood and saliva in the dirt and looked up at his daughter.

"Jules," Donnie said. "It's not . . . I know how it looks . . ."

The orange light winked off. The banshee came screaming out at them.

Julia didn't slap her father. She closed her fist and punched him in the face hard enough to knock him back a few steps, where the gray fabric of the banshee prop flapped around his face before drawing back into the woods.

"You piece of shit," Julia said. "I don't know what Mom ever saw in you. And if I were married to a woman who would let you in her bed, that would tell me all I ever needed to know about what a woman like that thinks of herself, never mind what she thinks of me."

Donnie looked stung for a moment, but then his drunken ire flared up. He sneered. "Listen, goddamn it. You don't talk to your father like—"

"Oh, fuck you, Donnie. I'm gonna spend the rest of my life trying to wash off the stink that comes with being your kid."

Julia seemed to want to say more, but she lost the ability. Overwhelmed, choking back more tears, she moved around her father and ran the rest of the way along the trail. By then, yet another group had come through the black tapestry on the trail, obviously wondering what the hell had happened. The Haunted Woods was seriously malfunctioning, but even numb as he was from learning about Donnie and Alice, Tony couldn't see pain like Julia felt and not try to help. He started to go after her, letting the rest of them work out their own problems.

"Dad, no," Chloe said quietly. She jogged past him, shot him a glance. "I've got this."

The banshee shrieked again as she went in pursuit of Julia, and Tony knew it would be okay. Chloe had a big heart. She was a smart girl and so kind. If anyone could give Julia the comfort she needed right now, Chloe could. If she wasn't too busy with her own sadness.

He looked over at Alice, still hiding in the shadows. For a moment, while she watched her daughter run off, she looked like the woman he'd married, whom he had loved for so long. But when she glanced at him, she flinched, and her gaze filled with shame and anger and even a little disdain. Despite the tensions the past year had driven between them, he had been laboring under the impression that she was still the Alice he had always known and loved, but now he saw he was wrong. He didn't know her at all anymore.

Suddenly, he wanted the night over with. The Haunted Woods, Halloween, the whole thing. For the first time, he couldn't wait to be out of their house, out of this neighborhood, all of it behind him.

"Right," Tony said, turning to Donnie. "Get the fuck out of here before I call the cops."

Donnie Sweeney spit again, a bit of blood that spattered next to Tony's boot. Tony stepped toward him, but Donnie muttered a fuck-you and shot him the middle finger in farewell as he trudged up the path.

Tony gestured to the Sullivans. "You, too."

"I'm sorry, Tony," Catherine said, and it felt so awkward having her apologize that he couldn't even meet her gaze.

"I'm sure we all are," he said. "Please, hurry up. We've got a traffic jam going."

As if nothing had happened. As if they hadn't all just learned far more than they wanted to know about their neighbors, as if Julia had not just passed judgment on both Alice and the Sullivans, just as she had passed judgment on her own father. Neither Catherine nor Kev spoke up to defend themselves against a teenage girl's insults, but what could they have said? What had Julia said that wasn't true?

Just minutes ago, they had been laughing. The thing that had been rotting away at their relationship had been put aside. They seemed to have been trying to repair their love.

Now it was broken. Shattered. After this, there could be no repair.

Kev hurried up the path after Donnie, but not with any violent intention. He simply wanted to leave his wife behind. Alice took Catherine by the arm, making quiet, sympathetic noises as Catherine wiped at her eyes, barely able to put one foot in front of the other as she grieved the end of her happiness. Alice didn't look at Tony again as she escorted Catherine away, and Tony made no effort to call after her. What was there to say?

The two kids who had been with Chloe and Julia followed behind Alice and Catherine, and the traffic through the Haunted Woods started moving again.

But the magic had died.

Nothing in these woods could be more dreadful, more terrifying, than the selfish cruelty of ordinary people.

RICK BARBOSA

When they reached the firepit, Rick and Billie stopped to catch their breaths. Leonard might have been smaller, younger, and barely aware of his surroundings, but somehow the kid didn't seem nearly as winded as they were from racing through the woods. Rick had been tugging him along, but for the past hundred yards, it had been an effort to keep up with him.

Now Leonard dropped to his knees on the leaf-strewn path, head drooping like a puppet with its strings cut. His shoulders rose and fell, and Rick could hear the weird, rattling breath coming out of his mouth, but beyond that, Leonard seemed as if someone had just flicked a switch and shut him off.

"You think he's still following?" Billie asked, hands on her knees. She stared back along the trail the way they'd come. Her white wig had come off somewhere back along the trail, but she barely seemed to have noticed its absence. Either that or running for her life was more important than keeping her Halloween costume intact.

Rick kept silent, listening to see if Zack Burgess had followed them. Seconds ticked by. The woods were filled with sounds. Peepers from the pond. Night birds rustling in the branches overhead. Turkeys roosted in trees at night to avoid predators, and he sometimes pictured how absurd they must look, the big, unwieldly birds plopped among the branches. He could hear the wind through the trees, the creak of bending branches, the sound of a fox or a raccoon moving through the undergrowth.

But no footsteps.

If Zack had kept after them, they would have been able to hear his boots pounding up the path, or his breathing. With all the cigarettes he smoked, he'd have been wheezing by now for sure. The trail behind the Burgesses' house went pretty deep into the woods before it hooked to the right, headed west, roughly parallel to the road but much too far to see the lights of any houses. Somewhere off in the trees, Rick knew trick-or-treat would be winding down. They might have found help at the Mathiesen house, or any of the other half dozen or more along the way, but that would have meant forging through the trees and underbrush, leaving the trail. Fear had driven them, and sticking to the path had been the fastest way to escape. But now that they had a moment to breathe, Rick could only think of getting home.

"I think we're okay," he said, turning to Billie. He mustered a smile, both for her benefit and his own.

A whisper made him shiver. He glanced around, thinking it might just have been the wind rustling leaves, but of course it had come from Leonard. The kid was the only other person with them, so who else could it have been?

"Hey, buddy," Rick said, recognizing his father's tone in his own voice, suddenly the responsible adult for the first time in his life. At thirteen. He went down on one knee beside Leonard. "You're okay now. They're not coming after us. We're gonna take you to my house and call the police."

Leonard's lips moved. Almost imperceptibly. The whisper seemed even quieter than before, and with the night sounds around them, Rick could not make out the words. But he shivered again, and a queasy feeling roiled in his belly. Something was wrong with this kid, and not just a reaction to what had just happened at the Burgess house.

"Hey," Rick said. He gave Leonard's shoulder a shake.

"Let him be," Billie said quietly. "Whatever set him off before, you don't want him going at you like he did with Ruth."

Whatever set him off? Rick thought.

They knew what had set Leonard off. Ruth and Zack had tried to hurt him or molest him or mess with him in some way. But the thought didn't ring completely true in Rick's head, because there had been more to it than that. The things Leonard had been saying and the savagery in the way he attacked Ruth. He'd never seen a little kid behave that way or have the strength and wildness to do anything like that.

The kid whispered again. Rick glanced at Billie, and she gestured impatiently for him to approach the smaller boy, to figure out what he was saying.

Twigs snapped beneath his shoes as Rick moved nearer.

"You're okay, Leonard," Rick said. "But Ruth . . . the lady back there . . . I think you might've hurt her bad. When we talk to the police, they're gonna ask you about that."

Leonard still had his head down, chin on his chest, completely deflated. When he raised his head and turned to look at Rick, he did it slowly, as if the process required caution, or as if he were frightened of what he might see. Rick saw tears glistening in the boy's eyes.

"The children were there," he said, loud enough to be heard at last.

Billie stepped up beside Rick. "What children? The Burgesses don't have kids. And how did you get there to begin with? Were you lost in the woods?"

A thin smile. "Yes. Lost in the woods. Completely lost."

Rick shook his head, confusion starting to irritate him. "So who are these kids you're looking for?"

"The hopeless ones!" Leonard roared. He sulked, crossing his arms, and couldn't stop his tears from coming. "You two are so stupid. I could feel the kids there, but I guess it was only echoes of the kids that Ruth lady hurt. I thought if there were hopeless ones, maybe he would take them instead of . . ."

Something snapped, off in the woods. Rick glanced over his shoulder. The dark breathed and animals scurried, and that was normal. But this kid—Always Leonard—nothing normal about him at all.

"Instead of what?" Rick asked.

Leonard's face crinkled, and he cried. "Me. Instead of me." He buried his face in his hands.

Billie knelt and took Leonard in her arms.

"We're going right now," she promised. "And we'll call the police with you. Come on."

Leonard took her offered hand and began to rise with her. Rick wasn't quite ready. "Okay, we're going. But first, Leonard . . . this guy you're so afraid of. Who is he? Who's coming for you?"

Leonard hugged Billie, pressed himself against her as if she were a life preserver. He looked pale and small beside her. Rick had always admired his best friend, but in that moment, she seemed like a hero to him. Like she could protect Leonard from whoever wanted to hurt him.

"Who is he, Leonard?" Billie asked, her tone much gentler than Rick's.

The kid mumbled something into the crook of her arm, but the words were too muffled for Rick to understand.

"The Cunning Man," Billie translated. "That's all he said." She held Leonard away from her. "Does this guy have a name?"

Leonard wiped snot from his face. "That *is* his name. He's coming after me, Billie. It won't be long now, a few hours." He looked around at the darkness as if it might be spying on them. "But there's something here already. Like his shadow's come ahead of him, sniffing around like a . . . like a hunting dog."

The kid faltered, as if words had failed him. Leonard hugged Billie a little tighter, but the expression on her face made Rick uneasy. She always knew what to do when there was trouble, but right then, she seemed worried and scared. Rick had been feeling so good about being thirteen, mature enough to handle his parents' impending divorce. Life could be hard, but you had to carry on. He and Billie were teenagers, not little kids like Leonard anymore.

So why did he suddenly feel so small?

Something shifted on the path behind them. A scritch against twigs. The tread of a boot. The night itself seemed to inhale sharply, ready for a scream. *The Cunning Man*, Rick thought.

But when he turned, he saw something worse than the Cunning Man.

Zack Burgess stood twenty feet away, back along the trail the way they had come. He snorted, gasping for air like a horse ready to run.

"All right," Zack growled, dappled by moonlight through the branches overhead. A ghost. A monster. An angry man with fists. "Which one of you little fuckers hurt my wife?"

Billie screamed for them to run. Rick bolted. Zack snatched at the back of his costume. Rick felt the tug of his fingers, but lunged ahead with all his strength and tore free. Momentum made him trip. He stumbled toward Billie and Leonard, who were in motion.

Rick knew he was falling, that he'd smash his face into the path or career into a tree, but neither of those things happened. On instinct, he reached for Billie, and she for him. The touch of her hand, the grip of her fingers, allowed him the strength and balance he needed to stay on his feet.

Zack loosed a stream of ugly profanity as they ran from him again. They had been fools to stop for so long, stupid to think he wouldn't try to sneak up while they paused to catch their breaths.

"Help!" Billie screamed as they raced along a trail they knew intimately, a path they could have run blindfolded. "Somebody, help us!"

But she didn't need to scream. They were faster than Zack, a middle-aged smoker who didn't know these woods the way they did. They would come to side trails soon, and that gave them options.

"You sick bastard!" Rick shouted back at him. "The police are gonna come for you!"

Between strained breaths and the thump of his boots on the trail, Zack shouted back that the cops would arrest them, not him. The kids would be in handcuffs for what they had done to Ruth. For a few seconds, Rick felt the shock of fear like he had dived into a lake of it, but he and Billie had witnessed the way the Burgesses had behaved with Leonard. And Leonard himself would tell his story. The police had to believe them, didn't they?

Rick didn't bother keeping the argument going. He needed all the air in his lungs.

How much farther to the edge of the woods? To the road? To the streetlights? Up ahead, they would find a narrow path off to the right that snaked through trees and then brought them out in the Kenneys' backyard, and the Kenneys lived right across the street from Rick's own house. They were going to make it, and then Zack would have a lot of explaining to do.

Off to the left, branches shook and cracked. Something

moved in the trees. Rick glanced over his shoulder as he ran, just to make sure it wasn't Zack Burgess playing some kind of trick on him.

No. Something else was there.

In the darkness, hidden from the moonlight, it looked at Rick with eyes of dancing fire. Those eyes, in fact, were all he could see.

Rick thought he might have heard it laugh.

Then it slowed down.

Rick and Billie and Leonard were maybe fifty feet from that side trail, with Zack Burgess in pursuit.

The twin fires, like flickering candle flames, drifted out of the trees to float above the path behind them.

The last thing Rick heard before hooking a right and crashing along the path toward the streetlights and safety of his neighborhood . . . was the screaming.

ZACK BURGESS

Zack couldn't have explained most of the emotions that drove him. Fury, desperation, wild self-preservation, and a violent, perverse hunger were all there in his head and heart, but it boiled down to *need*. He had to get the little one, Leonard. And the other two kids had to be stopped. Before he'd given chase, he had taken a look back at his house and seen Ruth standing in the darkness under their deck, one hand over the wounds Leonard had given her. She hadn't looked like his wife in that moment. Ruth seemed to grow larger, as if the act of breathing were the bellows in the furnace inside her, and she burned higher and brighter.

"Kill those fuckers and bury them deep," Ruth had said. "It's the only way."

And there it was—the one emotion he understood with crystal clarity—devotion. If he let these kids get away, then he and Ruth would end up in prison, and even if he someday saw the sunlight again, Ruth never would. There were lines she had crossed that Zack never had.

Tonight, that would change. Tonight he would cross any line, commit any sin, to protect Ruth. She was the only person who had ever seen him for who he really was and loved him anyway. When he thought of a life without her, he could barely breathe.

Focus, he told himself. *Get it done!*

Zack let the *need* take over, the hunger. He had always liked trains—steam trains the best—and as he chased those kids, he felt his insides bloating and smoking and blazing, driving him hard. When he knew the kids had slowed down, he slowed down, too. He'd learned long ago how to walk softly, and tonight, he had even taken off his boots. The rocks and roots hurt, but the slivers of moonlight were enough to run by.

On the pads of his feet, he had run. Being quiet did not come easily for a steam train. He wanted to pound the trail and let off the pressure inside him, wanted to cuss the little fuckers out, tell them how badly mistaken they were if they thought they could hurt Ruth and get away without being punished. But he could not give in to that urge if he wanted to catch these kids. Smart and silent, that was the way to win.

When he came near enough to hear them talking quietly on the path, the echo of Ruth's words blared inside his head. *Kill those fuckers and bury them deep. It's the only way.*

Zack had come close, but he had never killed anyone. Not an adult. Not a child. He loved them, loved the wonder and light in their eyes when he got to know them. But Ruth was right.

He quickened his pace, forgetting all about stealth, hurtling toward them on the trail. Little Leonard and two kids he recognized from the neighborhood. There would be so many questions. Police and volunteers would comb the woods. He knew he had to be careful, so careful, so much smarter than he had ever been. A voice in his skull tried to suggest that doing nothing would be better, doing nothing would be their word against these children's, and it might turn ugly, but it would not end in prison.

But the engine burning inside him kept the fire stoked, and then the kids saw him.

They turned and ran, and Zack kept after them. They headed for a side path that would take them out to Parmenter Road. Most people with small children were back home already. Others would be at Barbosa's Haunted Woods. Zack laughed at the thought, because now he recognized the boy fleeing in terror ahead of him. The Barbosa kid. The girl with him was Billie Suarez. It all clicked into place. Billie was the only Black girl on the street. Pretty, too. He didn't discriminate.

If the kids made it to the street, Ruth would be very disappointed in him. They would end up separated, maybe forever.

The Barbosa boy ran hard. Zack almost admired him. Might have, if not for the fact that these kids had hurt Ruth. Then he noticed the way the Barbosa boy kept glancing to his left, looking into the trees as if he thought help might be coming from that direction, and a shudder of dread ran through Zack. An alarm. If someone else was there, another adult, he had no way to explain any of this. The lies swirling in his head would not work.

He glanced into the woods, cocked his head to one side as he ran, trying to see what lurked back there in the trees.

An orange glow, keeping pace with them.

A little flame, flickering in the breeze, as if someone were running with a cigarette lighter in their hand, turned up high.

No. Two flames, side by side. Six inches apart.

Zack slowed just a little. He couldn't let the kids make it out of the woods, but the twin flames drifted across the path in front of him, seven feet off the ground, and he glanced up just before he ran beneath them, the same way he would look up at a yellow traffic light as he hit the gas, watching it turn red overhead.

The air turned thick as he plunged beneath those flames. Dense as water.

He passed through a spot colder than anything he had ever felt.

So cold that he screamed.

The kids were getting away, already heading up that side path.

Something snagged his clothes, punctured fabric and skin, like claws digging for bone. The cold raced through him as if it had infected his blood. Shadows surrounded him. Something had hold of him, but he could not see the hands that held him, the claws that lifted him, the arms that smashed him down onto the path. All the air burst from his lungs, and tears froze to a salty rime at the corners of his eyes.

The two flames swayed and flickered above him and then bent over to stare down at him. He could see it now, a silhouette against the darkness. Something tall and thin and hellish. The flames were holes in its head. . . .

No. They were inside its head, like the candle that burned within the jagged eyes of a carved pumpkin to make a jack-o'-lantern. The flames burned inside that skull of shadows, and for just a moment, Zack could see deeper, into the bottomless darkness beyond those flames.

This time when he screamed, no sound came out. Despair had stolen his voice. A sadness existed in the universe that he could never have conceived, and it waited for him in the fire that burned in that abyss.

A breeze caressed his face. It spoke to him.

"*The children,*" it said, "*have always been mine.*"

But the children had already been forgotten. Ruth had been forgotten. Only the cold mattered now. The cold, and that voice, and the abyss.

Zack died then, but he could still feel sorrow. His despair remained. Soon he would be nothing but despair, yet still he would linger.

Always.

JULIA SWEENEY

As she emerged from the Haunted Woods, Julia felt as if the world had vanished around her. She kept putting one foot in front of the other, somehow both numb and furious. Part of her knew she should also be thinking of her mother and her brothers—that to embrace her own hurt and pain and humiliation might be selfish—but right now selfish felt *right*. Her mother had put up with her father's emotional abuse and infidelity and drunkenness for way too long. Barb Sweeney ought to have kicked Donnie and his wandering dick out of the house years ago. How much pain would they have avoided if her mother had the courage to do that? Julia knew she ought to have more sympathy for her mom, but she had been sympathetic for years, and this time she only felt anger. Her home had been breaking for a long time, and tonight it had broken. Her father had left them. Her father had left *her*. Hurt her.

She didn't want him to come back. Not ever.

But goddamn it, why couldn't he have just loved her? Why couldn't she have mattered to him enough for him to act like a father was supposed to act? To come home and just be with them, to *want* to spend time with his children? With his daughter?

She knew the answer.

Julia knew.

Donnie Sweeney hadn't been born a piece of shit, but he had grown into the role and seemed to cherish it.

"Bastard," she muttered.

She blinked, glancing around. Someone had spoken to her, and it took a few seconds before her vision cleared and she realized they had left the Barbosas' front yard and crossed the street. She found herself in front of the O'Leary house, and now she saw who had come with her. Cynthia and Hunter were a dozen feet away, standing on the curb, having a whisper-fight that included a lot of hand gestures. Hunter sniffed and rolled his eyes and glanced away. Cynthia gave him a pouty face, that sweet, submissive girlfriend look that so many guys expected. Even if she hadn't known they were arguing over her—Hunter wanting to leave and Cynthia wanting to stay with her friend—Julia would have been soured by the sight of them. She ought to be kinder to Cynthia, since her friend obviously wanted to stay and comfort her, but the way she behaved around Hunter, she might as well have been a dog rolling over to show her soft, vulnerable throat.

Julia turned to see the rest of the kids who'd gathered around her. There were too many, and suddenly, she felt like a sideshow freak. How had this many people followed her from Chloe's house? Chloe was there among them, of course, and Steve Koenig from up the street, and a few others. A kid in an old-fashioned scarecrow costume stood beside Steve, cocking his head like a bird and studying her as if sadness were something inscrutable, instead of simple and common, shared by the daughters of shitty men the world over.

"Hey. You're okay," a soft voice said, and someone touched her arm.

Julia flinched.

Vanessa Montez drew back her hand, undone by that flinch. Her eyes were kind, and searching, and beautiful. "I'm sorry. I didn't mean . . . I was just trying to . . ."

"No. It's all right," Julia said, surprised to find herself talking. Surprised her voice worked to say something other than all the painful things in her heart or the angry curses she wanted to hurl at her father. But her father wasn't here with her now.

Vanessa smiled tentatively. "You had me a little scared, Jules."

Julia nodded. She could only imagine what questions had been going through Vanessa's mind—all their minds—when they followed her out of the Barbosas' yard and down the street. Julia tried to replay the past few minutes in her mind, but they were a blur, as if she'd blacked out. She wondered how often her father lost windows of time thanks to being too drunk to remember.

Her thoughts began to clear, but she still didn't remember gathering the rest of these kids around her as she fled the Haunted Woods. She took a fresh look at Vanessa and felt a rush of gratitude.

"Where did you come from? You weren't with us in the Haunted Woods."

"I was coming down with Steve and this kid Arthur. We were, like, next in line when I saw you coming around from the backyard," Vanessa said. She glanced away shyly as she continued, "I've never seen you cry before. You were really upset, and I guess I just wanted to make sure you were okay."

Julia smiled, some of the feeling coming back into her body. "That's sweet. I mean . . . that's really kind."

"Don't tell anyone," Vanessa replied. "You'll ruin my image."

"If your image is supposed to be 'adorable punk ruffian,' you've got it down."

"This is a Halloween costume, remember?" Vanessa said. "Siouxsie Sioux."

Julia had never been brave. Or, at least, never been braver than she had to be to keep living in a house full of tension and arguments. But tonight, she had jumped on her asshole father's back, and he had tossed her off. He had hurt her, more than once, and in more ways than one. All the rules of how her family was supposed to function had been tossed out the window, and everything seemed out of control—which also meant anything was possible.

"I'm not talking about the costume," she said. "I'm talking about the girl wearing it."

Vanessa's mouth opened in a shocked little O, as if the words surprised her as much as they had Julia. The two of them stood staring at each other, waiting to see if Julia would say anything further—something to clarify that she hadn't meant that to sound as flirty as it had—but Julia had nothing to add. Vanessa looked in her eyes, and Julia didn't look away. She had little experience with feeling bold, and she wanted to hold on to it, to be sure that Vanessa understood her.

She had been crushing on Vanessa all through high school. She had known Vanessa would never make the first move—the risk would have been huge. Rumors had flown about Vanessa, but Julia had dated two guys in high school, one nerdy sweetheart and one absolute prick. She had dumped them both, never had sex or gone down on either of them. Yes, they'd been naked and other things had happened, and all along, she had been wondering if this was *it*, shouldn't there have been something more exciting? Primal urges were one thing, but she had found no joy, no quickening of the heart, with either of those guys.

"I'm not used to being called adorable," Vanessa said.

Julia glanced around to make sure nobody else was close

enough to hear. She had been friendly but not close friends with Vanessa for years and had never uttered any of the words she'd really wanted to. There were risks involved, social repercussions she was not ready to face—in school, with her family, with friends who might not understand. But she wanted to make sure Vanessa understood. Tonight, she was angry with the world and sick of living for what other people thought.

"My father's been cheating on my mother with at least two of the neighborhood moms," Julia said very quietly, so Chloe could not possibly hear. Chloe's mom had been one of those women, but Julia didn't think she'd heard that part of the conversation back in the woods and did not want to be the one to break it to her.

"Pretty much the whole town's gonna know about it in the morning," Julia went on. "My dad's a drunk, my parents are getting divorced, and tonight, I'm gonna say whatever's on my mind."

She could always claim confusion later. Emotional trauma. Whatever it took to make people forget.

"I guess I'm not who you thought I was," she added.

Vanessa glanced nervously around at the others—the same anxious look Julia had given them—and then she smiled. "I guess not. But I think you might be exactly the person I hoped you'd be."

The night seemed to brighten, the blues and blacks and grays turned sharper, the golden moonlight more brilliant. As awful as this day and night had been, it felt like waking from a nightmare—not that the sun had come out, but Julia felt alert and alive.

Then she blinked, thoughts whirling. This was definitely not the time or place to let this conversation go any further. These other kids had followed her out here because of the ugly spectacle that had just unfolded behind the Barbosas' house. Some of them were worried for her, sorry for her, and others were like gawkers at a car crash. Either way, they were paying attention.

"Thank you," she said to Vanessa, giving her a quick hug—a friendly hug, short and sweet—before she looked around at the rest of them. "Thanks, everyone. It's been an awful night. My folks really had it out earlier, and I don't know what happens now. But I appreciate you all watching out for me."

Some of them looked uncomfortable, which Julia figured was a natural response. What they'd seen and heard tonight had been intimate—the mess her father had made of things, the lurid shouting match—that stuff should have been private. Julia hoped that was the reason for their discomfort and not because they had sensed the nature of the exchange she'd just had with Vanessa.

"Okay," Vanessa said. "If Julia's okay with it, I suggest we move on to the next portion of this exciting evening. Steve's dad wants everyone to show up for the block party."

Steve clapped his hands once, like a quarterback breaking the huddle. "Let's head up there now, before this night gets even crazier."

He led the way. Footfalls echoing up and down the street, the group shuffled along behind him.

The end of October could be unpredictable, and earlier it had been warmer than expected, but now the air turned crisp and chilly. Julia hugged herself, trying to warm up. She loved this time of year, all the scents and emotions that came with autumn. Sweater weather. Halloween, orange leaves crinkling underfoot, ghost stories. But she wished she'd worn something warmer.

They passed from the glow of one streetlamp into a dark patch that separated it from the next. In that momentary darkness, Vanessa moved closer, keeping pace beside her. Their hands brushed together. Julia's heart fluttered. People could say whatever they wanted about her father fucking the neighbors and leaving his family, but if the connection she'd just made with Vanessa became the stuff of whispers, it could make senior year difficult for both of them. People already gossiped about Vanessa—that'd been half the reason Julia had the confidence to flirt with her. But she could just imagine the sneering and slander, the mocking to come.

On the other hand, maybe she didn't care. Maybe her liking girls was just one more piece of gossip to come out of tonight. In less than a year, she would be in college, and everything would be different.

The worst had already happened tonight. Awful shit that she would remember the rest of her life. But Julia thought maybe the worst night of her life might also turn out to be the best.

CHARLIE SWEENEY

The back porch had baseboard heating but still got a little too cold in the winter, mainly because of the windows. They were made of horizontal panes of glass that opened and closed like blinds. For most of his life, Charlie had thought they were called "jealousy" windows, but over the summer, his mom heard him using the word and realized what he was saying. *Jalousie windows*, she'd explained, were perfect for a back porch like theirs, letting in plenty of sunshine during the day and allowing the breeze to flow through in the hot weather. His mom was right about that, but the jalousie windows made it tough to keep the porch warm.

Tonight, for instance. It had been warmer a few hours ago, when the bad stuff happened. Now Charlie sat with his brother, Brian, on the old sofa on the porch, eating chocolate on autopilot and watching *Taste the Blood of Dracula* on Channel 56. He loved the bright red of the blood in these old Dracula movies, and he would never have said it out loud, even to Brian, but the boobs got his attention as well. His mom had brought dinner out to them earlier—tonight wasn't the night for her to be strict about the rules, she'd said, so eating out on the porch was fine. She'd taken one look at the screen, seen Dracula hypnotizing a woman with his scary red eyes, and said something about "heaving bosoms." Charlie had thought maybe she would get mad that they were watching a bloody movie, so he had been surprised when she laughed. But he had been happy, too. They all needed to laugh, his mom more than anyone.

Brian batted him on the arm. Charlie flinched and looked up, ready for a fight.

They fought a lot. Brian was his brother and his best friend, and nobody knew him better. They loved so many of the same things, had so much fun together, but Brian never let him forget who was the older brother. Charlie still felt exhausted, kind of emptied out from all the crying he had done tonight. Normally, he would have been embarrassed, but Brian had cried, too, and if a guy couldn't cry on a night when his dad proved his assholery beyond a shadow of a doubt, on the front lawn where people could see, and left the house probably never to come back . . . Well, if you couldn't cry tonight, then what was the point of having tears, really?

So he didn't feel embarrassed, and he felt pretty close to Brian tonight. Halloween usually brought them close. Sitting out here watching Dracula and bright red blood and boobs, eating candy, and generally feeling like a deflated balloon—except for the achy bellyful of chocolate—this was the best part of having a brother, even on the worst of all nights.

Even so, when Brian batted his arm, Charlie flinched and shot him a guarded, defensive look. "What?"

Brian looked at him like he was a crazy person. "You've been sitting there with an uneaten Reese's in your hand for twenty minutes. If you're not gonna eat it, hand it over."

Charlie huffed his irritation, but then glanced down at his right hand. In his open palm, he held a Reese's Peanut Butter Cup, its bright orange wrapper halfway peeled back.

The candy sat in its little brown paper cup. Somehow he had stopped in the middle of opening it and forgotten all about it.

He shrugged. "I was watching the movie."

"Okay," Brian said. "But are you gonna eat it?"

Charlie glanced at the bowl of uneaten Halloween candy on the table near the TV. He could tell his brother to grab the bowl, but he understood that neither of them felt like moving and the bowl was halfway across the room. There were times when he might have been a jerk about it and popped the Reese's into his mouth or eaten half of it and handed over the other half, but he didn't have the energy. And Brian had come out to search for him tonight—if that didn't earn him some brotherly love and a Reese's, nothing would.

"Knock yourself out," Charlie said, handing it over.

Brian took the Reese's in silence, finished undressing it, then popped the peanut butter cup into his mouth whole. On-screen, one of the girls lured another into a dark, abandoned church, where Dracula waited. Charlie thought vampires couldn't go into churches, but maybe because this church had been kind of dilapidated, the rules didn't apply. Not that he cared either way. The danger mattered more than the logic behind it. Dracula waited like a lion in one of those animal shows Charlie's dad watched on Sundays. Anyone would have known what would happen next, but still, his chest felt tight and his pulse sped up.

Dracula stepped out of the shadows.

A voice whispered Charlie's name.

He jumped in his chair, swore in ways his mom would have hated, and whipped around to stare at the darkness outside the jalousie windows.

"Who's there?" Brian asked.

Also standing. Which meant he'd heard it, too, and that scared Charlie even more.

A soft rap came on the glass at the porch door. Charlie flinched, but then took two steps toward the door. Through the louvered glass panes, he saw the glint of dark eyes. The light from the television reflected back at them from that pair of eyes, and the shape resolved itself out in the darkness.

"It's a kid," Brian said, his voice turning gruff. The biggest, tallest boy in his class, he seemed like he had just remembered he was supposed to be tough. The fact that the person outside was a child certainly helped.

Charlie sighed in relief. "It's Sarah Jane."

BARB SWEENEY

In college, Barb had eaten magic mushrooms exactly once, at a party at the Arts House. She remembered the Rolling Stones song "Angie" playing, and even that night, it seemed like the only song coming out of the speakers. Barb felt pretty sure it was the mushrooms messing with her head and that "Angie" had not, in fact, played over and over, ad infinitum, for the duration of the party. She had stood in a corner nursing a cup of rum punch as the room turned liquid around her. Barb remembered feeling lost at sea, powerless to do more than float.

She felt the same tonight.

"Mom?" Brian said. "What are we gonna do?"

Barb couldn't even muster a smile for her son. She would think of that later and feel guilty, as if she had let him down. She had encouraged Julia to go out with her friends, to seek distraction, but Barb and her boys only had one another here, with nothing to distract them from the sadness of abandonment.

Except now there was.

A little girl sat on the porch sofa, wrapped in a blanket Barb's grandmother had crocheted during the Second World War. Nine o'clock had come and gone, and surely this little girl's parents would be crazy with worry about her. Trick-or-treat had ended, the Haunted Woods would be shutting down now, the party up at the Koenigs well underway. . . .

"The party," she said out loud.

Brian and Charlie stared at her.

Ignoring the ominous music coming from the television, Barb sat on the edge of the couch. "Sarah?"

"Sarah Jane," Charlie reminded her, his eyes pleading with her to do something, to be the adult and force the world to make sense. To protect and heal and be wise.

"Right, yeah," Barb replied.

Her heart ached from the trust in Charlie's eyes. Brian seemed a bit less certain that his mother could solve this—or anything, for that matter. And why wouldn't he feel that way? Why did they think she could fix anything? Barb felt herself floating just like that magic mushroom night. She halfway expected to hear Mick Jagger singing "Angie" in the background. Instead, she had screams and melodramatic orchestral music from the Dracula movie on the TV.

"Brian," she said. "Turn that down, please."

Her eldest boy went to obey her, and Barb focused again on the little girl.

"Sarah Jane. Talk to me, sweetheart. What's your last name?"

The girl's damp, frightened eyes opened, and she peered at Barb over the top of the blanket. In the flickering light of the television, her eyes seemed too pale, as if instead of blue, they were the gray of worrisome clouds.

"Charlie," Barb said, turning toward her younger boy. "This is the girl from . . . from the bushes, tonight? Have you ever seen her before?"

"I don't think so." He shot his older brother a dark look.

Barb could see he felt a little resentment at Brian having given away the existence of this secret hideout, and she understood. Kids needed their secrets. She wasn't going to try to find out more, and she'd never want to spoil it for them, but the one thing that couldn't stay secret was this little girl's name.

"Honey, listen," Barb said. "I've got to call your parents to come and get you. To do that, I need your last name. Unless you know the phone number?"

Charlie tapped her on the shoulder. "Mom. She ran away from home. I told you. If you call there without knowing what's going on, we have no idea what's gonna happen to her."

Exhaling, Barb let the word *fuck* slide out as a sigh. She closed her eyes and took another deep breath, then let it out. How was she supposed to deal with this tonight? The only reason they were even home in the first place was because Donnie had blown up their lives. If he had finished cleaning out the garage and helped the kids put away the painting supplies, she would have come home and gotten everyone ready for trick-or-treat, then happily sat around and given out candy to the little ghouls and goblins who showed up at their door. None of that would have erased her knowledge of what kind of husband he had always been, but she had been pretending to be okay for so long that she certainly would have been able to pretend for another night. Another year. Another lifetime, maybe, if Donnie could calm himself down and not be so cavalier about his drunken philandering.

Philandering. What a goddamn word. So playful and sweet, people might as well have said her husband was out frolicking with water nymphs by the riverbank. Even *cheating* didn't give the act the malicious power it carried. There ought to have been a word that summed it up better than that, that captured the feeling of being stabbed in the throat and the heart and the gut all at once.

Barb swallowed hard. Her eyes began to brim with tears.

"Mom?" Brian began, taking a worried step toward her.

She waved him away, forcing a smile. Finally able to do that for her boys.

"Sarah Jane," Charlie said, so gently that it broke her heart all over again. At least her boys were sweet. "Tell my mom what you were tryin' to tell me before. About the man." He looked up at Barb. "I don't remember what she called him. But he's after her."

The little girl had gone so still and pale beneath the blanket, she almost seemed dead. Her eyes stared straight ahead, looking at nothing. Barb followed her gaze and realized no, that wasn't right. She stared at the louvered panes of glass set into the porch door and at the darkness outside. The girl wasn't dead, she was terrified.

"Okay," Barb said, patting Sarah Jane's leg. "You just sit tight, sweetheart. I'm going to make a call."

The sofa creaked as she stood up. On the TV, Dracula ran through some kind of church or castle. Her boys had no idea how much she loved those old movies, and suddenly, she felt foolish for never sharing that with them—for trying to nudge them away from horror stories. Her parents had done the same to her, and it only made her more interested. It was foolish, the things a person would do because their parents had done the same. Putting up with a cheating drunk for a husband, for instance.

Barb wished her mom were still alive. She would have liked to apologize for how harshly she had judged her for staying.

"What are you doing, Mom?" Brian asked. "Who can you call?"

At the open door that led from the porch into the kitchen, she glanced back at her sons and the stray little girl they'd let into the house. "The police, bud."

Charlie stood up. "Mom, no!"

"You're not little anymore, Charlie. Use your head. Sarah Jane's run away from home. Maybe she has a good reason, and maybe she's in danger. I'll tell the police all that, but I can't just keep her here and not tell anyone. It's not right."

She went into the kitchen and plucked the phone from its cradle on the wall. The long, coiled cord drooped at her side as she began to dial. Not 9-1-1; this wasn't an emergency. She would just call the Coventry PD and have them send someone over. There would be a social worker or someone who would look after the girl.

Four numbers into dialing, Barb's finger hovered in front of the phone. It was Halloween night, closing in on 10:00 p.m., and she wondered where Sarah Jane would end up sleeping. If she hadn't been reported missing and the police could not figure out her identity right away, the girl might be left to sleep in the police station or some kind of foster home, and that felt cruel. But could she really let the girl spend the night here? If she handed Sarah Jane over in the morning, the cops would have the whole day to sort out where she really belonged.

Barb hesitated, but after a moment, she started dialing again. What would people think if she kept this kid overnight without calling the police?

She dialed the last number. As she listened to the ringing on the other end of the line, she walked the phone through the doorway onto the porch, long cord trailing behind her. Sarah Jane remained under the blanket, but had turned to stare at her, lower lip trembling.

Poor thing, Barb thought.

Which was when the little girl launched herself off the sofa. A confused Charlie reached for her but only caught the blanket, which Sarah Jane shed as she ran across the porch and reached up to grab at the phone with both hands, shouting the word *no* over and over.

"Stop it!" Barb snapped. "I'm sorry, but—"

On the phone, a male voice answered. "Coventry Police. This is Sergeant Pucillo."

Sarah Jane sank her fingernails into Barb's hand. Barb hissed in pain and yanked her hand away, losing the phone in the process. The girl hauled on the long, coiled cord like a sailor weighing anchor, and yanked it right out of the wall unit.

"Goddamn it!" Barb snatched the end of the cord, but the damage was done.

Brian and Charlie stepped into the kitchen just as Sarah Jane sank to the floor, clutching the useless handset to her chest and crying.

Trembling, the little girl looked up at Barb. "The Cunning Man is after me. The police can't help. If you send me back out, he'll find me. He'll *get* me. I just need a few hours, and then he can't hurt me anymore—"

Barb frowned. "A few hours? But what does that—"

"Please!" Sarah Jane cried, turned to look at Charlie and Brian, then back at Barb. "Just let me stay till midnight, and then I'll tell you everything. You can . . . you can call my mother and father then."

Barb held the end of the broken phone cord, while Sarah Jane held the phone itself. She looked at her sons, wondered what her daughter would think.

"Look, I'm not making any promises," she said, "but I'm guessing you must be hungry. Do you like grilled cheese sandwiches?"

Charlie's face lit up with love and pride in his mother, and tonight that was something Barb needed more than she ever had before. A little spark ignited inside her chest—a fire that had been snuffed out earlier tonight coming back to life.

"I love grilled cheese sammiches," Sarah Jane said, quite adorably.

"You're the best, Mom," Charlie added.

"I know. I also know that you'll have to find something a little less adult to watch if Sarah Jane is going to hang out with us until midnight."

The boys promised they would. Barb took the useless phone from Sarah Jane and put it on the kitchen table, then set about making her a grilled cheese. But when she glanced back at the girl, Barb noticed that Sarah Jane had turned her attention to the porch door, and the darkness outside the glass.

The Cunning Man, Barb thought. *Whoever the hell that is.*

Once she had the sandwich grilling in the pan, she went into the porch and made sure the door was closed and locked. Through the jalousie windows, she could see only darkness, but she put the chain lock on the door, too, just in case.

After all, the girl was running from someone. Whoever it was, Barb did not want them paying a visit.

RUTH BURGESS

Ruth couldn't stay seated anymore. She had tried to force herself to be patient, had sat on the downstairs sofa in the TV room, but she'd been bouncing her knee for half an hour. Every muscle felt tense with the anticipation of catastrophe. If the phone rang or someone banged on the front door, she thought she would take off like a rocket, right through the roof.

"Fuck a duck," she muttered to herself as she sprang up from the sofa. It came out the way kids with Tourette's had outbursts. She said it again, louder, with the same kind of expulsion. "Fuck a duck!"

Zack hated when she swore. He had gotten used to it over the years, but somehow it still felt as if she had stored up loads of profanity for when he wasn't around. Often, they were absurdities like this one. She knew there had to be something not quite right about her wiring, because sometimes she got into a groove where she kept saying the same thing over and over, unable to stop herself, forced to just let it run its course. Once, in an argument with Zack, she had said, "What do you want from me?" forty-seven times in a row. She had counted.

Now she gritted her teeth and enunciated the words clearly and quietly between them. "Fuck a duck."

Nodding, Ruth went to the locked room that led into the

back half of the basement. They had split the space shortly after moving into the house, finishing one side to use for their TV room, a place to relax and not worry if they left empty glasses around or spilled beer on the sofa. The other half of the cellar had been walled off and a lockable door installed. All the ugly things typical of home basements were on that side—the furnace, the water tank, the breaker box—plus lots of metal shelving, a stainless steel worktable, a deep industrial sink, drawers full of sharp tools. Soundproofing.

No cameras. Not much lighting.

The things that happened in the back basement mostly went on in the dark.

Anger roiled in her gut. Twisted into a sour knot. Ruth had never wanted to marry Zack, but it had seemed safer to work together. That first time, with his nephew, they had only been dating six months, but they had watched each other behave in ways each recognized in the other. Ruth felt humiliated the first time they had spoken of it, exposed, naked in a way that nudity never accomplished. As a little girl, she had imagined that her body was nothing but a giant robot, and the real her a little black fish with sharp teeth, like a single piranha swimming in a lightless pond, but aware of the robot's actions and sometimes able to control them. The little black fish with sharp teeth was *Ruthie*, and the robot was Ruth. Ruthie felt vulnerable at all times, despite her teeth, and there was only one way for her to feel strong—to use her teeth. To rend and tear the softness of others.

Being Ruth could be exhausting, but walking around inside the fleshy robot version of herself was the price she paid for the better times, when something soft and vulnerable would be dragged into the dark place where Ruthie lived, the little black fish with its sharp, sharp teeth.

A trill of laughter bubbled up from her throat, and she started to pace the TV room, nodding as she went, as if to some music audible only in her bones. Ruth often became frustrated with Zack the way some people did with their siblings, and though they fucked occasionally, their relationship did sometimes make her think of siblings. Or business partners. People with shared interests who usually enjoyed each other's company but who mainly relied on those shared interests to hold them together.

That didn't mean she trusted Zack not to destroy everything. When they were being honest, they both acknowledged that she was the smart one. That without her, he would have been caught years ago.

Cussing under her breath, she kept pacing the room just like the little black fish swimming in that dark pond, deep down in the shadows within her. Right now, Ruthie swam much closer to the surface than she ever had before.

She diverted from her course, went to the back door, and stared out at the darkness. The hinges squealed—twisted, broken by the way that kid had barged into the room. Fucking kid, brave and stupid, but she would show that boy his soft belly, show him the parts of himself that were easiest to hurt. He thought he could make Ruthie hurt, but she hadn't even had a chance to show her teeth yet.

With a huff, she strode back to the padlocked door that led into the other half of the basement. She didn't need to go back there. She knew what waited for her, knew what had been cleaned and what should be removed. The manacles and leg braces, the straps—almost everything else in that room could be explained, but those things had to vanish. But thoughts were tumbling in her mind now like river rapids, rushing among the rocks. If Zack had been caught, and she put those things in the car and was also caught, that was tantamount to a confession to complicity. What she needed was denial.

Denial would be her only safe place.

There were no pictures. No evidence. How many wives lived under the thumb of cruel husbands? Brutal, dictatorial men? Millions, surely. Simple enough for her to say she had never been allowed in the back room, never even had a key to that padlock. She'd been forbidden to enter.

A smile stretched her lips, bared the teeth of a little black fish named Ruthie.

Forbidden to enter. Poor Ruth, she thought.

She rested her forehead against the cool surface of the padlocked door. What had the little boy, Leonard, said about being able to smell the children? Ruth breathed deeply, but she could not smell anything but the musty aroma of the TV room and the little bit of blood crusted around her nose where she'd slammed her face against the ground earlier. When that nosy fucking kid had smashed his way in. Ricky Barbosa.

There were things he would say to the police, if Zack didn't catch him.

Ruth could lie about everything, could put any newly discovered sins on Zack and play the timid, frightened wife. But how much had Ricky Barbosa heard back there, snooping around in the dark?

The sharp-toothed fish swam even closer to the top, and for a few seconds, it was only Ruthie there in the TV room. The person everyone thought of as Ruth had been eclipsed.

Sneering, she went to the back door and stepped outside. The only sounds were the rustle of leaves in the breeze and the call of night birds. Ruthie emerged from beneath the deck and stared at the rear of the property, where Zack had gone into the woods in pursuit of the Barbosa boy and his friend. *Billie,* she thought. The Suarez girl's name was Billie.

Truth was, Ruth had been keeping a curious eye on Billie Suarez for a long time.

She started toward the trees. When she reached the end of the path, she picked up her pace, following the trail. Moonlight sifted through what remained of the autumn foliage, enough to guide her along the familiar path, and she quickened her pace.

It was natural, she told herself, for a wife to go off in search of her husband. Zack had run off into the woods. There'd been a burglar, he had shouted to her, just before running off in pursuit, and she hadn't seen him since. When she grew worried enough, she feared he might have been injured in the dark and went after him.

Ruth felt free in the dark, on that path in the woods. Like swimming in that dark pond in her heart. She moved lightly and with confidence, all the plans coming together. Even her anger and frustration with Zack evaporated, because now that she had put her own body in motion, she knew he would also be doing something. He might not be the cleverest, but neither was he stupid. Perhaps Rick and Billie had eluded him, but he would be tracking them, making a plan to reach them. To stop them sharing what they had seen.

An owl cried in the dark. Ruth came around a turn in the path and nearly stumbled over her husband's work boots. Her heart quickened. She had not given Zack enough credit. He had removed his boots so that he could run quietly, so he could come upon the little spies without them hearing him until it would be too late.

Zack had never killed a child. Not without her help, anyway. But she knew he could do it now, with the stakes so high. Maybe that had been the thing to delay his return.

Ruthie smiled to herself, proud of her man. Yes, it had to be something like that.

Distracted, she rounded a corner on the path, came down a small rise between a pair of enormous pine trees that had created a carpet of needles underfoot, and she was within ten feet of Zack's twisted, ravaged, bloody corpse before she realized what lay before her.

The misshapen lump glistened in the moonlight. Ruth shifted her feet, and her shoes squelched in the bloody bed of pine needles underfoot.

All the air went out of her lungs as if she'd been punched in the chest. In the shock of that moment, she could not utter a sound. She stared at the wreckage of what had once been her husband.

In her peripheral vision, she caught the glimmer of yellow light, but for several seconds, Ruth could not manage to turn her head. When at last she blinked, the moment broken, she glanced to her left and saw a pair of small flames flickering among the trees, the burning wicks of invisible candles. Her mind had difficulty fitting what she saw into any logical setting. She saw no source for those flames, no way for them to simply float there, a few feet from the path, and when she stepped toward them—the bloody path sucking at her heels—it was almost as if she had no control over herself. As if the little burning lights lured her in.

A grotesque sucking noise made her glance down at the path again, and for a moment, she thought she had stepped in what remained of Zack. But the noise had not come from underfoot. She heard it again, that and worse—along with the wet, slippery noises came a sound like rocks being scraped together, punctuated by thick, guttural breaths and a rhythmic grunting that made her think of pigs rutting in the filth on her grandfather's farm, back when she'd been a little girl and her grandfather had first hurt her.

Ruth stared at those candle flames—and shifted her gaze downward. In the trees, just a few feet from the path, something hunched on hands and knees. If not for the noises, and the way it trembled with every grunt and shaking breath, she would have thought it part of the landscape. Leaves and pine needles caked its form. Roots wound about its arms and legs, layered like muscles and tendons. Now that she stood so close, she could smell the earth of it, the decay of autumn, and something else. An animal stink that did not belong here.

It jerked slightly, racked by tiny seizures, and in its grunting, now Ruth thought of childbirth, both the trauma of the emerging fetus and the primal release of the mother. The candle flames flickered, lowered, sank into the sodden leaves and mire that comprised its head—and the forest thing threw back its head and opened its mouth as if to scream.

What issued from its black throat was a chorus of children's voices, a cacophony of shrieks and laughter, the joy of toddlers and adolescents at play. The sounds were like spiders skittering down the back of Ruth's neck.

Still trembling as roots and mud and pine needles built it from the ground up, the thing turned and looked at her with candle-flame eyes, mouth still open, children still laughing in its heart.

Ruth opened her own mouth, as if her body expected, at last, to be able to scream. No sound came out, but her legs worked better than her voice. One stagger-step backward, then she twisted round and bolted back the way she'd come, heedless of the rocks and roots on the path or the low branches that whipped at her face. For as long as she could remember, she had been waiting for damnation to claim her for the things she had done.

At last, it had arrived.

VANESSA MONTEZ

Vanessa often thought about a story her mother had told her when she was a little girl. Mom had been coming home from shopping for her wedding dress, the sky low and gray, a light November rain falling. She had been on the highway, headlights spearing the dark as evening arrived. Coming over the top of a hill, she had heard the windshield wipers begin to scrape the glass and felt a tremor of fear. She tapped the brakes just once to test the road and felt the tires slide. As she crested the hill, she tapped the brakes very lightly again, and once more, enough to slow the car just a bit.

Just in time. As she came over the top of the hill, she had seen the accident beginning. Someone else had realized the rain had frozen on the surface of the road. Black ice. The first driver to notice had hit the brakes, slowed enough that someone else had rear-ended them, starting a chain reaction. But Vanessa's mom had already slowed down, and as other cars continued to careen into one another, she kept her foot off the brake and somehow managed to navigate through the ongoing pileup. Cars smashed and caromed, spun in circles, and slid off the road. Others came over the hill behind her and tried too late to slow down. She had to nudge her accelerator to avoid being struck from the rear.

She had felt that night as if she were inside some invisible, protective bubble, gliding through disaster without being touched by it.

That was how the Koenigs' party felt to Vanessa tonight.

Neighbors she had known all her life behaved like high school kids, and the high school kids observed them with the brand of horror usually reserved for girls overhearing the private conversations of boys for the first time. A woman who had been Vanessa's first grade teacher had drunk so much that she had slapped the ass of one of Mr. Koenig's friends and then tittered as if this had been some elegant Jane Austen flirtation. Seeing these people, in this state, felt like one long ongoing car accident. Her own parents were chatting amiably with the Colemans on the little patio beside the Koenigs' deck. They did not seem on the verge of bursting into song or dropping into an orgy or any other behavior that would humiliate her, but neither did they seem distressed by the boisterous drunks around them.

"This is a nightmare," Vanessa said.

She and Steve stood beside the wall of lilac bushes that would flower beautifully in the spring but were unremarkable in the fall. Owen O'Leary and two of his friends were a few feet away. As she glanced over at them, she saw Owen wink at her—nothing salacious, just a hello—and eat half a hot dog in a single bite. Which was a feat, considering the mountain of condiments he had stacked on top of that dog.

"If you hate it so much, we should go," Steve replied.

Vanessa frowned at him. "Like you're having the time of your life?"

"It's my house. My parents are throwing the party."

Vanessa felt stung. She sipped the rum and Coke Owen had fixed for her, hidden in plain sight in a plastic cup. Could her revulsion really just be a bad attitude? She looked around the back lawn and the patio and the deck. Most everyone seemed to be enjoying themselves. The Koenigs knew how to throw a party. The Halloween decorations were more elegant than gaudy, and the grill was still fired up so everyone had plenty to eat. The Halloween music had lasted an hour before someone had grown tired of it and now the radio blared music from WAAF, "kick-ass" rock and roll out of Worcester. It was a party.

She exhaled. Maybe she was being uptight. "Sorry. It's just been a weird night."

Steve laughed softly. "That's for sure. But you should be happy, Vanessa. You got what you wanted."

"What's that supposed to mean?"

He arched an eyebrow. "She'll be back. She just went to use the bathroom."

Vanessa felt her face flush. Of course he was talking about Julia. And he wasn't wrong. "She went with Chloe."

Steve glanced at Owen and sipped his own rum and Coke before lowering his voice to a conspiratorial hush. "It's not Chloe she likes. And as far as I know, Chloe doesn't swing that direction."

"I didn't think Julia would, either."

"Unless there's something in the water on Parmenter Road, I think the odds of all the senior girls in the neighborhood being lesbians would be pretty slim."

Vanessa laughed and felt a warm rush in her chest. She still could barely believe it. Her hand still held the memory of Julia's touch. The girl had been having one of the all-time shitty days, so Vanessa was not going to hold her to anything she might say tonight. But one thing was for sure, Julia liked girls. And at the moment, it seemed as if she liked Vanessa in particular.

Like a beautiful, ginger-haired dream. With a bunch of little nightmares thrown in.

This party, for one.

She wanted to leave. If Julia would go with her, she would do exactly that—except that she knew Steve would be hurt if they ditched him.

With a sigh, she took another swig of rum and Coke. Owen laughed uproariously at something one of his buddies had said, and then they were doing Monty Python voices and Vanessa rolled her eyes. Monty Python had never been her kind of humor.

She watched the door that led from the deck into the house, waiting for Julia to reappear.

"Calm down," Steve said. "She'll be back. Try not to jump her."

Vanessa shot him a hard look. "Hey, keep it down?"

She glanced at Owen and his friends.

Steve sighed. "Nobody heard me. You're fine."

"Wow. That sounded . . . a little mean." Vanessa studied his face, but he glanced away. "What's up with you? I know you were crushing on her, too, but are you mad at me? Or jealous or something? You are the only person I can share this with, the only one who'd understand—or I thought you would." Vanessa chewed her bottom lip, fighting the emotion that welled up, surprising her. "I never expected this. Can't you just be happy for me?"

"I *am* happy for you," Steve said. "I am."

"But?"

He smiled thinly, almost cynically. "I'm not jealous of you, Vee. I'm jealous of her." Steve must have seen the shock on her face, and he backpedaled quickly. "No, no. Not like that. Of course I love you. Probably more than I love anyone. You were my first kiss, remember?"

Vanessa smiled. They had been twelve and eleven years old, sitting in the bottom of Vanessa's bedroom closet with a flashlight and telling spooky stories, which somehow led to them wondering what it would be like to kiss someone.

"I knew you didn't have any romantic interest in me even then," he went on. "I could feel it, and maybe that's why I didn't have that kind of interest in you." He lowered his voice even further. "Honestly, it was kind of a relief when you told me you weren't into guys. Simpler."

"For you," she said.

Steve shrugged. "True." He reached out and took her free hand in his. "But back to jealousy. Yeah, I'm jealous. You're my best friend, my only real friend, since rum is making me super honest. In less than a year, you'll be headed to college—you're leaving me—and when I saw you and Jules looking at each other like that, I got a little bummed out thinking about having to share you for the next ten months and then losing you."

"You're not losing me."

"Things are going to change. I know that. This just speeds life up a little bit." Steve let go of her hand and took a sip of his drink. He smiled at her over the rim of his cup. "She is awfully cute, though."

"Isn't she?"

He glanced at the house, and Vanessa saw that Julia and Chloe had come out onto the deck. She watched while Julia scanned the yard. When her eyes lit on Vanessa, her smile brightened and she tugged Chloe by the wrist, the two girls heading toward their spot by the dead lilacs.

Vanessa turned to Steve. "You're my best friend. You're the person I trust the most in the world. Nothing's going to change that."

Steve smiled, but it was a sort of tired smile, like he knew better. "I think we need to get another drink."

Vanessa lifted her plastic cup and toasted to that idea.

"Let's just steer clear of the scarecrow kid, Arthur What's-his-name. The guy creeps me out."

"Oh my God. Me, too."

By then, Julia and Chloe had reached them. U2 was playing on the radio, and one of the neighborhood moms, who had no business even knowing who U2 was, had begun to sing along—loudly and badly. Nobody paid any attention when the four of them slipped casually over to Owen O'Leary and his friends, and then back into the woods where the secret under-twenty-one booze had been stashed.

Walking among the trees, Vanessa glanced at Julia, wondering if she might be having second thoughts about the connection they'd established. But then Julia slowed to walk beside her, letting Chloe and Steve go ahead of them on the path. When Julia took her hand, Vanessa glanced over her shoulder, worried someone might notice, but Julia rolled her eyes and bumped against her, just a pair of slightly drunk girls being girls. Nobody would think anything of it, Julia's reaction seemed to say, and Vanessa realized that was true. Girls were always intimate with one another. Her lips felt dry, and her pulse quickened. Julia had the most astonishing blue eyes, like ice, somehow gleaming despite the darkness of the woods.

"Hey," Julia said, leaning in to whisper in her ear, mouth so close that Vanessa could feel warm breath on her neck. "Before this night is over, I really hope I get a chance to kiss you."

Vanessa's whole body flushed. She felt herself shiver and pretended it was from the chilly evening instead of the trembling Julia's words had set off. She had never been shy, but suddenly, she couldn't face Julia.

"I think we can manage," she said.

Julia squeezed her hand. They stepped into the little clearing where Owen and the guys were smoking cigarettes and fixing fresh drinks. The music and voices from the Koenigs' yard were muffled by distance and the trees, so it seemed like they were backstage now and the rest of the world couldn't see behind the curtain.

Vanessa looked into the woods, heart pounding, and wanted to drag Julia off into the trees right then. Steve would cover for her, she knew, but Chloe might want to come along, not understanding that Vanessa and Julia wanted to be alone or why. She would have to be patient.

Something moved in the forest. A deeper shadow, back in among the trees. Vanessa narrowed her eyes, trying to focus, but someone said something funny and everyone laughed and she pretended to have heard the joke and laughed along with them, and the moment passed.

Still, something in the air had changed. The night seemed darker, as if the moonlight sifting through the branches had dimmed. The shadows had turned weird, the clearing a bit smaller, closer. This time when her skin prickled, it wasn't from the flush that Julia made her feel, but from the way the night seemed to hold its breath.

When the moment came for her to get Julia alone, she thought maybe it wouldn't be in the woods after all. She had never been superstitious—Steve was the scaredy-cat of the two of them—but something felt different. Just Halloween, she told herself, the spooky season getting under her skin. Maybe they would go for a walk, head back to her house, a little errand that would give them a quiet moment together.

But not out in the trees on their own. Not tonight.

TONY BARBOSA

Tony didn't have the heart to shut down the generators powering the Haunted Woods—not yet. He sat against the old birch tree that marked the entrance to the attraction. The birch was uncommonly thick, with a trunk that split into four on the way up, and bark that had begun to peel off and reminded him of papyrus. If he gathered it, he thought he could write the story of his life on those pages, and what a story it would be. Tragic comedy, and the joke was on him.

After the scene earlier, word had spread up and down the path through whispers and awkward laughter. The line out front had already begun to dissipate by then, as it was near their posted closing time, but the ugly drama had shut things down even faster. They would be moving soon, but Tony knew his family would be the topic of neighborhood gossip from now until the last living human on Earth had forgotten them.

He supposed it had been too much to ask, to have one perfect night. One happy moment to finish the story of the Barbosas of Parmenter Road. Now, instead of people remembering how nice it used to be when the Barbosas lived here, when they had put blood, sweat, and tears, and lots of monster makeup and screams, into the annual charity of the Haunted Woods, people would remember that his wife had been unfaithful to him with one of the neighbors. Eventually, it wouldn't matter who that neighbor had been. Other than his children, the Haunted Woods had been the one thing Tony had been truly proud of. Now it would be forever associated with his humiliation.

Happy Halloween.

"Jesus Christ," he sighed.

He put his head back against the rough birch. In the woods, evil laughter and spooky music continued to play to the empty trail. The fog machines were still on, billowing mist low on the ground. All his volunteers were gone—all the actors, many of whom had become his friends—and most of them had left without so much as a farewell, doubtless uneasy about looking him in the eye. What were they supposed to say after the way it had fallen apart?

Somewhere out in front of the house, a car door slammed and an engine roared to life. That would be Alice's sister, he figured. On a typical Halloween, she would have stuck around and had coffee and something to eat, but no sane person would want to stay tonight. Rick and Chloe were out, and that meant just Tony and Alice left to drown in the resentment and embarrassment of the evening.

Tony closed his eyes, yearning for some kind of respite from the poison he had swallowed tonight. Every married couple went through some kind of ordeal, a period of turbulence, and many didn't make it through. People grew apart or bored, or circumstances emerged to put new stress on the marriage—all just a part of the natural order of things. But until tonight, he had not realized how far things had gone. He could hear her voice in his head, telling him he didn't understand her, that his frequent brooding and disinterest in socializing made her feel suffocated. But, of course, she hadn't mentioned anything about fucking Donnie Sweeney.

If she needed to take another man to bed, then she was

welcome to it. An affair with someone Tony could recognize as a better choice than himself? He could have lived with that. He'd have been angry and resentful, but he would not have hated her for it.

But a charming drunk who'd bed any woman fool enough to open her legs for him?

Jesus.

"Everyone's gone."

Tony opened his eyes, and there she was, walking slowly across the backyard toward him. She had always been light on her feet, and he had not heard her coming. A breeze swept across the yard, and he shuddered.

Alice paused ten feet away. "Are you going to shut the gennies down, or would you like me to do it?"

Tony didn't rise. "I don't want you to touch anything, since you asked."

She glanced away. "None of this was supposed to happen. I want you to know that."

He scowled. "Donnie fucking Sweeney?"

"It would have been better if it had been someone else?"

Tony put one hand against the birch and levered himself to his feet. "Truthfully? Yeah. It still would hurt, but it would have been better if it had been someone less cliché."

"It didn't mean anything."

"That's worse, Alice. You broke your marriage vows for a guy who didn't mean anything to you. Well done."

The night grew louder. The laughter and ominous music in the woods seemed to swell, almost as if it were commentary on their conversation, their dissolution. The chill sank to his bones, and he let it happen, jaw set tightly against the cold. Just a couple of hours to go before the curtain fell on October and November took the stage, but still, he had not expected it to be this cold tonight.

Alice slid her hands into the rear pockets of her jeans. "I'm sorry, Tony. I love you, and I love our family. It's just sometimes I get skittish, like I'm a horse trapped in a barn and the barn's on fire. I get to feeling like I've got to run, on instinct, even though consciously I know I've got everything I should really want. I'm just wired wrong, I guess."

Tony stared at her, more sad than angry now. "Our family . . . our house that I couldn't hold on to . . . those make you feel like you're trapped in a burning barn?"

She looked pale, nauseous. "I don't know what you want me to say."

Tony realized she was right. What could she say that would matter?

Seconds ticked by, and the moment passed, the damage done.

"Getting kind of late," he observed. "I'm surprised Rick isn't back."

When he lifted his gaze, he saw gratitude in her eyes, and he wished he could take back the merciful change of subject. The bitterness nearly choked him.

"He and Billie probably went to the block party. I'll go up the street and bring him home," Alice offered. "I told Chloe to be home by midnight, but Rick knows he ought to have come back by now."

The laugh that bubbled up in Tony's throat seemed to shock her, but not as much as it shocked him. He tried to stop it, tried to erase the smile on his face so that she would not misinterpret it as lunacy or forgiveness. Alice started to speak, and he held up a hand.

"I'm not laughing because it's funny, I'm laughing in disbelief. You want to go to the Koenigs' house, where pretty much the whole neighborhood is going to be drinking and gossiping about you? About us?"

"Let them talk. We're moving."

"We have *children*," he said, sharpening the last word as if he could stab her with it. "Or do you not give a fuck how much you've humiliated them? You show your face up there and you're only going to make it worse. Just call the house, ask them to send Rick home if he's there."

Alice squeezed her eyes closed, and tears spilled down her cheeks. Tony felt a guilty ache in his chest and the urge to comfort her, to take his wife in his arms and give her a safe place to pour out whatever pain had seized her. Maybe he would be able to do that again someday, but not tonight.

"Do you think anyone will say something to the kids?" she asked, covering her eyes as if to hide her tears.

"I'd like to lie, for your sake," he confessed. "But I think maybe yes. There are some gossipy bitches in this neighborhood. Even if nobody says it to their faces, they might overhear chatter. And you can bet the kids won't hesitate to ask about it. That Cynthia What's-her-name, for instance. That's a girl who feels better about herself when other people feel worse. So, yeah."

"Oh my God." Alice sobbed loudly. "It wasn't supposed to be like this."

No, Tony thought. *It wasn't.*

"I'm going to shut things down," he said. "I'll come inside in a while. Please don't go there. Just call and have them send Rick home."

Alice nodded without meeting his eyes again, then turned and headed toward the back of the house. He watched her go, loving and hating her and wanting to run after her, not sure if he would embrace her or shake her.

Instead, he started down the trail into the Haunted Woods for the last time.

As he reached the first of the sound systems—the one playing the creepy music—he heard the back door close. It sounded like the end of everything.

Tony turned off the music, but he took his time strolling through his Haunted Woods, storing memories. Tomorrow, he and Chloe would bring out the boxes and begin to pack things away. Some would be kept as mementos of a happier time, but most of them would be sold or junked long before they moved away from the house on Parmenter Road.

There were two generators hidden in the woods. He left the path and made his way to the first one, pressed the red button, and listened to it cough and then go still. Behind him, the evil laughter continued. Half the lights in the Haunted Woods had gone dark, and the witches and goblins would not be shrieking in delight and zipping out of the trees—not without power. But the rest of the lights and the fog machine and the second sound system still hummed along, powered by the second genny.

Back on the trail, he found himself no longer looking at his surroundings. Suddenly, he didn't want to see the evil clown faces or the creepy carousel horse. He let them blur in his peripheral vision, choosing not to see them in the same way he avoided seeing his flabby belly in the mirror while he shaved. He was done here. The desire to be out of the woods flooded through him and he picked up the pace. *Shut it down, go inside, have a drink, go to sleep. In that order.* Tony would face it all in the morning, but he felt too depleted to spend another minute *feeling* all of this tonight.

His foot dragged something along the trail, knocked it into the leaves. Mocking laughter roiled around him. The mist swirled, but he could see the object on the side of the trail, and he bent to pick it up, staring dumbly at the soft, stained, faded Raggedy Ann doll that he felt sure he had left inside the house.

"What the hell?"

He frowned in confusion, wondering how it had gotten back onto the path. Nobody had shown up tonight to claim it as far as he knew. Had Alice or Chloe brought it out and forgotten about it? That seemed unlikely, but in the tension of tonight, he would not call anything impossible.

Standing, mist swirling around his ankles, he stared at the frayed doll. How simple things had been, once upon a time. In the era when children still played with Raggedy Ann, life had been so uncomplicated. Or at least it seemed that way. Though he knew, of course, that the past had its share of pain and ugliness.

Through the trees not far away, the banshee began to scream.

Tony jumped back, heart pounding, and then laughed at himself. The Haunted Woods had actually scared him. He'd caught himself in his own trap.

But his smile didn't last, because the banshee was on a motion sensor.

"Hello?" he called, starting along the trail. "Alice?"

No answer came. The banshee went silent. Tony kept along the trail, winding around corners, setting off a cackling skeleton. The second generator was off the path to his right, thirty feet into the woods, but he didn't want to turn out the rest of the lights just yet. He told himself it had been a skunk or a coyote, but the tension remained.

"Hello?" he called again, a bit more urgently.

Someone stepped from behind a black curtain just ahead. His breath caught in his throat, but he exhaled quickly, clutching the doll.

It was the little girl in the antique Raggedy Ann costume who'd startled him earlier in the day. Tony started to smile, happy she had finally shown herself, but then he remembered that he had no idea who her parents might be, that nobody had come back for the doll.

"Are you okay?" he asked. "You shouldn't be out here alone. Where are your parents, honey?"

She walked toward him in little, halting steps. In the garish light, her face looked gray, her eyes almost black and shining with tears.

"Help me, mister. Will you help me?"

"What is it, honey?" Tony asked, her voice and her fear breaking his heart. "Has someone hurt you?"

"Oh yes," she said, lip quivering as fresh tears fell. "And he wants to hurt me again."

Of course he asked whom she meant.

And of course she said, "The Cunning Man."

"I don't understand," Tony told her, going down on one knee so he could look her in the eye. He reached out and wiped some of her tears away. "Who's the Cunning Man?"

"He's trick-or-treat," she said. "He's Halloween. And he's almost here."

RICK BARBOSA

Rick stood in the darkness of his next-door neighbors' backyard, between the pear tree and Mrs. Panza's rusty clothesline, and eavesdropped on his parents speaking honestly about infidelity. They talked about whether he might have gone up to the Koenigs' party, and he knew he should have revealed himself right then, told them he had overheard everything, but he could not bring himself to face them now. Then his mother had gone into the house and his father into the woods, and the moment had passed.

His stomach hurt. He wasn't sure if he felt like throwing up or throwing a punch. His eyes burned as if he might cry, but there were no tears.

"Rick," Billie whispered, placing a gentle hand on his back.

He turned and pulled her toward him. Now that they were teenagers, they weren't as physically demonstrative with each other as they once had been, but all awkwardness fled as he buried his face into Billie's neck. His breath hitched, and he whispered some profanity. Only a few feet away, the kid he thought of as Always Leonard watched him hugging Billie, but said nothing.

Rick knew they had to move, had to do something about Leonard—about Zack and Ruth and what they had seen in the woods—but his ability to function had shut down.

"Hey," Billie whispered in his ear. "Let's go."

"Where?"

"We need to call the police," Billie said.

Rick shook his head. "I can't go in my house right now. I hate her."

"Your mom?"

"Both of them. I feel bad for them and I hate them at the same time, for making me feel like this."

Billie glanced over at Leonard, and Rick knew what she must be thinking—this kid might not even have parents, and the grown-ups he'd encountered tonight had wanted to do more than hurt him. Guilt washed through him. His mother had cheated on his father. They were real people with real problems and ugly emotions like everyone else, and yeah, it made him sick and angry, but now wasn't the time.

"Can we go to your house?" Rick asked.

Billie nodded. "My parents are at a Halloween party—not the Koenigs'."

Normally, Billie wasn't allowed to have friends in the house when her parents weren't home—especially boys, including Rick. But he knew none of that mattered tonight, and he could see Billie knew it, too.

He turned toward Leonard, who stood by the clothesline as if he thought the rusty metal post could hide him. "Let's go, kid. We can't stay out here."

The boy hesitated, but when Rick and Billie started to walk, he hurried to catch up. Rick watched the Panzas' darkened rear windows for any sign that they were awake and might notice trespassers, but none of the curtains twitched and no lights went on. When they reached Billie's house, they went around to the front, and she dragged up the garage door. The three of them slipped in, and she let it come rattling back down with a boom.

"It's very dark in here," Leonard said in a small voice.

"Just wait there. I'll get the light."

Rick stayed with Leonard while Billie made her way past the lawn mower and trash cans and years of accumulated tools and boxes and Christmas decorations—this garage had not been home to a car in a very long time. At the three wooden steps that led into the house, Billie clicked a switch that cast a sickly yellow light on the mess. She unlocked the door with her key, and the three of them went inside, closing the door and locking the terror outside.

"Oh, man. I like the sound of that lock." Rick flopped into a wooden chair beside the kitchen table.

"It won't keep him out," Leonard said.

"Not for long, anyway," Billie agreed, and she headed for the phone that hung on the wall next to the refrigerator.

As Billie lifted the handset from its cradle, Leonard crossed the room and took her by the wrist.

"No."

The kid held on to Billie's wrist, but she pulled free.

"What's your issue?" she said. "We have to call the cops. Zack and Ruth aren't going to just leave us alone. If my parents were home, I'd talk to them first, but I know they would call the police. If Rick's mom and dad weren't in the middle of their battle over there, they would do the same. We have to."

The phone had been off the hook long enough that the dial tone turned to a fast busy signal. Rick could hear it even from across the kitchen. Billie hung up the phone to get a fresh dial tone, then picked it up again.

This time, Leonard grabbed the phone, trying to tug it away. Billie swore, holding on.

"You can't," the younger boy said.

An ugly feeling filled Rick. He moved a bit closer to them

both. "What's going on, Leonard? You're more afraid of the police than you are of the people who tried to hurt you tonight?"

Billie hung up the phone. "What are you hiding from?"

Headlight beams washed across the front windows of the Suarez house like the eye of a lighthouse sweeping across the ocean. Rick froze, wondering if Zack and Ruth might be driving that car, but then the headlights kept going and the low rumble of an engine faded.

"That could've been them," Billie said.

"Or the next one will be," Rick replied.

Billie snatched up the phone and started dialing 9-1-1.

Leonard lunged, hitting her like some little Pop Warner football kid learning to tackle. Billie stumbled and fell, her head thumping off the kitchen floor. The phone went flying from her hand, slingshotted by its cord, and that fast busy signal blared from the handset again. Leonard raised one hand and slapped Billie across the face. The smack of skin on skin echoed in the kitchen.

He might have been little, but he'd hurt Billie, so Rick didn't hold back. He grabbed Leonard with both hands and flung him so hard at the refrigerator that the fridge door opened and a bottle of Mr. Suarez's favorite beer toppled out and shattered on the floor.

Rick pointed at the kid. "You just sit right there!"

Leonard stared at him, then picked up the broken end of the beer bottle and glanced over at the handset dangling from the phone on the wall.

"No police," the boy said.

"Then get the fuck out of here," Rick said, gesturing to the door that led back into the garage. "It's not just you who's in trouble. They're gonna come for us, too."

Leonard glanced at the door, but instead of looking relieved, as if the door might be an escape, his face turned paler than it had already been. The idea of going back out into the dark did not sit well with him.

Rick watched him, wary of that broken bottle, but he went to grab the phone, hung it up to get a fresh dial tone, and then called 9-1-1. Billie sat up, leaning against the cabinets where her parents kept the pots and pans. She touched the back of her head, and her fingers came away bloody.

Little bastard, Rick thought, glaring at Leonard.

On the phone, 9-1-1 went through, and Rick listened to it ring.

DONNIE SWEENEY

Donnie wished he had never given up smoking. He could have used a cigarette tonight. He tucked his left knee against the steering wheel of his Cutlass as he reached over to open the glove compartment. A glance over the dash to make sure he wasn't about to career off the road, and then he started digging around, hoping an old pack of Winstons might be tucked away in the back.

No luck.

"This fucking night," he muttered.

The glove compartment stayed open, the little door bouncing as he went through a pothole. He drove slowly, wondering if he ought to hit Lucky 13 Liquors—he could get himself some cigarettes and a six-pack of Rolling Rock, park somewhere, and try to figure out his life.

Lucky 13 closed in twenty minutes. He could drive over there, get beer and cigs, and then drive half an hour to his office and sleep on the little sofa in the waiting room—maybe put the cushions on the floor so he could spread out. But he had a terrible vision of waking up in the morning with empty green bottles and a full ashtray beside him while the receptionist and paralegals stood watching.

Not the office, then.

Which meant the Red Roof Inn.

If he hadn't felt sick to his stomach—if he didn't know his dreams would be haunted by the look on Julia's face tonight and the way Charlie had cried as he ran off—Donnie would have laughed. He had never stayed at a Red Roof Inn unless he had been there with one of his conquests. And he did think of them that way. Growing up, his whole identity had been built around his charm. His younger brother, Martin, had been the smart one—brilliant as hell, that guy. But their parents had behaved as if neither of the boys had other qualities. Marty was the smart one, Donnie the charmer. "He'll be a real ladies' man when he grows up." How many thousands of times had he heard that as a kid?

Donnie knew it made his parents happy. From the time he could be aware of the world's response to him, he had seen that charm as his value to the family. In school, he might miss a homework assignment or talk too much in class, or even mock a teacher, but behaviors that would get other boys stuck in detention had always been laughed off when it came to him. He would smile and talk the teachers out of their frustration or disappointment.

"It's like magic," he'd said to his little brother when he'd been fourteen and Marty eleven.

And it *was* like magic. Because by then, he had found it worked on girls, too. That had been 1959, in a time and place when mothers spent much of their energy reinforcing what it meant to be a good girl. But to Donnie, every good girl was just a challenge. He charmed them, he romanced them, he made them laugh, and eventually, he persuaded them to put aside objections and their better judgment.

Later, as a married man, he learned to appreciate the bad girls even more than the good ones. By then, he had turned his charm into a law career and spent all his time fighting the pressures of what society considered a normal homelife. The dichotomy of life had become perplexing and frustrating. He had seen more than his share of episodes of *Father Knows Best*, so he knew he was supposed to stay home and hug his wife and help his kids with their homework. But those were television dads, and in real life, men who were strong and successful were painted as irresistible to women, and fidelity was treated with derision. Something quaint, made for lesser men.

He knew the right choice, but he survived on adoration as if it were his oxygen, so he nearly always made the wrong one. Everyone saw him as having the perfect life—three great kids, a smart and lovely wife, a nice house in a nice neighborhood—but every time he went home, Donnie felt like running away. And many times, he had. It was the perfect recipe for self-loathing.

The solution to this dilemma, Donnie had found, was simple. Drink.

And keep drinking.

The more he drank, the more tightly he embraced the cliché that had become his personal motto, the ruling principle of his messy life. *The only way out is through*. There were no time machines, no way to reverse the slow-motion disaster of his marriage, no way to make his children forget all the fights, the times Barb had dragged them around to the parking lots of bars in search of their father, the screaming on the front lawn this afternoon or his display of temper and bad taste tonight. He could go to couples counseling with Barb, promise to get on the wagon and keep his pants on, but how long would he be able to be that man?

How long before they both came to accept the inevitable?

No. The only way out was through.

Donnie tapped the brake and pulled the Cutlass to the curb. If there was still ugliness to come, he might as well get it over with tonight. Barb had humiliated him by running around town searching for him, but there was plenty of humiliation to go around. Time to put it behind him.

He turned the car around. Chilly air blew through the windows and perked him up. When Donnie reached Parmenter Road, he spotted the Weisbarts walking along the sidewalk, probably heading back from the Koenigs' party. The husband lifted a hand to wave, and his wife nudged him, glaring at Donnie's car. His behavior earlier tonight, back in the Barbosas' Haunted Woods, had already hit the neighborhood grapevine. The sooner he uprooted himself from this place, the better off he would be. And maybe they didn't see it now, but Barb and their kids would be better off, too.

As Donnie approached his house, he doused the headlights and let the car glide to a stop at the curb. All the lights in the front of the house were off, the whole place dark. Which either meant his family had gone up to the party or had already gone to bed. Neither seemed very likely, but he couldn't imagine them all going to a Halloween party with the neighbors tonight. Not after Donnie had talked about fucking Alice Barbosa in front of a dozen people, including his own daughter.

Blame the alcohol. That's what he would do. What he had always done. But Donnie knew by now that he and the alcohol were one creature, and he felt pretty sure Julia knew it, too.

He turned off the Cutlass's engine and sat in the silence, staring at the house that would never be his home again. He wanted to go in, get the things he would need for a week or so, and to tell Barb and the kids he loved them but they would all be happier without him living there.

The engine ticked as it cooled. He hugged himself against the chill and wondered if any of the women in his address book might open their doors to him at this hour. He was free now. He could go anywhere. So why did it feel like he had nowhere left to go?

BARB SWEENEY

Barb stood in the doorway that led from the kitchen to the porch, which was illuminated only by the blue flickering of the television. The garish old Dracula movie that had been playing had given way to the black and white of Hitchcock's *Psycho*, which she thought might have been too creepy for Sarah Jane, but the little girl had fallen asleep on the sofa. Brian had stumbled off to the bathroom twenty minutes ago and then to his bedroom, where she assumed he was now sound asleep. Trauma like what her family had been through tonight could be physically draining, causing people to collapse with exhaustion. Others ended up wired, wide awake, unable to sleep, and she knew that would be her story. Anger was part of it—fury at Donnie—but mostly, she just felt sad and defeated. She had believed that she could turn things around, that she could remind him of the man they had both dreamed he would become. But she'd failed.

On the sofa, snoring in adorable little bursts, like a doll in her clown makeup, Sarah Jane was the other reason Barb was not going to get any sleep.

Just call the police, she chided herself.

She had taken the phone from her bedroom and plugged it into the jack in the kitchen, where she could hear it ring anywhere in the house. Yet somehow, she could not force herself to call the police. She had promised to let the girl stay until midnight, had told her sons she would stay up late and make sure Sarah Jane would be safe. Barb could make little sense of the girl's fears—they seemed like gibberish—but she had no question that Sarah Jane was genuinely terrified. So she would wait until midnight, as promised. That felt safer than making the wrong decision and inadvertently putting the girl in some sort of danger. As frightened as her parents might be, at least Barb knew that under her roof, Sarah Jane would come to no harm.

She had seen *Psycho* many times, but she still had an hour and a quarter until midnight, and the movie would make a fine distraction. There was a chair in the corner of the porch where she could sit and not disturb Sarah Jane on the sofa, or Charlie, who had a pillow under his head but lay on the floor with his Halloween candy scattered around him as if there'd been some kind of explosion.

Despite everything, Barb smiled as she looked at her youngest child and this strange, sad little girl.

Psycho beckoned and she started onto the porch just as the phone rang.

Nearly 11:00 p.m. on Halloween night, and her phone was ringing. The worst thoughts flooded her mind. Donnie had wrapped his car around a tree or ended the night in jail. God, she hated that as awful as he had become, she still loved him. And what would it do to the children if their father died tonight?

Only as she crossed the kitchen in three steps and reached for the phone did the other likely answer hit her—Julia still hadn't come back from the Koenigs' party. What if something had happened to *her*?

Barb could barely breathe. She answered the phone.

"Hello?"

All her fears were audible in that one word.

But it wasn't the police and it wasn't Julia, and nobody and nothing had died, except her pride and her marriage.

"Oh my God, Barb, I'm so sorry to call this late, but Roger and I just came home from the Koenigs' party, and I heard what happened at the Barbosas' tonight. You must be mortified. I just wanted to reach out right now and say I'm here for you, whatever you need. And that includes kicking Donnie right in the balls the next time I see him."

Barb felt sick. If she had Heidi Coleman in front of her instead of just a voice on the phone, she would have throttled the woman. They knew each other from the municipal pool and from passing each other on the street, but they were not friends. It surprised her to know that Heidi even had her telephone number.

"I'm afraid you have me at a disadvantage," she said, hoping the ice she intended came across in her voice.

"Oh, babe. It's Heidi. Sorry, I thought you would've recognized my voice."

"I do. I mean I'm not sure what you're talking about, Heidi. If the news that Donnie and I have split up has already made it through the neighborhood, I'd say people aren't wasting any time sharing bad news. Except it isn't really bad news. He doesn't live here anymore."

Heidi hesitated, stumbled over her words for a moment— but only a moment.

"I'm sorry, Barb. But after tonight, I can't say I'm surprised."

Barb smiled. She wished Heidi were there to see it, certain her teeth were showing. "I appreciate your concern—"

"I didn't know he'd already moved out."

Heidi sounded disappointed. Barb refused to give her the satisfaction of providing gory details about the fight on the front lawn, or the circumstances of Donnie's departure, or the fact that he had only "moved out" a handful of hours earlier. None of those things were related to the reason for Heidi's call. Something else had happened, something Barb had yet to learn, and from the tone of this call, the fake sympathy and insistence that Heidi wanted to be *there* for her, Barb knew it had to be something even more deeply humiliating than she had already suffered. Whatever had happened, she would hear about it eventually, but she did not want Heidi Coleman to be the messenger.

"I appreciate you calling," Barb lied. "It's so thoughtful of you. But the kids and I are doing just fine."

"You've got such strength," Heidi said, barely hiding the condescension. "I don't think I could keep my chin up if my husband made a drunken scene in the neighborhood with somebody else's wi—"

"Happy Halloween, Heidi. Trick or treat."

Barb hung up the phone.

Exhaling slowly, she pressed her forehead against the cool wallpaper in the kitchen, trying not to hear the phrase she had interrupted. But she knew what Heidi had been in the middle of saying. *Somebody else's wife.* Donnie hadn't just been sleeping with divorcées he picked up in local bars, he'd apparently been fucking at least one of the neighbors.

Barb poured herself an enormous glass of wine and walked it out onto the porch, where Charlie and Sarah Jane were miraculously still asleep. She felt hollow, as if emotional energy might collect in a rain barrel and she had poured out all her reserves. With no way of knowing how long it would take that barrel to fill up again, all she could do was sit and drink her wine and watch while Norman Bates murdered the private investigator sent in search of Marion Crane.

The music, Barb decided, was really the best part of *Psycho*.

She sort of wished Norman Bates would visit Heidi Coleman's house. Which wasn't fair, of course. Heidi might be a vulture, but Donnie was the real villain. Barb wondered if she would need to have the lock changed, just to keep him from entering when she wasn't home. Donald F. Sweeney, Esquire, would not hesitate to use his knowledge of the law to control whatever came next for them. Divorce, child support, alimony—he would manipulate as much as he could to make his exit as painless for him as possible, putting himself first as he always had.

Yes, on Monday, she would call a locksmith. When Donnie came to get his things, she wanted to be certain he only took what belonged to him.

Barb sipped her wine and forced Donnie from her mind. When her wineglass was empty, she thought about refilling it, and about finally calling the police, and then she wondered how much it mattered. Would it be the worst thing in the world if Sarah Jane just slept on the sofa tonight? At least here she would be safe from whatever had frightened her so profoundly.

By the time the credits rolled on *Psycho*, Barb had closed her eyes. She rested peacefully, snoring lightly, and mercifully free of dreams.

RUTH BURGESS

Ruth stood in the foyer of the house where she and Zack had been happy and where they had done things that would once have had them burned at the stake. Most days, she never thought about those things, and when she did, she felt sick. Sometimes she wanted to cut her own throat. In the tool drawer in her kitchen was a box cutter with orange electrical tape wrapped around it for a better grip, and at least once a week when Zack was already sleeping, she would go downstairs and quietly open that drawer, slide open the box cutter to expose its razor with a satisfying click, and hold the cold point against the softness of her throat, willing herself to find the courage she needed.

Her belly and inner thighs were crisscrossed with the results of the many nights she had failed to cut her own throat. Thin white scars revealed each time she had turned gutless and decided to keep living, but still needed to draw her own blood. It had become a ritual. Zack had never seemed to loathe himself the way Ruth did, but it had all started with him, hadn't it? She had loved him even after he had revealed to her what he had endured as a child—so similar to her own story—and she had loved him even after he told her of his obsessions and compulsions and crimes. Maybe loved him more, because she had done something similar, just once.

Well, twice.

But Zack's confessions had felt like permission, like she had the freedom now to take the horror inside her and put it on the outside. It disgusted her. She knew the monster in her heart would only grow darker and darker, and she wanted to die nearly all the time. There were times she convinced herself there was beauty in what she and Zack did, a kindness to these children, that it came from love. But afterward, she always wanted to throw herself in the path of a truck or off the bridge into the Merrimack River.

Tonight, the monster in her heart, what she'd heard called the lizard brain, had taken over completely.

"Okay, okay. What did you forget?" she whispered to herself, standing in her bedroom and looking down at the fat suitcase she had packed.

Only her things. Not Zack's. He would not be coming back.

She went to the window, tugged back the curtain, and held her breath. Nothing moved except the branches of trees that swayed in the breeze. The window was open just an inch, and as she turned her back on it, the breeze picked up and began to shriek through that gap.

How many times had she told Zack they ought to have suitcases ready to go at all times, just in case? He had always believed that would be equal to a confession when the police finally came. And they would come someday, Ruth had always known that.

She pushed her hands through the things in her suitcase. Shirts, pants, sweaters, bras, panties, makeup kit, toiletries. The zippered pouch with her passport had already been tucked into the outside pocket, but she looked again to make sure. The pouch also contained $1,000 in cash, a bankbook for an account Zack had never known about, and the key to Ruth's grandfather's cabin outside Chesuncook Village in Maine. It was about the loneliest place in the state and a good place to go if you didn't want to be found. Somewhere along the way, she would have to stop for supplies, but right now, she needed to think about how cold it would be when she got there, and that meant boots and gloves and a hat and coat appropriate for northern Maine in winter.

Socks. Damn it, she had known something was missing.

Ruth yanked open her sock drawer, and then she froze as the sound of the doorbell echoed through the house.

Police? Neighbors? Whatever that thing had been in the woods?

Ignore it!

Frantic, she grabbed fistfuls of socks and tossed them in the suitcase, reached into her closet for work boots, and threw them in as well, not caring if they got her clean clothes dirty. She smashed the suitcase shut and zipped it.

The doorbell rang again, three times in quick succession.

Ruth felt the lizard brain start to crawl, felt her mouth widen into a smile she could not control. A madwoman's smile, and she wondered if that was what she had become. And then wondered if that was what she had always been, because how could she have ever been anything else?

The doorbell rang again, and she bared her teeth. Picked up her suitcase, thinking she could get downstairs quietly in the dark and slip into the garage for her car, not caring about her winter things anymore. She could get more once she got out of here.

The lights were all off inside the house. She told herself that whoever it was, she could just stay quiet and wait for them to go away.

Somewhere in the house, a child began to laugh.

Mischievous, that laughter. Joined by another voice. And then . . .

"Trick or treat!" one of the children said, so close and yet so far away.

The next voice came almost as a whisper in her ear. "*Give me something good to eat.*"

Ruth put down the suitcase. It no longer mattered. She had seen that thing in the woods, had heard the sounds coming from it. Tears slid down her face, because she had always thought she would face justice someday, that she'd pay for the things she had done, but she'd expected prison. Or that box cutter across her throat, by her own hand.

"Trick or treat?" another voice asked, words slithering up the stairs.

And there were other sounds. Crying and noises that could not be issuing from anywhere in her house at that moment. Noises she remembered.

Ruth reached into the pocket on the outside of the suitcase and took the zippered packet that held her passport and money and other things she would need to survive. Nothing else here mattered. She quietly opened her closet, reached inside with her free hand, and took out the aluminum baseball bat she kept there just in case. So many things she had done *just in case*, never thinking the moment for them would arrive.

Quietly as she could, she slipped from her bedroom, checked the top of the steps, and then bolted down them.

The front door remained closed.

Voices floated from the basement, and now she wondered if they belonged to the children who had visited the locked room down there. The children they broke. All those children had found their way home eventually, drugged and left to wander a back road until someone came by to pick them up—all but one, and she had never told Zack about that. He might have broken, possibly confessed, maybe killed himself . . . or he might have decided that one dead kid was no worse than a hundred, and then the dam would have broken. No, she could never have told Zack about that one.

The doorbell rang. Ruth jerked backward so fiercely that she smashed against the wall.

The voices of children floated around her again. Trick-or-treat. Something creaked off to her left, where the door to the basement waited. With a click of the latch and a quiet squall of hinges that sounded like a grandfather's last rattling breath, the door began to open. Halfway up that widening slit of shadow between door and frame, an eye peered out at her, milky white, a fringe of black hair above it.

A child. Or something like a child. Not the justice she had expected, but here it was, just the same.

Ruth screamed. She bolted down the hall, past the cellar door. She slammed it shut, felt only the slightest air resistance, then raced through the kitchen to the door that led into the garage. A ripple of laughter filled the eaves of her home, this place that had now become damnation. The packet of ID in her left hand, she yanked the garage door open and jumped the three steps to the concrete in the dark.

The motion sensor made the garage light flicker on. She spun around, searching the corners for the thing from the woods, but saw nothing. What Ruth felt then should not have been hope—she deserved horror, deserved agony, and knew it—but cowardice had possessed her. She yanked open the door of her '81 Firebird, tossed her ID packet and the aluminum bat inside, and dropped into the seat even as she jammed the key into the ignition.

She hit the button for the garage door opener. The motor overhead rumbled to life. The lights flickered—and then went dark with a pop that stopped the garage door before it could open more than a few inches. The garage door opener stopped clanking. The only sounds in the garage were the wail of the wind that buffeted the house.

Ruth opened the car door and jumped out. The car pinged in alarm to let her know she'd left her keys in the ignition as she ran to grab hold of the dangling rope and yanked it to release the garage door so she could open it manually. She grabbed the handle and hauled it upward. The cold wind blew in.

The Firebird still pinged. She started back toward it.

The door from the kitchen opened with an almost hydraulic hiss. The giggling of children spread into the garage, but she could see through into the darkness of the kitchen, and there were no children there. None at all. Something whispered, "Trick or treat," and suddenly, the monster stood in the open doorway and started down the three steps into the garage.

She only glanced at the thing. It looked more like a man now, tall and rickety thin, much of it hidden beneath a long cloak the color of burning charcoal, gray and black and fire orange, even in the dark. Its fingers moved like spider's legs, twitching at the air.

Under its hood, those candle flames burned. When it looked directly at her, she could see shadows flickering inside its hollow head. Nothing there but twin flickering flames. It opened its lips as if to speak, raised one of those twitching hands, and the laughter of children spilled from its mouth—and the laughter turned to screams.

Ruth ran, then. It swept after her, slowly and inexorably, and she knew she would never reach the Firebird. Its door hung open, the car still pinging in alarm that she had left the key in the ignition, but there was no time to get into the driver's seat, start the engine, put it in reverse. She left that ID packet and her only weapon behind, the things she needed to escape what the law might do to a monster like her, and she ran out of the garage into the night on Parmenter Road.

Screaming.

The Cunning Man followed.

RICK BARBOSA

Rick had been using the Suarezes' phone to call the police. He'd listened to it ring, a weird tinny buzz not like the usual sound, but now it had gone silent. He thought it might start emitting the fast busy signal that interrupted when a call had been cut off, but he could hear nothing, not even the hissing of an open line. The handset had become nothing but a blunt instrument.

"It's dead," he said, turning to look at Billie.

"Try again," she said. She had removed the cape from her Storm costume, and now, with the wig long since left behind, she was just Billie in a black jumpsuit. A teenager, like Rick himself.

We're not superheroes, Rick thought. He had barged into the Burgesses' basement out of panic, afraid for a smaller kid, not fearful for himself. But fear had caught up to them, and now he wondered if by trying to play the hero, he had made a terrible, terrible mistake.

Leonard started toward them, maybe to apologize but probably to try to take the phone away from Rick. Either way, Billie had reached her limit with the kid. He might be little, but he was old enough to have hit her, and it seemed she didn't mind returning the favor. Billie grabbed him by the hair and propelled him across the room, tossed him to the floor. When he looked up, his eyes were full of tears, and Rick felt badly for a few seconds, until he remembered that the little shit had hurt Billie.

He listened at the phone again, tapped the lever on the wall unit to try to clear the line, but it remained dead.

"Nothing?" Billie asked, forehead creased with worry.

Rick hung up. "I know I said I didn't want to go home, but I think we have to. Even if the phones are out all over the street and not just here, I have to tell my parents what's going on. They'll call the cops, or take us down to the police station if our phone's out, too."

"I don't know," Billie said, glancing around the kitchen. "The doors are locked. I want to wait until my parents come home."

"But we don't know when that will be. And you can't call them."

On the floor, Leonard curled up and began to whine. It stopped Rick cold. After what this kid had already been through tonight, now they had turned on him. Yes, he had slapped Billie and gone a little crazy, but he was only nine or ten and he was frightened. He tucked his knees up to his chest and made himself a little ball.

"Leonard," Rick said. "It's okay, man. It'll be okay."

It surprised Rick to realize he meant it. They would be all right—and the sooner they turned these problems over to the adults who were supposed to handle things like this, the better off they would be. He didn't want to argue with Billie, and he didn't want to go back outside by himself, but if she would not come with him to his house, Rick decided he would have to go alone.

"Billie—" he began.

But she held up a hand. Her face had gone slack and slightly pale. She gestured for him to step closer to the wall as she dropped into a crouch.

"What are you doing?"

Billie shushed him and moved on her hands and knees from the kitchen into the living room. At the sofa, she raised her head, looking over the top of the cushions.

By then, Rick understood. "Who is it?"

He dropped to the floor and scuttled past Leonard.

"It's him," the kid whispered. His eyes were pressed tightly shut. "I told you he was coming."

"You said midnight. It's not midnight yet."

Leonard whimpered.

Rick propped himself beside Billie and saw what she had seen—a figure in the street, moving swiftly. The streetlight in front of the Panzas' house flickered, so the woman outside turned from human to silhouette and back again, but Rick saw it was Ruth, and he cursed under his breath. He had expected Zack to come after them, but here was Ruth.

She picked up her pace, almost running, and then cut diagonally across Billie's front yard, heading straight for the house.

He jerked away from the sofa. "Jesus. Here she comes."

Billie turned to stare at him. "What the hell do we do?"

"We run."

"The doors are locked. Everything—"

Rick shook his head. "No, Billie. Nobody's home, the phone is out. If she's out there, Zack's probably out there, too. They can't let us tell the police what happened. You think they'll stop at smashing a window or kicking in the back door?"

Billie clenched her fists, still on her knees. "Shit!"

She sprang to her feet, ran to the kitchen. "Get him up!" she barked, pointing at Leonard, but Rick did not need to help

Leonard up. The kid was already rising as she went to the kitchen, unlocked the back door, and swung it open.

"No sign of Zack," she whispered.

Before Rick could debate with her, she rushed out, and all he could do was follow her, with Leonard in tow. They bolted back the way they had come across the Panzas' backyard. Rick had never hoped Mrs. Panza would catch them back there, but tonight, he wanted to be seen. He would have screamed for the racist old bat if he hadn't been afraid of giving their location away to Ruth.

They passed the Panzas' house and ran toward Rick's own backyard. Some of the lights were still on in the Haunted Woods, which meant his dad must still be back there. He didn't care about his parents' fight anymore, didn't care about his mom cheating, he just wanted to see them, wanted them to be here with him.

"Dad!" he shouted.

But that one word was drowned out by Ruth Burgess screaming in terror. Rick turned toward that scream but tried to keep walking, backward, and tripped. He fell on his ass, partially broke his fall with his left hand, and propped himself up just in time to see Ruth run through the big plastic gates that had been set up for the Haunted Woods. A shadow stalked behind her, swift but gawky, moving like a praying mantis or a man on stilts. A long coat hung around it, a hood over its head. In the cavern of that hood was the orange glow of flame, as if someone had carved that hooded person's skull like a jack-o'-lantern.

In three more strides, it dragged Ruth to the grass. Her scream turned to a roar of pain, cut off mid-note with only a momentary echo left behind. The thing huddled over her, reached down with one long hand, and tipped her head to one side, where it flopped unnaturally.

Billie took a fistful of Rick's jacket and hauled him to his feet. Leonard looked as if he might have wet his pants, and Rick did not blame him. He took a glance at his house, gauged the distance, and then the shrouded figure standing over Ruth Burgess's corpse looked up at them.

"*Mine*," it said in a voice that seemed carried on the wind from far, far away.

Rick took Billie's hand and they ran for the woods behind the Panzas' house, where the trees grew more densely and the paths were less familiar. Rick thought about his parents and about his sister Chloe, but they would have to fend for themselves.

"Is that it, Leonard?" Billie asked, breathing hard as the three of them darted in among the trees and began to weave themselves deeper and deeper into the forest. "Is that the Cunning Man?"

The boy said nothing, but the terror in his moonlit eyes was all the answer they required.

TONY BARBOSA

In the eerie glow that still lit a section of the Haunted Woods, Tony sat on a stool and stared at Raggedy Ann. Beneath her pale doll makeup, he could see freckles on the little girl's cheeks. Her eyes were wide and pleading in a way that made his chest ache. His life might have been falling apart, but that did not compare to a lost little girl whose mind had broken.

That had to be it.

"Delilah," he said, as that was her name, "all of this is . . . I can see you're a smart girl, but you have to know even at your age how crazy this all sounds."

He had pulled the stool out from behind a curtain so that he could sit and be on the same level with the girl. This close, he could not have missed the disappointment in her eyes, and maybe a bit of anger, too.

"Mr. Barbosa, that's mean. I'm not crazy."

He held up his hands, hating that he'd hurt her feelings. "I know. I know, but—"

"I'm telling the truth. The Cunning Man is coming."

When she said his name, she lowered her voice as if she thought he might be listening, and she glanced over her shoulder into the woods with such nervousness that Tony had to follow that glance. He believed none of this, but her certainty unnerved him.

Tony gave her wrist a little squeeze so that she looked him in the eye. "The other things you were saying? Where you're from? The time—"

Delilah yanked her hand from his grasp and backed up a few steps, ready to run. "I thought you were nice. I thought you would help me."

"I want to help," he assured her. "Some of that's a little hard to swallow, that's all. Please, kid, tell me how to get in touch with your parents."

"Can't you bring me into the house?" Delilah asked. "Just for a little while?"

He thought about that and how Alice would react. If he tried to explain the story this little girl had just told him, she would have him committed to a mental hospital. Obviously, Delilah had invented some kind of fantasy to process her fears, but her terror at the impending arrival of the so-called Cunning Man felt real enough.

Delilah cocked her head and seemed to be sniffing the air, her dirty antique Raggedy Ann in her arms. "Wait. Where are the children?"

"They're out for Halloween. But they'll be home soon. Rick should be back in a few minutes. I'm sure he'd be glad—"

"The other children. The ones who were here earlier, scaring one another? I need them."

Tony smiled. "They've all gone home. But let's get you inside, okay? You can meet my wife." His more or less ex-wife, but no need to explain to Delilah. "And we'll get you some help. It'll be okay."

The little girl took a step backward, as if she intended to retreat further. She had wanted to go inside, but now that she knew the kids weren't there, she seemed to have changed her mind. Her face was mostly in shadow, but he could see the glint of tears on her face. "No, it won't. Not ever."

Tony started to argue, but his words were cut off by a scream, somewhere out by the road. His breath hitched, and he turned to peer through the woods. Had he heard something else, another voice underneath the screaming? It had been there and then gone.

"Come on, sweetheart," he said, reaching out to grab Delilah by the wrist. "We've gotta go."

Clutching her Raggedy Ann doll, she dashed behind a black curtain. Tony shot a quick look toward his house and the neighborhood, but he could see nothing through the trees. The screaming hadn't sounded like Chloe or Alice, as far as he could tell, and it had stopped now. The urge to run toward it, to help whoever had cried out, tugged at him, but no matter how wild her story was or how much of a headache she had become, he could not leave Delilah out here alone.

He ducked past the black curtain and pursued Delilah deeper into the woods, past the last generator and beyond the Haunted Woods. Into the dark.

RICK BARBOSA

Rick and Billie had taken Leonard along one of the trails they often used. It ran through the woods behind the Panzas', then Billie's house, and then the next, the oldest home on Parmenter Road. The big colonial belonged to Mr. Xenakis, a grumpy old man who never gave out candy on Halloween, never had visitors, and snapped at any kid, even Girl Scouts, who tried to go to the door to sell him something.

The stretch of woods between Billie's house and Mr. Xenakis's had always felt safe to them. Quiet and hidden. The woods sloped down to a small stream that burbled into a little culvert that went underneath Parmenter. Big rocks jutted out of the sloping ground. In a spot where the rocks would hide them from prying eyes, hearts pounding, Rick and Billie pulled to a stop and drew Leonard into hiding.

Rick trembled, and it wasn't from the chill. His mind raced, trying to find an explanation for what they had just seen. His subconscious tried to persuade him that it had been some trick of his father's, some last perfect element of Barbosa's Haunted Woods.

"I think it was a prank," he said, growing irritated. Chloe must have been there, too, hiding. Instead of pranking her,

Dad had recruited her, and they'd done this to terrify him and Billie.

Billie didn't think so. "Don't be stupid."

Rick flinched. "Hey."

She grabbed him by the chin and brought her face within inches of his. Another night, he would have thought she meant to kiss him, but not tonight. Not with the hard glint in her eyes.

"Whatever that was, it wasn't a prank," Billie said. "Ruth came looking for us, and that thing broke her neck. You saw."

"My dad—" he tried weakly.

"No. You don't even believe that."

She was right, of course. Ruth had been after them. His dad could not have been involved with that. Which meant it had to be real—all of it.

"Jesus."

Leonard stood a few feet away, hunched over and watching the trees around them as if he thought bats might swoop down and drag them away. The kid had his hands in his pockets.

"What time is it?" he asked.

Rick stared at him. "What difference does that make?"

"We need to stay away from him until midnight."

Billie slapped her palms against the rock. "That's enough of that shit." She pointed at Leonard. "You talk to me right now about what we just saw!"

Leonard blanched. "I told you. It's the Cunning Man."

"That was no man," Billie said. She leaned against the stone and slid down until her butt hit the ground. Her eyes were wide and searching, as if the woods would offer up an explanation.

Rick huddled close to Billie on the ground. "Leonard. Sit down."

Leonard obeyed, and the three of them made an intimate triangle, there in the lee of those rocks, hidden in the woods above the stream.

"Ruth . . ." Rick began.

"Is dead," Billie said flatly. "Maybe Zack, too."

"They wanted to take me. Hurt me. The Cunning Man doesn't like competition."

"What the hell is he?" Billie asked, and this time, her voice was almost pleading.

Leonard peered up into the branches, and when he spoke again, his voice seemed older, a bit lower in register and thin, as if he had suddenly grown hoarse. His eyes seemed more focused, clearer, and Rick thought he was face-to-face with the real Leonard for the first time. Like the kid had been hiding his true self until now.

"My name is Leonard Blanchet. I don't know what year it is—"

Billie scoffed, shaking her head. "What the hell are you talking about?"

"Shush," Rick said. "Let him talk."

Leonard studied their eyes. "Last I knew, it was 1961. I was trick-or-treating with my sister, Nancy. I ran ahead because I knew the old couple at the end of the street liked to give out homemade chocolate chip cookies in little brown paper bags, but they only kept it up until the cookies ran out. I didn't want to miss those cookies."

"Where was this?" Rick asked.

Billie gawked at him as if he had lost his mind. "Did you hit your head? You can't—"

"Please," Rick said, reaching out to take her hand. "Billie, listen to him. You saw that thing. . . . You saw what happened to Ruth."

She bit her lip, but she held his hand more tightly and did not let go.

"I saw a big group of kids on the street ahead of me, and I didn't want them getting to those cookies before me. I didn't want them to run out." While he spoke, Leonard began to well up with tears. His breath hitched. "There was a turn in the road. Nancy shouted at me when I did it, but I ran into the backyard of this one house. I knew I could use it as a shortcut to get in front of that big group of kids.

"And that's when he took me. In the dark in the back of that old house, with a big dog barking at the end of his chain. I didn't call him the Cunning Man then. He has other names, but I learned that one later. He pulled me close, and I smelled something awful—like dirt and dead flowers and rotten apples—and I closed my eyes."

Leonard closed his eyes then, too. Tears slid down his face. "When I opened them, I wasn't in Iowa anymore."

For a few seconds, none of them spoke. The stream burbled and the wind rustled the branches. Yellow leaves blew around them.

"Where were you?" Billie asked.

Now, Leonard could only whisper. "He calls it 'Dubnos.' It's a dead place. The trees are burned black, and nothing grows. It's so cold, but there are places where fires burn in the ground. You never see animals, but you always know something is there, watching."

"Jesus Christ," Billie rasped.

Rick stared at Leonard. He knew none of this could be true, that it had to be the kid's imagination. But they had seen the Cunning Man kill Ruth—had seen the little flames that burned inside its head.

"You got away," he said.

Leonard nodded. His lower lip trembled. "It's Halloween. One of the older kids called it a . . . limal? A 'liminal time.' That means if you're quick, if you know where to walk, you can get from there to here."

"Christ," Billie said again.

"I know I can never go home," Leonard said, imploring. "But please just help me a little while longer. Just till midnight. After that, he can't take me back. I'd rather be lost here than trapped there, never changing, never eating, never drinking, never living.

"Please."

VANESSA MONTEZ

In the Koenigs' backyard, eleven o'clock had arrived, and the party began to wind down. Most of the partygoers had only been there a couple of hours, but Mr. Koenig and his friends had been on the deck since late afternoon, and their booming laughter kicked up every few minutes to disrupt the other guests, many of whom were already wishing one another good night. The music had been turned down, presumably by Mrs. Koenig at the request of one neighbor or another who had already gone home, maybe with a kiddie or two who might be awakened by the loud music in the Koenigs' yard. Vanessa had babysat enough times to know that once you'd managed to get a baby or a toddler to sleep, you might be willing to strangle anyone rude enough to wake them.

Owen's hidden alcohol stash had been depleted and some of his friends had departed, but he had stayed behind. Vanessa sat in an Adirondack chair by the firepit in the backyard and glanced at the circle of friends who remained. Steve was there—it was his house—along with Owen, Chloe Barbosa, Cynthia Walukevich, and Hunter Kenney.

And Julia Sweeney, of course . . . sitting on the arm of the Adirondack chair, laughing with Vanessa, comfortable together. They had both been drinking, but not so much that they could forget their surroundings. Still, it felt nice—just to be together in the way she had so often seen boys and girls together—like they were connected, at least for tonight, by a kind of tether, an energy. She might have called it desire, though that seemed so sexual and yes, that, too, but this was also something more. Desire for understanding, for appreciation, for the kind of knowledge of another person that went beyond simple friendship. Being friends with Steve meant hearing about his dreams, investing in those dreams, caring about them because she cared about him. But she yearned to be part of someone's dreams, to be the fulfillment of those dreams, even if just for a little while.

Owen started talking about what they would do after graduation, but Vanessa didn't want to think that far ahead. Not tonight.

"I'd like to backpack across Europe," Steve said.

Vanessa half smiled at him. "You've never told me that."

He shrugged. "I'm a year behind you. By the time I graduate, you'll have a roommate from Greece or something and be off on your own adventures. I'll have to make my own."

"What if I haven't had any adventures by then?" she said, half-joking, half-drunkenly earnest.

Steve smiled at her with a warmth and a wisdom that made him seem far older than the rest of them, though he was a year younger. She remembered, then, why they had been best friends for so long.

"You're like Indiana Jones. 'If adventure has a name, it must be Vanessa Montez.'"

"Oh, I like that," Julia said, turning toward her. "I want adventures!"

Vanessa linked arms with her, happy to be a girl. If she had been a guy, there would have been no misinterpreting this moment. But girls displayed this kind of affection all the time. It was a silver lining.

Steve raised his cup, which by now contained only root beer. "You are all invited to join me."

Chloe glanced at Hunter and Cynthia. "I don't know about you guys, but I'd like to see more of America before I go anywhere else. I want to drive cross-country. I've read so many books and seen so many movies, but I want to go into every diner and dive bar, swim every lake, and climb every mountain I can find."

Steve pointed at her. "You should be a travel writer, Chloe. Just, like, do it for a living."

Chloe blinked. "That's actually a really good idea. I never thought of it like that."

It was strange for Vanessa, looking around that circle at her friends. Steve had always been closest to her, and over the years, some of these people had been enemies, then friends, then enemies again. She had a visceral disdain for Hunter in particular. And yet this was senior year, and the thought of what came afterward turned bittersweet in her mouth. They had nearly seven months to go, but tonight already felt like the beginning of the end, and it was as if they all sensed it. Whatever they had meant to one another in the past, they were going through this moment together, and it brought them closer.

Vanessa lay her head on Julia's shoulder.

Julia bent down to whisper something, and they were not the words Vanessa expected.

"Do you smell hot dogs?"

Vanessa laughed. She sat forward and craned her neck to look toward the deck. Dozens of people were still at the party, but dozens more had already left. She was a bit surprised to see her mother chatting with the Kenneys, whom she usually avoided. Her dad stood on the deck amid a group of Mr. Koenig's business friends, arguing about the New England Patriots. The team's owner had fired coach Ron Meyer after the Pats had taken a drubbing from the Dolphins, and immediately hired a new guy named Raymond Berry. Berry had just won his first game, and Vanessa's dad had declared him the second coming of Jesus, insisting he would take the Patriots to the Super Bowl. Mr. Koenig and his friends were less confident.

Football. Vanessa rolled her eyes, but she did think her dad's enthusiasm was sort of adorable.

"My dad always does this," Steve said. "End of the night, things are winding down, one last round of beers and dogs before he kicks everyone out."

Vanessa glanced at Julia. "You want a hot dog, don't you?"

Julia's eyes lit up. "At least one."

"I could eat," Vanessa replied.

They rose together from the Adirondack chair. Vanessa marveled at how comfortable she felt already. She and Julia had known each other forever, but there had always been a wall between them, because Julia always seemed to find it so easy to fit in and Vanessa never had. Now she knew that both of them had felt alone and misunderstood in a world that didn't want to understand them. Julia had just been better at hiding it.

"Get me a dog!" Owen called to them.

Vanessa gave him a thumbs-up. Julia linked arms with her again as they walked toward the deck. Her mother spotted her and raised an eyebrow, a tiny glimmer of maternal excitement shining on her face before she covered it up. Mama Montez wouldn't want to draw attention to the girls, but she seemed to understand what was going on between them, and Vanessa gave her a little smile to confirm it.

"Hi, Mom!" she said as she and Julia mounted the steps to the deck. "Want a hot dog?"

"I'm all set, honey. Thank you."

The smell of the firepit smoke melded with the aroma of things cooking on the grill. Music and conversation were the soundtrack of the night. Vanessa felt exhausted, but good. Very good.

Then she glanced toward the grill and saw the way Mr. Koenig stared at her and Julia, and her stomach dropped. He seemed to focus on their linked arms, then he looked up at her with a sneer. His eyes were red from the smoke and too much beer.

"That's enough of that shit," he said, the edge in his voice sharp enough to cut through much of the chatter on the deck. His tone drew the attention of several of his friends.

Vanessa felt ice slide up her spine. She swallowed hard, separating herself from Julia as she picked up a paper plate from the table on the deck. "The guys sent us up for hot dogs," she said. "Steve said this would be last call."

"Oh, 'the guys' sent you?" Mr. Koenig said, dripping with disdain.

He glanced at his friends, and Vanessa saw the way they looked at her and knew that a conversation had already taken place here that concerned her. The realization made her want to throw up.

Julia had stiffened, glancing around in confusion, trying to read the tension and hostility that seemed to have come out of nowhere. Mr. Koenig used his bare fingers to pluck a hot dog from the grill and drop it onto a bun. He reached out and put it on Vanessa's plate.

"There you go. About the only way you like 'em, isn't it?" he said.

Vanessa wanted to scurry away, to hide under the deck

or run home and lock herself in her room. She had known this man her entire life. He might have been a blowhard, a conservative asshole who cared nothing for anyone who didn't look and think like he did, but he and his wife had been kind to her over the years. How many times had she been out to eat or the movies or to the beach with Steve and his parents? How many times had she played in the sandbox that used to be where the firepit now sat?

But Julia didn't have that history. Maybe she was braver, or maybe she just had less to lose. She took a step forward, straightened her spine, and for the first time, Vanessa realized how tall she was—nearly as tall as Mr. Koenig.

"What's *that* supposed to mean?" she demanded.

Mr. Koenig laughed. Some of his friends snickered.

"It means your friend here is a little dyke, and from the looks of things, she's converted you. I guess it's no surprise, though. Donnie Sweeney's such a pussy hound, why would his daughter be any different?"

Vanessa went numb. Her mouth hung open. The plate and hot dog fell from her hands as Mr. Koenig's friends whistled and laughed. One of them muttered something appreciative of the line the man had just crossed. Julia turned red, hands clenched into fists at her side.

"Oh, you're gonna cry now?" Mr. Koenig said to Julia. "Guess you should've thought of that before. A couple of abominations, you are. If it was up to me, you wouldn't even—"

He got no further.

Vanessa saw a shape moving out of the corner of her eye, and for a moment, she felt a chill, as she had in the Haunted Woods earlier that night. But this was no shadow—it was her father. Johnny Montez had a reputation as an amiable guy, a friendly neighbor, but he had come to this country as a child, had lived in poverty with his single Dominican mother. He remembered being spit on by neighborhood children who mocked his accent and his height and his mother, and anything else they could think of. Vanessa had heard the stories all her life from a father who strove for peace of mind and heart.

The man who crossed the deck was her father, but not any version of him she had ever seen. Johnny Montez reverted to speaking Spanish for a few seconds. He grabbed the front of Mr. Koenig's shirt. The white man tried to defend himself, and Vanessa's dad knocked his hands away. He hesitated long enough so there could be no mistaking the purpose behind what came next, so anyone watching would understand that he'd thought about what he was going to do, and then he punched Mr. Koenig so hard that blood flew from the white man's mouth.

"Papi!" Vanessa tried to grab him, but Julia caught her around the waist and held her back. All Vanessa could think about was the trouble her father would get into, no matter how glad she was to see Mr. Koenig hurt.

Mr. Koenig staggered backward, glanced down to see that his shirt had torn and blood spattered the fabric. He looked up at Vanessa's father with hatred in his eyes, all the alcohol seeming to have burned away. Or maybe he'd not been that drunk to begin with—and that made it all so much worse.

"You fucking spic," Mr. Koenig spat. "You got a lotta nerve. I thought your culture hated the gays, and here you are with a little dyke for a—"

Johnny Montez spat on him. Maybe a flashback to his own childhood or the only way he could express his disgust. Koenig gaped, so stunned that he couldn't speak.

Vanessa's father stepped toward him, ducked a punch from Mr. Koenig, and then hit him three times in quick succession, temple, kidney, gut. Mr. Koenig bent over, wheezing, desperate to get air into his lungs. Two of his friends approached

Vanessa's dad on either side, trying to tell him that he had done enough, that it was over, but Mr. Koenig roared and went at him like a bull, bent over and snorting.

And like a toreador, Vanessa's father sidestepped. He grabbed a handful of Mr. Koenig's hair and his belt and kept the man's momentum going, hurling him into his own tiki bar like he was throwing out the trash. A woman screamed—Mrs. Koenig or Vanessa's mom or someone else, she had no idea—and Mr. Koenig flopped to the deck amid the wreckage of the flimsy tiki bar.

Johnny Montez pointed at him. "You ever so much as speak my daughter's name again, and we'll pick up where we left off, you miserable prick."

He turned, walked toward Vanessa, and kissed her on the forehead, then took her mother by the hand. Wide-eyed spectators were already starting to whisper behind their hands as John and Lucy Montez went down the three steps to the lawn and headed toward home. Mrs. Montez glared murder at the women who were still gawking.

Breathless, Vanessa lowered her gaze and began to follow. Emotions were at war within her—so many painful feelings, but also a pure joy and love for her father and mother. Automatically, she went down those three steps off the deck, aware of Julia following quietly in her wake but unable to formulate any kind of thought about what to do next except to go home. To hug her parents, grateful for their love.

Then she lifted her head and saw Steve Koenig standing on the grass, watching her go. Steve. Her lifelong best friend. Pale and silent and expressionless, struggling with his own emotions.

And it hit her.

Steve.

Mr. Koenig had muttered something earlier in the day about her eating a box lunch, in retrospect a direct slur. Then tonight, he'd been telling his friends about her even before he had seen her come onto the deck arm in arm with Julia—something lots of straight girls might do. Mr. Koenig hadn't been guessing she was a lesbian, he had been certain. And there was only one way for him to be that certain.

"Oh my God," she said. One hand fluttered to her mouth. This hurt her even more than the hideous words and the public humiliation she'd just endured. This was so much worse. "You told him? You fucking told him?"

Steve started to shake his head, but it was halfhearted. He managed to say her name. "Vanessa."

Her best friend forever. She felt like throwing up. Wiping at her eyes, she turned and ran for the woods. Steve called after her—only Steve, nobody else.

Then she heard Julia's voice rising. "Stay there, asshole. You've done enough."

Vanessa crashed through the thin branches of trees, found a path, and jogged deeper into the woods. Hot tears slid down her face, and she stopped trying to wipe them away. The hurt of his betrayal cut deep and then became fury. Later, she knew she would feel the anguish again, but now the bright flame of rage kept burning higher. Steve had known how closely she held this secret, had known that he was the only person she had ever told, and he had revealed it to his parents? His macho prick of a father?

She wanted to do to him what her dad had done to Steve's father.

Her feet slowed. She heard footfalls on the path behind her and knew instantly that it would be Steve. Part of her screamed inwardly, not wanting the pain of seeing him, but the other half of her was grateful for the opportunity to hurt him back.

But when she turned, it wasn't Steve on the path. It was Julia.

"Vanessa . . ."

Her eyes were wide open, so blue even in the dark, as if the moonlight had sought her out. Vanessa thought she looked like an angel, and the cynical little voice that always seemed to accompany her every pure thought mocked her from within. But goddamn it, with that red hair shining in the dark, she *did* look like an angel. In the midst of her own drama, Vanessa had forgotten about what Julia had been through tonight. Her father had left his family, then shown up at the Haunted Woods and admitted to cheating on her mom. Now Julia had been outed along with Vanessa, almost as collateral damage.

"Holy shit," Vanessa breathed. "What the fuck is wrong with all the parents in this neighborhood tonight?"

"Not just tonight," Julia said. "They've been messed up for a long time. But not your dad. Your old man was badass!"

Vanessa wiped her eyes. "He kinda was."

"No kinda about it," Julia replied. She stood in a splash of moonlight that streamed through the branches above. As confident as she always seemed, just then she looked as lost as Vanessa felt. "Listen, why don't we go back to your house? Your folks are probably wondering where you went."

"I can't right now. I just need a minute." Vanessa deflated. "Fuckin' *Steve*. He outed me to his parents. I just couldn't look at his face for another second."

Julia went to her then, put her hands on Vanessa's arms. "I'm so sorry. I can't believe he did that to you."

Vanessa closed her eyes and listened to the sounds of the night. She felt Julia's hands on her arms. In the small space that separated them now, she inhaled a warmth that she thought might be Julia's breath, and the intimacy of that made her tremble.

"Are you cold?" Julia asked.

Vanessa couldn't help but smile, just a little. In spite of everything.

She knew she wasn't thinking straight, that someday she would look back on tonight as something cruel and painful, and that her first time kissing another girl—kissing someone she yearned so desperately to kiss—shouldn't be under these circumstances. But that caution also made her wonder if this might not be the perfect moment. After all, fifty years from now, what would she rather remember?

"You've got the most mischievous smile on your face," Julia said.

Vanessa opened her eyes. "You told me you were going to kiss me tonight."

Julia blinked in surprise, but when Vanessa slid her arms around Julia's waist and tilted back her head, the taller girl did not hesitate. When Julia's lips touched hers, softly at first and then more urgently, Vanessa felt as if the cruelty heaped upon her tonight—cruelty that had been meant to diminish her, even break her—had set her free. She pressed her body against Julia's, and time slipped away. She traced her fingers along Julia's face. How many times had she daydreamed about this and wished Julia felt the same way? And here they were.

The worst night of her life, and the best.

"Oh my God, how are you so beautiful?" Julia whispered.

Vanessa beamed. "That's supposed to be my line."

"Shut up."

They kissed again, and Vanessa let herself get lost in that moment.

In the woods, something shifted. Something big.

A branch snapped underfoot.

Holding each other, rudely awakened from this dream, the girls turned to seek the source of those sounds.

And they found it.

TONY BARBOSA

One of the primary factors in Tony's decision to buy this property was the inclusion of a stretch of protected woodland that could never be developed. It backed onto state forest with miles of hiking trails. People rode their horses in the state lands, and hikers used the paths year-round. Tony knew all those trails very well, but as he followed Delilah through the woods, he realized he had lost his way.

This path did not look familiar to him at all.

Despite the dark, and the way the trees screened out so much of the moonlight, that did not seem possible. Yet as he glimpsed the red mop of a Raggedy Ann wig again and quickened his pace, he knew it was true. The old hemlock and spruce trees around him were much taller, much older than he had encountered in these woods before. He would have remembered a section of old-growth forest like this.

"Delilah, wait!" he called. "I just want to help!"

Sweat filmed his forehead, and his hands felt clammy. The final hour of October had arrived, and the temperature kept dropping, yet the crisp chill in the air did nothing to allay the strange fever that had crept up on him.

A flash of red ahead. Delilah dashed around a turn in the trail. Tony swore under his breath and bent into a run, worried about the time it would take to find his way back home with this girl. The night had already been disaster enough, but now it seemed almost absurdly eventful. He wouldn't soon forget Halloween 1984.

Tony ducked a maple branch and darted around the same bend in the path, only to see that at last Delilah had come to a halt. Relieved, he slowed down, skidded on pine needles but managed to catch himself before he would have fallen.

"Kid," he said, sucking air to catch his breath as he slow-walked toward the clearing where she had stopped. "Please let's not run anymore."

In the dark, Delilah looked like a life-size Raggedy Ann doll, a fixture he might have put in his Haunted Woods, an animatronic whose eyes might light up or whose jaw would unhinge into a gale of high, shrieking laughter. It would have scared the shit out of the kids, and probably the grown-ups, too. He felt another moment of sorrow that the Haunted Woods existed now only in the past.

"You're creepy when you want to be, aren't you?" he asked.

Delilah said nothing. He could hear her breathing and felt some satisfaction to know that she seemed a little wrung out by the run through the woods. For the first time, he noticed the tree behind her, a massive white oak, gnarled and huge and ancient. That was definitely the word that came to mind, and it made him wonder just how old it might be. Centuries, at least.

"You're making me angry, mister," the little girl said. And though her voice was still that of a little girl, the way she spoke—brittle, deliberate—felt very mature indeed.

"I'm not trying to upset you, honey," Tony replied, walking slowly toward her, one hand outstretched, like she was a spooked horse he wanted to saddle. "The opposite. I want to help you."

"The police can't do anything for me."

"Okay. No police," Tony said, knowing it was a lie. "But how else can I help you?"

Delilah looked as if she might run again. Her body language seemed tensed to bolt. Tony went down on one knee, slowly, and then lowered his other knee to the ground, so she could see he no longer meant to chase her.

"You've made me very angry," Delilah said in that same, brittle tone.

Tony exhaled. "I seem to have mastered disappointing people. It's not my intention. But I'm tired, Delilah, and it's been a long night. A long year. So please just tell me—"

She darted her head forward. Her eyes shone in the dark. "You sent the children home."

He flinched. "Excuse me?"

"The children. The frightened children. The screaming ones. I stayed nearby because I knew they would come, but you sent them home too soon, and I need them."

"What do you mean, you 'need' them?"

Petulant, she rolled her eyes and blew out a frustrated breath.

Then she brought the rock out from behind her back and struck him in the left temple with a crack and a spray of blood. Tony felt the spike of pain that shot through his skull, felt himself tumbling sideways toward the ground, and then nothing.

The night swallowed him completely.

ALICE BARBOSA

Alice sat alone in her living room, trying to pretend it was a normal night. The eleven o'clock news had begun, but she found it hard to focus on Chet Curtis and Natalie Jacobson, the married couple who seemed always to be smiling behind the desk no matter how grim the news. Alice studied Chet and Nat, as locals called them, and wondered what their secret might be. How could they live together and work together and still smile like that? She had married a good guy—Alice had never doubted that Tony was one of the good ones—but that had not prevented their relationship from eroding.

"How do you do it, Nat?" she asked the news anchor.

Alice picked up the crossword book she had been working on and studied clue 37 Down. *Arcade game developed by Namco and first released in Japan in May 1980.* Alice sometimes brought the kids to Fun and Games, the arcade downtown, but she had no idea which game this might refer to. Six letters.

Minutes passed. The page blurred in front of her eyes.

She glanced at the little brass clock on the mantel, wondering what could be taking Tony so long. Had he decided to stay out there and freeze, just to spite her?

Alice tossed her crossword book onto the coffee table. The

last thing she wanted was to face Tony again tonight. They had both been humiliated by Donnie Sweeney's drunken revelations, but to Tony, it had been a slap in the face. After all, she had been the one screwing around behind his back. The hurt and humiliation of such a public spectacle would infuriate anyone. But even after all of that, Tony ought to have come back inside by now. It was late and cold outside.

"Damn it," she muttered.

She stood and slipped her feet into the loosely laced boots she often wore when tromping around the yard or the woods. The rest of the conversation she dreaded would happen one way or another, and she would rather get it over with so that she could go to bed and fast-forward to tomorrow morning. Christmas shopping, she would tell Tony, and she would definitely do some shopping, but she would get out of the house early, mostly to avoid being home.

Tonight, though—she wasn't coward enough to hide from him. He deserved better than that.

Alice pulled on a fuzzy sweater and started for the sliding glass door off the kitchen. As she opened it, she heard the rattle of the front door opening.

"Tony?" she called.

"It's me."

Not Tony, then. Chloe.

Alice's stomach dropped. But even as Chloe walked through the house in search of her and stepped into the kitchen, Alice frowned with another thought.

"Have you seen your brother?" she asked.

Chloe glanced around as if Alice had somehow misplaced him. "Rick's not home yet?"

"Not yet. He's probably at Billie's, but it's getting awful late."

"I guess. But it's Halloween, and he *is* thirteen." Chloe

opened the refrigerator door and bent her head to look inside, studying the contents of the fridge in the way teenagers did. She wasn't hungry, just considering. Alice had seen it a thousand times.

"It's after eleven, Chloe. Did he show up at the Koenigs'?" Alice asked.

Chloe closed the fridge. "I didn't see him. But if he did, it's over now anyway."

Alice noticed an edge in her voice. "What happened?"

"Mr. Koenig was an asshole to Vanessa Montez. The worst. Mr. Montez kicked his ass."

"Oh my God." Yet even as she reacted, in her heart, Alice was thinking this had to be good news for her. At least she wouldn't be the only object of gossip and ridicule on Parmenter Road.

Chloe studied her, eyes narrowed. "Sounds like the whole neighborhood's a mess tonight, huh? I heard things got ugly down here."

Sour bile rushed up the back of Alice's throat. No, no. She did not want to have this conversation. Fighting the urge to look away, she met her daughter's accusing stare.

"They were talking about it at the party?"

Chloe shrugged. "Not everyone. But I overheard Mrs. Coleman. I didn't let on that I'd heard anything. I didn't want anyone to try to make me feel better—that would've made it worse. I'm disgusted enough as it is."

Alice winced. "Chloe—"

"Don't, Mom."

"Can I just tell you I'm sorry?"

Her daughter stared at her. Her upper lip curled and her nostrils flared, but Alice couldn't be sure if what she saw on Chloe's face was anger, revulsion, or heartbreak.

"Chloe . . ."

"You're sorry. So you said. And now I don't ever want to talk about it again. Where's Dad?"

"He was out back shutting off the generators, but it's been a while. I was just about to go out and look for him."

Chloe seemed to notice her boots and sweater for the first time, and nodded thoughtfully. "You think maybe he took off or he's avoiding you."

"I couldn't blame him. But if he's out in the woods or trying to break down the props and things tonight, I'd like to talk him into going to bed and dealing with it tomorrow."

Chloe still looked disgusted, but she nodded. "Okay. Let's go."

"Maybe I should go alone?"

"You shouldn't go at all. I'm sure he'd rather not see you. But if you're going, let's go together." Chloe walked around the kitchen table and went to the sliding door. As she went outside, she looked over her shoulder at her mother. "Don't say anything to Rick. About what happened tonight. About what you *did*."

Alice hurried after her, closing the slider while Chloe was already descending the steps from the deck to the backyard. "Why would I do that? Of course not."

"Your behavior's turned out to be pretty unpredictable, Mom. So I'm just making sure."

Alice no longer had the heart to defend herself. She followed Chloe down the steps and across the backyard. There were still lights gleaming back in the woods, closer to the exit from the Haunted Woods, so Chloe headed for that path instead of the one they had always used for people to enter their homemade spooky attraction.

Chloe seemed to quicken her pace as they entered the woods, almost as if she might try to lose her mother among the trees. Alice thought of Hansel and Gretel, and the way their stepfather purposely got them lost in the woods. She wouldn't get lost back here, but maybe Chloe wished she would.

"It's so creepy in the dark, when everyone's gone," Alice said.

The banshee screamed out of the trees up ahead. Chloe didn't even flinch—so used to such things by now—but Alice jumped even though she was still a dozen feet away. The woods seemed strangely quiet, aside from that banshee wail. No more spooky music or unsettling laughter. Just the woods, and the last vestiges of a joy that Tony and their daughter had always shared. And now Donnie Sweeney would be what came to mind whenever either of them thought of the Haunted Woods. All those years of good memories, stained forever by the fallout from Alice's poor decisions. She hadn't seen it that way before, and now that she did, regret nearly knocked the air out of her lungs.

Up ahead, Chloe came to an abrupt stop on the path. "What are you doing back here? Did you get left behind, honey?"

Her tone confused Alice. Chloe wouldn't talk to her father that way. But when Chloe dropped to one knee, Alice saw the little girl coming toward her on the path. In her vintage Raggedy Ann costume, she should have seemed bright and cheerful, but instead, she seemed pitiful and desperate. The girl opened her arms as she rushed at Chloe, and Alice stiffened. Her own daughter might be growing up, but she remained a child, still in high school, and Alice was the mother—the adult. Seeing Chloe act as the grown-up made her feel old and alone.

"Hey, it's okay," Chloe said, hugging the child. "I've got you."

As Alice walked up behind Chloe, she saw the little Raggedy Ann shudder and sob.

"I was so scared," the little girl said.

"What's your name, darling?" Alice asked.

"Delilah."

"Did you see a man out here, Delilah?" Alice said. "My husband, Tony, should be here. He's tall—dark hair, kind of a big guy."

The girl did not look up. Alice felt strangely invisible. Her daughter did not want to see her, and this lost child seemed to have eyes only for Chloe.

"Can you take me home?" Delilah asked. She trembled, her lower lip quivering. "I'm scared."

Chloe took her hand and stood. "Yeah. Of course. We gotta get you to the house. Your parents must be freaking out."

Alice listened to the silence of the woods. The breeze had died down, and she realized she could hear the hum of the generator. As Chloe turned toward her, ready to guide the little girl home, Alice searched the darkness for Tony. Had he gone off in search of some time to himself? It hadn't occurred to her to check to see that both cars were still in the garage. Normally, he would never leave without telling her, but tonight Tony was liable to do anything, and she could never blame him.

As long as he doesn't hurt himself.

The thought swam up into her mind, and once there, she could not easily dispel it. As furious as he had been, as grievously as she had wounded him, would Tony consider taking his own life? Alice blew out a breath. No way. He would never do that to his children.

"Mom?" Chloe said, the single word prodding her to get out of the way. The tone of that one syllable said it all—she considered Alice an obstacle and maybe an idiot.

"Yes, sorry," Alice said quickly, stepping out of the way.

"You're not coming back to the house?" Chloe asked.

Alice glanced back into the woods. The eerie lighting still illuminated the creepy baby carriage just off the path. Every minute or so, the animatronic baby hand would come over the edge of the carriage, and the monstrously malformed baby head would rise. She hated even to look at these things that Tony had accumulated over the years, had never fully confessed how little she thought of his hobby. They were all ghoulish.

The sooner she could get back to the house, the better. But she owed Tony more than that. After tonight, the least she could do is show him that she cared enough to make sure he was all right.

"I want to see where your father's gotten off to," she said. "You go on. I'll catch up in a few minutes."

The little Raggedy Ann had both hands on Chloe's right arm as if it were a life preserver. Chloe smiled down, trying to comfort her, and the two of them went along the path, triggering the banshee one more time. The scream accompanied Alice as she headed deeper into the woods, listening for movement, worrying about Tony. No matter what might become of their marriage, she had no desire to hurt him any more than necessary.

She called his name.

Only the wind replied.

JULIA SWEENEY

Julia held on to Vanessa, lips still tingling from the urgency of their kiss. They stood frozen, listening to the noises in the woods, but then a branch snapped and something big moved amid the trees, and Julia let instinct take over. She stepped past Vanessa, putting herself between this beautiful girl whom she'd yearned to kiss for so long and whatever came toward them in the dark.

"Please . . ." a male voice said in the dark. "I'm sorry. I didn't mean . . ."

"Who's there?" Julia called, brow furrowing.

A tall, thin shadow came out of the trees and onto the path. He lifted his head, scarecrow makeup like dark slashes across his face in the dim moonlight.

"Arthur?" Vanessa said, voice tight with anger. She stepped up beside Julia. "You're spying on us? What the fuck?"

"No, it's not like that," Arthur said, glancing shamefacedly at the ground. "I saw you—yeah, I saw. But that's not . . . Please just listen to me."

He lifted his eyes. Makeup gleaming. Tears glistening on his night-scarred face.

Julia took Vanessa's hand, glad she didn't pull away. He'd seen them making out, so holding hands felt less like a risk and more like defiance. "We're listening. Make it quick, because spying on us is really creepy."

Arthur shocked her by unbuttoning his coat and untucking his shirt.

Vanessa put up her hands. "Jesus, keep your clothes on."

He ignored her. Wrestling his coat fully open, he dragged his shirt up to reveal a fish-belly-pale chest that nearly glowed, sickly white in the moonlight. Julia twisted away, took a step back, and pulled Vanessa with her. What kind of freak walked up on two people kissing in the woods and decided to disrobe?

But Vanessa resisted Julia's effort to tug her away. "Oh, God," she said, her voice suddenly small and sad. "Who did that to you?"

There were scars all across his chest. Ragged and badly healed, indents where divots of flesh had been dug out and the skin sutured. Torture scars. His scarecrow makeup turned his face into a slash of shadows, but his tears were visible.

"His name is Broghan, but they call him the Cunning Man," Arthur rasped. "I'm sorry . . . really. He's going to come for me, and I need help, just for a little while. An hour. Stay with me an hour, and then I'll be able to go back. I'll be safe."

Julia's thoughts whirled. "Come home with me. My mom will—"

"No!" Arthur snapped, yanking his shirt down as if ashamed of his exposure. His face contorted in frustration. "Nobody else can know. I shouldn't even be here. No parents, no police. Just please stay with me for an hour. Less than an hour. Just till midnight. And then I can go home."

Julia glanced at Vanessa, who gave a silent nod and squeezed her hand, so that Julia nodded, too.

"Okay," she said. "Just till midnight."

The smile of relief that touched his lips in that moment seemed warm, and soft, and true. Julia felt badly for not having liked the boy before, but now they would help him. How could they do any less, after seeing his fear and his scars?

He needed them.

Just till midnight.

DONNIE SWEENEY

Donnie hadn't quite nodded off in his car. All the alcohol he'd consumed over the course of the day had given him the same roller-coaster ride it always did, starting with a buzz, leading up to a giddy good time, then to frustration and anger, on to a blurry kind of despair, and now at last to surrender. Only pride kept him from thinking of this hour sitting in his car as sulking, but deep down, he knew there wasn't really another word for it. He'd shifted sideways behind the wheel, driver's seat back farther than usual, and huddled there with his knees slightly drawn up, not because he felt cold but because it comforted him.

He had to go back inside. Much as it might shock Barb, he had considered divorcing her in the past and had consulted a lawyer friend who specialized in family matters. The advice he had received was not to leave the house—not to move out—because that gave the spouse the upper hand in negotiating the split of assets.

"Fuuuuuck," he moaned, closing his eyes and burrowing against the seat.

Maybe if he just slept it off in the car, he would have a clearer idea of what to do in the morning. Did he care whether the neighbors spotted him out here, driving by him on the way to church or to the farmstand to get cider doughnuts on Sunday morning? He found that he did, but only a little. His reputation with the neighbors had been sealed earlier tonight, and there was no sweeping that back under the rug.

Despite the advice of his divorce lawyer friend, he did not want to stay living in the house. He knew enough judges and other attorneys that he figured moving out wouldn't hurt him too badly in the fight over alimony and child support. But he wanted at least to throw together some clothes and his shaving kit, some toiletries. He had about $500 in cash in a desk drawer in his little home office, and that would come in handy, too. For a couple of nights, he could stay at a decent hotel, clear his head, and start calling around to see which of his friends might be willing to give him a room for a few weeks. Jay Geldof had that enormous rambling Victorian in Nahant all to himself. Six bedrooms and only Jay there, most nights.

The idea brought a smile to Donnie's face. Jay owned a pub staffed by gorgeous waitresses who loved to flirt. Living out on Nahant for a while would make all of tonight's drama worth it. A wave of relief washed through him, and he felt the tension in his neck and shoulders loosening as he envisioned bachelor life with Jay Geldof. He'd still see the kids once in a while, but after all the anger and stress of being married to Barb, he deserved to be happy.

Donnie felt a lightness in his heart.

"Okay," he said to himself. "This is good."

He sat up straight, hands on the steering wheel, and looked at his house, which was just up the street and across the road. The hour had grown late. The party would be winding down at the Koenigs' house and most of the children of Parmenter Road would already be asleep, but Donnie wasn't surprised to see the costumed figure darting across the road up ahead, from the Panzas' yard toward his own. In his hooded robe, the man looked like some kind of grim reaper, and Donnie wondered how he had achieved the height effect, for he had to be at least seven feet, maybe taller.

Son of a bitch is fast. Donnie reached for the knob to turn on his headlights, but already the reaper had started across the grass toward his own house. The reaper slowed, moving with care, long as a praying mantis. Donnie saw its fingers as it reached for the living room window, brittle sticks that scraped along the glass as the hooded figure bent to look through into the dark interior of the Sweeney house.

My fucking house.

People talked about a chill running up your spine, but Donnie had never felt it until that moment. Real fear wasn't snapping awake when you'd nodded off behind the wheel or hearing a car in the driveway and having to rush a woman out of your bed before your wife caught you. That was just adrenaline. Fear was seeing a tall, shadowed figure peering through your window in the middle of the night and knowing your children were inside and vulnerable.

Donnie popped open the car door and practically fell out. The little alarm dinged to tell him the keys were still in the ignition, but he only heard it with some other part of his brain, some wide-awake and ordinary human part of his brain that had been shoved way down deep to make room for rapidly exploding panic. He cut across the street on feet he could barely feel. October wind whistled in his ears, and he thought he might have forgotten how to breathe.

The tall, impossibly thin man slithered around the side of the house, still bent over, still looking in windows. Donnie wanted to scream but had lost the capacity for words along with his breath. His children had been hurt by him, but this was different.

Donnie reached the corner of the house, came round the

side, thinking the wraith would be gone. But there it bent, peering through the window. Fingers like spider's legs caressed the glass.

"Bastard," Donnie seethed. "Fucking creep. Get away from my . . ."

House? Family? Kids?

When the thing turned to look at him, Donnie forgot what he meant to say next. He could see inside its skull, through the holes where its eyes should have been. Weird shadows flickered there, alongside candle flames. He could see the little fires burning, the charred black wicks that topped the small candles inside its head. His whole body went slack. Part of him knew he ought to be screaming, that he should turn and run, but shock made him drop his arms to his sides. He stared up at the face partly hidden by its hood, and a small sound came from Donnie's lips, the hiss of everything inside him simply surrendering.

Its spidery fingers lashed out so quickly he barely flinched. It darted its head toward him, fastened its lips over his. Donnie screamed into its mouth, thinking of his soul. All those years in Catholic school had warned him of this moment, and he had never listened. The devil had come.

But then he felt something moving inside his mouth, down his throat, filling his lungs like air but not air, and he began drowning in it. Donnie grabbed fistfuls of the thing's coat or cloak or whatever it was, but almost as soon as he had a grip on the fabric, it began to dissipate in his hands. Wool, then cotton, then cold embers, and then nothing but a kind of damp black mist on his fingers.

His chest expanded, his spine lengthened. Donnie felt ice around his heart, filling his chest. Pain shot down arms, the bones in his fingers cracked. His fingertips split and bled and lengthened.

With a smile, he threw back his head and sniffed at the air, searching for a particular scent, of rot and hunger, coppery blood and burning leaves. Of death and autumn. Then he strode off across the grass toward the back of the house. A long coat billowed around him, a coat he had not been wearing moments before.

He wasn't Donnie Sweeney anymore.

Donnie Sweeney was gone.

RICK BARBOSA

Rick wanted to go home. They were in the woods, trying to stay quiet, undiscovered, and he knew the slender, hooded man who had murdered Ruth Burgess might still be nearby, maybe even in the yard where Ruth had been killed. But he told himself the odds were that the killer had moved on, that the path back to his own house would be clear. The things he had overheard, his mom cheating on his dad—they were awful, heartbreaking revelations that made him want to scream or cry—but they were nothing compared to murder. To running for his life in the woods.

"I can't do this," he whispered. Earlier tonight, he had felt so brave. It felt like years had passed since then.

Billie took his hand. The two of them stared at Leonard. The pip-squeak. Leonard, whom they had rescued from Zack and Ruth, and who now said he had escaped something much worse. Rick believed him, because he had seen the thing Leonard talked about. The three of them had seen it murder Ruth, and maybe Ruth being dead was not the worst thing—the world must be better off without her—but the way it happened terrified him.

"Are you not listening?" Leonard pleaded. "I need you to stay with me for a little while longer. Then I'll be free. I'll be able to get away—"

"I heard you," Rick said, waving his hand as if that would make the words stop. "I even believe you, and maybe that's why I can't stay."

Only a crazy person would stay here, in the dark, with this kid.

A night bird called, and he flinched, heart thumping. "Jesus."

"Rick," Billie said. "Let's just take him to your house. That's our only choice now."

"No," Leonard said, voice dropping an octave. As if he were in charge.

The presumptuous little shit. Rick felt badly for him, but how dare he? They had already saved him once tonight, and now he acted as if they owed him protection, as if somehow they were required to risk their lives for him. To face that thing in the hood, that man.

Rick hung his head. "You said this guy snatched you off the street on Halloween—years ago—and he's been keeping you prisoner in some kinda . . . some kinda *Twilight Zone* all this time. The trees are black, and everything's cold and fire—*fucking fire*—burns in the ground, you said—"

"I said it because it's true," Leonard whined. "I told you. The place he's from, Dubnos, is closer tonight. It's easier to slip through."

Rick shook his head. Did this kid think he was making a persuasive argument? That saying even more terrifying stuff would win them over?

"And you want us to put ourselves between you and the Cunning Man, and risk him doing the same thing to us?" he asked.

Leonard turned even paler.

"I . . . I need . . ." Leonard said.

Billie shook her head. "We don't know you, kid. We helped you, but we're not gonna be stupid just because you said so.

Even if I halfway believe you, and maybe halfway I do because I saw that guy attack Ruth, too . . . I've got my mom's voice in the back of my head telling me to find an adult and hand the problem over to them. That's how this works."

"No," Leonard said.

"You know how this sounds, right?" Rick asked.

"I think it sounds like some kind of evil Peter Pan, dragging little kids off on Halloween night," Billie said, "to a land where they never grow up."

The kid's mouth hung open. All his earlier gratitude evaporated. "You saw him! You think that was just some normal guy? Some guy from your neighborhood just murdered that Ruth lady on the grass?" Leonard began to cry. "To a place like . . . like hell . . ."

Rick shook his head. "Billie and I are going back to my house. The Cunning Man has to be gone by now. You should come with us. If there's any sign of trouble, we'll go to the Spinales' or the Colemans' house. We'll find someone home, and we'll call the cops."

Leonard started to argue again.

Rick grabbed the front of his jacket, made the little kid focus on him. "Look at us. Me and Billie . . . we're older than you, but if that thing is really coming after you, how are we supposed to stop it?"

"We can't," Billie agreed. She reached a hand out to Leonard. "Come on."

Leonard glared at them both.

Billie sighed. "Fine."

She took Rick's hand, and they started back through the woods together. They had run far, but not so far that they would have difficulty making it back to a trail within a minute or two. Rick could not quite believe the kid was stubborn enough that he would stay out there in the woods alone. Night birds sang to one another. Rick felt his heart lighten, just a little. He wanted to be home, safe with Billie until her parents got back. Safe with his own mom and dad, no matter how bad things might be between them.

He heard the crunch of dry leaves behind him, light footsteps, and he felt Billie squeeze his hand. Rick glanced at her and saw she was smiling, relieved that Leonard had decided to follow. Rick shared that relief. In the morning, when the sun came out, it would be almost impossible for him to believe the things he had seen tonight, but for now, he just wanted everyone to be safe.

"You couldn't wait," Leonard said behind them, in that familiar, scared little kid voice.

That voice became an angry whisper. "You couldn't wait twenty fucking minutes."

Rick heard Leonard's steps quicken, and as the wind gusted, the stink of thick cider and rotting apples washed over them. Instinctively, he and Billie released each other's hands and turned toward the incoming steps and went to cover their mouths and noses to keep out the dreadful odor.

The stink came from Leonard. His cheeks were mottled and pitted, damp with rot. His lips drew back in a sneer that revealed black gums and jagged, broken teeth, stained brown and red. The stink came from his breath and from pockets of rot in his flesh. His eyes were the pale green of spring apples, the only part of him that seemed fresh and alive.

Billie screamed and cursed and backed up so quickly she stumbled and grabbed hold of Rick's shirt. He felt himself falling backward.

Leonard, the little rotting boy, reached out and caught him by the front of his coat with strength he should not have. Recoiling from the stink of moldering earth and dead, fermenting apples, Rick barely noticed Billie trying to pull him away, only that Leonard held on to him and would not let go.

The boy grinned, showing all those stained and broken teeth. Then he punched Rick in the chest.

Rick grunted, pain blossoming as he looked down to see the gnarled, pitted wrist twisting as the dreadful boy rooted around inside his chest.

For a moment, he felt nothing.

He looked into those beautiful eyes, spring apple green.

And he died.

BILLIE SUAREZ

Billie let go of Rick's coat. She didn't want to, did not even command her hand to do so, but when she heard the crack of bone and the wet squelch of Rick's insides, it felt as if she herself had died. Her fist unclenched, and the bit of bunched-up coat slipped from her grasp. One last breath wheezed between her lips, and she thumped to the ground, roots and broken branches digging into her backside.

Leonard seemed so small, but though Rick's knees had given way, his whole body slack, Leonard held him upright with one hand. With the other, Leonard thrust deeper inside Rick's chest cavity.

Tears filled Billie's eyes. Mixed with the stink of rotting apples that wafted from Leonard's gnarled and oozing body, she caught the scent of blood, rich and fresh and coppery. She tasted the salt of her tears on her lips, and she began to move, to push her boots against the dirt, shoving herself away from Leonard—and away from Rick.

Rick. My God, Rick.

I'm sorry.

Leonard tilted his head so he could look directly at her. Billie saw his eyes, bright green, clear and pure, and she froze in place, just about to leap to her feet but afraid he would come for her next.

With a grin of anticipation, Leonard ripped Rick's heart from his chest. Billie turned away, wanting to vomit from the sound alone. Unable to see him, she felt less transfixed by his presence, and she put one knee beneath her and then rose, at last, to her feet.

"Don't go, Billie," Leonard said, exhaling a cloud of rot. "It's not what it seems. Just watch."

She edged away from him, half a step at a time.

"I said, 'Watch,' damn you," Leonard growled.

Billie couldn't help it. She turned trembling toward him, ready to run with his very next word. But instead of speaking to her, the little boy held Rick's bleeding heart up to his lips and whispered to it in words that sounded like a snake moving through dry autumn leaves. As he did, he let go of Rick's coat, and the body collapsed onto the path. Billie gasped and covered her mouth, staring at the corpse of the boy who had been closer to her than anyone in the world, except her parents. And they weren't home tonight. They weren't here for this.

She said his name, because he was alone here, too, except for her, and someone had to mark this horror. She whispered it. "Rick."

The sound she heard then would remain with her all her life. A wet sound, a tearing. Billie pulled her gaze from Rick's corpse and saw Leonard holding his dripping heart. Leonard pulled his face back, lips smeared with blood, and he grinned with those horrid teeth as he began to chew. Billie trembled, felt another scream building inside her, but when she blinked, she saw what sat in Leonard's open hand was not a human heart at all but a rotten apple, skin burst in places, brown rot squirming out.

Leonard whispered to the apple in his hand. "Rick. You

belong to me now. We have much to do, and quickly, so that we can go home."

Confused, somehow numbed by the way Leonard had begun to ignore her, Billie still did not run. Not yet.

But then, on the ground, Rick's body twitched and settled. She heard him exhale, though he must be dead, having no heart in his chest. Again, Leonard spoke his name, and this time, Rick drew his hands and knees up beneath him, preparing to rise, and Billie noticed the skin of his hands and the back of his neck had become brown and rotten, and the smell of an early-winter orchard rose from him, the stink of dead apples, of poison cider.

Rick began to turn toward her, and that was the moment she broke. Billie could not see his face now, would not look at whatever he'd become. She twisted around and caught one more glimpse of Leonard. The little boy, the thing that wore the mask of a little boy, took another bite of the fruit in his hand, but it was no longer an apple. It had become Rick Barbosa's dripping heart once more, and the child chewed it with relish.

Billie ran screaming through the woods, felt as if she were flying over fallen trees and low rock walls, as if no root could trip her now. Terror drove her, and she knew where she had to go, the only place she could go now, with her mom and dad still far away from home.

She ran for Rick's house, and she prayed she would find his parents there. Their fights didn't matter now. Nothing that had mattered before tonight meant anything now. Nothing was real except for this. In her mind's eye, she could still see Rick beginning to turn to look back at her, and she could not scream anymore. The moment kept playing in her mind as she ran through the woods, and she feared . . . she knew . . . that it always would.

ALICE BARBOSA

Alice Barbosa heard screams in the distance, but it was Halloween night, and she told herself those shrieks must have come from teenagers partying around a bonfire somewhere. She had grown up in another era, a time that she always told Rick and Chloe had been more innocent than the rowdy decade they were living in now, but that wasn't entirely true. She understood the idea of kids cutting loose, getting wild . . . A little of that was probably healthy, if she was being honest.

But despite wishing she could brush them off as harmless fun, those screams from the woods didn't sound healthy at all. Alice hoped someone would hear them and call the police, but it could not be her. Rick had not come back from trick-or-treating with Billie, and that worried her. She assumed he had ended up at the Koenigs' and would be home soon, but midnight had almost arrived, and he knew that even with Billie, even tonight, he would be grounded for life if he didn't show up by twelve o'clock. Chloe had taken the little Raggedy Ann back to the house, and their father was nowhere to be found.

Alice paused on the path, in the midst of the Haunted Woods. Half of it had gone dark, the generator shut down, but the other generator still ran. She knew she ought to pull the plug, but then there would be no lights at all back here, just the moon peeking through branches that were rapidly losing leaves—and she didn't want to be back here in the dark.

"Tony, where the hell are you?" she called, fists clenched in frustration.

Too many things were happening tonight. The ordinary chaos of the Haunted Woods would be enough to make her want to hibernate, but then Donnie Sweeney had shown up and spilled their dirty laundry in public, and the whole night went to shit. Her fight with Tony had been sad and ugly, and now this lost child had shown up, and Tony had stormed out to sulk somewhere. Alice didn't blame him, but she had started to worry about Rick, and now they had found this little girl, and Alice would have to call the police.

The screams in the woods faded. Nothing felt right tonight. Nothing felt safe.

Reluctantly, Alice left the trail and headed deeper into the woods beyond the lights. Beyond the generator and the black drapes. She called her husband's name every half dozen steps, peering through the trees.

"Tony, if you're out here and just not answering, I've got to get back to the house. Ours isn't the only crisis tonight, and I need to help a girl who's lost."

She stood and listened a moment, then shook her head and turned to leave.

Leaves crunched. She heard a grunt behind her and turned. A silhouette blocked the moonlight between a pair of trees, but she had been married to Tony long enough to recognize his shape, even shadowed as he was. His left shoulder drooped and he leaned on one of the trees, his head partly hung.

"God, what happened to you?"

She walked toward him. Tony reached for her, stumbled, and

went down on his right knee in the leaves. The way he turned, his face caught the moonlight, and she saw the wound at his temple, the split in his skin, the blood that streaked his face and soaked his sweatshirt. His eyes were wide but unfocused, and her first concrete thought was, *Concussion.*

"The girl," he said. "Delilah."

Ice ran through Alice. "You saw her?"

He took her wrist, used her to steady himself, and rose to his feet. "Where is she now?"

"At the house with Chloe, but—"

Tony squeezed his eyes shut as if from pain. "Christ, no."

"What—"

"We have to hurry." Still holding her wrist, eyes wide again, he started back toward the Haunted Woods and their house beyond.

Alice tugged backward. "Tony, tell me what happened. What's going on?"

He let her go, but pointed at his bloody temple. "That girl. She did this! She's not . . ." He shook his head, stumbled dizzily, and caught himself. "We have to go!"

Tony careened along the path, hands out to balance himself like a sidewalk drunk. Alice tried to ask questions, but he could only focus on staying on his feet, and she followed, heart in her throat, knowing that somehow her daughter was in danger, that Tony was terrified for Chloe and that Raggedy Ann girl was responsible. It was best that Rick hadn't come home yet, she decided. He would be safer up at the Koenigs' or next door at Billie's. Wherever he was, he would be safer, because that wound on Tony's head was real, that blood was real, and *oh my God, Chloe.*

They reached the Haunted Woods and began to run toward the exit, helped by the lights that still burned back there. The banshee screamed, and this time, neither of them flinched.

Seconds later, they emerged into their backyard and ran across the lawn.

They weren't alone.

Alice heard before she saw. Footfalls and hitching sobs. She turned to see Billie Suarez barreling toward her, tears glistening in moonlight.

"Mrs. Barbosa," the girl managed, and then she threw her arms around Alice and began to wail, her whole body shaking. Her chest hitched, and she couldn't catch her breath to produce more than a syllable.

"No," Alice said, because she heard that syllable, and she knew that no matter what else had happened tonight, this was the worst. The very worst.

The syllable was just the first little sound, the *Ri-* that began her son's name.

Her son, who should have been with Billie.

Alice glanced around to see Tony limping back toward them, face etched with horror. On this night, he knew Billie's wailing could only mean disaster.

Could only mean, really, that the world had ended.

"Billie," Alice whispered. "Please, just tell me."

The girl shuddered one last time, exhaling. She leaned into Alice's arms as if hoping her best friend's mother would lift her and carry her away, like her own mother must have done when she was a child and exhaustion had taken hold. But there would be no respite tonight. Alice took Billie by the shoulders and shook her, snapped at her.

The girl stood up straight. Stared into her eyes.

And told Alice and Tony what had happened to their son.

Numb, Alice could only listen and shake her head. She released Billie and took a step backward, her whole body tensed to flee, as if she could escape this night simply by running from it. This was impossible.

"You're wrong," she said, and a terrible little laugh came from her lips. "He's . . . he's playing a trick on you."

Billie raised a shaking hand to cover her mouth, as if to stop herself from screaming. "I'm sorry. I'm so sorry. It's not a trick."

Tony stood six feet away, arms wrapped around himself as if caught in an invisible straitjacket. His head hung again. The blood on his face gleamed black in the dark. There might have been tears as well, but they would have been lost in the blood.

"Where is he?" Alice asked. "Take us to him."

Then she felt Tony's hand on her arm. She looked at him, saw the pale, slack mask of his face, and remembered what had happened to him and the little girl inside with her daughter.

"Chloe," Tony said.

Tears sprang to Alice's eyes as she turned toward her own home. According to Billie, her son was already beyond her help.

"Chloe," she echoed, and she started to run toward the house with Tony and Billie racing behind her.

This night. Goddamn this night.

VANESSA MONTEZ

Vanessa and Julia held hands as much for comfort as from affection. Arthur seemed to disapprove, but Vanessa refused to allow herself to be tamed by his disdain. He had been trying to hide it, and that was for the best. If he came right out and said the things she suspected were going through his mind, she would have had to abandon him. Vanessa also thought if he said what he really thought, Julia might kick him in the balls, and that wouldn't improve anyone's night.

The thought made her smirk. *Okay, maybe that wouldn't be so bad.*

The two girls could have gone home, of course. Arthur had spouted some fairly wild stories, some desperate paranoia, and he was virtually a stranger. They didn't owe him anything. But Vanessa could see his fear was genuine, and that tugged at her heart. In addition to that, she and Julia had just made the connection she had wished for on every star for so long, and neither of them was ready for the night to end just yet.

Now Vanessa glanced around and realized she had been distracted. The path Arthur led them along seemed unfamiliar. She told herself it was only that she was not used to being out there in the dark. She had only been out this deep in the woods at night for the occasional party at the firepit, and then she had always been with a big group of other kids. The trees here were huge and old and leaned at weird angles, as if they'd all been bent by a storm that pummeled each tree from a different direction.

She glanced at Julia, who looked as curious as Vanessa felt.

Julia squeezed her hand. "Hey, Arthur? I don't want to be the annoying kid in the back seat, but are we there yet?"

Arthur glanced over his shoulder. His scarecrow makeup looked like dried paint, thick and cracking on his face.

"As a matter of fact, we are."

They arrived at a clearing. In the center stood one of the biggest trees Vanessa had ever seen, so thick that the three of them could have made a circle around it with arms outstretched and not been able to touch hands. The tree had a slash in its trunk where something had cut into the bark, but so much time had passed that this split looked natural, as if it had just grown that way.

Arthur pushed up his sleeve and glanced at an old wristwatch. "Twenty-three minutes."

"Until midnight?" Julia asked.

He nodded. "I'll be able to go back where I belong then. But only from here. I have to stay right here, no matter what."

His expression had been flat, but now it filled with emotion, as if he'd just taken off a mask. "I can't thank the two of you enough for coming here with me. You don't know what it means. The Cunning Man may come to try to stop me getting back, and I'm . . ."

"Terrified," Vanessa whispered. She didn't mean to say it out loud, but it was impossible not to see the fear on his face, amid his gratitude and hope.

Julia released her hand. She dug into her pocket for a twisty and reached up to tie her hair back into a ponytail. "Don't worry, Arthur. There's nobody here but us."

Something about Julia's tone made Vanessa frown. Neither of them really believed the fairy-tale stuff he'd been telling them, but Vanessa didn't doubt the truth of Arthur's fear. The rest of it, this stuff about demonic beings from some kind of spirit world, might be invention or insanity, but either way, it had made her curious enough to find out. Julia's tone, and the way she studied Arthur now, suggested she thought the whole thing was an act, but Vanessa could not imagine why anyone would invent such a wild story.

"Twenty-three minutes?" she asked.

Arthur glanced at his watch again. "Twenty-two."

Vanessa smiled at Julia. "Well, we can survive that long, I guess. Nobody's going to turn into a pumpkin."

"That's true," Arthur replied.

Julia did not smile.

BARB SWEENEY

The first thing Barb saw when she opened her eyes was her uninvited guest. The little thing, Sarah Jane, had curled herself up into a ball on the sofa, more like a sleeping cat than a child. Her clown costume had been torn at some point, and Barb realized she must be cold. Charlie lay on the floor with a throw pillow under his head. The TV still showed a horror movie, but it fritzed with static that made Barb wince. A tightness in the back of her neck and across her skull promised a brutal headache on the horizon.

With a quiet groan, she sat up. Charlie gave a comical snort and grumbled in his sleep. Barb smiled at her youngest, sleeping on the floor because he worried about this stray that had shown up at their back door. He had a good heart, and she cherished that. All three of her children were good-hearted, and when she took the time to think about it, she knew there was no greater joy for a parent than the knowledge you were raising good kids. In her case, she had no idea how it had happened. She tried to be a good mother, to set a decent example, but she hadn't been anything close to perfect, and Donnie was not an example of anything except how to charm people into seeing past your faults.

A good mother, she thought. Idly, she reached down and

stole one of Charlie's York Peppermint Patties. He hated mint mixed with chocolate anyway, so she knew he wouldn't mind.

A good mother would have known that letting a runaway hide in her house was totally irresponsible. Even if the girl's fears were rooted in reality—and she had no reason to doubt it—she knew she should have called the police. A little voice in her head reminded her that the cops might just take the girl home, especially in the middle of the night, but Barb could call DSS, the Department of Social Services. She didn't know if someone answered the phone at DSS in the middle of the night, and she told herself the morning was soon enough.

She tore open the Peppermint Pattie wrapper, then froze with it in her hand. What if the law compelled her to report Sarah Jane? Would it be considered a crime for her to harbor the girl overnight? Barb hadn't considered that.

"Shit," she whispered.

Sarah Jane muttered in her sleep and shifted to find a more comfortable spot on the sofa. Barb stared at the girl and felt as if the mood of the night, her fury at Donnie and fear for her kids, had made her open to the idea of protecting this child herself, just as she wanted to protect her own kids. She wished she could talk to a lawyer about this, but she wasn't about to try to find Donnie, and the only other lawyers she knew were friends of his.

Barb popped the Peppermint Pattie into her mouth, relishing the chocolate and mint. She leaned back into the cushions as she chewed, trying to forget the problem of Sarah Jane for a moment, and as she did, another solution came to her. Anna Nathanson was the mother of one of Julia's friends, and while Julia and the girl had drifted apart during high school, Barb still ran into Anna at the Market Basket from time to time and said hello, and Anna was a social worker for Essex County. She would know what the law said.

It was very late. Barb got up from the sofa and walked softly into the kitchen to check the clock. Twenty minutes to twelve. Yes, late, but it was Halloween night and a Saturday and lots of people were up late, and Anna was a social worker. Barb imagined she must be used to the occasional late-night call.

Hand on the phone, she glanced back into the porch and watched Charlie and Sarah Jane sleeping. Brian would be asleep in his room, and she wondered if Julia had come home yet. But all those wonderings were just delaying the decision—she was either going to wake Anna Nathanson up or she was going to leave it until morning.

Sarah Jane seemed to shiver and snuggled deeper into the sofa.

Barb decided. The girl needed a sweatshirt, something warm and bulky. She had a closetful of coats and sweaters and sweatshirts downstairs—and a cordless phone that she still didn't quite trust not to cut her off in the middle of a call. The drawer next to the refrigerator held her address book, so she dug that out and thumbed through in search for Anna Nathanson's number, even as she walked down the stairs.

The basement playroom had a musty smell that never quite went away, but they were all used to it by now. The big console TV in the corner had terrible reception, and she had promised to get it fixed or replace it, but she suspected that wasn't going to happen now—not with her going to court against Donnie for child support and alimony.

Sobering up, Barb flicked on the light switch, found Anna Nathanson's number, and held the address book down with one hand while she picked up the cordless phone from its base and punched in the digits. Again, she thought of the time, and by the fourth ring, she knew she had made a mistake. She was just about to hang up when Anna answered, groggily but not angrily. Instead, she sounded frightened, as most mothers would be when the phone rang late at night.

"Anna, it sounds like I woke you," Barb began. "I'm sorry. Of course I woke you. I'd never have called so late if it weren't urgent—"

On the line, Anna cleared her throat, still half-asleep. "Hello? Who . . . who is this?"

"Shit, right. I should've . . . It's Barb Sweeney."

"Barb. What's wrong?"

She sounded a little more awake now. Not exactly welcoming the late call, but concerned, and that was fine.

"It's been a pretty awful day. But that's a story for another time," Barb said.

She sighed and carried the phone across the room and out into the landing at the bottom of the steps. The coats and sweaters and things were in a closet that had been built under the stairs, a renovation she had suggested when they first moved in, using an otherwise wasted space. It felt foolish now, being proud of such a little thing. But maybe the little things were the only things they could hang on to.

"So my youngest, Charlie, met a little girl out trick-or-treating tonight," Barb went on. "She'd run away from home. The poor thing is terrified. She's hiding from her parents or whoever she lives with, maybe foster family, I don't know—"

"Barb, what do you mean she's 'hiding'? Where is she hiding?"

"Well, that's what I wanted to ask you about. She . . . Charlie didn't invite her or anything like that, but a couple of hours after he ran into her, the girl showed up at the porch door. Charlie and Brian—that's my older son—let her in. And now she's here and she won't tell me her address or a phone number, and I know I should call the police, but I'm worried that I'd be sending her back into danger. Maybe violence. I feel sick thinking about that, and I thought about waiting for morning, but then I wondered if I could get into trouble—"

Barb had been fishing around in the closet. She'd found an old sweater of Brian's, a fuzzy green wool blend that Charlie said was too scratchy and was too small for Brian now. This would do, if the little girl didn't have Charlie's issues with wool.

But then Anna cut her off, and Barb's hands froze, fuzzy green sweater in hand.

"You absolutely could," Anna said.

"Oh," was all Barb could muster. "I just . . . I was afraid something might . . ." Her breath hitched, but she refused to cry. "Anna, I can't get into trouble. I'm in the middle of a shitstorm. Donnie walked out on us today, and I—"

"My God, Barb, I'm sorry—"

"No, no. Don't be sorry. He's . . . Honestly, he's a terrible husband. This way he can get as drunk as he likes and stop trying to keep his affairs a secret."

"Oh my God."

"But that was just this afternoon, and this happened tonight, and I can't think straight."

"No, it's okay," Anna said. "Calling me was the right thing to do."

"So, what now? It's nearly midnight. What am I supposed to—"

Anna cleared her throat. "First, take a breath. You're okay. You're not in trouble. Second, I'm going to make this very simple. I will come and take the girl off your hands, and I promise you I will make absolutely sure that she is not put back into a situation where she will be in danger. I'll get myself assigned as her social worker."

"You can do that?"

"I mean, not officially, but my boss loves me. She'll go along with it."

Barb exhaled. She felt so relieved that she even let out a small laugh and hugged the green sweater to her chest. "You're a lifesaver."

She started back up the stairs, sweater in one hand, phone clutched to her ear with the other.

Anna kept talking. "You just have to decide if you want me to come and get her now or in the morning. I'll write a short report now about this call, and if you want to just go to bed, I'll vouch for your home as a safe place and you as having agreed to be responsible for the girl overnight. But if you don't want that responsibility—"

"You don't want to get out of bed any more than that little girl will want to be woken up from my sofa right now," Barb said, smiling.

"That's true. But I'm happy to come and get her."

Two steps from the top, Barb heard a sniffle. It didn't come from her or from the phone. She looked up and saw Sarah Jane standing at the top of the steps, pitiful in her wrinkled and torn clown costume, reminding her of Cindy-Lou Who from the Grinch cartoon.

The little girl's eyes were full of suspicion. She sniffled again. "Who are you talking to?"

Barb ignored the question. She would deal with Sarah Jane in a moment. She smiled to let the girl know all was well.

"No, Anna. We'll be all right. No need to—"

Sarah Jane's upper lip curled. Her eyes were black. She reached out with both hands and shoved Barb hard enough to knock her off the step. The phone flew from her hand. She tried to grab the railing with her left hand, but the sweater got in the way, and she was just falling.

She hit the steps with a crack of bone, and the back of her skull struck the tiles at the landing by the front door.

Everything went dark for a moment, then she opened her

eyes and her vision blurred, a cascade of shadows and dim lamplight. She could hear Anna calling her name on the telephone, asking if she was still there. For a moment, she was, but then the cascade of shadows went full dark again, and Barb was gone.

SARAH JANE

Sarah Jane stood perfectly still, listening to the dark interior of the Sweeney house. On the landing by the split-level's front door, the mother moaned quietly but did not stir. Her foot twitched, and blood trickled from the wound on the back of her head, running in a little rivulet that filled the path of the grout in the tile floor. Sarah Jane could hear the eerie music floating from the television out on the porch, but she waited a moment to see if Brian would emerge from the bedroom down the hall that he shared with his little brother, Charlie. Seconds passed with no sign of Brian, so she turned and started back through the kitchen.

On the threshold between the kitchen and the porch, she paused to study Charlie, who still lay on the floor with his head on a throw pillow, surrounded by his Halloween candy, neatly sorted by brand and type. There were many empty wrappers. He'd had a good night, Charlie had, in spite of the awful things that had happened to him earlier in the day, when his father had left, and in spite of the fact that he had not been able to trick-or-treat. Charlie had enjoyed sitting on the porch and watching scary movies with his brother, and then with Sarah Jane. That was good, she thought.

At least he would have a happy memory to hold on to.

Sarah Jane glanced at the clock on the kitchen wall and saw that time was running out. She hurried through the porch, unlocked the door with its layers of plate glass windows, and drew it wide open. The last of October's wind blew in, a few dry leaves skittering across the floor to mingle with Charlie's Halloween candy.

The boy stirred. He shivered but did not wake.

Sarah Jane stood over him. Part of her wished she had time to choose someone else, but midnight ticked nearer, and Charlie would have to do.

She bent and grabbed him by the hair.

When she yanked him off the floor, he began to scream.

CHLOE BARBOSA

Chloe had her own opinions, but during the months she and her little brother had lived in the cloud of tension her dad's long unemployment and the resulting financial turmoil had created, she had held her tongue. The last thing she wanted was to put any further stress on their marriage. Losing their home was awful enough. But tonight, she'd heard people gossiping about her family and that her mom had an affair with Mr. Sweeney. Humiliation had nearly drowned her, and then rage threw her a lifeline. But mixed in with those emotions was another ingredient—simple disappointment. Her mother had set the family up for this embarrassment, and it wasn't fair.

She hated her mother tonight, and had been eager for the fight she had intended to have when she got home from the Koenigs' party. But now her father had gone into the Haunted Woods and not come back, and her mother had found this little girl, so the fight Chloe wanted had to be postponed.

Chloe had done as she'd been told, brought Delilah back to the house to give her something to eat and keep her warm. She would rather have been out in the woods. Her dad had probably just grabbed a beer and decided to sit in the woods and take some comfort from the last happy memories in the

Haunted Woods. She hadn't thought to ask how long he had been gone, but after the fight they must have had, it would have taken her mom a long time to get up enough concern to go out looking for him.

But now this little girl had shown up in her Raggedy Ann costume, scared and alone, and other problems had to be put aside for the moment. Chloe thought maybe that was for the best. Maybe the girl had come along just in the nick of time to prevent worse from happening to her family tonight.

"Okay," Chloe said as she brought Delilah into the kitchen. "Let's see what kind of snacks we can rustle up for you. Do you like peanut butter?"

"No," Delilah replied as they passed the kitchen table.

Chloe heard the scrape of chair legs on linoleum. She turned around in time to see Delilah lift one of the wooden chairs. Much too heavy for a little girl to lift that way, but Delilah smiled thinly at her, hoisting the chair effortlessly. She swung it at Chloe as easily as if it were a baseball bat. Chloe tried to lunge out of the way, but the chair caught her across the back and skull with such force that she felt something inside her crack as she went sprawling to the kitchen floor.

Pain sang in her head and spiked her back, and she managed to roll on her side. It hurt like hell to breathe, and her thoughts felt scrambled.

"Please," she rasped as Delilah came toward her with the chair raised again, maybe to make sure she didn't try to run. As if she could have.

Delilah smiled with satisfaction and set the chair down. "You'll be perfect."

"What the . . . what the *fuck*?" Chloe gasped, the pain in her back stabbing into her.

Delilah crouched by her. Stroked her face. "Tut-tut. Hasn't your mother taught you better than that?"

She didn't sound like a little girl anymore. And behind her eyes, Chloe saw a gleaming intelligence, sharp and cruel and so sure of itself.

They both heard the squeal of the front door's hinges. Hope blossomed in Chloe's chest. Tears touched the corners of her eyes, partly from pain and partly from hope, which was a special pain all its own. But then she saw the way Delilah's smile sharpened and the pleasure she took in realizing that someone had come home, that Rick or Mom or Dad had just come into the house, and that meant someone else for her to hurt. Or worse.

Footsteps creaked on the stairs.

"Wait," Chloe called weakly. "Watch out for—"

Delilah slapped her so hard that her head bounced off the linoleum again. Pain thrummed in her skull. She felt her hair sticking together in clumps and realized she was bleeding.

"Please," she managed to say, trying to pull herself into a ball, to find some way to protect herself.

The little girl did nothing. Delilah seemed to have frozen in place.

Thoughts a slurry, vision wavering, Chloe slid her head just enough to look up at the girl, and suddenly, Delilah seemed to have become a child again instead of whatever seething, cruel thing had filled out her little girl skin. She stared past Chloe, toward the kitchen entryway, at whatever member of the Barbosa family had just come in the door and up the stairs.

Chloe moved her head to have a look. The pain surged, so bad she nearly vomited. Then her vision cleared and she managed to make out the face of the figure standing in the kitchen entryway.

Donnie Sweeney.

Moments before, she would have wanted to strangle Mr. Sweeney herself for the things he had done with her mother and the pain he had caused her father. But now she whimpered in relief that someone, anyone, might help her.

But something was wrong with Mr. Sweeney. There were slashes on his face and arms and his fingers were bleeding and too long somehow, and she knew how badly concussed she must be, but there were little fires inside his eyes, or the place where his eyes should have been.

"She's mine, Broghan!" the little girl cried. "You can't have her!"

In two steps, Delilah grabbed Chloe by the wrist and dragged her skidding across the kitchen floor, out the back door, and down the stairs. Every step sent fresh agony bursting through Chloe's back and head, and she shrieked in pain, but then darkness floated in the corners of her vision, and her scream became a sigh as light and pain retreated.

She caught a glimpse, perhaps imagined, of her mother and father and Billie Suarez from next door, all running toward her, mouths moving in silent screams that might have been her name. But Delilah jerked her along and her body twisted and she lost sight of them, if they'd been there at all.

The last thing she saw before pain blotted out consciousness was Mr. Sweeney lumbering out through the back door of her house and those little flames set deep in the dark holes where his eyes should have been.

Then all Chloe felt was the grass and then the dirt and twigs and roots of the path beneath her, and the little girl's fingers clamped round her wrist.

And then nothing.

TONY BARBOSA

Tony went down to one knee. Delilah had hurt him, back there in the woods. But nothing she had done to him compared to the horror of watching the little girl run from his house and into the woods, dragging his daughter behind her. It felt like a nightmare, a scream inside him that he couldn't release. How could a little girl like Delilah have the strength to drag Chloe like that? How could she move with such speed? It was impossible. Inhuman. They'd taken half a dozen steps in the time it took Delilah to get Chloe out the door and into the woods.

"For Christ's sake, Tony, get up!" Alice cried. She grabbed him by the arm, one hand in his armpit, and helped him rise.

Tony spotted Billie, and the horror of the last minute nearly made him fall over again. His son, his boy, his Ricky was dead? Could that be possible? What Billie had told them, the little boy murdering Rick, and what Billie had said happened to him afterward . . . It seemed like a hideous lie, some dark imagining invented to inflict pain, but Billie would never do something like that.

And now Chloe . . . his daughter. If this little boy, Leonard, was some kind of monster, Delilah had to be the same. And she had Chloe.

Tony drew a breath, met his wife's eyes. "Let's go," he said. "We have to catch them."

But then he heard the rattle of his own back door opening again, and he looked up to see someone else coming down the steps to the yard.

"Mr. Sweeney," young Billie said.

Alice still held on to Tony's arm. Now she reached out to pull Billie toward her as well, protectively, the way any mother would. "I don't think that's Mr. Sweeney."

Maybe if there had been less moonlight, Tony would have made the same mistake as Billie Suarez. But he agreed with Alice. Whatever the thing was that stalked across his back lawn as if the three of them were invisible, it sure as hell wasn't Donnie Sweeney. Its face bore a resemblance to that drunken asshole, and it wore the clothes Donnie had worn earlier . . . but whatever this thing was, it wasn't Donnie anymore.

Alice let go of Tony. She ran to put herself between the thing inside Donnie Sweeney and the woods where her daughter had been taken. Tony swayed on his feet, but when Billie started after his wife, Tony held her back. There were pits where Donnie Sweeney's eyes ought to have been, and small flames flickered down inside them. His face and neck were split, and something showed through underneath, wet and slithering.

"Please?" Alice said, staring at those candle-flame eyes. "Leave my girl alone."

The thing inside Donnie Sweeney took two more steps toward her. Earlier tonight, Tony had despised his wife, wanted to humiliate her or hurt her the way she had done to him. But now he held his breath and prayed to a God he'd been ignoring for many long years.

The thing tilted its head. The candle flames inside its eyes remained vertical, while its head rocked on an angle.

"*You'll die for her*," it said in a voice like the wind or the death rattle of final words.

"If we have to," Tony said, stepping forward and putting Billie behind his back, as if he could protect her.

The thing did not look at him or seek out Billie. It kept its hollowed-out pits and candle-flame eyes on Alice. The question had been for her.

"*It will bring her to the Blackthorn,*" it breathed. "*You had better hurry after her. At midnight, it's too late.*"

The thing turned as if it had forgotten them and strode back across the yard, past the house, toward the road, as if Donnie intended to go home. Only then did Tony notice the thing's hands, the way its fingers had burst through Donnie's skin and hung down at its sides, thin and black and too-many-jointed, swaying like wind chimes.

It passed a body on the grass, but didn't bother looking down. Ruth Burgess, Tony figured. Billie had told them Ruth had been killed, and there she was.

Then the thing wearing Donnie Sweeney passed into the street and into the darkness, and Tony wondered how many minutes remained until midnight.

Alice whipped around to stare at Tony and Billie. "What did it mean? The Blackthorn. What is that? It said we only have till midnight!"

Tony realized he knew. "I've seen it. A blackthorn tree. I knew it was out of place. I was just distracted . . . always so fucking distracted."

He started for the path.

"Mr. Barbosa, you're still bleeding," Billie said. "You're not standing up straight."

Tony wanted to smile at her, but he didn't have the heart. Instead, he turned to Alice and took her by the shoulders, hoping she could see in his eyes that all the anger and spite were gone, replaced by simple need.

"You two stay here in case Rick comes back."

He turned to go, but Billie caught his hand.

"Mr. Barbosa, I'm sorry, but I already told you," she said, face crumpling with tears. "Rick isn't coming back."

Alice grabbed him by the wrist. "Chloe needs us."

He wanted to argue with her, but he couldn't do it anymore. They were out of time, and she was Chloe's mother.

"Billie—" he began, ready to tell her to lock herself inside the house.

"I'm coming," the girl said. "Let's go."

Then it was she, Billie, who ran for the path and into the Haunted Woods.

DONNIE SWEENEY

Donnie wondered if he might be a ghost. He knew he must be dead, but he remembered his own name and could still think, even if his thoughts were like waves on the sand. Wherever he floated now, he could still hear familiar sounds. The wind. Human voices. An engine, right now, rumbling as a car slowed down.

He couldn't see the car, of course. And he couldn't feel the air on his skin, because the skin didn't belong to him anymore.

A ghost, he thought again. But that didn't seem accurate. He might have been a bullshit artist in his personal life and standing before a judge in a courtroom, but if law school had taught him anything, it was the value of precise wording. No, ghost did not properly describe his current state of being.

A wave rolled in. He remembered screaming, though that might have only been on the inside, with his soul instead of his voice. He remembered the jack-o'-lantern eyes of the thing that had . . . that had killed him. Remembered those candle flames and the way it had carved into him with those spider-leg fingers. Burrowing under his skin.

Burrowing inside him.

First it had invaded his flesh, and now it occupied the body that had once belonged to him. All that remained was this flicker of awareness, these waves crashing on the sand, these memories.

And the sounds he could hear.

The car drove by, engine revving. Someone beeped the horn. People shouted to him, mocking him for being so drunk that he couldn't walk straight. Donnie focused on those voices, concentrated on them, and suddenly, he felt arms and legs, felt the wind against his skin and the pain of the wounds where his flesh had torn. His eyes were numb, and they burned, and he knew that whatever was inside his body, he himself was still in here, too. Donnie Sweeney.

"I'm . . . I'm me . . ." he croaked, making his old throat work. His old mouth.

But not his voice.

"I'm me!" he cried.

The Cunning Man roared inside Donnie's chest. He knew it was called that now, could feel its thoughts and bits of knowledge. *Broghan. The Cunning Man.* When the next wave washed onto the sand inside his mind, he knew that if the awareness known as Donnie Sweeney was composed of those waves, the Cunning Man was the sand.

Donnie cried out again as his legs gave out beneath him.

Not *his* legs anymore.

The Cunning Man smashed the palms of its hands against Donnie's skull—its own skull, now—trying to shake him loose. It bent over and pounded its forehead against the blacktop.

Another wave, and this time when it washed back into the ocean, it took Donnie with it.

He floated. No more hands. No more legs.

When he realized he could no longer hear the outside world, not even the wind, he would have cried except that he had no eyes.

Donnie had learned many things, however. He knew where the Cunning Man was headed now.

Home.

There were other evils on Parmenter Road tonight, and the Cunning Man still hunted them. *The children of Carmun. Witch-spawn.* The Cunning Man tracked the spawn by scent, and he had located one moments ago. It was inside Donnie's house, where Donnie and Barb's children slept. He didn't want the thing anywhere near his kids, but one of the witch-spawn had slipped into the house with them.

Donnie hated the Cunning Man, but now he urged him on. Prayed to God the creature would reach home in time.

Then the next wave crashed onto the sand, flowed in, and when it flowed out, Donnie Sweeney went with it.

BARB SWEENEY

On the landing by her front door, Barb regained consciousness. Her left cheek felt hot and sticky, and the rich stink of her own blood filled her nostrils. But the blood remained warm, and she knew she had not been out very long. Not even a minute.

She raised her head. Her cheek lifted from the bloody tile with a sticky slurp. Barb gritted her teeth at the pain all over her bruised and battered body, but she began to rise.

Her boys were upstairs with Sarah Jane. Or whoever she was.

Whatever she was.

Barb grabbed the banister and dragged herself to her feet.

BRIAN SWEENEY

Brian resented being awake. Usually when he fell asleep, he would be out for the night, unless something roused him. Tonight, he groaned as he slitted his eyes open. He had fallen asleep on his back, TV on quietly in the background, but at some point, he had turned over onto his belly. The left side of his face was buried in his pillow, only his narrowed right eye able to see the digital clock on his nightstand. The numbers glowed green—11:49.

His mouth felt dry and nasty. Brian made a face, wishing he had taken the time to brush his teeth after all the chocolate he'd eaten. Now he had a headache from the sugar crash, and even worse, he had to pee. The last thing he wanted was to get out of bed, so he shifted slightly to take the pressure off his bladder.

Out in the corridor, something thumped the floor. Or had that been on the stairs?

It was late. Mom should have been asleep by now. Dad was . . . Brian didn't want to think about it, but his dad was gone. He decided the noise must be Julia coming home, late enough that any other night she would have been in trouble.

For a few seconds, he managed to close his eyes and forget his bladder and the chocolate residue on his teeth, but he couldn't get comfortable. With a sigh, he turned onto his right side, facing Charlie's bed, only to find it empty. His little brother wasn't in bed, which made Brian come fully awake.

The little girl in the clown makeup, Sarah Jane. He'd been so lost in the fog of sleep that he'd forgotten about her. The noises in the house and Charlie not being in bed meant either she was still here or Mom had gone to take her home or to the police. But if so, where was Charlie?

Brian looked at his brother's messy, unoccupied bed another moment and then threw back his covers and sat up. Yawning, he sucked his teeth and decided to brush them after all. The sugar coating inside his mouth felt gross.

"Okay," he muttered to himself. "Okay."

He got up and went into the hall, heading for the bathroom, but before he got there he heard another noise coming from the stairs. A painful exhalation, almost a grunt. His brow furrowed in curiosity, and he walked past the bathroom. They lived in a split-level, with a dozen steps down from the upstairs to the landing at the front door, and another dozen from the landing to the playroom and cellar downstairs.

His mother stood six steps from the top, almost doubled over, one hand on the railing. Blood smeared her face. Pain and confusion and the effort of staying upright were all chiseled into her features. Brian opened his mouth in shock, staring at her.

"Mom . . ."

The word came out a whisper.

His mother whipped her head up to stare at him in something like fear. Her free hand came up to her face, and she held a finger in front of her lips to shush him, her gaze shifting rapidly between Brian and the entrance to the kitchen. Brian Sweeney might not have been the best student at Coventry High School, but he wasn't a fool. He saw her fear, saw that finger against her lips, and he turned toward the kitchen and the back porch beyond.

Charlie and Sarah Jane had been left out there.

He didn't know if his father had come back, drunker than ever, or if this had been done by some other intruder, but somebody had thrown his mother down the stairs. Brian didn't have the height or the muscle his father had, but his mom was *bleeding* and his brother was in trouble.

Somebody was going to regret that.

Barefoot, he padded through the kitchen. His mom whimpered behind him, and he knew she would have called him to come back if she hadn't been afraid of making noise. It would not have done any good. He went to the counter, slid the biggest knife from the wooden block, and then stood on his toes and looked through the window over the sink, out onto the back porch.

In the dark, in the flickering blue glow of the horror movies on the television set, Sarah Jane crouched over his little brother. Charlie had fallen asleep on the floor, his head on a small pillow from the sofa. The way the little clown girl bent over him should have looked playful, but the cant of her head and the gleam in her dark eyes made Brian think of things that had always fluttered around the edges of his nightmares. Things with black-feathered wings. She looked like a crow pecking at roadkill.

"Charlie?" Brian said softly, more to himself than to be heard by the kids out there on the porch.

Sarah Jane's head swiveled. Her black eyes narrowed. Her lips drew back and she hissed at him, through the window between porch and kitchen, and in that moment, Brian was glad for the glass and the wall that separated them.

But then she moved. Sarah Jane grabbed Charlie by the collar of his sweatshirt and yanked him around, toward the back door. For a second, Brian could barely process what he was seeing. Charlie snapped awake, confused, and started to shout at Sarah Jane the same way he always complained when Brian or Julia teased him, as if he expected Mom or Dad to come rescue him from his older siblings' bullying. But Sarah Jane wasn't his sibling. Dad was gone. And Mom . . .

Sarah Jane twisted the knob and whipped the back door open with such force that the jalousie windows shattered, glass shards showering onto the floor and out onto the steps.

Brian started to run after them, but hesitated, staring at the broken glass on the floor, feeling the vulnerability of his bare feet.

Behind him, his mother screamed. Brian twisted around to look at her, but she was already running past him. She wore slippers, not much help against the glass shards, but Mom didn't slow down at all. In four steps, she reached the back door, grabbed the frame to steady herself, and launched herself down the long, steep staircase to the concrete patio, racing after Sarah Jane and Charlie.

Brian had kicked off his sneakers by the sofa while they were watching horror movies. Now he hurled himself across the room, landed on the floor in a scattering of candy and discarded wrappers, and shoved his bare feet into those sneakers. Outside, his mother screamed for Charlie, screamed like her life was ending. Brian wore torn pajama pants and a T-shirt and unlaced sneakers, but he thought only of protecting his feet and protecting his brother. Laces flying, he bolted out the open back door with its shattered glass panes and ran down the stairs.

Mom had reached the woods at the back of the yard.

Sarah Jane had made it that far, but no farther. The little girl had a thrashing Charlie by one wrist, standing on the grass, facing off with a tall, looming shape that seemed to be blocking

Sarah Jane's path into the woods. The shape stepped into the moonlight, and Brian paused on the cracked concrete of the patio in confusion.

"Dad?"

His father reached for Sarah Jane.

DONNIE SWEENEY

The Cunning Man ruled his body now. Very little of Donnie remained, but the part of him that lingered began to scream. Down inside, where only the Cunning Man could hear him. *My son! That's my son! Let me out, you rotting fucker. Let me out!*

But Broghan, the Cunning Man, seemed not to hear him, as if the little voice of Donnie Sweeney, whose body it had infected, was not even as loud as a conscience. Donnie watched through the flicker of the Cunning Man's eyes as the sneering little girl lifted his boy Charlie by the wrist and slapped Charlie hard enough to make him cry out and then stop moving, not because he'd blacked out but in fear of further brutality.

Inside the Cunning Man, that little thread of Donnie Sweeney screamed again, heart breaking for his son. And there, the seed at the core of what the Cunning Man had become, Donnie began to pray for his boy.

"*Charlie,*" the Cunning Man said, with lips that had once been his.

Their thoughts were joined, somehow, Donnie's and Broghan's. The monster, this demon, saw that little boy and recognized his son.

The little girl yanked Charlie around in front of her,

wrapped one arm around his throat, and with the other, she dug a fingernail into the corner of his right eye. "Stay back or I'll blind him."

In his head, Donnie screamed louder than ever. He floated in darkness except for what he saw through the Cunning Man's eyes. He had no body, no hands to fight, no way to save his boy. He could not even cry for his son.

The Cunning Man laughed with a throat that had once been Donnie's. "*Blind him, then. That will not get you to the Blackthorn.*"

The little girl looked afraid. Her skin had changed. At first, it looked like a shift in the moonlight, but no, her face had become mottled and green, rough as bark, and her teeth when she spoke were little more than long, scarlet thorns.

"I will kill him if you don't move aside," the little girl snarled and shifted so that her fingernails now dug into Charlie's soft throat, puncturing pale skin, drawing blood.

"*And what will you bring home as an offering to Carmun?*" the Cunning Man asked. "*Will you go empty-handed?*"

"Let me by," the girl demanded.

"*Set the boy free and you can go on your way,*" the Cunning Man replied. But down inside that ruined, torn body, Donnie knew Broghan was lying.

Charlie blinked, staring at the Cunning Man. "Daddy? Is that really you?"

The Cunning Man wavered. Donnie felt that old, fierce mind lose its grip on what remained of his body, and for just a moment, he swam forward into his old flesh and blood, now warped and twisted but still his. Donnie surfaced.

"Close your eyes, Charlie," he rasped in the Cunning Man's voice. "I won't let anything happen to you."

The thing masquerading as a little girl dug claws deeper into Charlie's throat.

Then there came another scream, one that split the sky. Not a scream inside Donnie Sweeney's head but one that rang out across the yards and woods. The little girl and the Cunning Man both turned, but it was Donnie, down inside, who recognized the woman he'd married as she ran across the grass toward them.

"Sarah Jane!" Barb Sweeney cried, her red-dyed hair wild, half hiding her face. "I helped you! I wanted to save you. Whatever you are, don't do this!"

Save him, Donnie thought, sending the thought with all the strength his mind had left. He could not control the Cunning Man but needed the old demon to hear him. *Save my boy!*

Sarah Jane shifted sideways and began to shuffle toward the woods, dragging Charlie along with uncanny strength for one so small. The Cunning Man shifted, keeping himself between the girl and the woods, but Charlie kept bleeding and sobbing, and Donnie knew the girl would not hesitate to kill him. Except that she needed him. In the Cunning Man's mind, Donnie sensed that very keenly.

Then Brian came running across the yard. "No, please!" he shouted, a refrain Donnie shared, down in the bit of his ghost that still infused that flesh. "You can't take him. You can't—"

Brian tripped over his own laces and went sprawling face-first into the grass, groaning as he thumped the ground.

Sarah Jane turned her focus to him.

For that brief moment, Donnie felt as if he and the Cunning Man were one and the same. He remembered dancing around ancient fires and caressing the skin of the daughters of trees, and he remembered the rot that spread in the fruit and took the children who lived at the forest's edge. Donnie felt it all in his memory. He caught the scents of spring flowers and the rich earth of fall, felt the frost of autumn on his skin, heard the laughter and the cries of mourning, all of it at once. Those feelings and memories flooded into him so that he could not make sense of them. He only knew that his bones were now the Cunning Man's bones and that the long, many-jointed fingers of the Cunning Man belonged to him now.

Together, as one, Donnie Sweeney and the Cunning Man lashed out with those impossibly long fingers and tore off the hand that had been clawing at Charlie's throat. The boy fell to his knees, then scrambled up and bolted toward his mother and brother.

With the fingers of the Cunning Man, Donnie grabbed the hair of the creature that had called itself Sarah Jane and yanked back her head. He plunged those long, bony fingers into her mouth, thrust deep, and clutched at the twitching thing down inside her. With a grunt that made the candle flames in his eyes flicker, Donnie ripped it out of her throat. It caught on her lips, and he yanked harder, until it came away with a wet, tearing noise. The thing in his hand twitched, a cluster of black roots with wicked red thorns, and began to rot and shrivel and then flake away, all in an instant.

Once, she had been a living human girl, flesh and bone, snatched from the ordinary world by Carmun, the prehistoric crone-witch who festered at the heart of Dubnos, the other land. Her own children dead, the witch had stolen new ones, down across a span of years, and infected them with the autumnal rot that touched everything in the dark place. This little girl, her soul now witch-dark, survived only by slipping into the ordinary world and luring children through the Blackthorn as offerings to her mother. One per year, in exchange for another year of life. Soft children for her larder. Fresh children for her gullet.

Receding inside the Cunning Man, stunned by the knowledge available to him now that he and Broghan were one and the same, Donnie barely noticed as the body of the hideous Sarah

Jane continued to decay. Brown rot ate through her skin and split it open. The stink of foul cider filled the air. The body burst with other roots and strange seeds, and the Cunning Man stood over it and watched to be sure that nothing took root, that this rotted soul could not return.

But there were others nearby, and Broghan, the Cunning Man, knew he had only minutes to stop them.

When the Cunning Man turned and fled back into the woods, leaving Charlie Sweeney in the arms of his mother and brother, the last of Donnie flickered out like a snuffed candle flame.

BARB SWEENEY

Barb found herself on the long steps back up to her porch before she knew it. She carried Charlie in her arms, though at eleven, he was already too big for such babying. Too heavy for her. Brian had paused a few steps closer to the door and looked back down at her.

"Come on, Mom," Brian said. "Let's get him inside, okay? I don't want to be out here."

Displacement crashed over her like a wave. Somehow she had picked up Charlie and followed Brian back to the house without even being aware of it. The last minute or so had been blacked out completely from her memory. A little prayer issued from her lips, so quiet only she and Charlie could have heard, but though his eyes were open, Charlie was not paying any attention to her at all.

"Daddy," her youngest said. "Daddy saved me."

Brian had reached the porch door, with its shattered glass panes, and stood just inside. His sneakers crunched glass underfoot as he held the door open and looked back down at them.

"That wasn't Dad. It saved us, but it wasn't—" Brian began.

Barb hushed him. "Don't." She shot a meaningful look at

him, nodding to indicate his little brother in her arms. "He doesn't need to know that."

Brian stood back while Barb carried Charlie onto the porch and then on into the kitchen. She set him down there, on the linoleum, then kissed him on the forehead. Brian might be the older brother, but not that much older, so she steered him into the seat next to Charlie and kissed his forehead, too, before putting a pot of water on the stove. She would make them hot chocolate. It seemed absurd after the amount of candy they'd eaten tonight, but they were all chilled from being outside, and she wanted to put something warm in them.

"Mom?" Brian ventured.

Barb glanced at him. "I know, honey. Just give me a minute, okay?"

"Does this mean Dad's . . ."

Barb leaned on the counter, mostly to hold herself up. She had been trying not to think about the implications of any of the events that had just unfolded in her backyard, but of course that would not be good enough for her children. They were in shock, same as she was, and they wanted and deserved honest answers.

"Probably," she admitted.

She saw Brian's shoulders sink. He let out a whimper and dropped his gaze to the floor, and a moment later, he began wiping at his eyes. Barb found her hands trembling and busied them getting mugs out of the cabinet, and then the container of Nestlé's Quik powder. Three mugs—for Brian, for Charlie, and for Julia.

Only minutes to go until midnight. Julia should have been home by now. Another night, she could have come up with rational explanations for her daughter's lateness, but tonight, all her fears had been stripped bare and proven valid.

While the water simmered, she dug the telephone book from

a kitchen drawer and looked up the Koenigs' phone number. Barb dialed the number as the pot began to steam.

"Take care of the cocoa, Brian?" she asked, giving Charlie a worried glance and listening to the phone ringing at the other end of the line. It was late, so late, but the Koenigs could not complain about anyone calling at this hour when their party must still be going.

A click on the line, and a woman answered, sharply. "Hello?"

"Is this Stella? It's Barb Sweeney."

"Barb," the woman said dryly. "What do you want? If this is about what happened tonight, I've got nothing to say."

What happened tonight? There were so many things that quip could have referred to that Barb did not have the energy to attempt to decipher it.

"I'm sorry to call so late, Stella. I'm just looking for my Julia."

Stella Koenig replied with a nasty sort of laugh, "I'm sure you are. As far as I know, she's off with the Montez girl. Make of that what you will. The party's over, and they're both gone. And neither of them is welcome here again."

Despite everything she'd endured tonight, her fear and her grief and her numbness, Mrs. Koenig's derision was enough to wake the mama bear in her. Barb's skin prickled and flushed.

"What the hell is that supposed to mean?"

"Ask your daughter," Mrs. Koenig said and hung up the phone.

The line went dead. Barb stared at the receiver in her hand and then hung up, mystified. She turned to look back out onto the porch. Behind her, Brian had gotten up and was fixing three cups of hot cocoa, but Barb could not tear her gaze away from the darkness outside the jalousie windows or through the opening in the back door where the glass had been broken in. A cold breeze blew in, roiling and eddying about them.

"Where's Julia?" Brian asked.

Barb glanced at Charlie. Her littlest one sat sipping his cocoa, oblivious to the world. He thought his dad had saved him. Terror had driven him down inside himself, so this all must seem like a dream or a nightmare to him. But Brian was more direct, more practical.

"I don't know," Barb admitted. She went to an empty chair at the kitchen table, and Brian slid the third hot chocolate mug across to her. The warmth of the mug against her hands soothed her, but she had to fight the urge to cast it aside, smash it to the floor.

Somewhere out there, Julia still wandered. Her father was dead, or close enough. Wherever Julia was, Barb could not leave her sons to go and search for her. So she did the only thing she could.

"Boys," she said, setting down her cocoa mug without having taken a sip. "I want you to pray with me."

They hated being dragged to church. Usually, they groaned and rolled their eyes if she asked them to pray. Tonight, neither of them did that. Tonight, mother and sons linked hands and all prayed together for Julia's safe return.

And then all they could do was wait.

VANESSA MONTEZ

In the small clearing around the massive blackthorn tree, Vanessa winced as she watched Arthur slice into his palm with the sharp edge of a broken branch. It made Vanessa think of crucifixion, and she tried to remember what kind of wood the Bible said those crosses had been made from. Not that she had ever been very religious.

Until now, she thought. This might not have been Catholic, but it was some kind of ritual, wasn't it? What Arthur talked about—evil spirits, monsters, some kind of purgatorial limbo—that required faith. Vanessa felt doubt like a suit of armor around her, but there were definitely holes in that armor; otherwise, she would not have come here with him or listened to his story once it began to sound utterly insane. So maybe she had a bit of belief in evil, too. Maybe not enough to stab her open palm until blood drooled out, but fortunately, nobody had asked her to do anything of the kind.

"Is the fire ready?" Arthur asked, wincing as he made a fist, hastening the blood that dripped from his wound.

"It's my first blood ritual, so you'll have to be the judge," Julia replied.

Vanessa turned to see her crouched by a small stone circle in which she had lit a fire. The flames weren't much to celebrate—

a couple of logs, branches broken up for kindling—but Arthur had said they wouldn't need a very big fire. Even so, the way the flames flickered in the dark cast shadows across Julia's face that added new contours and mysteries to her beauty, and Vanessa felt her pulse quicken. *What the hell are we doing out here in the woods with this guy?* The thought sounded in her skull like a trumpet. In the midst of a record-breakingly shitty night, she had learned the girl she had been crushing on for ages liked her back. The odds had been so hugely against such a twist of fate that it felt storybook, and she realized she was squandering it out here. What if, in the morning, after the humiliation of tonight, Julia decided to deny it all? What if Julia decided the only safe course would be to avoid Vanessa from tomorrow until they'd graduated and gone off to college, at a safe distance from each other and from malicious local assholes?

Arthur stepped up to the little firepit, raised his fist above it, and squeezed until the blood coming from inside that closed fist turned from a few drops to a thin stream. The blood appeared black in the dark, but as it passed into the firelight, the flames themselves were streaked with the familiar bright crimson. Off to Vanessa's left, the blackthorn tree seemed to tremble. The branches shook, and dozens of autumn leaves floated down, whipped by the breeze, falling all about the clearing.

"What now?" Julia asked.

Vanessa watched her across the fire. Julia studied Arthur with the expression of someone working hard to detect the secret of a magician's trick. Vanessa was about to echo Julia's question when a puff of black smoke billowed up from the small fire. It stung her eyes and made her choke. As she backed away from the flames, trying to waft away the smoke, Vanessa saw that the flames and smoke and the shadows themselves coalesced into shapes and images, and told them a story.

They watched as smoke became a boy, perhaps a bit younger than Arthur looked now, but still Arthur. A car drove past, and to Vanessa, it looked antique. Arthur and other children were trick-or-treating, but while Arthur's scarecrow costume looked the same, the others were old-fashioned, cowboys and hoboes and ugly sacks for masks. Arthur fell behind with one other child, who had to stop and tie his shoe, and while they paused, a figure emerged from a copse of trees beside the road. The smoke and flames were like a strange, blazing puppet theater, but what happened to those figures was unmistakable. The Arthur shape opened its mouth and screamed as the thing Arthur called the Cunning Man dragged him back into the trees.

Arthur sniffed as if he'd been crying. He kicked dirt onto the flames. Half the fire went out. A single log and some of the kindling continued to smoke and burn, but the fire was dying, and the spell Arthur had cast had been extinguished.

Spell? Did I really just think that word? A spell?

"So now you see," Arthur said. "My own blood went into that. Your blood can't lie. The fire can't show you anything but what really happened. It's like I told you. Broghan drags you off, and you're his prisoner from then on."

Vanessa saw the pain in his eyes. She might not have liked Arthur, but she felt his fear and that pain.

Julia and Vanessa started to speak at the same time. Vanessa motioned for her to go on, but Julia shook her head and gestured for Vanessa to continue. Despite the impossible thing they had just seen, Vanessa smiled.

"Maybe it's all some kind of trick," she told Arthur, "but if I'm playing devil's advocate here, let's say everything you said is real and what you just did wasn't like a magician's illusion or whatever. What do you want from us?"

"Just . . . someone to understand, I guess," Arthur said.

He reached over his head and plucked a partly withered leaf from the blackthorn tree. "Someone who will help me hide. I only have a few more minutes, and then all of this is over."

Julia crouched by the fire again and began feeding leaves and small sticks back into it, banking the flames, bringing it back to life. "He can't get you after midnight?"

"You can come through as soon as the liminal space begins," Arthur said. "But you can't go back until it reaches the zenith of its power. That's from midnight until one in the morning."

"So you want to go back?" Julia asked, shooting Arthur a hard look. "That wasn't clear to me before. You think you can go back in time?"

Arthur frowned and stared at the fire, now blossoming again. "I don't know, but at least I can return to the where, even if not the when."

Julia stood up. "You could do that on a bus."

Vanessa had followed it all. Some teachers underestimated her intelligence, assuming she couldn't possibly be as smart as white students, and certainly not smarter than they were. But she knew *liminal* meant some kind of threshold, like the moment the tone of a sound shifted out of the range of human perception, so maybe dogs could hear it but people could not. A liminal moment might be the instant between daylight and darkness. A barely perceptible place between places. That was this clearing and the blackthorn tree. They only had Arthur's word for it, but she had never seen either the clearing or the tree before, and this spot certainly felt different. She felt awake, alive, her skin prickling, nerve endings firing.

Vanessa did not always understand people, however. She might have been smart, but not about that. So while she could tell that Julia did not trust Arthur, she couldn't see why. He had irritated them and taken up too much of their time already, and Vanessa yearned for more time with Julia, but how could she not be fascinated by this? By *magic*, because they could call it whatever they wanted to, but they would just be coming up with other words to avoid calling it what it was.

"You still bleeding?" Julia asked.

Arthur stiffened. He backed toward the blackthorn tree, holding his wounded hand against his threadbare scarecrow costume. "It'll stop soon."

"I don't want it to stop," Julia said. Then she laughed, and Vanessa thought she had never seen a faker laugh in her life. "You kicked dirt over the fire awfully fast, Arthur. I think I believe what you said about using your own blood, that the fire can only show you something that actually happened. But I'd like you to squeeze out a few more ounces of blood onto these flames and let us see what happened next."

Vanessa clucked her tongue. After what Arthur had been through, this seemed very unfair. Even mean.

But then she noticed the way Arthur's eyes narrowed and the sneer that spread across his face.

"Maybe I'm through bleeding for tonight," he said.

Julia nodded. "Yeah, I thought you might say something like that." She walked over to Vanessa and took her hand, gently but firmly. "I don't know what you're hiding, but I don't want to stick around to find out. Vanessa and I are leaving."

We are? Vanessa wanted to ask. Was about to ask. But then she saw Arthur's expression darken even further, saw him scowl, revealing a glimpse of sharp red teeth inside, as if he'd started to bleed from his mouth instead of his hand.

"Have a good night, Arthur," Vanessa said. She squeezed Julia's hand, and the two of them started out of the clearing.

"No," Arthur told them. "You'll stay with me. We'll count down the last few minutes together."

"The last few minutes of what?" Julia asked.

Arthur only smiled.

This time, painted with that hideous scarecrow makeup, his smile was horrible.

STEVE KOENIG

S teve felt like a bomb had exploded in the middle of his life. He knew he should have followed Vanessa immediately, but in the aftermath of the scuffle between his dad and Vanessa's, he had felt pinned in a spotlight. Awkwardness had always had a paralyzing effect on him, but that moment had been worse than any before it. His father had outed Vanessa and Julia in public, and worse than that, he had revealed a hatefulness that Steve had never imagined. He knew his father could be an asshole and said nasty, bigoted things sometimes, but he had always told himself that was a generational thing and that his father didn't really mean it.

For the first few minutes after Vanessa and Julia had left with that Arthur kid, Steve had simmered with rage, but not at his dad. Yes, his father had done something unforgivable, but he wasn't to blame for the pain Vanessa would be feeling— that was all on Steve. He had betrayed her trust, broken the confidence of the girl who'd been his closest friend all his life. He had known how important it was to Vanessa to keep her feelings private, and still, Steve had confided in his parents.

It wasn't your secret, he thought for the hundredth time.

Within minutes of the ugly scene ending, most of the people at the party had left or were awkwardly saying good night. Even the few young people who had hung around made quick exits. Cynthia and Hunter left without a word to Steve, whispering to each other, and Steve had the idea that Cynthia was busy assuring her boyfriend that she'd had no idea Vanessa was gay. Only Owen O'Leary—of all people— hung back a moment to speak with Steve.

"You want me to come with you?" Owen asked.

Steve frowned. "Huh?"

"To find them. You're gonna go look for them, right?"

He would have thought it impossible to feel worse, but Owen's question made him deeply ashamed. Of course he would go after Vanessa. The fact he hadn't already gone made him feel like he'd swallowed a beehive and it had gotten lodged in his throat.

"I'm good," Steve said. "I know these woods."

But now he was stumbling around in the dark, searching for signs of recent footsteps on the path as if he knew something about tracking. Like he was the last of the fucking Mohicans. Steve had gone by the two spots in the woods where he and Vanessa sometimes hung out, but he had found no sign of her. He had destroyed their friendship tonight—he knew that— and he had no illusions about the possibility of being forgiven. But even if she never forgave him, Steve would not be able to sleep tonight without first apologizing to both Vanessa and Julia. He told himself it wasn't purely selfish, that it wasn't about making himself feel better, that he just wanted her to know he had never imagined his parents could be so awful. But of course that was mostly a lie. He wanted Vanessa to feel better, but he also wanted her forgiveness, or at least to be able to tell himself he had tried.

Hands in his pockets, Steve made his way west, wondering if he had gone the wrong direction from the start. The girls had started in this direction, but maybe Vanessa had changed her mind and decided to go home instead. He kept trudging along, leaves crunching underfoot, but with every step, he began to think he might be moving farther away from her, and with every second, he feared his chances of making up with her were slipping away. He should have gone to her house, knocked on the door, apologized to her parents for his stupidity, and then just waited for her. A phone call wouldn't do it, not when they lived two doors away from each other.

Steve slowed on the path and then halted. A low stone wall ran along on his right—an old property boundary from the eighteenth century—and he sat on the stones and let his head loll back. Staring up at the partly denuded branches and the indigo sky, he took a deep breath. How long would he search before he decided all this had been fucked up beyond his ability to fix it—at least for tonight?

"Shit," he muttered, and he stood. There was no point in just wandering the woods in the middle of the night. He would go to Vanessa's house after all. The idea of facing her father made him feel nauseous, so he would sit on the swing set in her backyard and wait to see her bedroom light go on. How many times had they thrown stones at each other's windows, then had whispered conversations in the dark, like Romeo and Juliet without the romance and suicide?

He took a deep breath, started to turn, and a frown creased his forehead. Someone had started a fire in the woods. It wasn't that unusual—there were a few safe firepits, and some neighbors had them in their backyards—but it was late. A flicker of alarm went through him. Had someone left a fire burning or not put it out completely? An unattended fire in these woods could be devastating.

Grateful for the distraction, he started along the path again. Fifty yards farther, he came to a narrower trail on the left that he did not remember seeing before, but the smoke—

and he had no doubt it was smoke now—came from that direction. Steve followed the trail, seeking that fire, just to make sure.

He didn't want anyone else getting hurt tonight.

JULIA SWEENEY

Julia saw the smile on Arthur's face and knew she'd been right not to trust him. He had shown them a little magic, and she felt sure that bit with the fire and his blood had been no trick. She had watched Arthur cut himself, had seen the images forged by smoke and fire. That had not been an illusion or a hallucination—that was *magic*. It should have delighted her, but instead, it made her skin crawl. All night she had felt his presence as something oppressive, no less malignant than a predator spying on them from the bushes. She had no evidence, no reason not to trust him, but if he could do that with his blood and a little fire, what else could he do?

"We should go, Vanessa," Julia said.

Arthur's grin turned to a sneer. "*We should go, Vanessa,*" he echoed, mimicking her in a voice that sounded almost like a parrot.

Vanessa stepped between them. "Cut that shit out right now. Who do you think you are?"

"Someone who needs your help," Arthur said, but he had stopped pretending to be timid or kind or even frightened. He didn't seem like he needed anyone's help. "And that means you can't leave this clearing until the stroke of midnight."

Who talked like that? *The stroke of midnight.* Julia took Vanessa's elbow, and the two of them backed toward the trail opening. They would run if it came to that, anything to be away from Arthur, now that he'd turned out to be such a creep.

"I wanted to help you," Vanessa said. "But we don't owe you anything."

Julia moved Vanessa behind her and gave a little shove to get her moving down the trail.

"Little bitches," Arthur snarled.

He lunged past Julia, latched onto Vanessa with both hands, spun and hurled her through the air. She struck the blackthorn tree and cried out as she fell through its branches to land at its roots. Thorns tore her skin all the way down.

Julia had never thrown a real punch in her life, but she played soccer and kickball and back in middle school had routinely booted the kickball from the recess yard all the way across Route 125. She grabbed Arthur's hair with both hands, and as he turned, she kicked him in the balls as hard as she could, Vanessa's scream still ringing in her ears.

"You nasty fucker!" Julia said as Arthur grunted in pain and dropped to the ground. "I don't care what you can do. I don't care what kind of danger you're in."

Arthur pulled himself into a fetal ball as she kicked him in the back and head, once, twice, a third time. The fourth time, he whipped around and grabbed her ankle, then yanked hard, so Julia tumbled to the dirt beside him. Julia tasted leaves and rot in her mouth and tried to spit them out, but he was on top of her before she could blink.

He smashed her wrists to the ground on either side of her head, held her down, straddling her—he bent and hissed in her face, and when Julia got a good look at him, all logic went out of her. She stared at the bruised, veined face, the green-and-brown skin, the black lips and red shark teeth, and she screamed. Not the kind of scream she used on her brothers but, for the first time in her life, a real scream.

"I only need one of you," the Arthur-thing whispered.

He released her wrists and wrapped his cold fingers around her throat. The stench of his breath choked her. She tried to rip his hands from her throat, but they were like stone, coated in something slick and cold. Skin sloughed off his arms where she fought him. Julia could not breathe, black dots appeared in her vision, her thoughts slid away as if sluicing down a drain, but worse than all of that was the pain in her throat as his thumbs began to cut her skin, crushing something inside her. With her last gasp, she clawed his face and peeled skin and muscle away. It was soft and split like rotting fruit.

A scream erupted in the clearing, and it was not her own.

Something flashed in the corner of her vision, and then she could breathe. Arthur had been struck, tackled, dragged off her, and as Julia gasped and wheezed and rolled onto her hands and knees, she looked over to find it was not Vanessa who had saved her but Steve Koenig.

Julia tried to rasp his name, but only a kind of sigh came out. Her voice, now, just that sigh.

Hatred rippled through her. What if this thing, Arthur, had done permanent damage to her? Better than being dead, yes, but that didn't stop the rage. She glanced over at the fire, where one of the smaller logs jutted out of the edge of the small stone circle. Julia staggered toward it, one hand on her throat as she wheezed. She wrapped a hand around that log and lifted it, holding it like a club.

Arthur rose from the ground, holding Steve's jacket in his left fist. He was so much stronger than any kid his age should have been, but Julia had seen his real face, and whatever the fuck Arthur might be, he was no child. With his right hand, Arthur struck Steve hard enough to split the bone over his cheek. Steve's blood spattered the ground and his own jacket.

Julia hoisted the burning log, holding the unburned side in both hands like a sawed-off baseball bat.

Behind Arthur, Vanessa rose from the shadows. Her face and neck were scratched and bleeding badly from the thorns, but she raised one of the broken branches from the blackthorn tree and called Arthur's name.

He turned toward Vanessa just as she smashed him in the eyes with that thorny branch. She yanked the branch back, raking those thorns across Arthur's eyes.

The thing screamed. Black fluid burst from its eyes. Steve tore free from its grasp, and then the three of them were together—Vanessa, Julia, and Steve—all wounded, but alive. The Arthur-thing turned toward them. It had gaping, rotting holes where its eyes should have been.

"I don't need to see you to kill you," it said. "Remember, I only need one alive."

Julia held up the burning log, still with both hands, thinking to attack.

Then she came to her senses. "To hell with this," she said. "Run!"

None of them knew there were two of them—Arthur, and another thing, who would have looked like a much younger boy if not for the rotting skin and yellow, putrid eyes. He came out of the trees, grabbed Steve by the arm, and twisted, broke bones, and smashed Steve to the ground, all so fast that Julia and Vanessa barely had time to shout his name.

"Leonard, no!" the Arthur-thing screamed.

But the other thing, the rotting little boy-thing Arthur called Leonard, took Steve's skull in both hands. Steve's eyes went wide, and he cried out something like a prayer, then Leonard twisted his head so hard that the snapping of his neck resounded across the clearing, and Steve was dead.

Vanessa screamed his name, her eyes wide as she fell to her knees. Julia could not scream, only stare. She felt frozen, unsure if she continued to breathe or her heart continued to beat. How could this be?

Leonard turned to look at Arthur with murder in his eyes. "Now you have two," he said. "And we need them both alive."

"You bastard!" Arthur snarled.

"Enough," Leonard replied. "We're out of time. The Cunning Man is here. He's come for us. We've only a minute or two, and then we can be gone from here, but I need one of these children."

The Arthur-thing darted forward and backhanded Leonard across the face. His cheek split, and brown rot dribbled down his chin. Leonard crouched, ready for a fight.

Julia's breath hitched and she snapped alert, like waking from hypnosis. She glanced over at Vanessa, who had crawled to Steve's corpse and now wept silently at his side—a little broken, but still alive. Vanessa bled all over from where the thorns had cut her, but unlike Steve, she had a chance to survive this. Julia had waited so long for the moment when she could tell Vanessa how she felt, for the moment when they would look into each other's eyes and feel the connection Julia always hoped would develop. She was a high school senior, so what the hell did she know about love? But she had felt something for Vanessa for the longest time, something that stirred deep inside her. Love or not, she could never have lived with herself if she left Vanessa there. Running away was out of the question.

"You're meant to find your own offering!" the Arthur-thing sneered.

The Leonard-thing shoved him away. "I chose one, but I had to kill him. I've tainted him. I've got him out searching for a substitute, but we are out of time. I told you, the Cunning Man . . ."

Leonard's voice trailed off. Something had begun to happen to the blackthorn tree. Both of these things, these hideous rotting boys, turned to watch as the split in the trunk of the blackthorn cracked open all the way, as if the trunk had once grown apart and then back together, creating a vertical window shaped like a teardrop. Cold wind swept through from the other side of that window, blowing freezing rain through. Drops of ice flecked the otherwise dry clearing, pattered autumn leaves. Whatever showed through that window was not the other side of the tree.

"Midnight," Leonard said. "No more time. Give me one of them."

Arthur looked as if he were considering it.

Julia took Vanessa by the wrist and helped her stand. Vanessa seemed reluctant to leave Steve, but only for a second. Her best friend he might have been, but nobody could save him now.

Julia tugged Vanessa toward the open woods—not a trail, just the trees, anyplace but here. The two rotting boys were glaring at each other. Julia stepped on a few dried leaves that crinkled beneath her heel.

The things turned as one to stare at Julia and Vanessa.

"Run!" Julia shouted.

She and Vanessa bolted for the trees.

They would not make it.

CHLOE BARBOSA

Pain racked Chloe's body. She had smashed her nose on a thick root jutting out of the trail, and now her nostrils were clogged by her own blood. Her back and arms and ribs throbbed, and she felt sure she must have a concussion. She had screamed at first, when the girl had dragged her out of her house. Not a little girl, of course, not really. Delilah had strength and speed that could not be natural. She'd hurt Chloe, and the hurried race from the house had done so much more injury.

Chloe gasped, tasting air as if for the first time. She sucked it in, and silent tears sprang to her eyes. Tears of pain and rage and humiliation, and of shock.

They had stopped moving.

Dragged over grass and roots and dirt as she'd been, panic had shut her down. But in these moments of stillness, her thoughts and voice seemed to work again.

"Please . . ." she said, very softly, and then she choked on the blood that had been dripping down the back of her throat from her shattered nose.

But Delilah wasn't listening. Someone had made the little Raggedy Ann stop on the trail.

"Get out of the way, dead thing," Delilah said, with none of the sad, lost, pitiful little-girl tones she had used earlier.

The voice that replied sounded like the buzz of angry wasps inside their paper nest. "*Give her to me.*"

Delilah laughed. "I don't know which of the others made you—which of them would be so stupid—but if you've got a little of their spark in you, then you know I can't do that."

The voice only repeated the same four words. "*Give her to me.*"

But something about the voice, buzz of wasps or not, seemed familiar.

Chloe lay on the ground, relieved to breathe, thinking any second she would have the strength to stand up and run. A thousand questions churned in her brain, trying to force her to pay attention, to sort out what had happened tonight— what Delilah really was, if her father was okay—but her body pulsed with enough pain to distract her.

She started to rise. On hands and knees, she glanced up at Delilah's back. Beyond the little girl, someone else stood on the trail—the person who had blocked their way, who spoke with the voice of wasps.

"Rick," Chloe whispered.

Something awful had been done to him. His face looked green and brown, one cheek caved in. One of his eyes had sunken, and amid the tatters of his coat and shirt, his chest looked bloody and concave, and she wondered how he could even still stand.

Then Delilah ran at him, and Chloe didn't have time to wonder anymore.

She reached out and grabbed the back of Delilah's Raggedy Ann costume. The little girl might have been impossibly strong, but she was small. So much smaller than Chloe, who picked her up in fistfuls of velveteen red costume, turned, and hurled her into the trees. Delilah struck a thin birch tree, spun around, and landed on the other side of a fallen oak.

"Rick," Chloe said, turning to her brother. "Oh my God, what is going on—"

He snatched her by the hair and slapped her hard across the face, striking her broken nose. Fresh blood showered the trail as pain burst like fireworks in her brain. Her vision went dark, and she began to stumble, the pain bad enough to black her out for a moment.

Her little brother did not speak. No spark in his eyes suggested that he had any idea who she was. This close to him, the stench reached her, a stink of weeks-old compost, and Delilah's words echoed in her mind. *Get out of the way, dead thing.*

Her brother was dead.

If this thing had been Rick, it wasn't him any longer.

"She's mine!" little Delilah shrieked, stomping back toward the path in her Raggedy Ann costume. It would have been comical if not for the gleam in her eyes and the red teeth she bared, sharp as a saw blade.

Rick ignored the girl. Chloe tried to fight him, but when she punched him in the side of the head, the skin split open and her fist sank half an inch into the putrid mash of his flesh. She would have screamed, but her stomach revolted at the stink and the horror. Trapped by Rick's fist tangled in her hair, Chloe twisted around and vomited onto the trail, blood still dripping from her nostrils.

Again, the little Raggedy Ann shrieked for Rick to stop, but the dead thing—*My brother, oh my God, my little brother, not Rick, this can't be real*—grabbed her by the back of the neck and began to propel her along the path in front of him.

But then they heard Delilah cry out in alarm instead of fury.

Chloe stopped. Rick tried to push her from behind, and she stumbled and they both fell, him on top of her. Disgust roiled through her, and fear gave way before it like a dam. Grief swept in as she tried to push the dead boy away.

"*Chloe*," the dead thing said.

Her eyes opened. Her head spun from concussion and shock, but she felt a glimmer of hope. Rick knew her. Some part of him remained inside the dead thing.

Hope ran out of her like blood.

As he hoisted her to her feet, Chloe saw motion on the trail. Someone else had arrived. A tall figure, looming over a snarling Delilah, whose Raggedy Ann costume looked torn and filthy. The first time she'd seen the man, she had mistaken him for Julia's dad. But this thing was no more Mr. Sweeney than the dead boy was Chloe's brother. Her mind felt as if it were tearing itself apart—first Delilah, then Rick, and now this thing that wore Donnie Sweeney's face like badly applied papier-mâché.

Delilah fought the thing that wasn't Mr. Sweeney. The little creature ripped away from him and darted into the woods, fleeing in silence, abandoning her claim to Chloe. Whatever the little Raggedy Ann girl might be, she had not been frightened of Rick, but the thing wearing Mr. Sweeney's face obviously terrified her.

Chloe stole one last look at the Sweeney-thing, and then Rick dragged her along the trail. She heard voices calling her name. Her mom and dad, strident and panicked, shouting for her.

The thing with Mr. Sweeney's face rushed after her, impossibly fast. He shattered the dead boy's wrist and twisted her away. Dizzy with nausea and pain, Chloe went to her knees on the trail. The dead boy and Mr. Sweeney fought, but all Chloe could focus on were the voices crying her name.

They came around a turn in the path—her mom and dad, together, and Billie Suarez behind them, all three wide-eyed and desperate with hope.

When they saw the Mr. Sweeney-thing and their dead son fighting, it was Chloe's dad who screamed the loudest. That did not surprise her. Their mother had loved them just as much, but their father's heart had always been more tender more vulnerable, and Chloe knew this would destroy him.

She almost laughed at the absurdity of the thought. None of this could be real. None of this was possible. If this were really happening, she thought they were probably all going to die.

TONY BARBOSA

Tony had never been stoic. Even as a child, he had been full of passions and hobbies and recruited as many friends as he could to share those things as if they were adventures on the high seas. As a grown man, so much of that enthusiasm had been packed away in a trunk and stored in the attic of his mind, gathering dust. Halloween brought it out, and so had the births of his children. Work and marriage and all the mundane obligations of life could not steal away the joy his children gave him.

When he and Alice and Billie came around the turn in the path and he saw the thing that looked like Donnie Sweeney running at his children, Tony shouted. There were no words in that shout, only fear for his children, and then . . .

Rick shifted on the trail, just enough to catch the moonlight.

He remembered what Billie had told them, what she had seen, and he knew it was all true—that his son was dead. Tony had sung Rick to sleep hundreds of times, had clutched the feverish baby against his chest at 3:00 a.m., had tried to talk him through his first crush and his humiliation the day he realized he couldn't hit a baseball if his life depended on it.

Billie had been right.

Rick was right there on the trail, in the fading moonlight, his once-handsome face a ruin of violence and strange gore, with what looked like fragments of tree bark jutting from the wreckage of his cheek instead of bone.

Tony broke. His heart went hollow. He remembered teaching Rick how to bait his own hook, the way his little son had pricked his finger and drawn blood, and how brave he'd been, just wiping the blood away and carrying on. The sun had risen only a short time before, a golden glow that lit the boy's skin and made Tony think of his father and the generations of Portuguese fishermen before him, and how one day he would bring Ricky to Aveiro, the little village where their family had its roots, and they would cast a line into the ocean and, in doing so, be connected in a single strand all the way back to the first Barbosa to fish the coast of Portugal. That morning, the salt breeze had swept Ricky's curly black hair into his eyes, and when the tip of his fishing pole had jumped for the first time, the boy hadn't been startled, he'd been elated.

The thing in front of Tony now was not his son. This was not Rick.

Father and son would never fish the coast of Aveiro.

The creature that had been Donnie Sweeney—the Cunning Man—ran at the dead boy who had once been Tony's son. Donnie shoved Chloe aside, and at least that was a blessing. Chloe had blood on her face, but she cried and called for her mother and father, and she looked like herself.

Alive, and herself.

But the Cunning Man grabbed Rick by the throat and lifted him off the ground.

Both Alice and Billie were screaming at the monster, but Tony started toward the Cunning Man and shouted louder than the others.

"Put him down, goddamn you!" The words were like a roar. And the next ones surprised him. "That's my son!"

The Cunning Man paused, still holding the ruin of Rick up by its throat. It twitched, one good eye staring at Tony. The Cunning Man swiveled its head to look at him.

"*This is not your son. It is a corruption of every good thing about your son.*"

"I know," Tony said. "But please . . ."

Alice and Billie came up behind him. Alice slid her arm around Tony. No matter what else they might be, together they were still mother and father.

"Please, Donnie," she said, pale with shock, "if there's any Donnie left in there. We know it's not Rick anymore, but please just leave him to us."

The Cunning Man narrowed his eyes, then turned to toss what remained of Rick into a sprawl at the feet of the dead boy's father and mother and best friend. Billie whimpered and crouched, reaching for him. The thing that had been Rick sprang up as if to attack her, but Tony Barbosa had expected that. He dropped down onto this thing that had infected his son. It was strong, but Alice came down beside him, and together they held their son's thrashing body against the dirt and leaves of the trail.

"*You should destroy it,*" the Cunning Man said. "*It will only cause you pain.*"

He turned and ran deeper into the woods, along the trail, in search of other things that didn't belong in this world.

Tony and Alice held their son down while Billie stood to one side. She hugged herself and shook her head, unable to tear her gaze away from the dead thing her best friend had become. Chloe had picked herself up. Now she went to Billie and opened her arms, and the two girls embraced, both of them shuddery with tears.

"What do we do with him?" Alice asked.

"It's *not* him!" Billie cried. "I told you. That's not Rick anymore."

The dead boy thrashed against his parents, but he didn't have the strength or speed of Delilah—whatever she might be. Numbed by shock, all Tony could think in that moment was that they needed to stop Rick from fighting them, because every time he struggled, more of his skin sloughed away. The stink made Tony's eyes burn even more than his grief.

His son's eyes sought him out.

"*Dad*," Rick said. "*Please, let me go. How can you do this to your son? Mommy? Why are you hurting me?*"

Alice reeled away from Rick as if she'd burned herself on him. Her hands trembled as she tried to find words and managed only the stilted, muttered prayers of the bereft. Right arm free, the dead boy tried to force Tony off him, but Tony straddled him now, knees holding the dead thing's arms down. He unbuckled his belt and snaked it through the loops, fought the dead thing but managed to get Rick facedown.

"Help me with him!" Tony snapped.

But Alice could not. She stayed where she was, half turned away, a piece of her broken.

Chloe and Billie hurried over, and in moments, Tony had belted Rick's hands behind his back and held him there, face in the dirt. For a moment, the boy didn't move, and Tony stared at the so-familiar back of his son's head, at the curve of his ear, the way the hair at the nape of his neck made little S-curls, and he felt just how cold the body beneath him had become on this chilly night. Reality carved out Tony's insides with merciless claws. He had experienced grief before, but nothing like this.

"What are we supposed to do?" he asked.

Deeper in the woods, someone began to scream, and Tony's head snapped up. "Christ."

"Oh no." Billie let go of Chloe and took a step along the path, staring into the trees.

Alice didn't even look up.

Tony looked at Billie. "You told us about that boy—"

"Leonard," Billie replied.

"And there was Delilah," Chloe said. "Dad, what if there are others? You guys saved me, but how many kids have they tried to drag into the woods?"

Billie stared at Rick, who jerked against the belt that bound his wrists and struggled against his father's weight on his back. "Leonard did this to Rick. But he didn't want to. He wanted us with him at midnight for something. Wanted us alive."

"Midnight," Chloe replied. "Delilah said she would be safe then."

Tony stared at his wife, the mother of his children, the living one and the dead. She seemed to feel the weight of his stare because she flinched and turned her head farther away.

"Alice, you need to stay with him," Tony said. "Keep him here. Put weight on him, hold him down."

"I can't do it," Alice said quietly.

Chloe went to her. "You have to, Mom. Or other kids are gonna end up like Rick or just vanish completely. We're out here and we know what's happening. Most people are home asleep. We can't pretend there's nothing we can do."

"Alice," Tony said again.

She looked at him, then forced herself to glance down at Rick. Sorrow painted her features, but she stood a bit taller and then came to kneel by them.

"Go," Alice said. "Save someone else's kid."

"Jesus. That's not fair. How can you—"

"No, I mean it. We've done what we can here. We've got Chloe back. See if you can do the same for someone else," Alice said.

Tony stared down at Rick. He'd twisted his head so the left side of his face was visible, and the rot had continued. More bark showed where bone ought to have been. He slid over and let Alice take over for him, and then Chloe and Billie came and knelt on either side to help her.

"You'll be okay?" Tony asked them.

It was Chloe who looked up at him. "Hurry, Dad. Please."

Tony turned and ran along the trail, pursuing the Cunning Man. Behind him, he heard Alice and the girls trying to comfort his dead son, who was already beyond comfort. But there might still be some good he could do tonight.

JULIA SWEENEY

The blackthorn tree irised open to reveal another world. Evil things with the faces of boys fought over Julia and Vanessa, each wanting to drag them through as some kind of offering to what they called their mother, a witch called Carmun. They'd killed Steve Koenig. Julia and Vanessa were both injured . . . but they could run.

Julia had Vanessa by the hand. Her body ached and blood filled her nostrils, and later she would scream and tremble and weep, but first she had to earn herself a "later." Fear fueled her, panic made her strong, and in two steps, Julia darted between a pair of oak trees, yanking Vanessa behind her. She glanced at the ground, fearful of fallen logs in the dark, and when she looked up, she saw a little girl in a torn and dirty Raggedy Ann costume, a mop of red wig on her head.

This time, Julia understood instantly that the little girl was not human.

Vanessa tried to stop, shying from Raggedy Ann.

Julia refused. If they stopped now, they would never get away from these creatures. They would end up dead here, or maybe on the other side of that blackthorn tree, which she feared would be even worse. She tightened her grip on Vanessa's hand and lowered her left shoulder, aiming right at the little Raggedy Ann. No matter how strong these things were, Julia thought if she could just knock the girl down, they could keep running. If they could get out of the woods, find other people, make it difficult for the rotten things to follow, they might live.

And something's hunting them. The Cunning Man. Broghan, that's what Arthur called him. They're afraid of him and out of time.

If she and Vanessa could get away, right now, they still had a chance.

Raggedy Ann dodged as Julia went to knock her over, and as she did, the little thing shot a tiny fist into Julia's gut. Crying out, Julia let go of Vanessa's hand. Her foot caught on a stone or root or deadfall, and she went sprawling into leaves and pine needles. She rolled and fetched up in the scraping needles of a drooping pine, but she kept herself in motion, scrambling out the other side.

Julia lurched to her feet and spun in search of Vanessa, ready for them both to run again.

Raggedy Ann stood a dozen feet away, one hand in Vanessa's hair and the other locked like a manacle around her wrist. "If you're running from the Blackthorn at midnight, I wager you've got some idea what you're running from. We'll go back there now, or your friend will die in front of you and I'll still have *you* for the witch."

Julia hesitated. Shame washed over her for that instant of cowardice, but she could not deny she felt it. Vanessa had been a part of her daydreams and fantasies since the seventh grade, so strong and smart and beautiful, but it had only been hours since the walls had come down between them and the spark of real possibility had ignited. They weren't in love. Julia only had the slightest inkling of what actual love might feel like—as if she were at the base of a mountain and could see the peak, but love was on the other side. And if this wasn't love, was she supposed to die at Vanessa's side when there might be a slim possibility that if she ran, right now, this Raggedy Abomination might not bother to chase her?

Every muscle wanted to run, but her heart wouldn't let her, not because she was in love but because she knew she would never be able to live with herself if she survived and Vanessa died tonight.

As she started toward Raggedy Ann and Vanessa, Julia saw the rotting boy, Leonard, step up behind Raggedy Ann.

"Hello, Delilah," the rotting boy said. "Your timing is perfect. I'm grateful for your intervention."

Raggedy Ann twisted around, hauling Vanessa with her. She gave a feline hiss as she faced him, like an animal who'd just caught her prey and didn't want to share. "You're not getting her, Leonard."

The rotting boy smiled. "I don't need her. One is enough."

Julia felt as if she had turned invisible. The way the creatures, these dead Halloween children, faced off against one another, it seemed they had practically forgotten her. "Delilah" and "Leonard." But where had the third monster gone? The scarecrow kid, who'd said his name was "Arthur" and who'd pretended to befriend them?

As Julia watched, Raggedy Ann released Vanessa's wrist but still held on to her hair, driving her forward, bent over, like the cruel owner of a dog who'd misbehaved. Vanessa had given up on tears and whimpering. Instead, she bared her teeth like a wolf and growled until that growl became words.

"Little bitch," Vanessa snarled. "I'm gonna tear you apart."

Leonard laughed, amused by Vanessa's bravado. But then his head swiveled and he smiled at Julia, and she realized he had not forgotten her after all. *I don't need her*, Leonard had said to the little dead Raggedy Ann, and now Julia understood why.

He didn't need to fight Delilah over Vanessa . . . not when he could catch Julia anytime he wished.

Leonard came toward her, and in spite of everything she had seen, reality seemed to tilt into dreaming. Despite flesh like rotting fruit and the row of red shark's teeth, he still had the size and features of a little kid, no more than ten. Delilah looked even younger. Julia and Vanessa should not fear them, should be able to overpower them. They were absurd, impossible children . . . but Julia knew they weren't children at all.

"Come here, girl," Leonard said. "Don't make me chase you."

He needs you alive, Julia reminded herself. That gave her enough strength to obey. As Delilah forced Vanessa into the clearing with the blackthorn tree, Julia followed them, walking slowly toward Leonard.

Steve Koenig's body lay on the ground, limbs splayed like some discarded doll, skull caved in, but now she saw that his corpse was not alone. The scarecrow kid, the thing that had introduced itself as Arthur, lay dead just a few feet from Steve. Its head had been torn off and split open, rotted on the outside but papery like a wasp nest on the inside. Its body had been eviscerated, insides tossed around, strange organs that looked as if they came from some bizarre orchard. Whatever Arthur might really have been, it was dead now.

Which meant only two of these things, twisted golems who procured children for the witch, remained alive. Two rotting things, and Julia and Vanessa—an offering for each of them to bring back to their hellish mother.

"Jules," Vanessa said quietly.

Julia glanced at her as the two monsters marched them toward the iris that beckoned from the blackthorn tree.

"We'll be okay," Vanessa said.

Julia felt sick. She wanted to laugh. She stared through the opening in the heart of the Blackthorn. The wind and rain blasted through into the clearing, and she shivered as the first drops reached her, face and clothing spattered by the rain of another place.

"No," she rasped, unable to look at Vanessa. "I'm sorry, babe. I wish that were true, but it's just not."

"Jules?" Vanessa said again, the one word now a plea for her to take it back, to share some hope.

But Julia could find none to give her.

Something must have snapped in Vanessa—dark reality waking her up to their fate—because she screamed, then, and launched herself forward. Julia cried out, thinking Vanessa had surrendered, that she would hurl herself through the opening in the blackthorn tree. The rotting little Raggedy Ann must have thought the same, because she grinned and hastened her own steps, happy to get through the tree faster, still holding a fistful of Vanessa's hair.

Vanessa dropped to one knee. The little rotting girl crashed into her, and Vanessa flipped her into the tree. The impact shook Delilah's grip loose, and Vanessa found herself free.

Julia saw the opportunity. "Run!" she screamed.

But Vanessa didn't run away. Instead, she picked up a fallen branch and hurled herself at Leonard. She swung the branch with such ferocity that Leonard could not dodge. It struck his head, splitting rotten flesh on the side where it had been mostly unbroken.

Julia pulled free.

Vanessa took her hand. Together they started to run.

Leonard leaped on Julia from behind, and she fell to the ground. Vanessa screamed her name, but Leonard only pushed Julia's face into the dirt and bent to whisper into her ear.

"Nowhere to run," the rotting boy said, the words on a wave of nauseatingly awful breath.

But then someone else ran into the clearing and clomped to a stop.

Leonard jerked backward, scrambled off Julia's back as if suddenly she didn't matter to him at all. Julia heard Vanessa say, "Oh my God," in the smallest breath, and then Julia looked up at the thing that had just arrived.

"Broghan," the little rotting Raggedy Ann said, striding across the clearing toward him. "You won't save them."

Julia shook her head. She crab-walked backward across the clearing. Her left hand slid in the dry crust of what had once been false-Arthur's face, and she barely took note. Broghan was the Cunning Man, the creature that frightened these monsters so much. Arthur had claimed the Cunning Man would take him back to some other world and keep him as a tortured captive. For the first time, Julia realized that had been true, but it took on new meaning now. These rotting things were terrified of the Cunning Man, and she could see why. Seven feet tall, the creature had eyes that were little flames in the dark. His fingers were monstrously long and thin, with sharp claws for tips. But if he had come to destroy these rotting children, she refused to fear the Cunning Man.

Until he stepped into the moonlight and Julia saw its face.

Her father's face, but torn and twisted, little more than a mask over a skull. For just a moment, the Cunning Man looked at her, and the expression on that face looked so much like her father that she thought he might still be inside, looking out, but then it passed and she understood that her father was dead. Donnie Sweeney, dead.

He had hurt her tonight, both physically and in her soul, and he had been like poison to his marriage to her mother. Yet there had been so much laughter in Julia's childhood, so many times when he'd made her smile, when he'd played with her and made her feel loved.

"Daddy?" she said, though she knew he was gone.

The Cunning Man glanced at her again, but so briefly it might have been her imagination. Then he started toward Delilah.

"*Go back to the witch*," the Cunning Man said, his voice like branches cracking in high wind. "*Leave these to their lives.*"

"You know we can't do that," the putrid little Raggedy Ann said. "Our punishment if we return empty-handed—"

"*Is better than the death I will deliver*," the Cunning Man said.

Julia saw his lips curl up at the edges, a smirk her father had worn every time he knew he had won an argument. She slumped onto the ground, defeated by grief.

Someone touched her left hand, and she flinched, then looked up to find it had been Vanessa. Bleeding, pale, face pinched with pain, Vanessa knelt by Julia and brushed the hair from her face. She bent and kissed Julia's temple, a heartfelt comfort, and if Julia could have found any comfort in that moment, it would have been with this girl, her friend, whom she so adored. But she could find only sorrow.

"Keep them," Leonard said, startling the others in the clearing—those who still lived.

Raggedy Ann spun and glared at him incredulously. "Leonard, no—"

But the rotting little boy waved her protest away. "It's the Cunning Man, Delilah. I'll risk Mother's fury over his."

With that, the boy walked five paces to the blackthorn tree and stepped through the opening in its trunk, passing from this world to a place where the darkness seemed more complete, where wind and rain howled, and a witch named Carmun waited for them all.

The thing that looked like a little girl in her Raggedy Ann costume turned to stare hungrily at Julia and Vanessa and then, without even a glance to telegraph her intentions, she launched herself at the Cunning Man. Festering with evil, rotting more with every moment she spent in this world, Delilah should have looked absurd. Instead, she seemed a primal thing, red row of fangs sluicing thick black saliva. Her strength and speed carried her with such force that when she hit the Cunning Man, he fell backward, and the little girl tore into him like some rabid beast. She clawed at his throat and bent to bury her teeth in soft flesh. The Cunning Man cuffed her in the head, and her shark teeth ripped into his lower jaw instead, gnashing and tearing flesh and bone.

Julia staggered to her feet. Vanessa had to hold on to her arm to rise.

"Dad!" Julia shouted. But what could she do? For her father, it was too late, and she did not want to be here when this fight ended, no matter which of these horrors emerged triumphant.

"Come on, Jules," Vanessa rasped in her ear. "I'm so sorry. I know it's killing you, seeing your dad like this, but we have to go."

The Cunning Man hurled Delilah off him. The little girl smashed against the Blackthorn and then rose as if the impact had not pained her in the least. Her eyes were yellow, putrid, and full of hate and spite. She could have fled, then, left the way Leonard had, but instead, she ran at the Cunning Man again. The creature, Broghan, managed to catch her in his hands and lift her off the ground, but Delilah screamed and started to dig her claws into the Cunning Man's face—the stolen face of Donnie Sweeney.

Julia wanted to look away, knew she had to run, but she took one last look and saw that face being ripped away. Revolting as it was, somehow that was better. Her father might really be dead, but at least now she did not need to care what happened to this perverse thing that had worn his face.

She grabbed Vanessa's hand. "Let's go!"

Vanessa looked even paler than before, like some sort of wintry ghost. Julia helped her along, but as they reached the opening to the trail that would lead home, Vanessa stumbled— not over a root or rock, but out of exhaustion. Julia looked over to see blood coming from both of Vanessa's nostrils.

"Oh, God," she managed, reaching out just in time to catch Vanessa in her arms, the other girl nothing but deadweight.

As Julia lowered her to the ground yet again, Vanessa began to tremble, eyelids fluttering open to reveal the whites as her body jerked and thrashed against the trail.

Frantic, she looked over her shoulder to see the Cunning Man grab Delilah by the throat, those spider-leg fingers wrapped around her neck. He lifted the little girl and shook her. Delilah's red mop wig flew off and became lost in the leaves and the dark. *Good*, Julia thought, on the verge of hysteria. *Good!*

But then tiny Delilah took the Cunning Man's forearm in both hands and wrenched it upward with such ferocity that the bone broke. The snap echoed across the clearing. The Cunning Man hissed in whatever pain he could feel, and he released Delilah, who fell to the ground. She scrabbled on the dirt and turned, aimed not at the Cunning Man but at Julia.

Vanessa wouldn't be any use to the little rotting girl now, not if she might die before she could become a sacrifice, so Julia was Delilah's last chance.

"No," she whispered.

Julia knew she ought to run, but instead, she held Vanessa's right hand in both of her own. She would not abandon Vanessa like this, helpless and shuddering, eyes twitching blindly.

Screaming, Delilah ran at Julia with her teeth bared. Her lips opened so wide that the sides of her mouth split. Her eyes were pure malice.

Julia turned her back on the shrieking thing. She thought of the banshee in the Haunted Woods. On the ground, Vanessa stopped seizing, and Julia bent to whisper to her.

"You were my dream girl," she said softly.

Branches snapped, but ahead of them on the trail instead of in the clearing behind. Julia looked up to see Tony Barbosa running at her. She jerked backward to get out of his way, and Mr. Barbosa leaped over Vanessa.

Only then did Julia see the shovel in his hand. The long-handled gravedigger's shovel from the Haunted Woods. It had been a rusty, sharp-bladed garden shovel long before it had become a Halloween prop.

Delilah saw him coming but did not slow. Her filthy yellow eyes gleamed in the moonlight, narrowed with malevolence. She hissed as she ran at him, reaching for his abdomen as if she could rip him open, and maybe she could have. The rotting girl had the strength.

Tony gripped the shovel's haft as if it were a baseball bat and stepped into it as he swung the blade at her face. Bone should have crunched, the impact should have been solid, a clang. Instead, Delilah's head caved in with a heavy, wet slop like a torrent of vomit hitting the floor.

She went down, skidded on pine needles, and then lay still. Not even a twitch.

Tony Barbosa stood over the dead thing. The shovel slipped from his hand. "Oh, Jesus. What did I—"

"Mr. Barbosa," Julia said. "Please. I need your help."

He stood frozen, as if he hadn't heard her voice. Julia shifted on her knees, slid her arms beneath Vanessa, and staggered to her feet, holding the other girl against her chest. She wouldn't make it far like this, not all the way to Parmenter Road—not all the way to the help Vanessa needed.

"Mr. Barbosa," she pleaded again.

But the horror in the clearing had not yet ended. Steve Koenig was dead. The rotting things that called themselves Arthur and Delilah were dead. Leonard was gone. But the blackthorn tree remained open, that window through its trunk showed darkness and freezing rain that had somehow turned to snow, eddying in through the passage along with the wind.

And the Cunning Man remained. Delilah had hurt him, and he leaned against the tree, a viscous kind of blood dripping from what remained of his face. Of Donnie Sweeney's face. Julia did not want him to turn to face Mr. Barbosa. She didn't want to see him again, not that ruined face or the eye sockets like divots in his skull, with those candle flames burning inside.

She didn't want to see, but when the Cunning Man turned around, she did not look away.

Hardly any trace of her father lingered in the countenance of that demon or conjurer or whatever he was. Julia exhaled, grateful for that, at least. And then she shuddered, a fresh wave of grief pounding at her.

The Cunning Man nodded to her, and then to Tony Barbosa, who raised a hand in a kind of wave. Was it gratitude? Farewell? A sort of beckoning, in hopes that the monster would stay and explain it all to them?

It mattered not at all. The Cunning Man stepped through the passage in the heart of the blackthorn tree. A gust of snow and wind blew into the autumn clearing, in that first hour of the first of November in the last year of Julia's childhood. And then he was gone, taking her father with him.

Mr. Barbosa turned toward her as if he'd only just heard her plea for help. He took Vanessa from Julia's arms, listened to her chest, but even as he did that, her eyes fluttered open and she mumbled a bit—not conscious, but not close to dead—and Julia's gratitude that the night hadn't taken Vanessa from her was enough to propel her toward home.

As they left the clearing, the opening in the trunk of the Blackthorn closed up, knitting back together until only a split in the bark remained. Half a dozen steps down the trail, Julia glanced back and could not see the clearing at all, as if neither it, nor the blackthorn tree, had ever been there. The forest had erased them.

TONY BARBOSA

The night turned colder, but something about the air had changed. It tasted cleaner, crisper, and Tony felt his back straighten a little, in spite of the burden he carried. Until right now, Vanessa Montez had been just another girl from the neighborhood, one of his daughter's classmates but not one of her close friends.

But tonight, Tony had helped to save her life.

He carried her in his arms and tried to pretend she weighed less than a feather, though his spine did not seem fooled. Vanessa had never been a big girl, but she was seventeen or eighteen years old, a high school senior. Picking her up had been the logical thing—get her out of the woods and into a hospital. If he had run back and called 9-1-1, they would have lost critical minutes waiting for an ambulance and then waiting for the EMTs to reach the clearing. Carrying her out had really been the only choice, but his back would not thank him tomorrow.

Tony marched on.

Julia Sweeney followed right behind him. She said nothing to him, and that was for the best, because Tony had no idea what to say to her. This morning, her father had just been a neighbor people gossiped about. Tonight, Donnie Sweeney had become his enemy, a hateful bastard who had slept with Tony's wife. Now, Donnie no longer existed in this world. Parts of his body might remain behind, scattered around the woods, but the man himself—his soul, spirit, whatever he was—was simply gone, along with the Cunning Man.

Impossible. All of it.

And yet.

"Mr. Barbosa," Julia said, hurrying to catch up with him on the path. "Is she . . . Do you think Vanessa's gonna be okay?"

Tony looked down at the girl in his arms. Vanessa had turned her head toward him, face against his chest. Blood had stopped flowing from her nostrils and begun to dry. Her chest rose and fell, so she was still breathing, but she was unconscious. The truth was he did not know the answer.

"Absolutely," he said. "We'll get her to a hospital. They'll take good care of her."

Neither of them mentioned Julia's father and the things he had done—and become. And that was good, because though he felt for Julia, Tony had only so much strength for grief and sympathy right now. Vanessa lolled against him the way his own children always had after they had fallen asleep on the sofa and he'd had to carry them up to their beds. Chloe . . . and Rick. His boy, Ricky.

His chest hitched with delayed grief.

Tony heard Alice crying as they came to a bend in the trail. The sound floated through the trees like the wailing of a ghost. Despite the exhaustion in his arms and pain in his back, he hefted Vanessa a bit higher and picked up his pace. His lips pressed tightly together as he fought the sob that yearned to erupt.

His boy.

Around the turn in the path, they came to the place where

Tony had left Alice, Chloe, and Billie to restrain the thing that Rick had become. He told himself now that it was the right thing to do, that if he hadn't gone, Vanessa and Julia would be dead. But when he saw how Alice and Chloe knelt together on the path—the way fallen trees sometimes rested against each other long after their leaves had stopped growing—he wondered if he had made the right decision.

Billie Suarez stood a few feet away, perhaps to give Alice and Chloe room to mourn. But Billie grieved, too. Her head hung low and she hugged herself, shoulders shaking as she cried in silence. Rick had been more than her best friend—Tony knew that. To Billie, Rick had been the closest thing she would ever have to a brother.

"Oh no," Julia said. "My God."

Tony felt blessed by her sympathy. After all Julia had lost tonight and the grief she must have been feeling, the idea that she had sadness left over for him and his family touched Tony's heart. He would never forget the kindness she showed in that moment.

Numb, Vanessa somehow now weightless in his arms, Tony approached Alice and Chloe. Just beyond them, Rick lay on the path amid leaves and pine needles. Moonlight painted his face in strange shadows, but nothing cruel remained. There was something peaceful in that partly ravaged face. He might have been fighting before, full of violence and malice, but now Rick was merely Rick.

Brave, smart, funny, but all those things in the past tense forevermore.

"What happened?" Tony managed to ask.

Alice glanced up but could not speak. She tried, but the grief stifled her, and she hugged Chloe more tightly.

It was Billie who answered. "A couple of minutes ago, he just . . . stopped. All that nastiness left him, and he just sort of . . ." She wiped tears from her eyes. "He sighed a little, and then he was gone."

Right around the moment the blackthorn tree left us. Tony thought about the difference in the air, the sweetness. The evil had bled away somewhere, but the damage it had done remained.

"Mr. Barbosa," Julia Sweeney said, nudging his arm from behind. "Want me to take her?"

Alice didn't look up. For the first time, Tony noticed that all along she had been holding their dead son's cold hand, even while Chloe hugged her.

It was Chloe who looked up at her father, saw his hesitation. "You have to go, Dad."

Tony wanted to speak, to explain—to Alice and Chloe, even Billie, but especially to his son. To Rick. Who could no longer hear him. But then Alice glanced up at him and nodded.

When Tony spoke again, his voice broke. "You'll take care of him, Alice?"

"Of course," she rasped, voice crushed by grief. "Of course I will."

Her betrayal had hurt him deeply, but on this, Tony trusted her completely.

He hefted Vanessa, got a better grip beneath her, and then nodded at Julia. She ran ahead of him on the path, but not so far ahead that she lost sight of Tony following behind with Vanessa.

Before he left his family behind, Tony turned to Billie. "Come home with me, Bill. Your folks will be back by now."

Billie stared at the still, gray body of her best friend. "No, I . . ."

"They'll be worried about you," Tony said. "Let's not put them through that."

Billie's breath hitched and fresh tears sprang to her eyes,

but she nodded, and when Tony started hurrying toward home, Billie followed.

They left the woods behind. Left Rick behind. Left October behind.

Tony's love for Halloween had come to an end.

BARB SWEENEY

S unshine.

Halfhearted November sunshine, yes, but sunshine nevertheless. Barb narrowed her eyes, trying to sort out what time the angle and golden hue of the light might suggest. It took a few seconds of blearily staring at the window before she remembered there was such a thing as an alarm clock, and she turned to look at the one on her nightstand.

2:13 p.m.

Her groan had no words, only emotion. No doubt she had needed the sleep, but now there were only a couple of hours of daylight left and then darkness would fall again, and she hated the idea of night coming so soon. The police had arrived at her house a little after midnight, and then the two officers had wasted valuable minutes trying to dismiss her fears, even though her sons were there to confirm the things she told them, about the girl who'd tried to drag Charlie into the woods. She'd been so afraid because Julia had still been missing at that point.

It hadn't been long before other sirens could be heard, and soon after, Julia finally came home. The story broke and spread and changed as more police arrived and the cops and neighbors tried to make sense of the shocking violence on Parmenter Road that night. Ruth and Zack Burgess had been murdered, and immediately the police—familiar with the Burgesses—suspected Zack had killed Ruth and then, somehow, himself.

Barb told the police about the little girl who had pushed her down the stairs and tried to steal her son, but then the EMTs had taken her to the hospital, concerned about her condition. She had a mild concussion, some wrenched muscles, no serious damage, but the concussion was enough for the investigating officers to twist and doubt her memories. By the time they let her go home, about eight o'clock in the morning, they had decided the little girl had somehow been Ruth Burgess in disguise, that the Burgesses had gone on some kind of murder spree. Already, the TV and radio news programs were reporting those allegations, and the names of the dead—Steven Koenig, Rick Barbosa, and her own husband, Donnie. Not to mention the so-called perpetrators, the Burgesses.

It exhausted Barb to think about trying to correct them. What would she have said that anybody who had not been on Parmenter Road that night would believe? If she tried to explain what had become of her husband, anyone would think she had lost her mind.

She threw back her covers, careful not to look at the pillow where Donnie had always laid his head. She wondered if someone with more experience taking charge of their life would know what to do next. Four hours of sleep would have to be enough, at least for today.

Barb grabbed a fluffy robe from its hook on the back of her bedroom door and padded down the stairs to find Julia asleep on the sofa with the TV playing a Burt Reynolds movie, volume down low. Tempted to wake her daughter, Barb forced herself to let Julia sleep. After what she had been through, what they were all still going through, sleep would be her best friend. Julia had bruises and scratches all over her body. Nothing broken and no concussion, but she had witnessed things that would give her nightmares forever and lost her father in the bargain.

On the couch, Julia's brow furrowed and she muttered in her sleep, troubled or even frightened, but Barb chose not to wake her. The nightmares would still be there when Julia woke up.

She kissed the first two fingers of her right hand for luck and then touched those fingers to her sleeping daughter's forehead. She paused at the kitchen doorway, composing herself. So much of parenting seemed to be comprised of learning when to let your children see your true emotions, if ever. She took a breath, hand on the doorframe.

"It's not a story!" Charlie cried.

Fear jolted her. She hurried through the kitchen to the porch, where the broken jalousie windows in the back door had already been boarded over by a kind neighbor. Another kind neighbor, an elderly widow named Peg Mathiesen, had come down to watch the kids while Barb had been in the hospital. The woman understood loss and trauma and how to be where she was needed, and Barb thought she would be grateful to Peg forever.

When she walked onto the porch, she saw Mrs. Mathiesen in the chair Barb herself had fallen asleep in last night. Charlie and Brian were on the sofa. Many empty candy wrappers suggested that the kids had enjoyed a small chocolate feast this morning or after lunch—or both.

"It wasn't Dad," Brian said.

"I told you it was. I saw him up close. He saved me!" Charlie barked at his older brother, furious tears in his eyes. At eleven, sometimes he seemed even younger.

Mrs. Mathiesen raised both hands. "Boys, please. Now really isn't the time to fight about this."

Both boys scoffed, then turned their anger back upon each other.

"Charlie, I know you wanna believe—"

Barb rapped her knuckles on the doorframe. Both boys whipped around to stare at her.

"Brian, I know you're trying to help. That's what you do. But Charlie saw what he saw. There's no harm in that."

Let him have this, she thought. *If he needs to believe his father loved and cared about him to go on, then let him.*

"I guess," Brian relented.

Mrs. Mathiesen seemed overjoyed to have Barb take back responsibility for her children. "Can I fix you something to eat?" she asked.

Barb felt grief seize her again, but she swallowed it down. For now.

"I think we'll manage, Peg. But thank you so much for your kindness. I don't know what I'd have done without you."

Mrs. Mathiesen got up and hugged Barb, told her to call if she needed anything from a hot meal to a ride somewhere, and of course that she was happy to look after the kids anytime. Barb thanked her again, fought back tears as she walked the elderly woman to the door, and had to take a moment to compose herself again before she returned to the back porch.

The boys were watching cartoons. No horror movies today.

Barb sat down between them. "We'll manage," she said again, as much to herself as to them. "We're going to be all right."

VANESSA MONTEZ

Later, Vanessa would claim it had been the painkillers that caused her to tell the police detective to fuck off. As accustomed to bristling against authority as she was, it still felt like stepping over a line, but she didn't care. The asshole had it coming.

The hospital smelled of illness and antiseptic. Her wounds had been bandaged, but most of her injuries could only be treated with time and rest. She had a severe concussion and three cracked ribs. When she had woken just before lunch from a drug-induced stupor, she had discovered that her left wrist had been broken at some point during the night's chaos and the doctors had put a cast on it. Rumor was that they planned to send her home tomorrow, but the doctor said he might keep Vanessa an extra day for observation, which she understood to mean they were worried a concussion might not be the only thing wrong with her head. Given the things she had said to the EMTs and police and nurses when the ambulance had brought her to the emergency room, she did not blame them.

All those things were true, of course. But Vanessa had quickly learned the folly of attempting to persuade anyone of the truth. Better to lie and say she couldn't remember, although that strategy was not popular with Detective What's-his-face.

"I know you're supposed to be resting," the cop said, not bothering to hide his irritation. "The nurses have made that very clear. But listen, Vanessa, I'm not just doing this because it's my job to find answers. I'm doing this because Steve Koenig's parents—his family and friends, of which you're one—they deserve to know what happened."

The shades were drawn down to cover all but the bottom few inches of window, but still, the sunshine that seeped into her room made her head hurt. Vanessa held her left hand up to shield her eyes and still squinted a little while looking at the detective, a short, stocky man with vivid blue eyes that almost made her want to put her faith in him. But what could he do? There were mysteries here that he could not solve even if he spent his entire life investigating, mysteries whose explanations would put her in a mental hospital for a very long time.

"I wish I could tell you, Detective—"

Cardiff, that was it. *Detective Roger Cardiff.* It was 1984, and nobody named their kid Roger anymore, but there were some Rogers from earlier decades who still walked the earth, like the last few dinosaurs after the Ice Age.

"Vanessa—"

"Please, Detective Cardiff," she said, squinting against the light and to let him know her head had started to hurt again. She had been pretending a little bit, earlier, but there was no playacting here. "We've been over this. I don't know what you want me to say."

"You were the last one to see Steve," the detective reminded her.

"As far as we know, yeah," she said. Memories of her last real encounter with Steve haunted her. For the rest of her life, she would have to live with the knowledge that their last conversation had been an angry one.

"His father said—"

Vanessa sat up a little in bed. Pain radiated from her cracked ribs, but she ignored it. "Steve's father is a massive asshole, Detective. He's the whole reason Steve and I left the party when we did."

Detective Cardiff had been standing at the foot of her hospital bed throughout his visit. Now he walked to the visitor's chair and plunked himself down with relief, as if he'd been yearning for that seat since he'd entered.

"Your parents left around the same time. I'm told there was some violence. He attacked Mr. Koenig—"

"Who had it coming," Vanessa interrupted. A different flavor of nausea tightened her gut. "If you're trying to suggest my father had anything to do with what happened to Steve and Rick—"

"And you."

Vanessa scowled. "Oh, fuck off."

The detective blinked and sat back in the chair in utter shock. "Excuse me?"

"I said, 'Fuck off.' Do you need to hear it again? Fuck off."

Anger reddened his face. Detective Cardiff stood. He might not have been a tall man, but with her in a hospital bed, he towered over her.

"You listen to me—"

Vanessa felt her lip curl in disgust. If he meant to intimidate her, it was working, but she was not going to let him see it.

"I've told you!" she snapped. "Mr. Koenig was being a drunken ass. He was rude and disgusting. My dad got into a shoving match with him on the deck, pushing him into that stupid tiki bar, and then Julia Sweeney and I left the party. I didn't see Steve after that, as far as I remember."

That last part was a lie. But considering the alternative, she could live with it.

"What about Donald Sweeney? Or Mr. Burgess or his wife?"

"Maybe."

Detective Cardiff didn't roll his eyes, but she could tell he wanted to. "Maybe?"

Vanessa sighed. "Look, I've told you what I can remember. I don't want to make your job harder—"

"You have a funny way of showing it, kid."

Vanessa closed her eyes and steadied herself, trying to drive away the increasing pain in her skull. The nurse should have come back and ushered the detective out of there by now, but she had seen how much the staff deferred to Cardiff. People had been murdered—two of them kids—so Vanessa understood. But that didn't make her head feel better. She wished her father were there with her, or her mother, and for the first time, she wondered something.

"Hey, Detective?"

Cardiff leaned in, maybe thinking she had remembered something.

"Are you even supposed to be questioning a minor without her parents in the room?"

"You're eighteen," the detective replied, but he sat up straighter, shifting his whole body away from her, deeper into the chair.

"Seventeen," she said.

Detective Cardiff deflated. For a few seconds, he buried his face in his hands, and she could see his exhaustion. It was November 2, about thirty-six hours after the first police had arrived on Parmenter Road, and she imagined this man had slept very little since then.

He stood, the chair legs squealing on the linoleum floor. The sound drove a spike through her brain.

"We'll talk again," he said. "If you think of anything or remember anything, please ask your parents to call me."

"I will."

At the door, he paused and looked back into the room at her. "Vanessa, I'm sorry about Steve. Your mother talked a lot about how close you were. Whatever else happened that night, I hope you won't mind a word of advice from someone who has seen young people die before."

Grief had snuck up on her while the detective spoke. Now it settled in her throat, so that she could barely do more than wave for him to continue.

"You may hate the Koenigs now—"

"Mr. Koenig," she corrected him. "But I'm not an awful person. They just . . . They lost their son. Even if I hate his father, Steve loved them both. The way I feel, I can't imagine how much worse it is for them. If she wants to come over and see me, if that'll make her feel better somehow, then I hope she does."

The detective gave her a thoughtful look. "You're a good kid. Again, I'm very sorry. I'm around if you need me."

Then he was gone, and as nice as he had seemed, there at the end, Vanessa hoped he stayed away from her for a very long time. Lying felt awful, as if it was a betrayal of some kind, even though the police could do nothing to get justice for Steve's murder.

A soft knock came at the door. She winced at the sound, but thought it must be the nurse with more painkillers. Vanessa would ask her to pull the curtain the rest of the way down.

But it wasn't the nurse.

Julia walked in. She had scratches on her face and hands, but otherwise, she seemed okay, except for the dark circles under her eyes and the gray hue of her skin.

"Hey," she said.

"Hey yourself." Vanessa smiled, and there was nothing sad or half-hearted about it. Julia's arrival made her headache recede. "You didn't have to come."

Julia came to the foot of the bed. "Did you not want me to?"

"God, no. I'm so glad you're here."

Vanessa wondered how much she ought to say. That night in the woods had been a horror that haunted her every time she closed her eyes. The screams still echoed in her mind. She wouldn't blame Julia for wanting to leave it all behind. And yet, there she was, standing at the foot of the bed. Her father had been killed, they had nearly been murdered themselves, had confronted something awful—something truly evil, when neither of them had really believed in evil before. And yet, Julia had come here.

"I saw the detective leaving," Julia said, settling onto the edge of the bed. "Was he torturing you?"

"He thinks I'm lying about how much I remember."

Julia smiled. "How much do you remember?"

Wincing in pain, ribs aching, Vanessa reached out and took Julia's hand. "Everything, Jules. I remember everything."

TONY BARBOSA

The FOR SALE sign went up in the Barbosas' front yard on the third of November. Tony watched the real estate agent hammer it into the grass, listening to the pounding echo off the Kenney and Gnecco houses across the street. Neighbors, only they didn't feel like neighbors anymore. In Tony's mind, he had already left Parmenter Road. They would stay in the house until Rick's funeral, and then they would move as soon as they could find a temporary apartment, just the three of them—Tony, Alice, and Chloe.

Somewhere close, so Chloe could finish her senior year in Coventry. But not here. Not in this house, on this street. Not with those woods in their backyard.

He held a mug of coffee in both hands as he watched the real estate agent drive away. The day had turned gray, and a light mist presaged the rainstorm the meteorologists were predicting for tonight. The FOR SALE sign swayed back and forth in the wind, creaking in a way that unnerved him.

Tony took a sip of his coffee and walked around the garage to the backyard. He held the mug tightly in both hands, warming them.

In the backyard, he stared at the signage he and Chloe had used to mark the entrance to the Haunted Woods for the past four Halloweens. Prior to that, they had used crappy cardboard signs every year, but these were solid wood, painted with creepy, glow-in-the-dark letters.

Tony never wanted to see the fucking things again.

Behind him, the screen door squealed open and banged shut. He jumped, spilled a bit of hot coffee on his hands, and cussed quietly.

"Oh no! Sorry, Dad," Chloe said as she descended the stairs.

Tony shook his hands dry one at a time. "It's okay. I was trying to get them warm anyway."

It was a joke, but neither of them laughed. Chloe walked over to stand beside him. In silence, they watched the woods. The wind of the past couple of days had stolen many of the remaining leaves from the trees, and some of the decorations and mechanisms inside the Haunted Woods were visible through the branches.

"Have the police said when we can take it all down?" Chloe asked.

"When the investigation is finished. That's all they've told me."

"I can't wait to pack it all away." She glanced sidelong at him. "I'm sorry if that makes you sad."

Tony sniffed. "Hell, kid. It all makes me sad. I'm with you, though—the sooner we can get all this stuff out of here and forget about it, the better."

Chloe slid her arm through the crook of his elbow, as if he were going to escort her to the dance floor. He flashed forward to the wedding he hoped she would have one day and what it might be like to walk her down the aisle of a church. It gave him a spark of good feeling, and then he remembered that Rick wouldn't be there. Chloe's brother would not be at her wedding, or anywhere else, ever again.

Loss spread beneath him, a bottomless pit into which he feared he would be falling forever. But he owed Rick better than that, and he certainly owed more to Chloe. If he allowed his own grief to prevent him from giving her comfort, he would have failed them both.

"Mom said there's a house we're going to look at on Saturday," Chloe said.

Rick sipped his coffee, but it had started to turn cold, and he tipped the rest of it onto the grass. "Across town, yeah. It's for rent, which suits us fine for now."

A silence fell between them. The sort of silence love allowed. After a moment, Chloe laid her head on her father's shoulder, one arm still looped through his. His heart broke and was healed, all in those moments.

Tony had a sense that Chloe thought this shared ordeal, and shared pain, had brought her parents closer together. She hadn't believed in fairy tales ever since she had figured out the truth about Santa Claus, and she knew they hadn't been happy in a while and that her mother's affair with Mr. Sweeney had ruined things between them. Tony felt badly that their decision to stay together now—which he and Alice had agreed they were doing for Chloe's sake and to share their grief—might be giving her the wrong idea. He knew he ought to remind her that grief, especially the loss of a child, often tore marriages apart, and had never been known to repair them.

Yet his marriage to Alice had already been fraying at the edges before any of this had begun. And nobody else in the world would ever be able to understand what they had been through on Halloween night, what they had seen and what they had lost. For now, they would retreat together, put the past behind them, and try to rebuild their lives. So was it possible that, somehow, after all of this, the three of them could remain a family?

Who was to say?

Stranger things had happened.

Perhaps they'd all go fishing in that little Portuguese village together one day and remember Rick, and somehow in that way, he would still be with them.

Clutching his mug with one hand, he took his daughter's in the other. "Come on," he said. "Let's get your mom and go for a drive."

Chloe squeezed his hand as they walked around to the front of the house. "Okay with me, but where are we going?"

"Maybe we'll drive by that house," Tony suggested. "We'll take a look from the outside. Be creepy people who peep through windows."

"That sounds good to me."

He glanced over at her. "It does?"

"Anywhere sounds good to me right now," Chloe said. "As long as it's far from here."

They left the Haunted Woods behind, along with everything it had ever meant to them. The wind picked up, gusting so hard that it sounded like a banshee wail coming from deep in the woods. At the exit, just a few feet along the path, a dirty old Raggedy Ann doll lay half-covered by rotting leaves, soaked through from the rain.

Perhaps forgotten.

And perhaps not.

Acknowledgments

Writing a novel like *All Hallows* is a bit like time travel. To get into the mindset of these characters and to really see the neighborhood of Parmenter Road, I had to open a door and step through. On Halloween night, 1984, I was seventeen years old—too old for trick-or-treat but the perfect age for mischief. I'm grateful for all those in or out of my neighborhood who participated in that mischief with me, but most of all to my brother, Jamie Golden. When I think of Halloween and childhood mischief—and when I write about it—it's always Jamie I think of first.

Enormous thanks to my esteemed literary agent, Howard Morhaim, and my film/TV manager and producing partner, Peter Donaldson, for all their work on my behalf. Special thanks to my editor, Michael Homler, and to the entire team at St. Martin's Press, especially Sarah Bonamino, Allison Ziegler, and Cassidy Graham. My thanks to Caspian Dennis, Cath Trechman, and Heather Baror. Thanks as always to the friends who get me through it all—you know who you are. Finally, and always most importantly, to Connie and the family we've built, Nicholas and Danielle, Daniel, and Lily.

And a thanks, in the end, to all of the neighbors who

answered the door when I rang the bell on Halloween night, all those years ago. Most of them are gone now, but I remember. Trick or treat!

About the Author

CHRISTOPHER GOLDEN is the *New York Times*-bestselling author of *Ararat*, *Road of Bones*, *Snowblind*, and many other novels. With Mike Mignola, he is the co-creator of such comics series as *Baltimore*, *Lady Baltimore*, and *Joe Golem: Occult Detective*. Golden has edited and co-edited numerous anthologies, including *Seize the Night*, *The New Dead*, *Hex Life* and Shirley Jackson Award-winner *The Twisted Book of Shadows*. The author has been nominated ten times in eight different categories for the Bram Stoker Awards ®, and won twice. Golden is also a screenwriter and producer, as well as a writer of audio dramas and video games. He lives in Massachusetts.

Twitter: @ChristophGolden
Facebook: ChristopherGoldenAuthor
Instagram: christopher_golden

For more fantastic fiction, author events,
exclusive excerpts, competitions, limited editions and more

VISIT OUR WEBSITE
titanbooks.com

LIKE US ON FACEBOOK
facebook.com/titanbooks

FOLLOW US ON TWITTER AND INSTAGRAM
@TitanBooks

EMAIL US
readerfeedback@titanemail.com